COLD CASE
INVESTIGATORS
The Kidnapping

MERRILL VAUGHAN

Cold Case Investigators: The Kidnapping
Copyright © 2024 by Merrill Vaughan

ISBN: 979-8-3305-8939-5 (Paperback)
       979-8-3305-8938-8 (Ebook)

All Rights Reserved. No part of this publication may be reproduced, distributed, or transmitted in any form or by any means, including photocopying, recording, or other electronic or mechanical methods, without the priorwritten permission of the publisher, except in the case brief quotations embodied reviews and other noncommercial uses permitted by copyright law.

The views expressed in this book are solely those of the author and do not necessarily reflect the views of the publisher, and the publisher hereby disclaims any responsibility for them.

Paperwrights

Paper Wrights, LLC
www.paperwrights.co

CONTENTS

Acknowledgments vii
Prologue ix
Chapter 1 1
Chapter 2 8
Chapter 3 12
Chapter 4 20
Chapter 5 25
Chapter 6 37
Chapter 7 42
Chapter 8 47
Chapter 9 49
Chapter 10 56
Chapter 11 60
Chapter 12 63
Chapter 13 66
Chapter 14 73
Chapter 15 77
Chapter 16 86
Chapter 17 89
Chapter 18 98
Chapter 19 106
Chapter 20 111
Chapter 21 117
Chapter 22 122
Chapter 23 130
Chapter 24 134
Chapter 25 139
Chapter 26 146

Chapter 27 154
Chapter 28 158
Chapter 29 170
Chapter 30 176
Chapter 31 180
Chapter 32 184
Chapter 33 188
Chapter 34 193
Chapter 35 199
Chapter 36 205
Chapter 37 209
Chapter 38 213
Chapter 39 217
Chapter 40 224
Chapter 41 228
Chapter 42 231
Chapter 43 237
Chapter 44 244
Chapter 45 249
Chapter 46 257
Chapter 47 260
Chapter 48 265
Chapter 49 271
Chapter 50 276
Chapter 51 282
Chapter 52 288
Chapter 53 291
Chapter 54 297
Chapter 55 300
Chapter 56 304
Chapter 57 313
Chapter 58 320
Chapter 59 326

Chapter 60..336
Chapter 61..349
Chapter 62..355
Chapter 63..358
Chapter 64..363
Chapter 65..368
Chapter 66..373
Chapter 67..382
Chapter 68..385
Chapter 69..391
Chapter 70..396
About the Author..398

ACKNOWLEDGMENTS

Grateful acknowledgments go to Elaine Maurice and Henry Ellis for their reviews and comments. I also wish to thank the Brandin' Iron management for allowing me to use their establishment in the book. I also wish to thank the Boston, Massachusetts, Field Office of the Federal Bureau of Investigation for their information on proper procedures in searching for kidnapped children. I would also like to thank my wife for her patience and support in my writing this book.

PROLOGUE

Roderick "Rod" Duval grew up in Southern California as a young troublemaker. His homelife was not what one might call stable; his father was gone more often than being at home. His mom was forced to work two jobs just to keep a roof over their heads, food on the table, and clothes on his back. He was more or less forced to fend for himself.

In high school, he had average grades except for physical fitness classes. He played on the football team as a second string and was an average baseball player. He excelled in the martial arts, where he used his mind over physical actions. He had trouble dealing with female classmates. None of the girls would want to talk with him, much less go out with him—except for one.

Sherrie Robertson saw him one day working out with the Martial Arts Club and decided that he was kind of cute; she liked him. She got him to talk after school one day, and he opened up to tell her about his home life and that he was working in a gas station to earn money to help his mom out.

They began going steady in their junior year of high school. Rod starting pushing the idea of getting married right after gradua- tion from high school; however, Sherrie did not feel comfortable get- ting married so young. Sherrie's best friend, Rose MacDonald, told her on many occasions that she thought Rod was "just plain creepy" and she did not trust him.

Just after graduation, Sherrie broke up with Rod, telling him that she was not old enough to get married and raise a family. She also told him that she did not want to see him again. Rod blamed

Rose for causing Sherrie to break up with him, and he told her that one day he would make her pay for things she had said about him. He left town, and rumor had it that he had headed back east. Almost all, including Rose and Sherrie, felt relieved that he had left town.

In 1988, while serving in the US Army, Rod met a young woman; and in 1989, they got married. Sandy did her best to make Rod happy and tried to be a good Army wife. However, nothing was good enough—with the exception of finally getting pregnant. On March 2, 1990, while giving birth to his son, Roderick Duval Jr, she died from heart failure due to complications from a breech birth. His son died the same day due to the cord being wrapped around his neck. Rod was devastated and could not cope with the death of his wife and son on the same day. All he wanted was to get as far away from anything that would remind him of Sandy and Rod Jr as possible, so he volunteered for duty in Iraq and other places most Americans never heard of.

In 1991, he met Josie Edmunds; and after they decided to get married, she told him she could not get pregnant due to a botched abortion she had as a teenager. They got married anyway. She brought up the subject of adopting a young boy that would be the same age as his dead son, but Rod declined to consider it, telling her that he had other plans for getting a son.

A few years after graduating from high school, Sherrie met and married Patrick Johnson, a non-Commissioned Officer in the Air Force stationed at Norton AFB in San Bernardino, California. He was exactly what Sherrie was looking for—a few years older, stable, and mature beyond his years.

1

Saturday, June 28, 1989, was a special day for Sherrie Johnson as it was her twenty-fourth birthday. She was not what you would call extremely beautiful, but she was pretty, with soft blue eyes that looked like pools of clear water. Her golden blonde hair looked like a field of wheat on a hot midsummer day. She had married two years ago to Patrick Johnson, a Master Sergeant in the 63rd Security Police Squadron at Norton AFB in California.

Since Norton was about six hours away from her hometown, she was lonely and had made only a few friends, most of them spouses.

That morning, around 1000 hours, Patrick came to her and told her, "I know today is your birthday and we were going to go out tonight, but I need to do a no-notice check on the new troops tonight. It is a normal shift tonight, 1500 to 2300. I'm sorry. I will make it up to you."

She looked at him and then she said, "Honey, Rose called and told me that she wants to take me to a special party if it is okay with you. She promised the dedicated driver and I will behave."

"It is no fun sitting at home on your birthday all alone. Go and have fun with Rose and the others. Just be careful of how much you drink."

"What about dinner for you? Are you going to eat at the terminal? You know it is not good for you."

"I will take my meal with me—sandwich, cookies, and grapes that I love so much. I might stop at the terminal to have coffee breaks and such, but none of those greasy burgers. Don't worry that pretty head of yours."

Sherrie spent the rest of the morning working outside so that Patrick could rest until around 1200. Patrick came out around 1130 and helped her finish cleaning up the yard. She looked at her flower garden and was happy with what she saw; there were no weeds, snails, or other bugs that would ruin her flower bed. Finding none, she put up her garden tools, and they both went into the house for lunch.

Patrick walked in behind Sherrie, grabbed her around her waist, and pulled her back to him. He whispered in her ear, "How about I wash your back, and I will let you wash mine?" Playfully his "Roman hands and Russian fingers" lightly touched her nipples, and he could feel them harden inside her bra and shirt.

"Now behave, or you will have no time for lunch." She laughed as she broke away from his grasp and ran down the hallway to the bedroom and bath.

After their shower, they lay down on the bed, snuggled in each other's arms, and talked about having a baby. It was short-lived talk as she rolled him over and lay on his rock-hard body and teased him until he could not stand anymore and told her to "stop playing around, or we will not have time before I have to get dressed and leave."

An hour later, Patrick came out dressed in his starched battle dress uniform (or BDUs) with his boots shined to a high gloss.

His web gear was in his GMC Sierra pickup truck in the garage. She had a quick meal for him—his favorite egg salad sandwich on white bread with lettuce, chips, and two sweet gherkin pickles. He did not need to look inside the bag she packed, for he knew what she had packed for him including her special homemade peanut butter cookies.

He looked at her, drank the last of his coffee, got up, and gave her a hug. He always did this before going on duty. He told her he loved her and said, "Have fun tonight, honey, and remember, some- one has to be a designated driver. I will see you tonight. I love you, babe."

She watched him leave and said a small private prayer to keep Patrick safe tonight because "I love him so much," she said aloud.

She went to the bathroom, took a quick shower, and then looked in the closet. She saw just what she was looking for—a white blouse and a knee-high light-blue skirt and black boots. She looked at herself in the mirror and decided that she did not look like someone looking for trouble; she was happily married now. She saw a small box on the counter and opened it. With a gasp, she saw that it had a ring in it. The stone was of agate to match her blue eyes. It was not a big stone but was a perfect fit for her finger. Underneath the box was an envelope. Inside the card, Patrick had written,

Happy birthday, my love,

I love you. You are the love of my life, my one and only. I love you, babe.

With tears in her eyes, she slid the ring on and thought about later tonight. *If he is not too tired from working and I do not get real drunk, who knows what might happen?* Then with a smile on her face, she went to wait for her friend, Rose MacDonald.

* * * * *

Promptly at 5:00 p.m., Rose MacDonald arrived and wished Sherrie a very happy birthday. "Come on, birthday girl, let's go." Sherrie made sure the door was closed and locked.

On the drive to the bar, Sherrie showed Rose her birthday gift from Patrick, letting Rose look at it with envy.

"Sherrie, you are in love with an incredible man who also loves you beyond all doubt."

Sherrie then told her about how much she and Patrick wanted to have a baby and "Hopefully, tonight will be our lucky night—if I am not too drunk and he is not too tired, that is."

Forty-five minutes later, they pulled into the bar called Brandin' Iron, a country Western nightclub which she and Patrick would go to on special occasions. They both knew which table to go to; it had balloons, heavy snack food items, and her favorite drink, a screwdriver, already on the table. The dance floor was empty. Saturday nights they had a live band and entertainment and a policy to let special people have the first dance. Patrick was not with her, so she was cautious until she felt a soothing touch on her bare arm—a touch she remembered from long ago. She quickly looked for Rose and found her at the bar, getting her drink before coming back to the table.

The thought was reinforced when she heard him say, "Sherrie, you still are the most beautiful woman around."

She wished Rose and her friends would hurry back, but they were talking with guys. She turned her head. It was her old boyfriend, Roderick "Rod" Duval.

How in the hell did he know I would be here tonight and without Patrick? she asked herself.

"Rod, I am married now—to a wonderful man that treats me like a lady. There is nothing anymore between us. I am here with Rose and friends for my birthday, so please leave me alone."

"Come on let's dance—just one dance for old times' sake."

With a forceful grip, he pulled her from her chair. What she did not see him do was slip a pill into her drink behind her back. With one hand on her arm and his other hand now on the small of her back, he moved her to the dance floor, where a slow song was being played. He pulled her to him, though she was not relaxed in his arms. The song ended, and she broke away from him and went back to the table and took a healthy slug of her screwdriver.

They made small talk, with Sherrie telling him about Patrick and his job at Norton AFB, just outside of San Bernardino.

"But tell me where you have been. You look good, by the way, much better than the bum you were when we split."

As she talked, she was feeling a strange buzzed feeling. *They must have given me a double shot of vodka for my first drink*, she thought.

"I went into the Army, and after boot camp, I went to Army Ranger training where I earned jump wings. From there it was Special Forces, where I earned my Green Beret. I am still on active duty, which is the reason for the short blond hair."

What he did not tell her was that he knew she came in here with Patrick, and remembering her birthday, he stopped by earlier; and the bartender, who was his friend, told him about the party.

He ran his hand over his extremely short hair and smiled sheepishly at her. He looked into her eyes and asked, "You okay?"

"I need to find Rose. I need to go to the bathroom. I am not feeling too stable." She looked around but did not see Rose nearby, so she asked him to please help her through the crowd so she could get there safely.

Holding her close while going through the packed crowd near the dance floor, he got her to the bathroom. He opened the door slowly and called in, "Is anyone in here?" Hearing nothing, he opened the door for Sherrie, pulled her in, and blocked the door with the large metal wastebasket.

He leaned her back over the counter, kissing her, then moving his hands up underneath her skirt, pulled her panties off and raped her. Afterward, he made sure that there were no marks on his pants. He wet a towel and cleaned her up and then slid her down off the counter.

He was waiting outside the restroom when Rose (who knew and did not trust Rod) walked up and asked him where Sherrie was. "Inside. She must not be feeling well. She said she wanted me to escort her to the bathroom since she could not find you. How about if you go in and see if she is okay."

Looking at him with a skeptical look, she told him, "Yeah, I think I will." She glared at him, knowing that she did not trust him, for Sherrie had told her all about him and how he treated her in the past.

She went inside and waited until Sherrie was finished washing her hands. "Girl, what's wrong with you? You look like crap."

Leaning against the sink, she told Rose, "I'm not feeling well. I felt dizzy and somewhat confused earlier. I could not find you, so I asked Rod to walk me to the bathroom. He is probably waiting outside."

"Yeah, he is, but I still don't trust him. Both of us will walk you back to the table."

Quickly after being back at the table, Rod disappeared, and a cake arrived with two candles on it showing the numbers 24. The band played, and everyone sang "Happy Birthday" to Sherrie.

She then told everyone that it was a grand party tonight and thanked everyone for the party.

On the way home, Sherrie told Rose, "Rod seemed sure of himself. He has grown up and matured, I think. Yet he simply disappeared after I went to the bathroom." Suddenly she looked at Rose and told her, "I hope Patrick is home and not too tired. I want to make mad, passionate, no-holds-barred love tonight. I am terribly horny in the worst sense, and I want a baby before I get too old."

Rose looked at her, not saying what she was thinking but just told her, "I hope you had a good time tonight seeing some of your old friends, and the atmosphere was electric!"

* * * * *

At the main gate to Norton Air Force Base, Sherrie showed her ID card while Rose showed her visitor pass to the young airman. He looked at both, smiled, and then said, "Happy Birthday, Mrs. Johnson." Startled, she smiled back and said, "Thank you." After they cleared the gate, they both laughed, and within five minutes, they arrived at her quarters. Sherrie gave Rose a hug and a peck on the cheek and thanked her for a great time.

As she left, Rose waved back at Sherrie, but something else was on her mind—Rod. Her concentration was such that she did not see him parked around the corner of Sherrie's street.

As Sherrie opened the door, she looked outside one last time and saw a red pickup truck pull out and follow Rose back toward the gate.

She thought nothing of it as she flew into her husband's arms just as he was getting up to greet her at the door.

"Thank you, my love, my husband, for the ring. Everyone loved it. Now if you are not too tired from working, I want to end this day having wild, passionate, no-holds-barred sex tonight."

After he made sure the door was locked and the chain was in place, Patrick grinned as he followed his wife's clothing on the floor, found her on the bed under the covers with just a hint of the bare skin of her thigh showing. Their lovemaking was so intense that they both came together twice within an hour. They fell asleep in each other's arms.

Two days later, they read in the paper that Rose MacDonald was dead. She had died from an accident in her apartment parking garage.

* * * * *

On March 4, 1990, they had a nine-pound seven-ounce baby boy whom they named Patrick Johnson Jr. The baby had her soft blue eyes and Patrick's hair, but who was the father?

2

March 4, 1992, 10:00 a.m., Sherrie Johnson had just put Patrick Jr., or just "JR," as they called him (now two years old) down for his nap; he had been cranky all night and just now fell asleep in her arms. Sherrie leaned back in the kitchen against the sink, drinking her iced tea. Normally she would not be drinking iced tea at this hour, but there was a freak weather system that was pushing early "Santa Ana" winds, causing it to be extremely hot in the day and cold at night. She was glad that Patrick was working in the Investigations section of the Security Police today. He hates the hot weather, especially in his BDUs, which brings back unpleasant memories of assignments in his past and are better left alone. That reminded her that tonight she had to iron his blue shirts not because she dreaded it but because it was out of love. No matter what she did for him, it was for love. Taking another glass of iced tea, she went into the living room and sat down near the fan.

Knowing no one was going to come by until Patrick would come home for lunch, she unbuttoned three buttons on her loose-fitting blouse, and minus her bra and thinking of Patrick, her nipples hardened quickly under the cool air of the fan. She turned on the TV to see what was on, and she ended up watching a silly game show that almost put her to sleep. She had been up almost all night with JR and his coughing. He seemed better, so there was no need to go to the doctor.

Suddenly she heard the doorbell ring; she jumped up and quickly buttoned her blouse. She went to the door and peeped through the security hole Patrick had insisted on installing. She was glad she did. She was looking at a face from hell. Even though the person looked like someone else, she knew who it was. It was Rod Duval. She hesitated to call Patrick. He knew Rod from her early years as her boyfriend, but she did not tell him he was at the bar that night.

Just as she reached for the phone, he rang the doorbell constantly and started to bang loudly on the door. She was afraid that the ringing of the doorbell would awaken JR, and she did not want the neighbors to see him pounding on the door. She had no choice; she let him in.

"You sure got a nice house, Sherrie, for base quarters that is. Too bad the base is shutting down in two years. I hear Patrick will be a new senior master sergeant in a couple of months. Where are you and your wonderful family going next?"

With a confused, terrified look on her face, she wondered how much about her family did he really know. Then she remembered Patrick's name was on the new E-8 listing in *The Air Force Times*.

Suddenly she had a terrible thought. Was Rose's death due to Rod? After all, Rod was seen by Rose near the bathroom at the party, and then she died. She wondered if Rod had anything to do with that. Sherrie could only think of protecting her baby boy, for she thought she knew what Rod wanted.

"I suppose you want to look at my son, correct?" she asked, hoping either he would leave after seeing JR or Patrick would come home early. "You have to be quiet. He is sleeping after having a bad night last night."

At the door to JR's bedroom, they both looked in on the sleeping boy. Rod put his hand on her shoulder and said, "The three of us—you, me, and the boy—could have been a happy family, but no, you had to dump me and then marry someone else."

He squeezed her shoulder hard enough to make her wince. His touch, the tone of his voice, and his personal appearance caused her to be uneasy. She was wishing she had called Patrick or the LE desk. Hopefully, now that he had seen JR, he would leave. Even though her nipples had flattened out, she wished that she had put on a bra. She did not want to entice him to rape her in her home.

"Let's go into the kitchen and have some water. I'm thirsty," he directed her.

As they walked through the quarters, he looked around and saw a few photographs of the boy and his parents. He saw one photo of Sherrie and Patrick on their wedding day with Patrick in his mess dress uniform. His first thought was that Patrick was much better looking than he was, but then Rod thought that he was a better cocksman. After all, he had gotten Sherrie pregnant—or so he thought.

In the kitchen, filling the glasses with cold water, she asked, "You bastard. You raped me that night in the bathroom, didn't you? You somehow drugged me and then raped me in the bathroom, didn't you? Rose told me all about seeing you near the bathroom." She looked deep in his eyes and told him, "You killed Rose, right? How did you do that? They said it was due to a faulty brake hose." Then as an afterthought, she told him, "You killed Rose so she could not tell anyone about her thoughts after learning I was pregnant, you bastard!"

He noticed a kitchen knife holder on the countertop, and with her back to him, he selected one that was just what he wanted. As she turned back to him, he put his arm around her head and plunged the knife into her upper left abdomen between the tenth and eleventh ribs. He did not intend to kill her but to keep her quiet while he made his escape with the boy. He gently laid her on the kitchen floor and placed two kitchen towels on her wound, making sure he had the knife with him and did not step into the pool of her blood.

He quickly saw the time as ten thirty and knew her husband would be home for lunch in about fifteen minutes or so. He quickly went through the house, collecting pictures of the boy, and then went into JR's bedroom. He put on plastic gloves and found what he was looking for—a small suitcase with Mickey Mouse and assorted Disneyland stickers. He pulled everything from the dresser into the suitcase. The only stuffed toy he saw in the bed was a teddy bear clutched deeply in the boy's arms, so he made a mental note to make sure he takes that with him when he puts JR in his truck. He placed the suitcase in a large box along with all the pictures and took it out to the truck and went back inside only to emerge five minutes later with the boy in his arms. As he closed the door, he put his head inside and said loudly, "Sherrie, I promise to have my favorite nephew back for his party."

He made sure the sleeping boy was placed into a car seat and secured tightly. He waved at the neighbor across the street as he exited the cul-de-sac while noticing a white Ford Bronco pulling into the street. Knowing it was Patrick Johnson, Rod smiled and prayed silently that he would be allowed off base before it would be locked up tighter than a drum.

Well within the base speed limit, he stopped off at the main gate, turned in his visitor's pass, and left the base just in front of the main gate closing. All he could think about was, *That was cutting it too close. I need to get going.*

3

As Master Sergeant (MSgt) Patrick Johnson turned onto his street, he noticed a red pickup truck with a dent in the left front fender that had a visitor's pass in the lower left corner of the windshield. Being the good-natured person that he was, he waved at the visitor and smiled when he returned the wave. He wondered whom he had visited but did not remember it until later that day.

Patrick arrived home for lunch ten minutes early that day but knew something was amiss as Sherrie did not meet him at the door as she normally did.

JR must be sleeping, or she is resting after a long night last night, he thought to himself.

As soon as he opened the door, he definitely knew something was wrong. He noticed the distinct coppery smell of fresh blood—a lot of it, from the strong odor. Just to the right side of the entry hall was the kitchen. He looked in there and saw Sherrie lying on the floor in a large pool of blood.

"Oh my god, no!" he cried out as he went to her, grabbing a towel to press against the wound. He grabbed the kitchen phone from the countertop and called the Law Enforcement Desk while applying pressure on the wound.

"Sixty-Third Security Police Squadron LE Desk, Staff Sergeant Brown speaking. How may I help you?"

"Aaron, this is MSgt Patrick Johnson. I need for you to contact a full response to my quarters. Someone has been here and tried to kill my wife by stabbing her in the upper left abdomen. She has lost a lot of blood already."

While applying another towel over her wound, he heard SSgt Brown making the notifications to the correct individuals.

"All units stand by for a full response to 11 Starlifter Circle, LE flight chief and medical response, stabbing of Mrs. Patrick Johnson. All responding units go to Tactical 2. All others resume normal communications. Gates 1, 3, and 4 secure the base. I say again—secure the base."

Patrick could also hear him contacting the squadron commander and First Sergeant. "MSgt Johnson, you still there? The commander and shirt (First Sergeant) are on their way. Please keep this line open."

"Roger that, Aaron, and thanks," Patrick replied.

Hearing SSgt Brown in his cool and professional tone comforted him as he had trained him a year ago. He knew that with the base secured, all traffic in and out was now stopped, waiting for further instructions. As he waited for the responders, he looked at his wounded wife. Even though he had seen other assault victims in his career, this one was different. It was his wife, his soul mate.

"Who did this to you, honey? Tell me who did this to you," Patrick asked. "Hang in there, babe. I will take JR next door and be with you at the hospital. Help is coming. Just hang in there, babe. The medics are here now. They will take care of you."

The door banged open, and the medics told Patrick to stand back now that they were there. They carefully stepped around the pool of blood as best as they could, carrying in the gurney to where Sherrie was. They put her onto the gurney and placed a heavy strap over the kitchen towels that Patrick had put over the wound. The young medic told Patrick, "You did the right thing, sir, trying to stop the bleeding." They carried her out to the ambulance, and as he heard the mournful sound of the siren, they left for the base hospital. Just as the ambulance left, the first two LE patrol cars arrived.

Patrick stopped them at the front door and told them to call in the Investigations team.

"Do not go inside until they arrive. There is possible evidence in the scene," he told the young airman.

Shortly afterward, Senior Master Sergeant (SMSgt) Paul Gibbons and Technical Sergeant (TSgt) John Sommers from the Investigations Unit arrived.

Since they all worked together, Paul told him, "Patrick, the rest of the 'A Team' is now here."

Patrick's grin was a forced grin, and Paul knew it was not a good sign. He had Patrick lead them inside. The pool of blood was evident on the kitchen floor, and they walked to the living room where Patrick remained standing since he had Sherrie's blood on his pants. "Patrick, where is JR? I do not see him, so I suspect he is with

a neighbor," Paul asked as he took in the living room. Paul did not see anything outside of place except for gaps where pictures were normally hung, but he decided to ask about them later.

Patrick explained that JR was probably sleeping since he had had a bad night the night before. "He did not sleep much last night with his coughing. Sherrie was up all night with him so I could go to work today."

Paul looked at John and motioned for him to go check in JR's room. John went down the hall to JR's room then stepped back then, with a grim look on his face, motioned with his head for Paul to come down.

With an ice-cold grip in his chest, afraid to guess what John discovered, Paul told Patrick to sit tight and went down and looked inside JR's room.

He whispered to John, "Oh Jesus, don't tell me what it looks like."

The fear that he felt as a father was all too real, for we both saw a barren room that essentially was now a crime scene. It appeared JR had been kidnapped, and the only witness is his mother, who is now in the Base Hospital Emergency Room. Everything was now empty—the closet completely devoid of clothing and hangers, and the dresser drawers were pulled open and empty. The bed was stripped, and even his small toy box was empty.

"Let me tell him, John, I am JR's godfather, just as we are to each other's kids. Go outside, contact the desk, brief them, and have them call Office of Special Investigations (OSI) and FBI."

With an anguished look on his face, went back into the living room.

"Patrick, I have bad news to tell you. It appears that JR has been kidnapped. All his clothes are missing along with his toys and that small suitcase that he had in the closet. Everything is gone but the furniture. Do you know of anyone—family or otherwise—that would take JR?"

"Paul, what the hell are you telling me? You are telling me that along with my wife being knifed, our son is now missing and presumed to be kidnapped?" He sat down, his head in his hands, and then looked up at Paul with tears streaming down his face.

"Paul, you and I have worked cases like this before. We both know the drill. I know that I cannot ask the questions or lead the investigation. It is up to you and John now. What about OSI and FBI?"

"Patrick, I just had John go outside to contact the desk to have them contact OSI and FBI although I believe OSI are on their way. You know they monitor our radio frequencies. Once OSI gets here, it will be a big circus. Then when the FBI gets here, it will be a true 100 percent muddled mess."

Patrick told him, "Just do the job we normally do by the book—that is all I ask. And no, I have no idea who did this to me and my family. Find the bastard!"

Paul told him there was a 100 percent vehicle check on all vehicles leaving the base, but his gut told him that whoever did this was long gone. "We can't keep the gates locked all day."

Patrick, torn between the bitter feeling of not being with his wife and trying to find his son, knew he could not leave until he gave a statement to both OSI and the LE patrolman who first arrived on the scene. He knew he could give a statement to Paul later on.

Just then, Patrick's squadron commander, Lieutenant Colonel (Lt Col) Burns and First Sergeant (First Sgt, Shirt, or Top) MSgt Penkowsky arrived. They both stopped at the doorway and waited until Patrick, John, and Paul came out.

Patrick looked at the commander and told him, "Sir, I have sixty days on the books. I want thirty days' leave starting today."

The Old Man nodded in agreement. Patrick then looked at his First Sergeant and asked him for a favor. "Shirt, could you contact the hospital and find out what the status is on Sherrie? I want to get there, but I know I have to wait for the OSI and FBI clowns to get here."

Penkowsky nodded and left for one of the patrol cars to have them check.

Meanwhile, Paul briefed Lt Col Burns on the crime scene and the barren look of JR's room.

"Sir, Mrs. Johnson was stabbed in the abdomen, and it appears their son, Patrick Johnson Jr., or JR, as he is called, has been kidnapped. His bedroom is completely empty. I mean everything but his bed and dresser is gone. Whoever did this knew exactly what they were doing." He paused and then asked him, "Sir, may I suggest we initiate a recall of all off-duty personnel to walk through the fields throughout the base?"

Burns agreed and used his radio to contact the LE Desk to initiate a recall of all off-duty personnel for a special tasking and to have all personnel report to the Guard Mount Room for a briefing in forty-five minutes.

John came up to Patrick with a big grin on his face. "We have a witness! Seems that a neighbor across the street told one of the patrolmen that she saw a red Ford pickup truck that had a dent in the left front fender parked outside your home with a visitor pass taped to the windshield. I just put the word out to the desk. They will pass it on to the gates and visitor control."

At that, Patrick jerked his head up and asked, "A red Ford pickup with a dent in the left front fender with a visitor pass? I saw him leave as I turned on to the street. Did the witness get a plate number or a description of the driver?"

Paul's pager went off, and he went to the car to call the desk. All Patrick and the others heard was "u-huh" and "Are you sure? Thanks."

Paul went back and told Patrick the bad news. "It seems that a red Ford pickup with a dent in the left front fender dropped off his pass and went through the gate just before it closed. And get this, he had a young boy in a car seat next to him. I'm sorry, Patrick."

Penkowsky came back and told Patrick Sherrie was now being prepped in the ER and getting ready to go up to the operating room. He told Patrick that as soon as he was finished here, he would take him to the hospital since he would not be able to get to his truck. He nodded his thanks and turned to Paul.

"Okay, let's presume he is no longer on base. Let's go talk to the witness. Maybe she can provide information for the civil authorities to catch this guy."

He then realized what he had said and apologized to Paul. "I am not doing the investigation on this one. It's up to you, my friend."

Paul, John, and Patrick went across the street to join the crowd around the primary witness who was being interviewed by Sergeant (Sgt) Jones, one of the responding patrolmen. Jones introduced the witness.

"SMSgt Gibbons, this is Mrs. Rosemary Smyth, wife of SMSgt Gregory Smyth of the Civil Engineers Squadron (CES). She has a good description of both the individual and the vehicle." He then turned to Mrs. Smyth and introduced Paul as the lead investigator.

Paul looked at her, told her to take her time and to tell them exactly that she saw.

"I saw a red pickup truck. It had a rather large dent in the left front fender and a visitor pass in the lower corner of the windshield. I heard him talking to Mrs. Johnson through the front door as if she knew who it was. She opened the door and let him in." She looked around somewhat sheepishly and continued.

"When he left, he had what I took to be little Patrick Jr. in his car seat and a cardboard box with some words on it. I think it said something like 'bric-a-brac,' but I cannot be sure."

"Anything else you might remember?" Paul asked.

"Now this is a little strange, but he talked to her through the closed door, telling her that 'I'm taking JR to the park' and that he would have him back in time for the party. They were both in his truck, and they left just before you got home. I hope this all helps."

Paul asked, "Mrs. Smyth, could you give a license plate and description of the person you saw or anything else that might be helpful?"

Mrs. Smyth declared regretfully, "I can't remember the plate number, but I can give you a description of him. He was about twenty to thirty, tall, about six foot six, about 210 pounds with short blond hair. He wore an old pair of blue jeans and a long-sleeve light-blue Western shirt and hiking boots, and he was clean shaven. I feel so embarrassed that I can't remember the license plate, but I am sure it will come back to me later. This is such a tragic episode for our small street."

She looked at Patrick and told him, "If you need anything, let me know, and please let all of us know how she is doing." With that, she gave him a hug and went back in her home.

Patrick looked down and realized his uniform and shoes were covered in Sherrie's blood. He told Penkowsky he needed three things: "Top, I need three things in this order: one, a smoke; two, a trip to the hospital; and three, a clean uniform. However, I can't get inside my quarters right now. I have a clean set of BDUs at my office."

He gave Patrick a smoke and said, "I thought you quit," as he lit it for him. "If you are cleared to go now, I will take you to the hospital and have your clean uniform brought to the hospital for you. "What you need and we do not have at the shop, I will take care of it."

For some reason, Patrick looked around; and at the small hill behind his home, just outside the fence line, with a chill up his spine, just as in Iraq when that same feeling had saved his ass—did he see something up there, or did he long to see something, maybe a suspect? Was the suspect up there in the hills overlooking the base watching him? With those thoughts, he got into Penkowsky's vehicle and drove off to the hospital to be with his wife when she wakes up.

4

Duval went no faster than the speed limit when he reached the main gate. He put the visitor's pass in the box and then moved off base. No sooner had his tail gate left the base boundary than he saw the gates slamming shut, imprisoning all those who wanted to leave and stopping all from entering. He waited until the left-turn signal came on so he could be above the boundary fence line and he could pull over. Just by chance, this one spot was above the Senior NCO Housing Complex, and he could see all the flashing blue-and-red lights in front of Johnson's quarters. Then he saw the medics carry Sherrie into the ambulance and race off to the base hospital.

He knew that Sherrie would be okay, maybe losing her spleen but nothing else. After all, he had to learn where the vital organs were in case he had to intimidate a captured bad guy and did not want to kill him outright. "Mad Dog" is what they had called him and his Special Forces unit in training. However, his smile soon retracted as he heard a siren coming up behind him and watched a California Highway Patrol car scream past to the turn off to the main gate.

Must be calling in all the heavy-hitters on this. Time for me to beat feet, he thought.

He pulled out onto the town road, watching his back to see if he was being followed. When he made it to the storage lockers and opened one side and backed the truck inside then closed and locked the door and looked around, nothing had changed, but that would soon cease. He looked at JR and saw that he was sound asleep in his car seat. He opened the door to the next locker, and picking up JR from his car seat, he put him in a new car seat in the 1992 Ford Ranger that was registered in his real name. Duval had previously put in fresh clothes for him and a rough idea of clothes and snack food that JR might like. He finished moving everything else he would need and then closed the door. He had installed a speaker so he could hear JR if he cried out.

He removed the license plates from the Ford pickup and put them to the side. He would dispose of them away from the scene. He then removed the vehicle identification number plate and placed everything else, including the vehicle registration, near a drum of caustic acid. Even though he knew the fumes could not get to him since the lid was still on, he took no chances now that he was close to completing his crime and having his son. He put on the white coveralls, a special respirator that would keep him from inhaling the fumes and face mask, followed by rubber gloves.

He opened the lid, and using special chemical-resistant tongs, he placed the vehicle registration and the VIN plate into the drum. Next went his rubber face mask that included his wig followed by his clothes and tennis shoes. He looked around, certain that nothing was amiss, clamped the lid down tight, picked up the plates, and walked to the wall door and closed it quickly. There he quickly removed his protective clothing. He would dispose of them later.

He went to check on JR, making certain that he was still sleeping and not overcome by any fumes that might have leaked through the doorway. He pulled on his new Levi's and Western snap-button light-blue shirt that was common for the area and his old scruffy cowboy boots. He put his everyday cowboy hat on the front dash. Then Duval opened the door and, seeing no one (he knew the owner was not around), drove out and closed and locked both locker doors.

He knew better than to drive near the base, so he took a long trip through town and set out heading north to Sacramento by the quickest route, I-215 to I-5. The distance was 435 miles, and he knew he should not attempt it, but he was going to try it in eight hours. The first order of business was lunch for him and JR. He hoped that JR liked what most kids liked—PB&J with an apple fruit drink. For Duval, he was going to eat a PB&J with his son and drink coffee. He pulled into the first rest stop with inside restrooms.

"Hey, buddy, time to wake up. Daddy has to go to the bathroom. What about you? When we come back, we can have some lunch. How about PB&J for both of us and for you apple fruit juice? That's all I have for now, but we will eat a burger for dinner, okay?"

With that, JR's eyes lit up.

JR looked at Duval with fear in his eyes. "You are not my daddy. Where is my daddy?" He started to cry and wail. He did not know this man. "I want my daddy," he cried out as Duval reached inside the truck to unhook him from his car seat.

"I know it is hard for you to understand now, but it will easier in a couple of years as you get older. The people you were with that you thought was your mom and dad were really your aunt Sherrie and uncle Patrick. I am your daddy—always have been, always will be your daddy. They were taking care of you until I could take you to my home."

JR looked at him with a quizzical look and asked him if he now had two daddies.

Duval laughed and told him no, that he had only one daddy, and that his aunt and uncle love him very much; that is why they took care of him while he was away.

"You okay now, buddy? I know it will take some time to get used to each other, but we will get along just fine."

Duval unhooked JR, pulled him out of his car seat, and put him in his stroller. They headed toward the doors. Duval's head was constantly looking around, trying to see if anyone noticed him.

Just outside the door, Duval heard a screech of tires. He quickly turned his head around, fearing the worst, but only a car pulled up and a young teenager quickly got out of the car and ran inside the building. Making sure no other vehicles had followed him into the rest stop, Duval and JR went inside. Duval headed for the men's room, and just as he finished peeing, he looked at JR and saw him smile.

"Uh oh, did you do a stinky just now, son?" He quickly washed his hands then put JR on the changing table and changed his diaper, added a fresh dose of powder, and put him back in his stroller.

"Let's get back in the car now, have lunch, then start driving again."

He stayed in the Jeep with him, giving him a half a PB&J sandwich and his fruit drink.

Before they started on the road again, Rod spoke to JR to see if he had understood that he was his daddy and that the man and woman he had been with were his aunt and uncle and that they were now going to get his mommy and then finish driving home.

JR looked at him with what an adult would say "skeptically," but he accepted it. Rod knew it would take time.

"Okay, son, we are off again. Hopefully, we can make my planned stop before you need to be changed again." He made sure JR's pacifier was connected to the seat.

Before Duval started the Jeep, he checked around, saw no one suspicious, then pulled out. Just as he took the on-ramp back to the interstate, a California Highway Patrol car entered the parking lot. Duval maintained his entry speed onto the highway, but not three minutes later, he saw the same CHP car come up behind him with his red lights on. As he pulled over, he thought to himself, *I will not try and evade him and possibly kill my son.* However, the CHP car went screaming past him.

Five miles later, traffic backed up and stopped. He was caught in a traffic jam, and that was not good. Like everyone else, he got out of his car, trying to see what happened, when two ambulances went past with lights flashing and sirens blaring. Someone came up and told him that he heard over the radio there was a bad accident up ahead and wreckage was all over the highway. All he could think of was the young kid in the speeding car at the rest stop.

Ninety minutes later, the traffic finally began to move; and as he looked at the car, it was the same one that had rushed into the rest stop. He could see where the car had collided with a tree, but the view of the carnage was blocked by a blue tarp.

His next stop in three hours or so would be for supper.

5

As Patrick and the First Sergeant headed to the base hospital, they saw two unmarked cars with flashing blue lights behind the grills of the cars come up.

"Now the fun begins," Penkowsky told Patrick as he pulled to the side of the road to let them swing onto the street. "FBI and OSI working together? I seriously doubt it, but you never know. Paul just might have to put the fear of the Wing King in them, and everything will be calm, cool, and professional, but I bet you lunch at the club that does not happen."

Patrick looked at him and replied, "You're on, pal."

Not another word was said as Patrick thought about this crime. Something just did not fit right, but damned if he could figure it out. When they got to the base hospital, the Shirt pulled into the First Sergeant's reserved parking slot. Patrick was out of the car and sprinting toward the ER entrance, leaving the car door open for the Shirt to close and shaking his head as he took off after Patrick.

Patrick ran up to the counter. The startled nurse looked at him and saw the blood on his uniform and asked, "Sir, are you okay? Do you need any help?"

Patrick, looking around, found the area where they must have first put Sherrie. The bloody kitchen towels were still on the floor.

He walked over to the treatment area as the nurse arrived after him. He looked at her and said, "Where is my wife? Is she dead? Where is Sherrie?"

"Sir, I am Captain Middleton, the chief nurse on duty. Is your wife's name Sherrie Johnson? She is upstairs in surgery. The Hospital

Commander, Dr. Thompson, is with her now. He is an excellent trauma surgeon, and I can assure you she could not be in better hands."

At that point, Penkowsky came in and asked if First Sergeant Brownlie was in.

Captain Middleton looked at the command listing and said he was.

"Would you please call him and tell him that First Sergeant Penkowsky is here with MSgt Johnson? We need to put him someplace to calm down, and I do not think this is the right place to do that."

She called MSgt Paul Brownlie and explained the situation. She hung up the phone and told them that he was coming right down.

The Medical Squadron First Sergeant arrived and stopped when he saw Patrick and Bill Penkowsky and realized what the situation was. "Patrick, why don't we go up to my office while Bill gets you a clean uniform—right down to your skivvies, socks, and shoes." He looked at the bloody mess on the floor, looked at Middleton, and jerked his thumb at it. The scowl on his face was not good, and she could only hope he would not say anything to the Old Man as her evaluation time was coming up.

Upstairs, as they walked past the orderly room, the clerks tried to look busy, but word on something like this traveled fast on a base. However, curiosity got the better of them, and they could not help but look at Patrick in his bloody uniform.

Inside Brownlie's office, Patrick smelled coffee; Brownlie poured him a cup and watched him drink the hot coffee.

Penkowsky, shaking his head, told Patrick, "I will go to Clothing Sales. Anything else you might need from your office or Clothing Sales? I will take the cost out of the squadron fund."

Patrick told him thanks and watched as he left the office. Brownlie told him that he would see if Patrick could change into a set of scrubs and take a shower. Then they would go to lunch after he changed.

Johnson looked at Brownlie and asked him to point him in the direction of the nearest shower so he could clean up before his clean uniform arrived.

Brownlie called down to supply and asked for two sets of scrubs to be brought up to his office. Johnson removed his blues and stepped into the first set of scrubs then walked down to one of the wards to take a shower. He put on the other clean set and went back to Brownlie's office.

Just as he got back to Brownie's office, Penkowsky came in with his clean set of BDUs and all the accessories. "Your BDUs will stand up to long hours better than your blues would, and don't worry about getting your uniform cleaned up. An off-duty patrolman came by and picked up your uniform and already took it to the cleaners for you. He says it is the least he could do for you after you helped him last year with a personal problem."

Patrick nodded to him as he started to get dressed.

"As soon as you are dressed, we will go to the club. Paul and John will meet us there with the FBI agent as well."

Just as they started to leave, the phone rang.

"I told them no calls except for my wife and the Old Man." "First Sergeant Brownlie, how may I help you?"

He listened then pulled the phone away from his ear. "Yes, dear, he is in here now, and his wife is still in surgery. Honey, I do not think that is a good idea now. I doubt Patrick is going to be eating at home for the next couple of days. Tell the wives to hold off on cooking any meals until he is allowed back in the house. We are on our way out the door to go eat at the club. If I hear anything, I will call you as soon as I can. I love you too. Bye, hon."

As they left, he told his chief clerk, "No release of information on the condition of Mrs. Johnson until you get the word from me, do you understand me? Make sure everyone gets the word."

The clerk replied with, "Yes, Top, I understand."

He nodded at his clerk and bragged to Penkowsky, "I have the best orderly room NCOIC on this base. In fact, he will be promoted next month to E-5 first time out. Now that is confidence in my people. I have the right people right here right now!"

All Johnson and Penkowsky could do was look at each other and smile. They knew they had the right people, but the way Brownlie was bending over backward for them, they were not going to get into a pissing contest—especially if they were going to lunch with him.

Penkowsky told Johnson he had his radio with him and that if anything came down from the hospital, Paul would get the first word.

They climbed into Brownlie's station wagon as he told Penkowsky, "My car is much more comfortable that your old vehicle is. My lower back is still killing me from that Saturday we had up in the hills last month, and don't you deny it either, or you will pay for all three lunches."

"Does that mean you are paying for all three lunches today?" Penkowsky asked with a large grin on his face. Even Johnson got into the act by smiling.

They pulled up to the NCO club, from which they could see the main gate where television trucks were nose to bumper on both sides of the street and the gate guards were trying to be as profes- sional as they could, trying to keep the entry and exit drives clear for base traffic.

Just then they saw two peacekeeper vehicles roll up at the gate and parked on each side of the gate guard shack.

"I guess I need to make a statement after I talk with the FBI, OSI, and Public Affairs," Johnson grumbled as they went inside. "Maybe Public Affairs will have one made up for me—or at least I hope they will."

He passed neighbors and coworkers that he and Sherrie went out to the club to eat and party with. They asked him the normal questions of how Sherrie was and how he was holding up.

His mind was in total confusion. One part wanted to be with his wife, and the second part wanted to get his son back. He knew, however, that the longer it took for the return of a kidnapped child, the harder it would be to have a normal life.

Just after they finished going through the food line, Penkowsky received a message to call Sommers at Patrick's quarters.

"I'll be right back. I need to make a phone call."

Five minutes later, he returned with a message for Patrick. "TSgt Summers, SMSgt Gibbons, and an FBI Special Agent Donald Abernathy are on their way here for lunch. The FBI wants to talk to you. That's all I know."

Patrick looked for and helped push two tables together. Soon Gibbons and Summers entered the dining room with a guy who must have stood seven feet tall and looked like he was a large oak tree.

His size caused everyone to stop eating and try to figure him out. One thing was certain—he was not assigned to the base; otherwise, he would have been remembered as he stuck out like the proverbial sore thumb.

Johnson looked at the new guy as he began to go through the lunch line and said out loud, "If he were the FBI agent, I would seriously have second thoughts about meeting him in a dark alley at night."

Both First Sergeants agreed with his assessment. The three of them waited to see them come through the doorway.

Gibbons came out first, shaking his head. He went over to the tables and told them, "You know that Summers eats a lot, right? Well, the other guy eats twice as much as he does, and he says he will go back for dessert."

Summers came out with his plate full of chili mac, a side salad, and two slices of bread. Shaking his head, he mumbled, "I can't out-eat this guy. You see how much I have on my plate? He has three times as much, and he says he is going back for Boston cream pie. He actually asked them to try and save the whole pie!" Still shaking his head, he finally sat down but waited until the FBI agent came out and ambled over to the table.

Summers told them, "As you can tell, as heavy as he is, he does not make a sound walking. Utterly amazing, my friends, utterly amazing." Summers made the introductions around the table. "Patrick,

this is FBI Special Agent Donald Abernathy from the Los Angeles Field Office. Don, MSgt Johnson is the victim of the kidnapping and husband of the assault victim, Sherrie Johnson."

Johnson shook Abernathy's hand. It was a firm shake, just as he suspected it would be considering his size. "Okay, Special Agent Abernathy, tell me that you have found my son and the bastard that almost killed my wife. I want nothing kept from me from this point forward. Am I clear?"

Abernathy looked at him and told him, "SMSgt Gibbons told me you have had extensive training as an SP Investigator, so I will make you a deal. You do not hold anything away from me, and I will hold nothing from you, am I clear?"

Johnson nodded his agreement to the FBI agent.

"Okay, Special Agent, you have the floor first. Tell me you have found my son, damn it!"

"Slow down, son, I have had a bad morning and have not eaten since early this morning. That is why I have a lot here. Let me eat something first, then I will talk with you." And with that, Abernathy began to dig into his meal, attacking the large side salad which was covered with blue cheese dressing. Then he began to devour the pile of chili mac. All four airmen could only wonder what his stomach would look like after lunch.

He then announced "I am going back for the pie. Anyone want coffee? When I get back, we can talk."

While waiting for his return, a young airman came over to the table and told Johnson that he was Airman First Class Baker from the Wing Public Affairs Office. "MSgt Johnson, I was told you were here. I have a script you can go by if you want as we suggest you address the press outside the gate after your lunch."

Before Johnson could say anything, he left, leaving the notes and letting the four of them review the talking points from the Public Affairs Office.

Patrick commented, "I think I want to wait on this until after I talk with 'Paul Bunyan' buying out all the food from the club. I hope they charge him dearly for it too."

Patrick noticed his cup was empty, and when he went to get a refill, he noticed the agent talking with the food server, convincing her to let him have the whole pie. Shaking his head, he returned to the table and told the others "You won't believe this. First, my wife almost gets killed, and my son is kidnapped, then this clown eats everything in the club, and now he is trying to sweet talk the food server. Totally unbelievable day!"

"Patrick, calm down. What has happened to you and your family has affected us all, but you know how to control yourself in bad situations. That is what has made you an excellent Security Police investigator, so calm down, or I will have the Shirt take you out of the building and face the gate crowd alone!" Paul told him in no uncertain terms. He turned and looked at the doorway from the food line and saw Abernathy with a whole chocolate cream pie in one hand and plates for all in his other hand.

"I could not sit here and eat it all by myself. I mean it would not look right, and besides, the gal I was talking to said this is Patrick's favorite pie, and considering what has happened, there is no charge today and for you to consider it 'comfort food.'" He sat down and passed the pie down to Summers to cut and serve.

He looked at Johnson and told him, "Sir, what I have seen happen on base today and how everyone respects you and your wife is beyond comprehension for me to understand. I have yet to run into an agent that has the respect that you have. That is why I was talking to her in there. I heard you blow off steam. Perhaps that was the first time for you today?" He paused then told him, "Before you ask, yes,

I have spoken to the OSI agent at the scene. He gave me some basic information, but not much."

Patrick said, "You're right, it is the first time, and I apologize, and yes, that is my favorite pie here in the club. Let's eat before it melts." He sat there, eating and talking with the agent, giving him some background information but no ideas, clues, or reasons why the attack and kidnapping happened.

"Right now, we have a forensics team in your home going over everything with a fine-tooth comb—so far, nothing. We have also installed a phone monitoring team to record any calls coming in. You can stay there if you want, just don't push the teams, okay?"

"Thanks anyway, but I will find someplace else to stay until the investigation is over with. However, you are telling me there is no forensics evidence at my quarters of who did this? No footprints outside or inside my home? What about my son's room?"

Patrick tried to remember what he had seen earlier. "Wait, there was a glass on the kitchen counter, and one of the kitchen drawers open a little. Sherrie never left any kitchenware on the countertop; she always puts things in the dishwasher or puts them away. And she never left drawers open because of JR."

"Yes, we noticed all that and checked them out. No prints, whatsoever, anywhere inside or outside."

Looking at Johnson again, he told him, "Now I know you know the drill and all the questions, but I have to ask them. If you want to expand on a question, go ahead."

Johnson nodded, looked around the table, and said, "I have one thing that just came to mind. I did saw an old battered red pickup truck leaving my street as I pulled in. I did not give it another thought, but one of my neighbors, Mrs. Smyth, said she saw the same truck. Other than that, nothing."

The agent looked at his notes and nodded then asked him, "Sir, have you or your wife received any phone calls that might have been out of the ordinary? Any nuisance phone calls or threats on your life or your family?"

"No, sir, none of those calls. No threats on my life or harm to my family."

Johnson looked at his watch and saw it was only 1330 hours. "God, it has only been two and a half hours since I arrived home. I think the pie did all of us some good. Thank you, Agent Abernathy." With that, he got up from the tables, started to leave, telling everyone he would be back.

The agent looked at Johnson and told him, "I have written up a few notes if you would consider letting me say a few words, give them the perspective from the eye of the FBI."

He thought about it and said, "Let's do it this way. Paul, you first then FBI then me. However, I want to wait until MSgt Brownlie comes back with current information on Sherrie."

"That sounds like a good plan and will give me a chance to find out anything from the team at your home. Excuse me, gentlemen, I need to make the call." The agent stepped away from the table and went to a corner to talk on his radio.

"Paul, what is your take on him? Do you think he is competent enough for this case? He seems so damned laid-back—almost too cocky—but then that is the image of the FBI, correct? Too cocky?"

"Patrick, both John and I watched him talk with OSI to gain control of the situation, and you know the rules. We have to give everything to the FBI, and they, in turn, will decide what they want to pass on to us. On the way over here, Donald, John, and I agreed to work together on this no matter how long it takes. Both John and I feel comfortable with him."

Before Johnson could respond, both Donald and MSgt Brownlie came to the table. Johnson looked at Brownlie and indicated he was to speak first.

"Patrick, sorry that took so long, but I had to wait for one of the nurses to come out and talk to me. The surgeon is closing now.

Sherrie is going to live; however, she will be in recovery until late this afternoon or early evening. They already have a private room for her, and they will put an extra bed in the room for you to use while Sherrie is in the hospital. The surgeon will talk to you when she comes out of Recovery. Wish I could tell you more, but I can't."

All Johnson could do was nod his head up and down and then glanced over at the FBI agent.

"Guys, I do not have any news at all from the house other than what Mrs. Smyth has provided us. Patrick, I am sure SMSgt Gibbons told you about NIMS, or rather the National Incident Management System. I intend to do that with you guys. No matter how long it takes, I will attempt to keep on this case. I suggest we put our heads together and come up with something strong for the media circus outside. They will want something, and I think they need to hear it from Air Force's side of the investigation that their kids and spouses are safe and secure on base, that this is not some sick psycho."

Johnson took what Public Affairs gave him and started to write down his notes while the three investigators worked on their presentations.

It was obvious that Johnson did not want to interfere with the investigators. He knew what they were doing. He knew how Gibbons and Sommers worked because he had served with them.

Gibbons took out a fresh piece of paper and wrote down the following questions:

1. Knowledge of Visitor Pass program?
2. Knowledge of quickest routes off base?
3. Someone assigned to Norton or someone Johnson had arrested in his long career?

Sommers had done the same thing. On his paper, he wrote:

1. Knowledge of base procedures for closing the gates
2. Knowledge of Visitor Control and Vehicle Pass procedures
3. Knew street layout for quick escape

FBI Special Agent Abernathy was working on three questions himself that he thought might be valid:

1. Knew military procedures
2. If so, was the suspect a veteran or someone from the base?
3. Who?

All four returned to the table with the First Sergeants, who decided it was now time to leave. They asked Johnson if he would be okay to drive back to get his car with Paul.

Johnson nodded then stuck his hand out to MSgt Penkowsky, saying, "Thanks, Shirt, for all you have done for me today. I will check in with you later after I hear something. Please thank the young troop for me for getting my uniforms taken care of."

He then did the same to First Sergeant Brownlie. "MSgt Brownlie, thanks for all you did for me this morning. Sorry about any mess you ended up with." Brownlie nodded and left.

Johnson turned to the remaining three and said, "Let's go and feed the circus."

Unfortunately, as they neared the front door, they heard a sound they were too familiar with—sirens of law enforcement vehicles. They stopped at the door and watched two LE sedans and a peacekeeper head toward the main gate.

Gibbons looked at Johnson and Sommers and told them, "Uh, guys, I think we better wait and see what is going on before we hit the gate. Seems the media animals are hungry, and a few may have overstepped the boundary line."

They watched the gate and security personnel get things back under control.

In the parking lot was an LE sedan with the roof lights flashing.

They walked over to the patrol car, and the driver got out.

"SMSgt Gibbons, I was directed by the commander to escort you wherever you need to go. Someone said you were going to the main gate to address the media?"

"That is right. We are waiting until the crowd becomes more manageable, and then we are going over there to address the circus. Then we will be going back to MSgt Johnson's quarters, where he will pick up his vehicle. Then you are to resume your patrol."

Gibbons looked back at the gate and saw that things were much improved, but the peacekeeper was still there—except now it was behind the gate house.

They got into Gibbons's car with the patrol car leading them with his lights on. Gibbons turned on his rotating blue light on the roof, and they went to face the crowd that seemed to have grown since they went into the club to eat. As they pulled up behind the gate, the crowd grew restless as they saw the four of them move in front of the main gate.

6

Paul figured that since he was the lead investigator, he would speak first followed by Agent Abernathy then Patrick. "Ladies and gentlemen, I am Senior Master Sergeant Paul Gibbons of the Sixty-Third Security Police Squadron, Investigations Section. I am the lead investigator for this case. To my left is TSgt John Sommers, my co-investigator. To my right is FBI Special Agent Donald Abernathy. To his right is MSgt Patrick Johnson Sr., the husband and father of the victims." He paused to try and get a feel of the crowd, to see if anyone suspicious was mixed in with the reporters.

"I will give you a status of our investigation, then Agent Abernathy will present his status, and finally MSgt Johnson will speak to you. We ask that all questions be held until after we are all finished. Thank you."

Gibbons opened his notebook. "Before I begin the status of the investigation, let me reassure all who live and work here that you are safe. Your safety is our business. This is an isolated crime that happened. This *criminal act* has never occurred here before.

"At approximately 1100 this morning, an assault on Ms. Sherrie Johnson occurred. In addition, her son, Patrick Johnson Jr., was taken from his home by persons unknown. The investigation is in full swing with Security Police, the FBI, and the Air Force Office of Special Investigation, with the FBI being the lead investigating unit. The residents on the street where the crime occurred have been a tremendous help including one neighbor provided us with vital information. I now give you Special Agent Donald Abernathy."

"Good afternoon, I am Special Agent Donald Abernathy of the FBI Los Angeles Field Office. As it turns out, my specialty is juvenile kidnappings. This being a double crime scene does not change how we operate. First thing is the recovery of Mrs. Johnson, the only witness to the crime, and the return of Patrick Johnson Jr.

"As SMSgt Gibbons stated, we do have some substantial eyewitness accounts of an individual leaving the scene. The person of interest is described as clean shaven, age around twenty to twenty-five, six foot to six foot five, about 210 pounds, and short blond hair. He was wearing an old pair of blue jeans, a long-sleeve blue Western shirt, and white tennis shoes. He was last seen driving an older model red Ford pickup truck with a rather large dent in the left front." He paused for a minute then continued. "Based on the assault of Mrs. Johnson this morning, he is to be considered armed and dangerous. Please do not try to stop him. Contact your local police department or the Security Police Law Enforcement Desk with all the important information. After MSgt Johnson talks, we will give you a priority line directly to the Investigations Office, where we will be establishing a command center to handle all calls. Thank you." He then motioned to Patrick to step forward.

Everyone was quiet, waiting to hear from the husband and father of the victims.

"Good afternoon. I am MSgt Patrick Johnson Sr. All I want—my son, who turned two years old today, back and my wife to recover. As of a few minutes ago, my wife was still in surgery, and so far, there have been no demands from the person who did this. At 1100 hours…excuse me, I deal in military time…eleven this morning, as I turned onto my street for lunch with my wife and son at home, I noticed the red pickup truck mentioned earlier. I did not recognize it, but since we have many visitors on base, I looked for either a base decal or a visitor pass. The visitor pass was in the lower left corner of the windshield."

"When I entered my quarters, I found my wife on the kitchen floor, bleeding from a knife wound in her abdomen. I notified the authorities and applied first aid to the best of my ability. It was not until the investigators arrived that we discovered that my son had been taken." He paused before he continued.

"It was not until the investigator talked to the witness who saw the person leaving that I felt I should have noticed something. I am a trained lead investigator for the Law Enforcement Division of the Security Police Squadron. I have tried as hard as I can to think back, yet there was nothing that stuck out that should have triggered my senses."

The gate guard noticed a slight twitch in Patrick's voice, and she gave him a cup of water.

"That, ladies and gentlemen, is why we have the best in the squadron on the gates. They know, without being told, what to do. She did not ask if I wanted water, nor did I ask for water. She just knew!" He looked back at her and said, "Thank you."

He faced the crowd again. "To the person who took our son and assaulted my wife, I tell you this—we will not rest. We will not quit searching for you, and when you are found, you will be taken into custody, and I will see you appear in court." Patrick heard a noise behind him and saw the gate guard pass a slip of paper to John.

He showed the note to Paul, who addressed the media for the second time today.

"Ladies and gentlemen, I am going to give you the direct line to my office for information on this case. I ask that you get it out to the public immediately. As soon as we have any information, base Public Affairs will contact you. On behalf of the wing commander, Colonel Robert Williamson, please do not restrict the flow of traffic coming on or off base. If it does happen again, restrictions will be placed, so please work with us, and we will work with you. I have one last comment before I give you the phone number. At the present time, our pass and ID folks are going through the files of all visitors today, trying to find the license plate number of the red pickup. As soon as we have it, you will be contacted. Here is the direct line into the Security Police Investigations Command Center—714-382-2877. Tell the LE Desk you have information pertaining to this crime. Any information, no matter how trivial, might be important. We have given out enough information for now. Thank you for your support in getting the word out."

With that done, the four of them departed the front gate without answering several questions from the media.

"Paul, if you do not mind, I would like a ride to my quarters so I can pick up my truck and go to the hospital. I want to be there when Sherrie is in her room. You guys carry on with the investigation and hope we get a phone call with the information we can use to get the bastard that did this to my family."

Paul passed on his thoughts to the LE patrolman and fell in line behind him with lights no longer flashing. They arrived at Patrick's quarters and found the crowd that had been there when they left for lunch had departed, leaving just the patrolman outside and the FBI technical truck still in front. They got out of the car, and Mrs. Smyth came running over and told them some good news.

"I finally remembered the license plate number of the pickup truck. I hope it is not too late." She paused to read her notes. "The number is 5WQZ949. The three numbers are my birth month and year. I feel so bad I did not remember it before." She gave Patrick a hug and told him she was going to church tonight to pray for Sherrie's quick recovery and pray for the safe return of Patrick Jr. "He is such a good little boy."

"Thank you, Rosemary. Thank you for everything you have done for us today. I will let you know as soon as I hear anything."

They walked across the street to Patrick's, and Paul promised to let him know as soon as he had an update.

Paul told him, "I want you to contact us when she is awake and alert, probably tomorrow morning. You know the drill, Patrick."

The FBI agent told Patrick, "I need you to come inside for a few minutes. I need to go over a couple of things including the numbers of friends and family members. This will help us isolate any of the incoming phone calls."

"Let us go. I need to get to the hospital. Time is almost there for me to be with her. Paul, I will call you."

Inside the house, Patrick gave the agent a list of friends and family members that called on a regular basis. "I have also done some thinking about anyone suspicious that might do this, and I still cannot think of one. Is there anything else?"

"MSgt Johnson, I look around the house and see that there are photos of you and, I guess, your wife, but none of your son. I find it strange that there are no photos at all. Do you have any photos of him we can use for the press?"

Patrick looked at him, then around the living room. The two photos of the three of them were gone from the walls; only a faint outline of a frame was left.

"Agent Abernathy, whoever did this knew exactly what he was doing. If I find one in our family files, I will get it to you. The missing photos can only mean one thing—it is going to be twice as hard to find him. He is damn good. My bet is that he is either military or is a veteran of special operations. That is my professional opinion as a security police investigator. Now if you do not need me anymore, I would like to leave and be with my wife when she comes out of surgery."

The FBI agent watched him leave for the hospital and knew that Patrick was right; he needed to be at the hospital.

By the time Patrick arrived at the hospital, he knew the individual that did this to his family was long gone by now and was nowhere in the local area. Patrick did not know how right he was. His mind was like a large compartment, and inside were three smaller compartments. One was labeled Crime Scene, the second one was Sherrie, and the third but most certainly not the last one, Patrick Jr. This was the way he always worked different scenarios, which helped him solve crimes; however, this time it was different. There were no clearly defined clues, no actual suspects, and no rhyme or reason for this crime. Somewhere out there was his son. As he walked inside the hospital main door, he prayed that JR was okay and was not going to be harmed.

7

By 3:00 p.m., Rod and JR were now close to three hours north of San Bernardino. He did not realize just how many red pickup trucks there were on the road. He saw so many red trucks that he lost count, and almost all had a small child in the truck. All the trucks that had been pulled over by the highway patrol had the child or children out of the truck, and in two cases, the car seat was removed as well.

He was glad that he had thought to purchase a new car seat and to change vehicles. He told himself, "I believe that I have everything covered. On second thought, maybe not everything is covered. I need to somehow change his hair color, but at only two years of age, maybe I should just leave it alone for now."

He realized that he had forgotten to turn on the police scanner he had purchased so he could listen to CHP calls. So as not to wake JR, he turned on the scanner to the CHP frequency then put in the earpiece. Now he could listen to all the CHP calls without awakening the boy. It would also help pass the time, he thought.

He was amazed at the constant stream of calls coming in from the public on red pickup trucks with boys and girls in the bed of the truck or kids in the front seat. Didn't these people understand that it was a red pickup truck with one child in a car seat? It seemed that mass hysteria had taken over common sense.

He looked in his rearview mirror and saw flashing red lights coming up on him, so he pulled over, and the CHP patrol went past him; he prayed it was not another accident. That last accident traffic jam had sent his nerves and timetable into a serious tailspin.

Thinking of accidents, he knew he had to get off at a truck stop, stretch his legs, and get something to eat. He also wanted to catch any news reports about the kidnapping. His son, whom he now called Rodney "Rod" Duval Jr., was still sound asleep. Maybe the motion of the moving car let him sleep. Sure, it had cost him some big bucks, but he had been able to get a birth certificate with the boy's correct name and date of birth. Just then, he saw a sign for a truck stop that looked like a chain which would be perfect.

His dad had told him, "Son, if you are on the road and get hungry, look for a truck stop with lots of trucks and cars. That means the food and service is good." The first thing he did was to gas up. He was still at half, but he did not know how far the next truck stop was. He paid cash for the gas, parked the Jeep, got JR out of the car, and went inside.

Walking inside, Duval found a small booth and put the car seat on the bench next to him. Just then, one of the counter waitresses turned up the TV when it showed the news conference from the gate at Norton AFB. He swung his head around to listen as everyone else did. A waitress came by with a glass of water and asked if he wanted anything to drink while he was looking at the menu. What really got her attention was his son sleeping in his car seat. "Have you heard the news about the kidnapping?"

"First, coffee, and yes, I heard it. My son will not be out of my sight. I would like a burger and fries along with a PB and grape jelly sandwich for him. He likes it in small cut pieces, please."

She repeated the order and quickly brought the coffee. She commented what a handsome young boy JR was, but he was trying to catch most of the news conference. From what he could gather, it was pretty much what he had hoped for.

I am the master of the universe, the master of this crime. If everything holds like this until I get home to Wyoming, I will be okay, he thought. *At least until they open the storage garages, then they will know they lost a lot of time in searching. By that time, I should be out of the state.*

He looked ravenously as others had their meals brought to them; he had not eaten since early this morning, and now the excite- ment had caused him to be extra hungry. Finally, his meal came to him, but just as soon as he bit into his burger, he almost gagged.

Two CHP officers stepped out of their patrol cars, and after looking at the parked vehicles, they entered the restaurant and looked around. They walked down toward him. He nodded as he bit into the hamburger, trying not to bolt out of there, but they walked past him and talked to another customer and asked him what type of vehicle he had. They asked him to step outside for a minute.

As they went by, one of them stopped and looked at the baby and told Duval, "Sir, you have a handsome son there. You know about the kidnapping today? Keep close tabs on him. Have a good day."

"Yes, sir, I am keeping him close to me now especially after the news today. Thank you for your advice." After the CHP officer left, it was all Duval could do to not lose his stomach over it, but he passed the test. He turned his attention back to the TV to hear Patrick's plea for the safe return of "his son."

He then used the phone at the table to call his wife, Josie, at the hotel she was staying at in Sacramento and told her he was on the road but had stopped for something to eat. "I should be there around 10:00 p.m. I can't wait to see you again. And yes, he and Nanna had enjoyed their time together. Right now he is sleeping like a little lamb. I have a PB&J sandwich which I will cut up so he can eat if he wakes up while I am driving."

The boy began to fuss a little, so he told her, "Rod is starting to fuss, and I need to go and probably change and feed him before I get back on the road. I love you and will see you in a few hours." He hung up the phone and told the waitress he would be back but needed another cup of coffee.

She showed him where the family restroom was and made sure there were no mothers nursing in there. "He really is a handsome devil," she said.

He left to change him, and he also warmed up a bottle of milk in the special bottle warmer. As he was giving the little guy his milk, he thought that this place could set high standards for truck stops what with the family room, phones on the tables, and of course, the excellent meal he had just finished. Just as he was leaving, a mother came in with a real small bundle of joy. "Looks like I am leaving just in time," Duval told her as he quickly left the room.

Back at the table, he broke up some of the PB&J sandwich for his son as he drank his coffee. He had signaled for another cup of coffee and another sandwich for his JR when a Breaking News sign came on the TV screen, interrupting the afternoon talk show.

"We seem to have a break in the kidnapping this morning of Patrick Johnson Jr., son of Air Force MSgt Patrick Johnson from Norton AFB whose wife was also seriously wounded this morning. It seems there was a red pickup truck found abandoned on the east side of San Bernardino that matches the description of the eyewitnesses at the scene." The news anchor held the earpiece tighter in his ear as if he did not want to lose any of the report.

"There is an empty baby seat in the cab of the truck that might be the same as was taken this morning. The license plate is off by one digit, but there is no dent in the front fender."

Suddenly he shook his head and told the viewers, "Folks, we apologize. Seems this pickup has been tagged before being in the wrong place at the wrong time. The vehicle has not, I repeat, not been located yet. We apologize for the inaccurate report."

Everyone just shook their heads, murmured in discontent, and wished the kidnapper would be found before tonight. No one wanted to think of the possible outcome if he was not found.

As long as his son ate the finger food and drank his milk, he was content to sit and drink his coffee before the large dinner crowds came in. He asked the waitress to fill his cup one more time.

"As soon as he is finished eating, we will be going. I want to make a purchase in the store. Can I pay for everything there?"

She paused then said, "Do you need another sandwich for your son, or do you think he will fall asleep in the car?"

He told her that he would fall asleep once he got started. Rod went to the store and bought a thermos and some candy for himself to chew on to keep alert. He then had her fill the new thermos with fresh hot black coffee.

Once everything was done, he went to the Jeep, buckled JR, and made sure his pacifier was tied to the seat and his glass was connected to his tray. Rod then then left the truck stop, back onto Interstate 5 north; it was now 4:00 p.m., so he knew he would be there around ten.

8

Patrick arrived at the hospital before Sherrie was sent to the recovery room. He checked in with MSgt Brownlie to thank him again for his orderly room and the support he had given to Patrick with the shower. He then went to the ward Sherrie would go to, and they told him what room she would be in. There were two beds in there—one for her and one for him. Already there were plenty of flowers. A large planter of flowers was from the squadron with a note from the Command Section, one smaller planter from the Enlisted Spouses club, and one from the neighborhood.

Probably from Mrs. Smyth, Patrick mused.

Just then one of the nurses came in and told him, "Sherrie is out of surgery and will be in the recovery room for about three hours. Being as you cannot visit her in the recovery room, I suggest you get a bite to eat if you want to be in here when she comes in."

Patrick looked at his watch and saw it was after 4:00 p.m. and decided the nurse was right. The only problem was he did not want to eat at the club and definitely not at home, so he decided to eat at the dining hall. But first, he needed to call Paul to see if tips had come in yet.

He used the room phone and called the Investigations Office. Thankfully, Paul answered the phone. "Paul, it's Patrick. Any tips or news come in yet?"

"Patrick, the answer goes both ways. Yes, we have had tips, and no, they are not valid. The CHPs have been pulling over every red pickup on the highways, and every one of them is a valid truck and driver. They are going to back off a little tonight unless they see the license plate. The locals thought they had the truck in the eastern part of town right down to the dent in the left fender, but it was not the case." He stopped talking then told him, "Patrick, I have a feeling this is not going to be solved in the next week or month. I hate to tell you this, but I hope I am wrong."

Patrick thought long and hard on what his best friend in the squadron had told him. "Paul, I know what you are thinking. I am in the room Sherrie is going to be in. I am going to the dining hall for dinner. I do not want to eat at the club tonight; it was hard enough at lunch. Call me if you hear anything. I will be jotting down ideas I might have when I come back here. I feel so lost not being out there investigating this crime. It has hurt more than just my physical family. It has hurt my neighbors, wondering if it will happen to them as well some time. I want this bastard, Paul. I want him really bad!" At a loss for words, all Paul could do was to agree with him.

Then he told him, "Oh, by the way, I sent Anne to the commissary. 'Paul Bunyan' is coming over for dinner. I told her to buy out the place. He will probably eat everything in sight."

It took Patrick a few moments to try and remember who "Paul Bunyan" was until he remembered that he had given that name to the FBI agent, Abernathy. "Here is the phone number for the room." He then remembered. "Hey, Paul, thanks for the flowers. They are great. I am sure Sherrie will enjoy them when she comes to. Give my best to Anne. I am on my way out now. Hopefully, you and the agent will come up with some ideas. Talk to you later."

Patrick stepped out of the room and went down to the nurse's station and told them that he was going to the dining hall.

9

The dining hall had just opened when Patrick arrived. Those that were in his unit asked him how Sherrie was doing—not just out of kindness but because of genuine concern. At Christmas, Patrick and Sherrie would make up a batch or two of homemade fudge and bring it out to those who were working. Whether it was on the LE Desk or on patrol, they were there for them regardless of the hour. Now it was their turn to show concern for one of the best supervisors not only in the Security Police Squadron but on base.

It saddened them to have something like this happen when the base had pulled an "Excellent" rating from the Headquarters Military Airlift Command inspector general visit. Patrick told all who expressed concern that Sherrie was now out of surgery and in recovery and would be in her room in a couple of hours.

One group of airmen asked if there was anything they could do for him at his quarters. Patrick knew it was a thin gray line, for he could not have those in junior rank to him used for manual labor, so he told them, "Thanks anyway, guys, but my neighbors are going to watch the house for me. Plus, the FBI guys are in there monitoring the incoming phone calls."

One young airman, on base about a week and not assigned to a Law Enforcement flight yet, asked him, "Who was that towering giant we saw there today? I was on the search in the open fields near your quarters and saw him. I have never seen anyone like him."

"First, Airman Hopkins, if my memory serves me right, you are going on to patrol pretty soon, correct?" Without waiting for a response because he knew the answer, he continued, "Describe that person for me. What color was his hair? What was he wearing? How tall and what did he weigh? What kind of car did he have? A good patrolman will remember and answer those questions without hesitation."

Airman Hopkins thought about two seconds then answered all of Patrick's questions except for the car. "MSgt Johnson, that indi-vidual did not have a car. He left in the First Sergeant's car when you all left."

With a stern look, Patrick asked him "Airman Hopkins, how did he get to my quarters? Were there any cars there that looked like Federal agency cars?"

"Oh, shit, I blew it! Yes, there was a tan Ford Victoria at your quarters. I completely dismissed it. I just learned an unbelievably valuable lesson. Also, he did not leave with you and the First Sergeant. He left with the investigators after you left the scene."

"Yes, you did. However, you aced everything else. Good job, and welcome to the squadron. But now I need to get back to the hospital." With that, he was gone, hoping he would get back before Sherrie was moved into the room.

* * * * *

When Patrick arrived at the nurse's station on the ward, the head nurse saw him and told him, "MSgt Johnson, your wife will be coming down shortly. I need to ask you to sit in the waiting room while we get her settled in. She is not completely awake, but you will be able to talk with her at times."

"I understand. I need to go somewhere anyway—just as long as I know she is doing okay."

Patrick knew the Base Exchange (BX) flower shop was still open, so he went and looked at what they had left. He had started to leave when he spotted exactly what he wanted. They were flowers which were the same as her wedding bouquet—simple daisies and small roses. He went to the clerk and told her he wanted a small planter of pink roses and daisies.

"Is your wife the assault victim, and was that your son who was kidnapped? Is there any news on your wife or son?"

"No, unfortunately, nothing on our son. My wife is coming out of recovery just about now. I will wait for the planter and take it with me. I will be in the BX. How much time will you need?"

The clerk told him fifteen minutes and it should be ready.

In the BX he wandered around and bought a book to read, a get-well card, and a notepad. He paid for them and received some words of support from some of their friends and then went to the flower shop. The planter was on the counter ready to go.

"Considering the situation, I am going to give you a 10 percent discount, so your total is $15.25," the clerk told him.

He just nodded, gave her the money, and put the change in a can asking for donations for the "Help our Homeless Veterans" drive that was going on. He thanked her and left and headed back to the hospital.

Just as he turned into the hallway, Patrick saw the nurses and medical techs walk out of Sherrie's room. Her nurse saw Patrick and went over to him.

"Sir, I am Captain Holland, your wife's nurse for this evening. She is having some pain now, which is to be expected. Dr. Thompson will be in shortly to talk to you. If you have any questions, please feel free to ask."

He nodded his thanks and looked at the hospital bed that held his wife—his wife, his beautiful wife, with IV fluids flowing in her arms, but most disturbing was the tube in her nose that drained a brownish liquid into a suction device.

This does not look good, he mused to himself. He reached over to the chair and pulled it close to the bed and put the planter on her tabletop which, for now, lay across her lower legs. The sheet was pulled up even to her shoulders, which he knew she would never do; she never liked the sheet up all the way. He would fix it later. He heard a noise behind him, and he saw a doctor in white scrubs. "Dr. Thompson, I presume?"

"You must be MSgt Johnson. I was told that you had eyes in the back of your head and could tell who it was behind you. Yes, I am Dr. Thompson, also the Hospital Commander, but in here, the working side of the squadron, I am Doc."

He paused then asked Patrick to step outside the room. "I have several things I need to tell you. One, your wife will survive. Two, the spleen had to be removed. She suffered a puncture, and it was your quick thinking that saved her life. Three, your wife may not be able to bear any more children. Her attacker knew exactly what to do. Of course, puncturing her spleen was bad enough, but one ovary was nicked and could not be repaired. I'm sorry."

He paused and finished by telling Patrick, "As for her spleen removal, it is not life threatening, per se. She will need to get her flu shot annually plus a pneumonia shot when required. She already received it today during surgery."

Patrick held up his hand and suggested no more be said until Sherrie was awake. He asked if there was a handout he could read about spleen removal. Also, he asked for a copy of her injuries that could be forwarded to the SP Investigation. "I know it is not normal that you would provide a copy to the spouse, but in this case, I am asking for an exception to the rule."

Dr. Thompson thought about it for five seconds and told him, "Patrick, I had planned on doing so as soon as they are typed. Whatever goes to the investigators, you will get a copy as well." They went back into the room where Doc bent over Sherrie and listened to her lungs and heart. "Her lungs are clear, and she has a strong heart. She will be fine in a couple of days. The tube in her nose is to keep her stomach empty. We had to move her organs around, so to let everything return to normal, the stomach needs to be kept empty and small. In a day or two, she will be put on a liquid diet and then moved to a regular diet. Is there any type of food she is allergic to or does not like?"

Patrick shook his head. "No, she does not have any allergies, and there is nothing she does not like. Sometimes she likes to put hot sauce on her eggs in the morning. She likes everything she can eat."

"I will return later before I go home to check on her, but I am sure she will make a speedy recovery. The staff on this floor is top-notch. They told me you would be staying in here until she is released. That is okay with me. You can order your meals from here as well or eat in the dining room."

"Thank you, sir. I appreciate everything your squadron has done for my wife and me today." He shook hands with the doctor and watched him leave. He heard a rustle behind him and saw his wife trying to open her eyes.

"Patrick, what happened to me?" Her eyes looked around the room and especially the IV needle in her arm and the tube in her nose. "Where's JR? Is he okay? Who is he with?"

"Honey, JR is okay, and he is doing well. Dr. Thompson will be in to talk to you before he goes home. Go back to sleep."

Patrick watched his wife's eyes flutter as she surrendered herself to sleep. He had to ask a question but not here in the room, so he hurried down to the nurse's station.

"Captain, I have one question for you. What do I tell her when she wakes up for a longer period and asks about our son? What do I tell her if she asks me again what happened? I do not want to say the wrong thing right now while she is a bit wacky from the anesthesia." Patrick was torn from lying to her for the first time in their marriage or telling her the truth, not knowing what would mean for her recovery. Captain Holland told him, "You need to judge each question.

You would be safe to tell her what happened to her, but not about the kidnapping of your son until Dr. Thompson thinks it is safe to do so." She looked at Patrick and told him, "It will be a rough time for her. Sometimes the smallest upset can delay an excellent recovery time. Wait until the doc can let her be interviewed by the FBI and your office."

Patrick nodded at her. He had already figured that part out. To change the subject, he asked her, "Is there a smoking area outside? Where can I purchase a pack of cigarettes tonight? I forgot to get a pack at the BX when I was there earlier."

The captain looked around, opened a drawer, and pulled out a pack. "Which brand? We have Camel Filter, Marlboro Light, and Winston. We keep these here out of sight for patients that need them real bad. As for a smoking area, you have to go out the ER doors and turn right."

"I'll take a pack of Marlboro Light. Here is a dollar for it." He started to walk away then stopped and asked, "Do you have a coffee fund here? With as much time I will be here, I will need coffee. If so, here is my first donation" as he pulled out his wallet again and gave her five dollars. "Please no arguing. I have had my share of upsets today." He felt in his pockets and found his old zippo. "Thank you very much, Captain. I appreciate everything." He headed for the ER, went out the door, and hung a right. Surprisingly, he found the room occupied with patients and visitors.

He went outside, looked at the sky, and marveled at all the stars. Patrick said a prayer: "God, please let Sherrie heal quickly and let us have our son back. He is most important in our lives now. Please keep him safe. Amen."

He then heard a deep voice. "MSgt Johnson, would you please come over here?"

He knew that voice from somewhere, he mused, as he walked toward the voice. It was none other than John Sommers.

With deep trepidation, he walked over to him, thinking that JR was dead. He walked up to find out what was going on.

"What's up, John, any news at all? Any news at all, my friend?" "Nope, nada, none, not one useful tip has come in. We are now set up in the Investigations Office, and we have a dedicated line to come in to the LE Desk so that the number can be covered twenty-four seven. We know that you will be in Sherrie's room. So how is she?"

"She just came into the room from recovery and is still kind of drowsy and confused. She wants to know what happened and if JR is doing okay and where he is. No questions until at least tomorrow after I get the okay from the doc, and then I will call you to come in and talk to her." Patrick paused then continued. "At that point, I will leave the room. We need to make sure everything is on the up and up with no interference by me as it goes for her."

John nodded his agreement and told him he needed to get back to the shop. Before he left, he asked Patrick for Sherrie's room number even though he already knew it. He did not want Patrick to feel alone right now. They both said good night, and John left Patrick standing there, lighting up his second cigarette.

Patrick walked back to the smoke room, thankful it was empty except for one patient and his visitor. They both kept to themselves, away from Patrick, which allowed him to be by himself and to think. Trying to recall all the questions that FBI Agent Abernathy had asked: "Did he know of anyone who could have done this?" None came to mind. "Any strange phone calls or threats?" Again, none that he knew of, and he was sure that Sherrie would have told him so. "Could it be anyone in the military that he had arrested and had been recently released from custody?"

Patrick thought long and hard on this one and decided he might have to go into the office tomorrow and go through the files to see, but he did not think so.

10

John walked back into the squadron and to the office only to find a very disgruntled crew. The LE Desk had not had any phone call tips come in since the end of the evening news; in fact, all the base patrols were having a very calm night even though for the past two weeks the night shifts had all been very busy. In the office the mood was much the same. Even though they had the television on and special reports had been on throughout the day, not one tidbit came in.

"Hell, people," John announced in a loud voice at the door. "If we have not had one iota of a tip, and the CHiPS and local law enforcement (LE) has not picked up the truck, then we are dealing with a 100 percent expert at this. We need to be the same." He looked around the room and went to see Don.

"John, I know exactly what you are going to say. I agree with you, and I have already been in contact with the field office and FBI headquarters, trying to match up what we do know with any previously unsolved kidnapping with no demands within twelve hours of the crime. So far, nothing. Either this guy is one cool dude and he is laying low in the local area, is out of state, or God forbid, out of the country. My guess is he is or was military. In which case, if we do not have a sighting on him quickly, this case is going to end up as a cold case and be solved probably by some private eye."

At the mention of the two words *cold case*, Paul and John looked at each other, for they had discussed a couple of weeks ago starting a business after retiring from the Air Force to handle cold cases for the local law enforcement agencies. Paul looked at Don and told him what he and John had talked about. "However, that does not mean we will delay solving this crime. Patrick is our friend, partner, and in some cases like a brother to us. We want this bastard that did this to Patrick's family and all the families on this base." He then looked at John and asked him if he had seen Patrick and what was the news on Sherrie.

"Yeah, I saw him out in the hospital smoke room. Sherrie is in the room now, still real groggy and does not know what happened. She asked about JR and if he was okay and with a neighbor. Patrick lied to her and told her JR was fine. He also told me that once the doc clears her for questioning, he will not be in the room. He wants this to be done by the book without his possible interfering or influencing the investigation."

Don looked at the two of them and told them, "I wish I had you two guys working with me in my job. You show professionalism, yet you also care about your people—I mean everyone on this base. So what's next?"

Paul picked up the phone and called his wife. "Hi, Anne. Sorry about missing dinner tonight. We had a quick bite at the terminal. I am bringing Agent Abernathy home with me to sleep in the guest room. I know you went shopping today, so we will have dinner tomorrow night. Honey, I need to go. I am being waved at. I love you." He quickly hung up the phone as John motioned him over.

"Paul, Don, we have a possible hit. Seems our guy rented two storage lockers side by side for almost a year. The address of the lockers is 2025 Industrial Street, San Bernardino. The owner also tells us this guy has an older model Ford pickup, and get this—it has a dent in the left front fender."

Paul looked at John and Don and asked them, "Okay, gents, how do we do this? John, does our perp have an address?"

He looked at his notepad. "Yeah, he lives at 111 Juniper Court, San Bernardino."

Don was immediately on the phone, calling the field office to request a monitor team at 111 Juniper Court and the storage lockers to monitor the comings and goings until further notice. He hung up and said, "We have a monitor team going up to both the storage lockers and his home. All they will do is monitor—nothing more unless they get the word." He took a swig of coffee and then told them, "Guys, I need to coordinate with city and county as well, but they will do that from the office. I have a feeling he is not home. When do you want to go to the lockers?"

Paul looked at John and Don. "How about 0700? That will allow all that have to be there to be in place after breakfast. The place will be monitored between now and then."

The direct line from the LE Desk rang, and John picked it up. John took down some notes and dropped the handset. "Don, cancel the house monitor team. San Bernardino PD went to that address, and it is a broken-down old crack house. I suggest you keep the team at the lockers though."

Don spoke up after phoning the field office again with the update on the residence. "They suggest that we hold off until 0700 tomorrow. The advance monitor team will be in place, and we can have a smaller version of the Hostage Rescue Team (HRT). We will use a scaled-down version as we do not feel the child is there, but it will be good to have all segments of the team including the forensics team."

Paul looked up from a notepad and said to both, "Here is what we are going to do. I will take Don to my place and crash for the night. John, you go to your place and crash. We will meet back here tomorrow morning at 0530. That will give us plenty of time to get ready. Don, once we get there, you will be in charge. John and I are along for the ride because the crime was committed on base. Is that okay with you?"

"What you have described sounds perfectly okay to me. The local PD will have perimeter control set up at 0645. County will be a bit further out, and CHP will be on the on-ramps near the storage locker area. It is 2100. I also suggest that we do not—I can't emphasize this enough—tell MSgt Johnson about this tip. It may not be a valid tip, or he might get himself into a position he should not be in. I am sure you know what I am talking about."

On one hand, Paul felt Patrick should know, but he understood the risks that were caused by letting victim's families know ahead of time of a procedure. "You are right. Of course, even though Patrick is considered one of our primary investigators, we need to treat him as a victim and not a fellow worker with a need to know." He looked at the clock and changed his mind about going home to sleep. "We might as well break out the cots and sleep here tonight. Both John and I have our tactical gear here anyways, and we have showers for us. John, break out the cots, and let's get some sleep."

Paul called Anne again and told her of the decision to stay there. John called his wife and told her the bad news as well. MJ took it all in stride, and she told him to be careful.

Meanwhile, Don, not being married, filled out some papers for tomorrow and called the office to make sure everything was set for "kickoff" time of 0700 tomorrow.

11

While the planning was going on, Patrick kept an eye on Sherrie, wishing she would wake up, but they had given her some pain meds to help her sleep. He had questions to ask her, but he also knew that it was not his job to do the questioning this time. He had seen enough victims' families to know that this is what he is, a victim. She woke up once and asked why he was in a strange room with her. When she dropped back off to sleep. Patrick told himself he needed to get out of the room.

He went to the nurse's station for a cup of coffee. He then asked where the hospital chapel was located. Once he found out, he went out to the smoke room—and who would be there but First Sergeant Penkowsky. He took a deep drag off his smoke and asked, "Patrick, how are things with Sherrie? Does she know anything?"

"Shirt, it is good to see you. It's nice to see someone out here instead of medical people always tiptoeing around me, wanting to talk but afraid to." He paused to light his own and told him, "Sherrie is in her room now. She's been there about five hours or so—at least I think it has been that long. It might be longer." He decided to look at his watch and saw how late it was getting. "I came out here for a quick smoke then I am going to the Hospital Chapel for a prayer for her and JR. I am staying in Sherrie's room for the next couple of nights." He then gave the room number to MSgt Penkowsky in case Lieutenant Colonel Burns would want to stop by. He shook his hand then walked out. He went back inside to find the chapel and then back to Sherrie's room for some much-needed sleep.

He found the Hospital Chapel and went inside. He went toward the altar railing, where he knelt and prayed. "Forgive me, Father. It has been many years since I was last in chapel. Let the person who did these evil acts to my family be found and punished. I also ask for you to place your healing hand on Sherrie's body to make her well. I ask this in your beloved name, amen." He then felt a light touch on his shoulder. Startled, he turned around and found the Hospital Chaplain, a Catholic Priest, looking at him.

"I am sorry, my son. I did not mean to startle you. I heard your opening comments. I am sure He knows that you will not receive the best attendance marks at the silver gate with St. Peter, but He knows you are a Christian, and that is what matters, or you would not be in here." He looked at Patrick and said something that made them both smile. "Your opening is an indicator that you were raised as a Catholic. With the name of Patrick, what else could you be?"

"Yes, sir, I was raised as a Catholic. I came in for the first time today to pray. I have not done so in some time, but I feel better now, and I know He will help my wife to feel better soon and He will watch over Patrick Jr. and keep him safe. I feel he will not even be harmed. How does that sound?"

"Son, that is your God talking to you. He is already watching over him for his safe return—whenever that will be."

"Thank you, Father."

They both smiled at each other, and Patrick walked out of the chapel. He turned to wish him a good evening. He was nowhere to be found. Patrick shrugged his shoulders and left to head back to the ward and get some sleep.

He returned to the ward and asked the new nurse on duty who the Catholic Chaplain was in the hospital chapel. "He and I had a good conversation."

"Sir, we do not have a Catholic Chaplain assigned to the hospital chapel this week. We use whoever is on call, and this week, it is a young Protestant Chaplain. Why do you ask?"

"I was just in the chapel, and this Catholic Priest was there. He made me feel comfortable in knowing I was with God."

She explained to him that was not a real person. "He was not real. Some say it is Jesus that comes to those who pray in there in time of need." She smiled and said his wife was doing okay and he needed to get to bed. It was after midnight now.

He shook his head, said good night, and walked down the hallway quietly, not wanting to wake any of the patients. He entered the room and stripped down and went to bed, said one more prayer, then fell into a dream-filled sleep.

12

About ten miles south of Sacramento, Rod had to pull over to change his son's diaper. The best part of the whole trip was that he slept all but a few miles, and even then, he was quiet. With the pacifier and Tippee glass, he was happy. He called Josie so she would be waiting for him in the back of the motel; this way he would not have to go through the lobby, which would be locked. He had to move off Interstate 5 to Route 50 East, and then there was the motel.

It's going to be good to lie down in bed tonight, he thought. He swung in back, and there she was, Josie Duval, his loving wife, but he still took no chances. He carefully scanned the different parked cars, anyone else outside, and so forth.

He got out of the Jeep, hugged his wife, and then went to the other side and opened the back door. He pulled JR out of the car seat and held on to him for a second. This was the first time he held him, comfortable no one else could see him.

Josie looked at them both and reached around and hugged them. For now, they were a complete family—but how long would it last? One month? Ten months? A year? No one knew, but they would try for as long as they could. She could not get pregnant due to a problem with an earlier pregnancy, but now she had a baby to take care of, and he did look like Rod.

"Let me grab your bag and the car seat. He can sleep in that tonight, right?"

"Yeah, he can—at least until we get home, then he will have the crib we bought for him before we came out here." He looked at JR, still sleeping, then turned to his wife. "We need to look at the map tonight. We can leave early, stop for breakfast, and be on the road early. I don't want to be hanging around in this state any longer than I have to."

Once in the room, he pulled the map out of his carry case and spread it out on the table. "Okay, according to the map, once we get onto I-80, we can be home in two days. If both of us drive, we can make it into Rock Springs tomorrow night." He looked up at her and saw she nodded in agreement. He then continued, "After that, it is a straight shot into Cheyenne. It will sure be good to get home. This is beginning to wear me out—all the flashing red-and-blue lights on the interstate and I thought it was me they were after."

"I saw the big accident scene on the news. They say one sixteen-year old and a fifteen-year-old were killed. So damn senseless." She looked at sleeping JR and cried for the parents of those kids who died. She then went into the bathroom and washed her face.

They checked JR to make sure he did not have to be changed. Josie looked at him and asked Rod, "Do you think he sleeps all night? What do we do if he wakes up in the middle of the night and starts to cry and the night clerk wants to check and see about the noise?"

With a hard, tired look, he replied rather testily, "I guess I forgot to ask Sherrie before I stabbed her." His look softened when he realized what he had said. "Honey, please forgive me. I'm tired and exhausted. If he wakes up, one of us will have to get up and take care of him as soon as we hear him. We are on the end of the floor, so I doubt there will be a problem. Right now, I need to get to sleep." Within minutes, the immediate stress was off him, and he fell into a deep, dream-free sleep.

Josie, on the other hand, could not sleep. Every sudden noise she woke up thinking it was JR. It was not until 5:00 a.m. that he woke with a wet diaper. They both bounded out of bed at the same time only to start laughing. While he changed JR's diaper, Josie went to the office to use the bottle warmer.

She explained to the clerk that her husband came in late last night with their son after seeing his mother. "She totally hates me."

She also told him they would be checking out in a couple of hours for an early start. She then went back to the room and held the bottle for JR as Rod had shown her.

By six, Rod had the car packed; and since they were ahead of schedule, they decided to eat a leisurely breakfast.

They pulled out of the parking lot and saw a Denny's restaurant nearby. Inside, they got a booth quickly where he could keep an eye on the parking lot and the front door. He looked at his watch and saw it was six thirty, and he felt a hard chill up his back. "I guess they found the locker. *Oh well, it would still take some time before they finish up there, and by that time, we should be in Utah*, he thought to himself.

13

The three investigators were up at 5:00 a.m., unable to sleep with the off chance they could possibly catch the suspect, but they did not really believe it. Paul stopped to check the LE Desk to see if there were any other leads that might have come in overnight; unfortunately, there were none.

Shortly after gathering their gear, they went to the dining hall. Most of the early troops eating there were Security Police, and they knew what investigation they were involved with. John spoke up for the three of them to all who could hear: "The investigation is ongoing and, as you know, not well. We will be following leads today both on and off base. As far as MSgt Johnson's wife is concerned, she had her emergency surgery yesterday afternoon and was taken to her room last night. I have not heard any more information. The LE Desk will be up-to-date on it. There is a card going around the squadron if you want to sign it. If you miss it while on duty, there will be another card at the desk. That is all."

He joined the other two at the table, once again amazed at the amount of food Don was going to ingest prior to heading out.

"Guys, this is a normal meal for me when I am in the field and going on an operation especially of this magnitude." He went on to tell them of one time on the hostage rescue team: "I was the lead person in through the door. I had a quote normal unquote breakfast. The breakfast gave me the momentum to go through the door and not get shot. So it is second nature for me to eat big before a big op."

John and Paul could only shake their heads and continued to eat since John and Paul needed to draw rifles, 9mm sidearms, extra ammo, and radios. They left as soon as they finished eating. Don would get his from the FBI team at the rally point.

Paul made another check at the desk and left word that "If MSgt Johnson calls and asks for us, tell him we are out investigating some possible leads and will contact him later on."

He also informed the flight chief, "If this operation gets back to MSgt Johnson before I tell him, you will no longer be a flight chief. You will be on permanent third shift until you get out of the Air Force!"

The flight chief assured him, "No one will leak, or they will join me on third shift."

Paul joined the two others in the pickup truck and left for the rally point. They reached the outer perimeter ring of San Bernardino County Sheriff deputies, and they told them, "No one was between the city cops and us. That was their intention. This way no one from inside the first perimeter could get out. We made it to the next ring, the most critical of perimeter lines. This is the first line the suspect would encounter if he tried to leave. As it was, no one was able to leave. They were advised to call their employers and explain the situation."

They finally made it to the FBI assembly area and conferred with other agencies and the owner of the storage lockers. In addi- tion to law enforcement vehicles, there was an ambulance and a fire engine.

"I don't normally go into the lockers, but I do have keys for them. However, I made a search last night, and he changed the locks on me, so I cannot give you the key for the locks."

The FBI team leader explained how he might have encountered the suspect and been injured or even killed. The leader's phone rang, and he was told the press was at the outer ring, clamoring for access. He looked at Special Agent Abernathy. "Don, this is really your op. How do you want to handle the media? My suggestion is that we let the field office public relations staff handle it. We have a representative from there with us in the van.

"Let him make a media line outside the outer perimeter. This way they won't get in the way. Have him in constant communication link with the van. We need to get this op going so we can break down the lines and the residents can get to work."

He looked at his watch. "Okay, people, listen up. It is now 0655. I want the entry team at the locker for entry at 0700, but make sure there are no wires or booby traps before we go in. We do not know what we will find."

Don cleared it with FBI HRT Team Chief Robinson to accept John and Paul into the team since they both had both Security Police HRT and SWAT team training.

The entry team, whose sole responsibility was to scale the door and create an opening, moved cautiously to the door. The second team, with Donald, John, and Paul had their weapons pointed to the roofs of the lockers and the building behind the wall. One agent from the entry team slid a small thin fiber-optic wire underneath the door to see if he could see anything.

"Oh, shit, boss, we got a problem. Along with what appears to be the suspect's truck is a fifty-five-gallon drum with visible vapors. We are going to need to go in with masks and have the fire engine brought up in case we need water and their exhaust fan."

Donald looked at John and Paul as they started to go for their masks. "Guys, are you sure?"

Paul looked at John and told him, "We train to use our masks in wartime. We both used it during Operation Desert Storm. We are trained and qualified to be here today, so we go."

"Okay." He looked around and told everyone to mask up and be ready before breeching the door. It would not be an easy breech, and they could not blow the door in because of the possible chemical gas inside.

Donald called for the heavy-duty bolt cutter to cut the new padlock, which was stronger than most locks. Even though he was the biggest agent, he had trouble cutting the lock hasps.

Finally, the door was unlocked and raised. They could see that no one was inside. Donald sent two agents inside to the door against the wall. The door was not locked, and since an assumption could get a guy killed, they opened it slowly only to find fresh stains on the floor but nothing else. They called out, "Clear," and went into the locker to see if they could find anything—anything at all. They came back and told both Donald and Robinson that nothing was found in the other locker, not even fresh dust. It was as if the person they were looking for had cleaned the place before he left; not even a footprint existed.

Yet as they looked around the first locker, they could see dust all over, the red truck, the old car seat that had been taken out of Johnson's quarters, scraps of paper, and other debris. They pulled everyone outside and waited for the forensics team to get there before they would go back inside. "It is just two damn dangerous to have us in there any longer," Donald to Robinson.

"Yeah, I agree, but now we have a new dimension here. It seems we are up against a smart guy who has every angle, every turn, and every minute thought out. This is going to be a tough one. Why do you think he left the car seat with Johnson's name on it?"

Paul joined them and added his two cents' worth for the heck of it. "I think we are dealing with someone either in the service or is now out of the service. He seemed to know the road layout on base well plus the visitor pass procedures, which to me says he has been on base several times."

He took a deep breath as he knew he was going out on a limb. "And he knew how to do this in plain sight. That is how he pulled it off. Do I have proof? No, not any more than what you have, but it all fits."

They all looked at Paul as if he had arrived from outer space when the FBI Forensics Team pulled up. They moved over to the truck and talked to the team leader about what they had found inside. Don let out a sigh of relief when he said, "Oh good, it's Timmy." He looked at Paul and said that Timmy was the best they had at the field office.

"How you guys doing? I understand you found a barrel with something in it that was giving off fumes, and you had everyone masked up, right?"

Donald nodded at him that everyone inside had been masked before going in.

"That was a good move. Now let us experts get in there and see what we got."

He got out of the truck and his team put on rubber suits, slipped into rubber booties, and sealed their cuffs with duct tape, followed by their arms in rubber gloves, masks, hoods, then finished sealing any possible gaps. Once all the masks were tested, they went inside and closed the door. They looked around the space and the barrel. Two members, opposite of each other, lifted the lid with two heavy-duty tongs, and they gazed into the barrel. Not knowing what they would find, they exhaled a deep breath, seeing only dissolved items of what they did not know.

They laid out a triple layer of plastic sheet, and two members of the team, using special tongs, began to pull out what they could—a glob of plastic, a few remains of clothing, and a smaller piece of metal.

Timmy addressed his team. "Drain this into another container to see if there is anything else at the bottom. I'll go out and brief Robby and Don. As soon as we can get the barrels sealed up, we can have the fire department come in and blow the fumes out so we can finish our job."

Timmy opened the door a small amount, ducked underneath, and closed the door right away. He went to Robby and Don and looked at Paul and John. Don nodded, so Timmy began to give them a brief about what was found inside. "Guys, whoever this suspect is, he knows his shit. That barrel contained caustic acid, which left a glob of plastic, some remnants of clothing, and some metal, we don't know yet. They are now draining the barrel so we can make sure we are getting it all out, then we can have the fire department blow out the fumes. Then we can go back in to do our normal forensics job. Can we identify anything? Maybe Washington can, but not us in the field. This one is too intensive. One thing is for certain—the kid is not in there. I need to go back inside."

Paul was the first one to speak up. "This is another reason why I think this guy is military. Put it all together. What civilian would understand and could use these tactics?"

Don told Robby, "He has very solid points for us to consider. Maybe we need to check and see if there are any AWOL or deserters that might be in the area. I will put it in my report when I get back to the office on base." He looked at Paul and continued. "Their commander has set up a command center in their office, so I have fax, phone—the whole works."

At that time, the door opened, and we heard the call for the heavy fan to come in. We all waited until the fumes were gone to go inside.

What was left of the fumes would not bother us unless we stuck our heads inside the barrel. We bent down and saw the stuff they got out of the barrel, the remnants of clothing, the glob of plastic, and the small piece of metal which appeared to be flattened as if hit by a hammer, defacing what was on there. It had what appeared to be two small holes at the ends of it.

Paul looked over his shoulder at the truck. He stood up and walked over to it and looked at the left front corner of the dash and could see two metal fasteners were broken off. He called for Don and John to come over.

"Take a look at where the VIN number is normally located. It's gone, and the fasteners have been broken off. On the plastic sheet is a small piece of metal about that size. If, in fact, that is the VIN plate there on the sheet, this is the truck, but will you be able to find out the owners without the VIN number?"

Don looked at the truck and called Timmy over. He asked Timmy the same question Paul asked him. "Timmy, if the VIN number and plates are missing, can you still identify who the owner or owners are or have been or if it is on a hot sheet as stolen?"

Timmy looked at the same spot on the truck dash and then at the plastic sheet. "You know, I was thinking the same thing. We might be able to figure out the VIN in the lab, or if not, Washington will." Timmy continued, "Guys, this one is going to be one son of a b—to crack. Whoever he is, he is very smart."

Leaving the site to the forensics team, Don, Paul, and John decided to head back to the office and see if anything came in while they were gone.

Paul asked John, "Do you want to tell Patrick? I know he would want to know, and I believe that he would tell us if the roles were reversed. Also, see if Sherrie is awake and willing to answer questions for us."

14

Patrick, after a rough night sleeping, having tossed and turned whenever they came in to check on Sherrie, finally decided to get up around 6:00 a.m. as was his custom whether he was working or not.

He shaved and showered in the room's bathroom, dressed, and as he was starting to go out the door, he heard a muffled sound behind him. He turned and smiled at her—a face filled with pain and sorrow.

"Hi, babe, how are you feeling?"

Sherrie looked at him, then her eyes opened wider at the room around her. She asked three questions: "Patrick, where am I? What happened, and where is JR?"

Before he answered her, he hit the nurse's call button. "Honey, you are in the base hospital. You were attacked yesterday morning. They had to do emergency surgery. As to that part, I will let the doc tell you about it when he comes in." There was a light tap on the door. He turned around and saw the nurse and told her to come on in.

The nurse told Patrick he had to leave the room and that the hospital dining room was open.

She then turned to Sherrie and told her that she needed to check the bandage over the incision and that there was nothing to be afraid of. She lifted the sheet, looked at the bandage, and told Sherrie, "It is nice and dry. It will be changed when the doctor comes in to look at you later this morning." She saw her grimace a little when she touched the bandage, so she gave her a pain shot through the IV. "Oh, and one more thing, the line coming out of your nose is to keep your stomach shrunk so that everything will move back in place, then the tube can come out in a day or so. If the doctor okays it, you can have coffee or tea, but nothing solid yet. Okay?"

Sherrie nodded and started to drift off again. Memories of the day before started to run through her mind like a bad nightmare. Her last conscious thoughts were that something had happened to JR and seeing Patrick in the doorway with his cup of coffee. "I love you, Patrick," she murmured as her eyes closed, blotting out everything in her sight.

Patrick, seeing her eyes close, told the nurse's station he would be out for breakfast but that he had his pager with him, and he gave them his number to call him if the doctor came in the room or if anything happened to Sherrie.

He went to the hospital dining room and had just sat down when he saw First Sergeant Brownlie come into the dining room. Patrick waved at him, and he waved back and nodded.

Brownlie came to his table, his tray loaded with an old warrior's breakfast which consisted of a ham and cheese omelet smothered with chip beef gravy, toast, orange juice, and coffee. "Ahh, a good warrior breakfast. However, I see that they will be stopping this type of eating at some point in the future, and I hope it's long after I retire. So, Patrick, how was your first night in our 'hotel'?"

"Good morning to you too." Smiling, he continued, "Hospital beds are not good for a hotel, but I will consider the situation and not make any complaints. I tossed and turned every time they came in to check on Sherrie. Before you ask, Sherrie woke up just as I was going to leave the room. She asked some questions I could not answer." He went on to describe the questions especially the one about JR. "I can tell from her eyes she might remember what happened yesterday, but I do not want to push it with her still being drugged." He paused to eat some of his own breakfast. "I know deep down in my heart JR is okay. He is not dead nor has he been harmed, but damn if I know why someone took him and almost killed my wife."

Brownlie listened and drank some coffee, looked at Patrick, and said, "Patrick, I have been a First Sergeant for more than five years, and I love my job. One of the keys to trying to figure out what one person is really saying is in the eyes. Yours right now are empty. I know you are on the Senior Master Sergeant list for next month, so you have attended Senior Non-Commissioned Officer Academy, and so have I. Unless they have changed the curriculum, you can spot nonverbal gestures. I cannot find any from you. Are you a robot that has no outward feelings?" He looked at Patrick harder to see if he had hit any trigger points, and when he mentioned the E-8 list for next month, he noticed Patrick's eyes flickered a little.

Patrick asked him, "Do you mind if I call you Shirt?" He acknowledged he could.

"Shirt, I took that class there, and I aced that block. I know what you are looking for. I do it all the time in my job and talking to those that need to be counseled." He took a gulp of coffee and went on.

"Last night, I went to the Hospital Chapel to pray and ask for guidance from God. I ended up having a conversation with a Catholic Chaplain. When I got back to the ward, I asked the nurse who the Chaplain was, and she told me there is no Catholic Chaplain assigned this week. Tell me who I talked to in your chapel?"

Brownlie looked at Patrick and knew he had to tread carefully. "Patrick, the nurse was correct. We have no chaplains assigned to the hospital staff. We borrow from the Wing Chaplains Office, and there is no Catholic Chaplain assigned to us this week. Now I am going to tell you the truth here, so listen carefully. You asked me a question, so I will answer it to the best of my ability." Here he paused and emptied his cup. "How about if we both go up and get a refill?"

Patrick slid out of the booth seat, and as they both went for the coffee, some younger troops said, "Good morning, Top," an old term used back in the old cavalry days. It means you are the Top NCO for the enlisted troops, a sign of respect. Brownlie acknowledged the greeting with a wave.

Patrick looked at how the troops here respected their First Sergeant; even though his own First Sergeant wanted him to put in for it, he never felt the urge for it. *Maybe after we find JR, I will consider it*, he thought to himself as they walked back to their table.

"Patrick, back on the subject of the chaplain that you saw. There are many different stories about him. Most have seen him just as you did last night. He is not real. The best we can figure out is that it is a Heavenly Spirit that comes to those that are having problems such as what you are going through right now. You can check with the Wing Chaplain if you want, but they will tell you the same thing. Do you understand what I am trying to tell you?" He drank some coffee, looked at Patrick, and felt like a piece of shit trying to talk to him as if he were a young airman just coming into the squadron.

Patrick looked at Brownlie and thought long and hard how to respond. "For some strange reason, I believe you. I will make an appointment to see the Wing Chaplain. It has been so long since I was in a church I do not know what to believe anymore." He drained his cup and said he was going out to the smoke room then check on Sherrie. He thanked him for the talk. "I know I needed it. I will tell my First Sergeant about this so he knows someone yanked on my chain because I deserved it." He stood up and shook hands, took his tray to the return window, and left the dining room.

Outside he breathed the fresh air. Since it was a beautiful morning, the sky was clear of smog and clouds. He thought about the investigation, Sherrie, and where was JR now.

15

They sat down at Denny's for breakfast, Rod ordering steak and eggs and Josie ordering ham and eggs with toast, no potatoes, and coffee for both. Rod ordered oatmeal and apple juice for JR. He had fallen right back asleep after being changed and fed but was now waking up and acting fussy. Josie put a rag on her shoulder and pulled him out of the car seat with his head on her shoulder. As she patted his back, talking softly to him, he started to gurgle, burped, and then started to laugh. Both Rod and Josie smiled, knowing that they had just passed a test in public. She was now glad that she had read baby books in the motel waiting for Rod to arrive.

The waitress brought their food and looked at how happy the three of them were. As she put the meals down, she looked at JR and remarked at how the boy looked like his father. "Watch out though. Before you know it, he will be in school then out on his own." Just then she happened to look at the door, which Rod had lost sight of due to the waitress. His heart stopped, and Josie's blood turned to ice.

Two California Highway Patrol officers walked in, looked around the room, glanced at the three of them, and then went to sit at the counter. "Well, that's my husband over there. I guess I need to go over to him. You take good care of your son. He's going to be a heartbreaker." Rod, because of his training, maintained himself well and told Josie to go into the bathroom and wash her face. "We will be okay.

Just go wash your face and think of our ride home to the ranch. If we keep our composure, we will be okay."

Just as Josie was leaving the restroom, another guest came in and asked her if that child with the guy in the checkered shirt was her son. "I noticed how he smiles every time you look at him. How do you get him to do that? Mine never smiles or laughs."

Josie smiled inwardly as she had read a book in the motel on this very subject. Not wanting to appear to know too much, she told her, "It might be a medical problem. You should have him checked with the doctor, or your tone of voice may bother him." She paused as if to gather her thoughts. "Or it might be that it shows how he will be when he grows up, but then your doctor will be able to tell you more. Remember, one child is different from another." She quickly left the restroom, knowing Rod would be worried. He gave a look to her that was relieved that she was okay.

"Honey, you okay? I was getting worried."

"Yes, my dear, I am okay. There was a woman who wanted to talk to me about how JR smiles when I pick him up. I will tell you later. I am starved."

They quickly finished eating and asked for the check. They left the money on the table for the tip. Rod was at the cash register when one of the CHP officers came over to look at JR and asked them how old he was. Josie said he was twenty months.

"He is going to be a big boy if he is this big at twenty months." He paused and told her, "Take some advice—when you get home, have his fingerprints recorded and photographs taken with your local PD or sheriff's office. That way if he is missing, it will be easier to locate him. I am sure you have seen on the news about the kidnapping manhunt going on now."

Josie nodded, a knot forming in her stomach.

The officer continued, "Well, unfortunately, they did not fingerprint their son, nor do they have any photos of him. That makes it tough to find the little tyke. Have a safe trip." He went back to his counter seat and asked for more coffee.

Rod finished paying the bill then turned and looked at him. "Thank you, sir, we will do that. What you said makes sense. I do feel for the family of the little one. I hope they find the baby and the person who took him." He put his hand out to shake the officer's hand and said, "Goodbye, sir. Thanks for the tips," and they walked naturally to the Jeep, put JR in the back seat, and they left, heading for the freeway to connect to I-80 then home.

Once on the Interstate, Rod looked at Josie and told her, "Honey, you did great back there. You handled the situation in the bathroom well. And then checking out, the damn cop could not shut up and let us leave. He had to give us advice that I had been thinking of yesterday. Damn nosy cops anyways."

He looked at his beautiful wife and told her, "Honey, it's a straight shot now. If we drive smart, we should be in Salt Lake City by"—he looked at his watch and saw it was 8:00 a.m.—"6:00 p.m. if we trade off at lunchtime. We can get a room there, and then tomorrow late afternoon, early evening, we will be home." He looked at her, and she was gazing out the window at the passing landscape. "What's wrong, hon?"

She turned and looked at him. "You ask me what's wrong? We almost got caught back there, that's what's wrong. First it was that idiot woman who can't figure out why her child does not smile like JR does. Then it was those two CHP cops. Is it going to be like this from now on? Always looking behind our back every time we go into town with JR? What happens when he gets older and wants to do things on his own like school and stuff? What happens then? You seem to know it all."

Stung by Josie's comments, Rod thought long and hard before he responded. "Honey, we talked about it for several weeks before I came out here, right? I know you are under a lot of stress right now—we all are including JR." He took a wide glance at Josie and a look in his rearview mirror and smiled when he saw his eyes flicker open then shut again. "Once we get home, everything will be okay. No one knew us before we moved there, and we already planted the seed of honesty that JR is really my son whose mother died at childbirth and that my sister was watching him. If we stay with that line, we will be okay with anyone that asks questions. All we need to hope for is that his hair is like mine, blond, and it probably will be."

Rod added to himself, *Of course, Josie does not know that I raped Sherrie two years ago, and she asked no questions about the line I gave her about my previous wife who died at childbirth.* He got his mind back on track; he had to concentrate on the freeway traffic.

They soon hit Reno, but it was not quite lunchtime, and they did not want to have JR visible in a major town right now. They were still too close to San Bernardino. If he figured it out right, when they stopped for gas, they could stop to eat.

"Honey, there is a small town called Battle Mountain away from Reno, and we can gas and eat there. You can take over and drive into Salt Lake City where we will stop for the night and have a fresh start in the morning."

"Yeah, maybe that is the smart thing to do. This way we can be closer to home by tomorrow night." She looked out the window and looked back at JR and told Rod, "Even though this is dirt, it is real pretty up here—the different colors and such. I am darn glad that I did not come out here by covered wagon like those poor people did. It took them forever to go cross country."

"Yeah, no music to listen to while driving the wagon, plus they had to worry about Indians, no real good medical care, and so forth. Man, we got it made here in the last decade of the twentieth century." Rod then grew quiet as he saw brake lights come on the cars in front of him. His internal alarm bells began to ring—the same alarms that kept his sorry ass alive in all those out-of-the-way places that the US Army sent him to and most Americans did not know about. He then saw the flashing red-and-blue lights up ahead. He slammed the steering wheel with his hand and muttered to himself, "Aww shit, not again!"

Josie looked at him. "Honey, what's wrong? What do you mean when you say, 'Not again'? All it is up ahead is nothing more than an accident scene. Please calm down, or you will wake the baby."

Rod quickly turned the radio to an all-news format to see if up ahead was in connection to him and the baby. He also turned the police scanner on. "Honey, I have a bad feeling this time. Just remember to just be cool and act naturally. If the baby wakes up, tell me. With any luck, he won't. As for probably nothing, my internal alarm bells are going off like crazy. Just follow my lead." He looked at Josie, and as she nodded, a special report came over the radio.

"This is an update special report repeating the liquor store robbery this morning. The suspect is described as being twenty to twenty-five, with brown hair, brown eyes, and weighing around 180 pounds. The Reno Police Department has received tips that he is travelling in a white Jeep last seen travelling eastbound on I-80. He is armed and considered dangerous. If you see him, do not attempt to stop him. Contact your local law enforcement. Updates as it occurs." "That's great, simply great. They have a roadblock ahead. Just act normal. In fact, pull out your book. I think we will be here for a while." He looked back at the baby with a sigh of relief. JR looked so calm and peaceful. He sighed and turned around to face the front and put the Jeep in park.

He suddenly remembered he still had one of the plates from the damn truck he had used. "Those damn plate will be the nail in the coffin if I do not get rid of it real quick, and a rest stop today is not going to be the answer," he mumbled to himself under his breath.

He decided that "it will have to be at the motel tonight when we stop. I only hope that the cops up ahead will not look inside. After all, we are a family on vacation."

He pulled out his book and pretended to read, turning the pages absently, hoping Josie did not know the new danger.

She turned her head and looked at him as he absently turned the book pages. "Rod, what is the matter with you? I know you are a fast reader, but you turned five pages in less than a minute. Talk to me, dang you!"

"Daddy!" they both heard JR cry out.

"What is it, son? Is it because the car is not moving?"

"Uh-huh, and I wet."

Josie looked at Rod with a look of "What now? How do we handle this? It was not in the book you gave me to read."

"Mommy will get back there and change you. When we can, we'll make a real bathroom break. I need to go also. Then we can take a short break, okay, son?"

Josie got out of the front and got in the back and changed his diaper. She gave him fresh pants and got back into the front seat. "Leave the windows open until we get to a rest stop, and we can throw the diaper away."

Josie went through the package in front and got out his cookies and gave him one. This next moment was going to be the biggest test yet. "Here you go, son. As soon as we get past this roadblock, we will find a rest area, okay?"

JR took the cookie, looked at her with a quizzical look, and nodded as he reached for the cookie. A smile was all he gave her, but it was enough—no questions asked.

When they finally reached the roadblock, the Nevada Highway Patrol officer looked in the Jeep and was about to say something when Rod asked him, "Sir, I take it the bad guy is still on the loose? My family are on our way home, but we need to find a rest stop fairly quickly. Our son needs to use the bathroom—in fact, all of us do. Is there a stop nearby?"

"Sir, I apologize, but it is necessary. He is still on the loose and is now threatening to kill anyone who stops him. The nearest rest stop is about a quarter mile ahead. It might be busy though. Other families are in the same predicament as you, and I have a son about your son's age, so I know what you are going through. Safe travels, sir." He waved at JR and watched him wave back at him.

Rod put the Jeep in gear and proceeded down to the rest stop and followed the cars into the parking lot. "We will now have to wait our turn. It seems everyone is having the same problem, but we will let you out so you can stretch your legs with Mommy and me." He looked back, and the smile on his face said it all.

Josie went to unbuckle JR from his car seat. "Hey, Rod, we better not play right now. He needs to get changed again. You want to do it, or do you want me to do it?"

Rod looked at Josie. "You do it. I want to check out a few things with the other drivers and the big map they have here, plus I want to hit the snack machines." He got out of the Jeep and went to the large map that was on the wall of the visitor center along with other drivers trying to figure out how to make up the lost time.

Someone hollered out, "They got the guy."

The question rang out, "Where did they get him?" from several drivers.

A woman's voice hollered out, "Gawd, I hope it was not back at our roadblock. He could have killed us and our kids."

Hysteria ran rampant especially among the women.

Rod went inside and spoke to the clerk behind the counter. "Do you have any idea of where they got the liquor store robber? Someone heard on a car radio that he had been caught. I hope it was behind us."

"Yes, sir, I heard the call on my police scanner. He was caught at the roadblock that hung all of you up."

Just then the scanner erupted with voices yelling then gunfire and then the worst words in police calls: "Officer down. We need an emergency medical at this location. Officer down. We need a medevac pronto. We also have a civilian with a fatal gunshot. Suspect is also wounded."

The clerk looked at Rod. "They will probably fly in a helicopter from a Nevada National Guard unit. I hope the civilian was not with a family."

Just then he heard a familiar sound overhead. It was a UH-1 Huey medical helicopter arriving. Rod ran outside, and he pointed it out to Josie and JR: "That is what I flew in while going to various Special Forces camps in South Vietnam." Memories of his tours flashed through his mind until he shook them off.

Rod looked at his wife and JR and asked if everything was okay. Josie nodded, and JR squirmed in her arms. He led them outside and told her, "Let's take him to the grass area and see how he is doing walking. We will be on each side of him." This was the first time they saw him walk. Although unsteady, he had a good sense of balance. The three of them looked like a happy family. It was time to leave, but they would have many more days of being happy.

Rod and Josie led JR to the grass area so he could stretch his stubby little legs. "With all the excitement, I forgot to hit the snack machine. I want to get a couple of candy bars and a soda. Do you want anything?"

Josie shook her head and watched JR, hoping they could get home quickly and out of the public view. Back in the Jeep, she put JR in his car seat, refilled his bottle, and put some cookies where he could reach them if he wanted them. She got into the front seat, and as Rod got in, one of the highway patrol cars from the roadblock came into the parking lot and parked near them.

The officer got out of the patrol car and started to head for the restroom. He came over to talk to Rod and asked him not to leave until he came back out so he could talk to him. While the officer was inside, Rod wondered what he wanted to say to them.

He came out and went to the Jeep. "Sir, I apologize for holding you up, but I was wondering if everything is okay with you and your family now? You remember what I told you about the robber being dangerous? He shot and killed a civilian and then killed a highway patrolman. Again, I am sorry for the inconvenience, but I just wanted to let you know why we had to do it. I wish you safe travels and enjoy the rest of your trip."

"Officer, please accept my condolences on the dead patrolman and I will pray for the dead motorist as well—and again, thank you for keeping the roads safe for us." Rod waited until the officer went back inside before he backed out and joined the line of cars getting back onto the highway.

He looked at Josie. "Honey, I know we had talked about a break and then you drive, but that break put us way behind schedule. I am rested enough to drive all the way tonight." As he eased onto the highway, he wondered what stage the investigation was now going into and how Sherrie was doing. Could they make it all the way home without getting caught? Could they really do it? How good is that FBI agent he saw on the news yesterday? So many questions and no simple answers.

16

In the investigation office, Paul, John, and Don went over the information that they had been able to retrieve, which was not very much. "Don, have you had any experience in profiling? I mean so far, this bastard is an expert at what he has done, and I know that there must be a weak link somewhere. Have you checked with Washington to see if there have been any crimes like this one?"

Don took a large gulp of coffee and thought before he replied. "Unfortunately, I have never done any profiling in my career with the FBI. However, my thoughts match up with what Patrick and you mentioned earlier. This guy has had military experience, possibly a special operations type. He knows the drill on visitor passes. He had the time to drive from the crime scene to the gate and then how to destroy any chance of an easy investigation." He took another drink of coffee and asked Paul, "Did Patrick arrest anyone with a major crime within the past year or so?"

Paul looked at John, who shook his head no and told Don, "MSgt Johnson has not made a major arrest in the past year. We already checked our files and Patrick's personal files." Before Don could say anything, he quickly explained, "Each of us here in this office have personal files that we all know about and have access to, but no one else can get into them."

John put his cup down and told them, "I think it is time we went to the hospital and talked to Sherrie. Knowing Patrick, he will probably come in here while we are gone and go through the files. I suggest we leave our notes locked up in the safe at the LE Desk. The desk personnel will know that Patrick is not allowed to look at them."

He collected all the information they had—notes, pictures from the crime scene and the storage locker, and witness statements and put them in the LE Desk safe. As he left, he turned toward the LE Desk supervisor and told him, "Under no circumstances are you to open the safe for MSgt Patrick Johnson unless SMSgt Gibbons or I are with him."

After getting affirmative nods, he left the desk area and rejoined the other two in the Investigations room. "Hey, guys, I just thought of something. We spent so much time with Patrick yesterday that we forgot to talk to the responding EMTs and the ER staff. I think we need to do that today. Paul, you know Sherrie a little better than me. I will cover the ER side if you take Don to see Sherrie and hope he does not scare the crap out of her."

Laughing in front of everyone as they left the office, drawing looks as if they had turned completely nuts, they went outside to the Investigations staff car and went to the hospital. John got out of the car at the ER entrance and told them he would meet them in Sherrie's room and if he did not show, to find him in the ER.

John was lucky enough to find the ER nurse that was in charge yesterday, Captain Middleton. "Capt, I am TSgt Sommers, Sixty-Third Security Police Investigations. If you have a few moments, I need to talk to you about yesterday." He looked around and saw they were not busy, so he looked at her again and arched his eyebrow, which got her to smile.

"Do you do that at the beginning of your investigations? Come on back to the break room. You look like you need a cup of coffee."

"Thanks, I do need it. I've been up since before the roosters."

He watched her pour a cup of black coffee and offered him cream and sugar.

"Okay, TSgt Sommers, you have my attention now as long as we have no customers," she told him with a smile.

He told her that her statement would be tape recorded and he would also write notes. She nodded in agreement. He began by asking her, "Please state your full name and duty title and the events yesterday when you were notified of a stabbing incident at an on-base quarters."

He leaned forward so he could write down what she was saying. "I am Captain Brenda Middleton, USAF. I am an emergency room nurse at the base hospital, Norton AFB, CA. Yesterday, 4 March 1992, at approximately 1100 hours, we received a call of a stabbing victim, and we dispatched an ambulance to 11 Starlifter Circle. Once the ambulance was dispatched, we went into trauma team notification and advised the squadron commander, who is also the trauma surgeon, of the victim. When the ambulance arrived, we put her into the first cubicle and could see that she was still bleeding from her abdomen. We could see where someone had put dish towels over her abdomen to try and stop the bleeding. We could see one deep puncture that caused the bleeding. Other than that, there is nothing else for me to add."

John looked over the notes he had written and looked at Captain Middleton. He took in her beauty and the fact she wore no wedding ring and told himself to calm down because he was happily married. "Ma'am, did Mrs. Johnson happen to regain consciousness and say anything? Anything at all—a name, something for us to go on?"

She looked at him, liked what she saw, and told him, "No, she did not regain consciousness. You need to realize, with the injuries she sustained, her mind was working to keep everything functioning so she could come out of this alive. I'm sorry I do not have more information for you."

John shut off the tape recorder and looked at his notes and told her, "Capt, you have been a great help." He gave her a business card and told her, "If you think of anything, give me a call. If I am not there, SMSgt Gibbons will take your information." He told her that a typed statement would be given to her for her signature later on. He thanked her for the coffee and commented that it was a great picker-upper. He then left for the elevators to take him to Sherrie's room.

In the elevator, he read over his notes and hoped that Sherrie was providing more information to Paul and Don. He knew one thing—the key to solving this crime would boil down to one person, Sherrie Johnson, and not to all the years of investigating experience of Don, Paul, and himself.

17

Don was asking Sherrie a question when the door opened. Paul looked up from his notebook when John walked in. He motioned for John to leave the room and told Don he would be right outside.

"John, you and I both have had uncooperative victims before, but this one is a real bitch and a half. Sherrie is not helping. Even Don is having a hard time. I don't know what to think right now." Shaking his head, he asked him what he found out in the ER.

"I spoke to a Capt Middleton that was on duty yesterday when Sherrie came into the ER. When the call came in of an assault with knife wounds, the ER initiated a Trauma Alert team notification, which included the hospital commander as the lead trauma surgeon." He looked at his notes and continued, "Sherrie did not say any- thing that would pinpoint any one person or group of people nor did she regain consciousness." He closed his notebook and told him, "Paul, this one is a definite loser as it goes. No forced break in, no scratches around the door handle or other openings, and then we have what the witness, Mrs. Smyth, said about him walking out the door and saying that he would be back."

He put his notebook in his back pocket and shook his head, scratching as he always did when confronted with a bad problem.

"What does Don think?"

Paul told him he had no clue yet as he had not been able to talk to him privately since we started to do the questioning. He started to say something else when Don came out, shaking his head.

"Guys, this is the most confusing victim that I have ever interviewed. She does not ID anyone nor any type of relationship with the attacker. According to your one key witness, she let the person inside, which means she knew the person." He rubbed his crew cut and muttered, "I need to sit down and have a cup of coffee and talk to you guys. Then we need to talk to the husband again." They headed to the hospital dining hall for free coffee.

Once the three investigators sat down with coffee, Paul took charge of the little meeting. He first asked John to tell them of his interview with the emergency room nurse, Captain Middleton.

Don followed up with his experienced thoughts and ideas after he had visited the crime scene and questioned all parties so far.

He flipped through his notes and told us what he thought of the whole sordid mess.

"Well, from when I first arrived yesterday, I figured something was amiss based on five points of view. One, I noticed there were no scratch marks around the door handle, which showed there was no forced entry; two, in the child's room there were no fingerprints, no clothes, no toys—nothing." He took a sip of coffee before he continued. "Three, no pictures of the boy or of the family were on the walls. All that was visible were what we call shadow marks of photos obviously taken from the home; four, no demands of any kind were placed by the kidnapper, and five, the witness, who saw Mrs. Johnson let him inside. Based on this, I have to say that the boy was taken by someone who knew him quite well. However, Mrs. Johnson states that there are no family members alive that could have done this. Then there is this morning at the locker—same person." He paused and looked at both Paul and John.

"I need to ask this, and I will ask MSgt Johnson the same question. Is he the natural father of the child? Now before you go off on me, this is something to consider. Could Mrs. Johnson had become pregnant by someone other than the husband and he did not know it? It is not uncommon to have this problem."

Both John and Paul looked at each other, their mouths wide open in shock and surprise. Paul spoke for both of them. "Agent Abernathy, we both realize we need to consider all possibilities, but this is going out on a very thin limb. Sherrie and Patrick have been married for a number of years, and they love each other very much. I am JR's godfather, for crying out loud. Neither one would cheat on the other. Just be careful how you ask Patrick this question."

Paul and John made eye contact, agreeing not to say anything about the picture that Patrick gave them with the promise they would get it back that day.

After refilling their cups with more coffee, Don led off with "This morning at the locker, I reemphasized the fact that I was thinking the suspect was Special Forces or one of the other Special Operations troops, remember?" Both John and Paul nodded in agree- ment. "The locker was done by an expert—an expert with the will to do the crime and escape right under our noses, probably yesterday." He paused and, like John, looked at Paul with an arched eyebrow as if to say, "Your turn."

Paul always hated the arched eyebrow that John gave him. It was as if he was saying to him, "What now?"

"Don, I have pretty much the same feeling as you. My gut feeling is that we are dealing with a member of the military, one who knows the ins and outs of base protocol for visitors, coupled with the way he cleaned out JR's room and assaulted Mrs. Johnson without killing her. If I am right, this is a Spec Ops individual being successful at his job, with the thought of hiding in plain sight. Then at the locker this morning, he had us delayed since we had no knowledge of what type of chemicals were in the drum. Then there was the issue of who was the owner of the truck. This guy is totally diabolical, I am thinking. He just might have pulled off the perfect crime, and it is going to be one son of a bitch to solve it." He added, "Is there a way you guys can dig into the Pentagon's files to see if any Spec Ops troops have left the service for any reason and are residing in the area? Also, include if anyone was kicked out of the Air Force as a result of an investigation by Patrick, err, MSgt Johnson?"

Don nodded and made a notation in his notebook and said that he would forward that request when they get back to the office.

"Of course, the call will be made after we talk to MSgt Johnson. My boss will want to know how the interview went. I know deep down that he has no clue, but I have to follow standard protocol on this one including the one irritating question if he is the father."

Paul asked the next key question: "Okay, where do you want to interview him? The office is too friendly a place since he works there.

How about the club? I am sure we can use the office and then we can have lunch." They both agreed, and Paul left to have the LE Desk page Patrick to meet them at the NCO Club, not giving the reason; he was quite sure Patrick would know why.

John went by Sherrie's room, and through the closed door, he could hear Patrick's pager going off. They were pretty distinctive. He caught up with us in the ER, where he waved at Captain Middleton. It was pretty obvious her face turned red, and John smiled when he got to the car. "What, can't an expert investigator like me not make a good impression on a female anymore?"

"Yeah, just as long as MJ doesn't find out you are making female captains blush. But don't worry, I will not tell her," Paul replied, laughing. Paul used the car radio to tell the desk that they were on the way to the NCO Club to meet up with MSgt Johnson and probably be there for lunch as well.

When Don heard the word *lunch*, his eyes lit up at the thought of the good food he could get there and said, "Who knows? Maybe a certain young lady might be working today."

Both Paul and John looked at Don, and Paul told him, "Don, I am not running a dating service here. If you want to talk to her, do it on your time, not ours."

When they arrived at the club, Paul talked to the club manager, and he agreed they could use his office. John and Don went to get some coffee for the four of them, and Patrick arrived. Paul took him into the office for the questioning. Don and John came in shortly afterward.

Paul told Don this was strictly between John, Paul, and Patrick. "You will have your chance to ask after us; however, the two of us will be in here also."

After Don stepped out, Paul started the interview. "MSgt Johnson, even though you are not a suspect in this case, I still need to ask if you desire an attorney during this interview." They could see in his eyes he was hurting, but he declined representation. "MSgt Johnson, you have the right to decline making statements if they will incriminate you. Any statement you willingly make can and will be used against you in trial. You have the right to a military attorney at no cost. If you wish to hire a civilian attorney, you will bear that cost. Do you understand these rights, and do you desire to make a statement now, or do you wish to wait for an attorney?"

Patrick looked at Paul and said he was willing to answer questions now without a lawyer present.

Paul had Patrick go through what happened the day before—from when he left for work to when he returned home at lunchtime.

His answers were the same as yesterday without deviation. He then told them that, "JR had a bad night the night before, and Sherrie had been up most of the night with him. Yesterday morning, he was fine." John indicated he had no questions. Paul then asked John to bring in Don, knowing the one question he would ask.

"MSgt Johnson, you heard yesterday Mrs. Smyth stated that she saw your wife let the suspect inside your home, correct?"

"Yes, that is correct."

"Then it would be safe to presume that she knew this person from her past or present?"

"Agent Abernathy, just what the hell are you getting at here? Come right out and ask me the question. Don't play games with me right now. I am not in the mood."

John started to intervene, but Paul put his hand on his arm and shook his head. "It is his questioning, and here it comes."

The FBI agent looked at Patrick and told him, "I am going to ask you a question, and I ask that you remember that you are an investigator as well." He paused, looked at both Paul and John, then hit Patrick with "Is it possible the suspect might be the boy's father and came to pick him up for the day and then took off?"

Patrick looked at him stunned then looked at his two best pals in the squadron. With fire in his eyes and clenched fists, he looked at Don in the eye and told him, "My wife and I have been married for years. She never cheated on me, and she did not have JR before we got married. If that is your question, the answer is no, I am the father." He paused to catch his breath and calm down.

Then in a complete turnaround, he told them, "Guys, I'm hungry, let's go eat. I know you had to ask those questions."

They could all see the hurt and pain in his eyes. Paul then announced the interview was finished and it was time for lunch.

Patrick concurred as he was tired of eating dining hall food, sitting all alone. Once they had gotten their food, the three went to find a table and to wait for Don, joking that they were having to make a special heavy-duty tray for him to handle all the food he would order. Sure enough, when he came out, his tray was loaded with a salad and main dish of shepherd's pie and two rolls.

He looked at his tray and told them, "Yup, she's working and has my favorite pie—Dutch cinnamon apple pie." He sat down and started to eat. With a twinkle in his eye, he commented, "Maybe I ought to have an office out here nearby so I could enjoy this good food all the time."

All three started to say something then but decided to let Patrick have the last word on this. "Uh, Don, maybe you forgot one thing. Norton is closing in another year or two. That means the club closes as well. That means all of us will no longer be here—no more military, no civilians, nobody."

"You are right. I forgot about that. I got used to the idea of the way you guys can get things done." He then dug into his shepherd's pie and salad like there was no tomorrow. He quickly finished then went for his pie while the others went for coffee refills.

Don came back with a whole pie and plates for everyone. "Lydia heated it for us, so it should be really good."

Paul could not resist it, "Lydia now? I know of some guys who tried for months to get to know her, and she turned them down.

I suppose you got her phone number, and you have a date with her?"

The smirk on Don's face said it all.

"Boys, we need to teach the G-Man some manners on an Air

Force base. Let's hurry and eat our portions before he eats it all." With all of them laughing, they felt good. It was the first time Paul had seen Patrick laugh since he was at work yesterday morning.

"Okay, guys, what's up with the investigation now? I have not spoken to Sherrie yet about it. I wanted to hear it from you first. I want the straight stuff—no hiding anything from me. And the desk guys were great. They would not let me know where you were, just that you were quote investigating unquote. I want nothing held back including this morning."

Paul looked at him then at John. "Go check and see if we can have more coffee. It is going to be a while here." He came back with a pot of coffee and set it on the table.

"Patrick, things have not been going well. Every corner we turn, we run into a dead end. Whoever it was that did this to you and your family is good, damn good. He destroyed the outfit he had on yesterday, and it appears that he had a rubber mask on. We have no idea who he is nor where he is. Don, why don't you tell him about this morning?"

Don looked at Patrick and told him everything from the phone call last night, giving them a possible tip on a storage locker and the procedures they did with local and state law enforcement agencies.

"Patrick, as Paul said, this guy is damn good. He and we are going on the premise that the subject is a male, has covered his tracks well. We have no clue who he is or where he is, much less what he is using for transportation." He paused to gather his thoughts.

"Hell, he could be using a tractor trailer rig for all we know. What we do believe is that he is either military or is a veteran trained in special operations, with the motto of "hide in plain sight and you survive." This case will remain open until it is solved one way or the other. One last thing, the phone guys at your place have told me that there have been no phone calls demanding a ransom of any kind. The only calls have been from women from the NCO Wives Club that want to make you meals. Some of them have brought food over for the phone guys, and they are grateful."

Patrick told Don, "Tell them the kitchen is open to them as long as they clean up after themselves and they are there. What of the interview with my wife?" He saw them sharing looks until Paul spoke up.

"Patrick, the questioning of Sherrie lasted for about an hour and a half. It had to be cut short as she was getting tired and the nurse had to change her dressing anyway. She denies knowing the attacker even though there were no signs of forced entry." He paused to take a drink of coffee and he saw the pain in Patrick's eyes. He knew he had to continue, and it would not get any easier. "She stated that she one hundred percent did not know who he was, why, or how he entered the house. Patrick, we all know you are the expert in these types of cases, but we doubt that even you could solve this one. Let us not forget Mrs. Smyth's account that she saw Sherrie let him in herself." He then turned it over to Don for the fed's perspective.

"MSgt Johnson, we are of one mind that the individual who did this is either serving in the military or is a veteran that has had special operations training. I have placed a call to my office asking the FBI Headquarters in Washington to pull files from the Pentagon database of any Spec Ops veterans who have separated or retired and now live in the local area. They will also go through any possible veterans who were kicked out of the Air Force based on investigations lead by you in the past year. Right now, we are grasping at straws." He paused and then hit him with the news of the locker this morning.

When he was finished, Patrick looked up from his notepad and told the three of them, "Okay, gentlemen, this is what I see. The individual is highly trained and possibly Spec Ops qualified—I agree with you there. As for Sherrie, she might be suffering from PTSD right now. As for JR, she feels responsible for him being kidnapped. Why and by whom, I have no idea right now. One thing I did notice in the house is that some pictures that were in frames on the walls were missing. If there were no prints, this guy is a pro—plain and simple, a pro." He looked at them and told them he was going to the hospital if they needed to get hold of him. He picked up his blue Security Police beret and walked out of the dining room.

"Don, that is why he is chosen to lead investigations that are a bit sticky. If we did not tell you before, and if we did—it is worth repeating—he is due to be promoted to senior master sergeant, which is the second highest enlisted pay grade, next month and is slotted to attend FBI academy training in two months. I am sure he will accept E-8 but not the FBI training." Paul finished his cup of coffee and had to get back to the office.

18

Patrick arrived at the hospital, checked in with the nurse's station, and with a fresh cup of coffee, he went into Sherrie's room. She appeared to be sleeping, so Patrick quietly pulled the chair up close to her bed and started reading his book. For some reason, he felt calmer now than yesterday morning. Yes, he thought of JR, but he knew he was safe; it was Sherrie he was worried about both physically and mentally.

Looking at Sherrie, he had two questions that came to mind; one, who did this despicable act to his family? And two, why did she let this person into their home while she was alone? No one was scheduled to come in from housing maintenance, so who was it? He knew deep down that what the investigation was showing was that the person who did this was smart and resourceful.

What was the phrase he had heard from a couple of Special Forces troops in Saudi Arabia before Desert Storm? "To survive, we need to hide in plain sight."

This person did this and did it well. He knew the procedures right to the timing from his quarters to the main gate, which meant he had been in his neighborhood several times. Was he in the same pickup or a different car? He sensed that Sherrie had stirred in bed as she quickly turned her head away from him.

"Honey, I am here with you until you are released." He had hoped that she would turn toward him to talk with him not as a Security Police investigator but as her husband, her confidant, her best friend, but it did not happen.

He wondered if she would be able to handle going back into the home that had been violated. Based on this thought, he wrote a note to call his First Sergeant in the morning to see if he could get different quarters. A new home might be just what she needs.

Just then he heard a tapping on the door. He no sooner got up to answer it than the door opened and in came Mrs. Burns, his squadron commander's wife. In her hands she had a small bouquet of flowers that Sherrie liked to have around the house.

Patrick stood fully upright. "Mrs. Burns, thank you for coming with those flowers. I am sure we will find room for them here. I know that Sherrie will like them as they are like what she has in the house." He looked at her and smiled. "Lt Col Burns told you what she had, right? She is resting now. The surgery yesterday was a long one. Can I speak to you outside please?"

They went outside, and he told her that there had been no word yet on JR and told her there were no indications of who may have done this. He did ask her one favor.

"Mrs. Burns, could you please speak to your husband to see if we can move into another place? Our current place will need extensive cleanup and will hold too many powerful memories for Sherrie when she is released from here."

"Of course, I will. If there is anything else I can do for you, please ask. By the way, both of the spouses clubs are willing to make you meals, but I guess you are staying here with your wife. Tell you what, I will tell them to hold off until we find out what is going to happen about your new quarters. How's that sound to you?"

"Ma'am, I am grateful for your visit today, and please tell the spouses clubs that we are thankful for the thoughts, prayers, and support. Once we know when she will be released, I will let you know so that the ladies can help Sherrie with the new quarters and such." He gave her a grin that made Mrs. Burns almost melt. They shook hands, and as she left, he pushed open the door to see Sherrie looking at all the different flowers in the room.

He smiled at her and said, "Hi, beautiful."

With sad eyes wet from crying, she looked at him and said, "Hi." She then blinked back the tears from her eyes. She unexpectedly asked Patrick if the visitors this morning were real or if she was in a dream.

"They were in here this morning—your coworkers, Paul, John, and some big guy that looked like a mountain from the FBI."

She started to smile at the comment about Don but quickly shut it down. Before Patrick could say anything, she told him what they had been there for—her assault and the kidnapping of JR on his birthday.

Before she could interrupt him, he leaped at the opening to say something. "Honey, it is true. They were in here to ask you questions about yesterday. They think it was someone you knew as there were no forced entry marks around the door or the windows, and a witness said you opened the door and let him in." He looked at her, and her brown doelike eyes seemed to grow in size as she looked at him in fear.

She looked up at her IV bags and at the tube running out of her nose. "What really happened to me? Paul told me I had been stabbed, but that was it, and the damn nurses won't tell me nothing."

Patrick went on to tell her that she had been stabbed, they had to take her spleen out, and the tube was to keep her stomach shrunk so other organs could move back into place on their own. "Soon, you will have the tube removed and be put on liquids then a soft diet then regular. You had the best trauma surgeon work on you. He is the hospital commander. I do not want to say much more until he comes in tonight to check on you."

He stopped, not wanting to say the wrong things to her now.

The most important task right now was her getting better.

"Honey, yes, JR was kidnapped. We do not know who, but the FBI is working on it along with Paul and John. They have been working on tips that have come in and are utilizing all possible resources. I need to go eat, but I will be back. Do you want anything, hon?"

He bent down to kiss her forehead and told her he would be back to watch TV tonight.

"Patrick, I need something for pain." She then rolled her head toward the wall, not looking at him, which was not normal for her. She had never kept secrets from him as long as they had been married. One thought stuck in his mind. "She knows who did this, but

I cannot prove it." He was going to eat, but he needed to make one stop before the dining hall.

He stopped by the nurse's station and saw the same captain as last night. "Evening, ma'am. My wife is asking for pain medication, and I think she needs something to calm her down. She's starting to cry a lot now over what happened. I'm going to eat, and I will be back shortly."

The captain made all the important notes including a sedative request and how long before Sherrie would be able to eat something. With a sly smile, she said, "Sir, I know we will see you up here tonight for coffee. Enjoy your meal."

Patrick knew he had time before the dining hall closed, so he went to the hospital chapel again, wondering if he would see the priest he saw last night, but he was not to be granted that wish; it seemed it was a once-in-a-lifetime vision. He prayed for strength and guidance on the rough road ahead, for his wife to heal, and for his son to be safe and returned to them swiftly.

Afterward he went to the dining hall where he had dinner all to himself. It was a time for him to write down his thoughts about what had happened to his family:

1. Who did it?
2. Why is Sherrie not talking?
3. Where is Patrick Jr.?
4. Where can I do a blood test to prove I am JR's father?
5. Do I take the promotion to E-8?

The most important thing was Sherrie's recovery. He was finished eating. He picked up his tray and went to the tray turn-in slot and left the dining hall. He decided he needed to go out for some fresh air and a smoke, so he headed to the smoke area outside.

As he went out, he put his blue beret on and noticed that there were no clouds, the stars were bright, and there was a full moon. He looked up at the moon, knelt down and removed his beret and remembered a prayer he used when confronted by the stress of combat while serving in Desert Storm. "Heavenly Father, I come to you in prayer that you will watch over our military forces that are engaged in combat and in high-threat locations. I also come to you to protect little JR and keep him safe and return him to us. Protect my family as you would protect me from unknown sources. Amen."

He stood tall, put his beret back on, and dug in his pockets for his smokes. He heard a noise behind him as he lit up with his Desert Storm Zippo, turned around, and was happy to see John.

"Patrick, my man, don't you know those damn things will kill you? And before you answer me, you got a smoke I can bum?"

"Sure John, here." He waited until he was finished lighting up, and he asked him, "John, I know you did not come here after din- nertime to bum a smoke off me while your wife is at home. So what gives?"

John thought hard about what he wanted to say. He did not want to ruin a friendship that had built up over the years. "Patrick, Don has left to go back to his office, and the phone team will be in your quarters for another two weeks. You know what we said today about Sherrie not wanting to talk to us about who she let in."

He took a deep, long pull on the cigarette, looked at Patrick, and told him, "My personal opinion—and it is personal, not official—Sherrie knows who it is that assaulted her and took your boy. If she does not speak quickly, this is going to become a cold case and take years to solve, and you know it. If I were not so damn concerned, I would not be here saying this to you." He crushed out the cigarette and then told him with a grin, "And by the way, that tasted like shit!"

"John, Sherrie called Don a quote mountain unquote. I agreed with her, and I agree with you—she knows. I tried to talk to her today but met a stone wall. She turned away from me. I am hoping that the doc will have her see one of the shrinks here. I know she needs it, and even if she were telling us the truth now, she would still need it. God, how many times did I suggest the same thing to other victims?"

He then put his smoke out and told John he was correct about the taste, but "This is the only thing that calms me down and makes me feel sane." Disgusted with himself, he then crumpled the pack and threw it away in the trash can. "You will just have to bum smokes off others, my trusted companion. I am now going inside to watch TV with my wife." He gave a smile that John knew was sincere. They shook hands and Patrick headed back inside and John left to finally go home after not seeing his own family for over thirty-six hours.

Patrick stopped by the nurse's station to get his normal cup of coffee and threw in a couple of bucks for the coffee fund then turned and went to the room. As he got to the door, he heard some- one talking to Sherrie about the surgical procedure the day prior. He knocked and pushed the door open and saw the doc, who turned his head and saw Patrick.

He addressed Patrick as he entered. He then turned back toward Sherrie and explained what to expect without a spleen.

"Basically, you will live a normal life, but you have to ensure you get your flu shot each year and your pneumococcal pneumonia shot as required. You have already received both by IV. You may have problems fighting off a common cold, and you have to watch out for the flu as it can become pneumonia rather quickly. Other than that, you will lead a perfectly normal healthy life."

He turned to look at Patrick and asked him to step outside. Scratching his head, he took his cup of coffee and left the room, wondering what this was all about. He tried to think of all possible reasons and was debating calling Paul to have him come over if it related to the assault but decided to wait and see what was going on. Dr. Thompson motioned Patrick to come into an office with him. "Patrick, I did not want to tell your wife this, but there was another problem. Did you know that she was pregnant?" Gazing into his face, he knew he did not know she was pregnant.

"How far along was she? This might explain her crazy moods the past few weeks. I know she missed her period last month, but we thought it was just one of those quirky things. We've been trying for over a year and a half."

"I am sorry to tell you this, but she was six weeks. There was no way we could save the baby, and due to the stress of the attack, her system aborted the fetus. For the foreseeable future, I would recommend she not know this. I do not know how it would affect her." "Sir, with all due respect, I am really angry now. Why did you not tell me about this yesterday when we had our discussion while I was waiting for Sherrie to come from the recovery room?"

Dr. Thompson told him, "You were under a lot of stress yesterday, and there is no telling how you would have reacted. It was a judgment call on my part. I still feel I was correct."

"Sir, I apologize for my outburst, and you are correct as to my possible reaction yesterday and Sherrie's reaction. I will hold it in until there is a correct moment."

Patrick drained his cup then looked at the surgeon. "I want to thank you for your help in this. I know she is in capable hands with the people here. Everyone has been great with me in here. They have even let me join their coffee fund."

"Patrick, I do know that she is not really forthcoming with the investigators on their questions. I know she is holding back from me as to what really happened." He also told Patrick that he was doing up a consult for a mental health evaluation for possible PTSD to see Sherrie tomorrow alone. "In other words, Patrick, you cannot be in there."

Patrick asked him what was next as far as Sherrie's physical recovery. "I know the tube has to stay in, but when can she start walking? From personal experience, the sooner a patient begins to walk, the sooner they can be released. Correct, doc?"

The doc told him, "Tomorrow. I am going to have someone from Physical Therapy come by twice a day and start her walking. That is the quickest way to get her out of here."

Patrick left for the nurse's station for coffee then to the room to watch TV with Sherrie, hold her hand, and talk softly to her like they used to do in times of stress.

Sherrie was asleep when Patrick went back into the room, so he decided to go out for fresh air and a smoke.

There was a slight chill in the air, and Patrick had to go inside the shack when he realized he did not have any smokes with him. He was able to bum a smoke off another E-7: "Name is Arthur, but everyone calls me Art. By the way, I am in supply."

Patrick looked at him and thanked him for the smoke. They talked about Norton closing down and what their future plans were.

Art looked at Patrick's name tag and told him, "Wait, you're the one whose wife was assaulted and your son kidnapped yesterday. I am so damn sorry. How is your wife doing?"

"She's doing better, thanks, though they had to remove her spleen. Sorry, Art, I got to get back inside."

As he got up to leave, Art threw him the almost full pack of smokes. "Here, I got more in the car."

Patrick waved at him and went inside straight to the room. He moved the chair next to her bed, took her hand into his, and silently prayed for JR's safety and for Sherrie's recovery. He also asked for the protection of all Air Force Security Police around the world.

After the prayer, he turned on the TV to a show they used to watch before JR was born. He talked to her, said that he loved her very much and that they would work together for her to get well and for them to move on into the future without little Patrick Jr.

19

Rod, Josie, and JR made it to Salt Lake City that night without further incidents. The next morning, they left for Rock Springs, Wyoming. Even though Rod knew the FBI was now involved, he was glad to be two states away from the crime he had committed. He knew from hereon out he would have to constantly watch his backside. They spent an easy night in a hotel, knowing that they would be home the next day.

The following afternoon, after exiting I-80 onto I-25 north just outside of Cheyenne, they drove past F. E. Warren AFB, and he told Josie that was where they would shop at the Base Exchange and commissary. "It is a unique Air Force base. They do not have any aircraft except for helicopters, just missiles. Next year, when they have their open house, we will go. JR will love it."

Ten minutes later, they pulled up to their long entry drive. Rod stopped at the entry drive to their ranch and looked up at his sign overhead, which read TripleD followed by interlocking DDD. JR woke up after they stopped. "Dad, we home yet?" was the prover- bial question. Both Rod and Josie looked at each other, smiled, and laughed.

"Yes, we are home." He shut off the Jeep, Josie got out to check the mailbox, and Rod pulled the boy out of his car seat. Holding onto him, he pointed up to the sign above the driveway. "That is the name of our ranch, the TripleD. Tomorrow I will take you around the ranch, but it's getting dark now." He put him down, and JR went to Josie and asked her to pick him up to carry him inside.

Rod looked at them both. A smile came to his face, and he knew that JR would be good for not only him but Josie as well. He got back in the Jeep and went to the old barn that he was using as a garage and unloaded everything. Once he put everything on the back porch, he pulled the Jeep into the barn and closed the doors.

Before going inside, he thought about the past three or so days. "I can't believe that I got away with the whole thing. I did what I did and made it through roadblocks that I should have been caught in." He remembered the plates that were still in the Jeep. The plates that were in the barrel in the storage locker were from a truck he had found years ago.

As a lark, he had pulled the plates off it, and now they had come to good use. He figured he had time to think of a way to dispose of the actual plates, but not tonight.

As he finished thinking, he heard laughter inside the house where Josie was showing JR where things went and explaining about the house. He saw a post hole digger and knew what he would do in the morning.

Rod picked up the bags and carried them inside. His first stop was JR's room. He wanted to see his expression with a new bed and furniture. He was all smiles, looking at his bedspread with horses and cowboys on it. He put his small suitcase in the closet, away from him so he would not see the Mickey Mouse sticker. Rod did not want him to be asking questions right now.

Josie went to the kitchen to make mac and cheese with ground beef for supper as Rod put things away in the bedroom.

"Did your aunt and uncle start to have you use the bathroom at home?" Rod looked at him and asked if he needed to go potty now.

JR nodded, so Rod went to the kitchen and told Josie what had just happened. "We have a lot of learning to do—I mean all three of us do. We do not know all that Patrick and Sherrie did to teach him things, and the fact is that he is only two."

JR came out and told his dad he needed help washing his hands. They went back to the bathroom, and as he washed his hands, Rod told him, "Tell you what, I will help Mom set the table, and you sit and watch TV. Okay with you? I will put a cartoon on for you."

He watched him waddle down the hall toward the living room where he pointed out a small rocking chair between two larger chairs. JR sat in the chair and crossed his arms as if to say "This is mine" and was happy to see a Mickey Mouse cartoon come on.

Rod went into the kitchen to help Josie finish setting the table and whispered to her, "We need to be careful of watching the national news just in case they show Patrick or Sherrie's faces for a while. Just no TV during meals, okay, hon? We can watch the news after he goes to bed. That includes your favorite morning shows."

She agreed with him but also told him that they needed to keep abreast of what was going on with the investigation. She put the food on the table and went to go get JR and put him in his high chair. While Josie cut up his hamburger patty and began to feed him his meat and mac and cheese, he smiled and laughed at her facial expressions.

Rod smiled, happy that everything was working out so far. He told his son, "After supper, while Mom cleans up the kitchen, you and I will watch the cartoon, okay? Then Mom will give you a bath and then both of us will put you to bed. No arguments, you have had a long three days, and Aunt Sherrie said you had a bad night the day before I picked you up."

After they finished, Rod took his plate to the kitchen and then took JR from his chair. JR went straight to his small chair and sat down, waiting for Rod to turn on the TV, where they laughed together at Mickey's antics with Minnie Mouse. When Josie came in, they watched another cartoon, this one with Donald Duck with his three nephews. Then Josie told him it was bath time.

As Josie walked him to the bathroom, Rod pulled out a pad of paper and jotted down notes of what he had to do the following day:

Get rid of the plates.

Have Josie go to the post office to pick up the mail that had been held while we were gone.

Register the Jeep on base.

Set up an appointment on base to establish medical records for JR before I retire from the Army.

Find out where I could get a DNA blood test.

Later on, he could contact his buddy, a former Special Forces troop who was an expert forger, for a Wyoming birth certificate.

Josie came out wet from JR's splashing and told him that JR was ready for bed. They kneeled down against the side of the bed and said the bedtime prayers, turned on the small nightlight on top of the dresser, and closed the door after saying good night.

In the living room, they sat in their chairs and turned on CNN to see if anything was on about the kidnapping. There was a short item about the kidnapping, an excerpt of the press conference held the day of the kidnapping, and an update on the condition of the mother, who was improving. After that was the story of the shooting at the roadblock on I-80 and the families involved.

Josie looked at Rod and told him, "That shooting was so damn senseless especially killing the motorist and that highway patrolman. I wonder why he did it?"

"Sometimes it is hard to figure out why some people do what he did. Maybe he knew he had nothing to lose. Maybe he was hoping they would kill him before anyone got hurt."

Rod went over the list of things to do tomorrow and asked if he had forgotten anything. Josie just shook her head no. They watched a few other shows then decided to go to bed as they were both tired and they had a long week ahead of them.

* * * * *

Rod woke up, as customary, at the crack of dawn, checked on JR and saw he was still sleeping and went and turned on the cof- feepot. He then went to the barn, got the post hole digger and the license plates from the truck, and went where the next fence post would be. He dug the hole deeper than normal, put the folded plates in the ground and then the post on top of them and filled in the dirt. The rest of the fence would be set up that day with the barbed wire strung. Soon his land would be properly fenced, and he could then start planting crops before it was too late.

After he put the digger away, he went back inside the house to find Josie in the kitchen with JR sitting at the table. He washed up and took the cup of coffee offered by Josie.

"I had to go out to put a post in for the new area fence that I am hoping to have completed by this afternoon. Once the fence is finished, we can start planting."

As they sat down for breakfast, he told JR that he was going to be busy all day and he could go with his mom into town to see downtown Cheyenne, a real cowboy town. He told Josie that he needed to call the extension bureau to talk about seeds for the crops.

After breakfast, Josie told Rod that since she was going to be in town with JR, she might as well go shopping; but since the Jeep was not registered on base yet, she would go to Albertson's Supermarket for the few things they needed. Once the Jeep is registered on base, they could go to the commissary and BX.

Rod told her to be careful, watched them leave, and headed to the barn to talk with some of the help he had as to what needed to be done that morning, in particular the fencing.

20

Within days of no news and nothing to advance the investigation, everything seemed to grind to a halt. Special Agent Abernathy decided he needed to go back to his office in Los Angeles. The phone monitoring had received no suspicious calls, but they would remain for one more week. Even though he was going back to his office, he was still the special agent in charge of this crime, and it irked him terribly; this was his first case that he had not been able to crack or solve within a few days—no suspects, no nothing!

Out of the blue, his phone rang. It was his office in LA. They had a preliminary finding on the license plates that were in the barrel that was in the storage locker. With a surprised look on his face, he hung up.

"Guys, this case just got worse. Those plates we found in the storage locker? Get this—they belonged to a 1955 Chevy that was reported stolen from Fort Benning, Georgia, two years ago. Isn't that where Army Rangers get trained?"

Paul looked at him and told him yes and that it fit with their premise that this perp was Special Ops. With a shake of his head, he told both Don and John he was getting a headache, and he needed a break.

Paul suggested to Don, "Why not go to the club tonight for dinner with us and our wives? It will give you a chance to finally meet them."

John added his two cents' worth that he thought it would be s a great idea.

"Guys, it sounds like a great idea. I really would enjoy it, but I have a date tonight."

John suggested that he bring her to the club. He paused, looked at Don, then he said, "Wait just a minute. There are rumors that the best cook we have at the club is leaving after this week. You would not have any part of this, would you?" He cocked his eyebrow like he did when confronting a hesitant witness.

Don looked at both and bowed his head. "Guys, the rumor is true. Lydia and I are going to move in together in LA after I get back and clean up my place. I was smitten by her looks and her cooking. There is no way I can have her in the club for dinner. We both agreed to that. It would not look right."

Paul looked at him and said, "You like country music, right? Let's all go to the Brandin' Iron then. We can eat, listen to good country music, and maybe even dance. Hell, I bet Lydia does not even know that you can dance. You can dance, right?"

His face was turning beet red now. "Lydia and I love the Brandin' Iron. We have been there, and we dance just fine—thank you very much."

Both John and Paul started laughing so hard they had to close the door lest someone came in to check and see if they were okay.

John suggested they call their wives and tell them of the change and then added, "Okay, now that I know we are going to the Brandin' Iron tonight, I got to see you dancing with little ole Lydia."

Paul finally stopped laughing and suggested, "We should all go to the club for one last lunch, or is your personal cook not working?" He started to laugh again until he saw Don begin to make a move for Paul. John was going to pick up a chair when Patrick walked in. "What the hell is going on here? My wife has been stabbed a

few days ago, our son has been kidnapped, and you jokers are in here doing nothing but laughing?" He looked at the three of them and then calmed down and said, "You know, I have not had a good laugh in almost three days. Tell me what is so damn funny so I can laugh as well."

Paul told him what they were laughing about. "Honestly, Patrick, John and I just can't seem to visualize this tall mountain here dancing with little Lydia from the club and quitting to go and move in with him in a week. Hell, just about every single senior NCO, active and retired, has been trying to woo her away from here. I do not want to be around him when the word is out."

Patrick looked at him, thought about what he was going to say, and told him, "Okay, I know you have done your best on my case, but answer me this—will you take care of her and not have her cook for four people when it is just you and her?"

The three of them looked at Don, waiting for his response. He agreed. "Since it is my last day here, I am buying lunch at the club. Will you join us, Patrick?"

They clambered into their duty section's truck and went to the club. This would be Patrick's first time in the club since he was questioned the day after the attack on Sherrie and the kidnapping of his son. But, truth be told, he was tired of hospital chow.

After they went through the line and saw Lydia, they went to a vacant table in the back corner of the room where they would not be disturbed. Patrick was the first to speak up. "Actually, guys, I wanted to bounce something off you. I've been doing some deep thinking and talking to Sherrie. From the way she looks at me and her comments to the doctor that visits her every day, I have a feeling that she knows exactly who it was that did this to our family. I know a shrink comes in every day. She will not talk to me. I want each of you to give me your thoughts on what I just said and if there is a way to get her to talk straight with us or the shrink?"

Donald looked at the three of them and decided since this was his specialty, he would try and answer first. "Patrick, I am supposed to be an expert in juvenile kidnapping, but as you probably know, with each passing day, the trail goes cold. Deep down, I know she knows who did this, but other than the shrink giving her sodium pentothal, or truth serum, I do not have a clear-cut answer for you. The problem with this is that sometimes the information that comes out is not 100 percent truthful. It is sometimes what the interrogator wants to hear. I personally do not use it nor accept it for my job. Sorry, Patrick, but you asked." He shook his head and leaned back in his chair and looked at his lunch. He was not totally comfortable with this case.

Paul looked at John and at Don before speaking. "Patrick, you and I have been friends for so long I can't remember when we first met. You know I am a hardworking SOB especially when it comes to cases like this one, but I am stumped. What we thought was a surefire lead turned into more crazy confusion by a pro."

He stopped because he knew Patrick did not know about this lead.

"Patrick, the one lead we had was to a storage locker in town.

The manager called us the night of the kidnapping. We assembled all the right players including the FBI Hostage Rescue Team. The FBI had set up two containment rings around the area, no one out, no one in, until the op was finished. The perp, if that is what we want to call him, is good. He destroyed all the evidence. He put the license plates in a barrel of acid, which we found out this morning were from a 1955 Chevy that was stolen two years ago from Fort Benning, Georgia. The VIN plate was so damaged it is back at FBI Headquarters Lab. We have no idea what kind of vehicle he drove out of here sometime that afternoon."

He paused and continued, "I say again this guy is a pro. We think he might be Special Ops trained. He definitely knows military installation procedures."

Paul looked at Patrick again deep into his eyes and told him his gut feeling. "Patrick, deep down inside, I feel the same way as Don does. Sherrie knows who did it and why. You know as well as I do there was no sign of forced entry and no sign of running from the scene. Patrick, I am not going to let this sit and collect dust. It might turn into a cold case, but I will keep digging in between other active cases and if I have to after I retire."

"Don, I know you did the best, and other than spending the night in the office with these two clowns, your expertise was not enough. Perhaps what Paul said about him being Spec Ops qualified is right. If that is the case, what's next? I wish I had met you under other circumstances." Patrick drank some coffee and said, "I don't like the idea of drugging Sherrie."

Don spoke first, saying, "The telephone team will be removed from the premises in another five days. Someone is punching buttons all over the place on this case. We were told to keep it in place longer than normal. Personally, I do not think anything is going to come over the phone. Hell, Patrick, the only female phone callers are from the wives' clubs wanting to fix you dinner."

He paused, and then with a grin, he told him, "Since you were not home, the wives' clubs were making meals for the phone teams. That has never happened in my career. You are highly respected, Patrick."

Patrick nodded to him as a way of saying thanks. "I have asked the old man's wife to see if they can arrange other quarters for us. Sherrie is going to have a hard enough time recovering without having to be in the crime scene. They will keep her in the hospital until I find new quarters."

"Paul, I want to ask you to do this for us—you, me, Sherrie, our squadron, and the Wing. Keep this on the front burner, okay?"

"Patrick, you know that. The security flights are still doing walkthrough on all the open spaces on base. It is good exercise for them security pukes." Everyone laughed when he told them that he had started out in the security field and not law enforcement.

John was the only one who had not spoken; he had a troubled look on his face when he said, "Guys, if, in fact, this guy is spec ops trained, how can we beat him? We do not know where he is. Hell, for all we know, he might still be in San Bernardino or in Riverside. The only thing that is certain is that he is not on base. This may be worse than the Lindbergh kidnapping although that was finally solved." With that, he went back to eating his lunch.

Don told Patrick he was leaving to go back to LA in the morning. "I will not rest until this one is solved, Patrick. The resources of the FBI are available to you and your investigation team. I wish I had met you under better circumstances. I wish there was more we could tell you. This is especially hard when it hits someone you work with." All three stood up, shook hands, and Patrick thanked them once again for all they had done, knowing they would continue to do so. Patrick sat back down, alone in his thoughts of JR and Sherrie.

Would she ever tell him what she knows? More and more questions come to him. Some were questions he had two years ago that he always pushed away in his mind. Then he knew what he needed to do. He needed to go to the gym and do a hard workout. He always worked out in the gym when he had pressing problems. Maybe this would help. Sherrie still could not eat solid food, so he knew he did not want to eat in front of her. He would eat someplace else tonight. He was tired of dining hall and club food. He knew of the perfect place, the MAC Terminal, where he could see people arriving and leaving and the lumbering C-141 Starlifters landing and taking off. The noise and confusion were like a large opera performance. But first, he had to see his commander.

21

Patrick arrived at the commander's office, where the secretary told him he would have to wait a few minutes as the commander was on the phone. He flipped through an old *Airman Magazine* that brought back memories of Operation Desert Storm. His picture was in an arti- cle showing him sitting in a Humvee at a security checkpoint in Iraq. He put it down, trying to erase the memory of that night, rubbing his lower right leg where he took a piece of shrapnel from an RPG explosion that left only a glancing wound which required a few stitches.

The secretary asked him how his wife was, and glancing at the phone, she told him he could go on in.

He knocked on the doorframe, walked in, and saluted Lieutenant Colonel Burns, who told him to have a seat and asked what he could do for him.

"Sir, I spoke to your wife yesterday at the hospital to ask if she would speak to you about getting me new quarters. It will take a lot of cleaning, and the memory of the attack and kidnapping is still strong. You know that I do not normally come in and ask a major favor, but this is different."

"Patrick, since I assumed command of the Sixty-Third Security Police Squadron I have never seen you in here asking for anything that was not important. Yesterday, I took the liberty, before my wife asked me, of calling the Civil Engineering Squadron Commander Lieutenant Colonel Blackwell, and he approved your change of quar- ters. We both felt it would probably be best to move you to com- pletely different quarters. The end result will be up to you, and when you put your next stripe on, you will be eligible for a single house, which means you will have to move to a new street and new neighbors. The choice is yours."

Patrick thought about it and told him that it might be a good idea to do it that way. He also had to decide what to do with JR's stuff that remained. He then advised him what had transpired at lunch and what was going to happen now.

"The FBI phone team will not leave for a week. They are getting fat and happy with the fresh cooked meals from the neighborhood." "Patrick, you have plenty of leave on the books. Take what you need. I hope you are taking the stripe and staying with us until the base closes. I will let you know your new quarters' assignment by this time tomorrow. Now go spend time with Sherrie. She needs you now and, stay away from the squadron until you come back to work." With that, Patrick stood at attention, saluted his commander, and did a smart about face. He stopped by the secretary's office and thanked her for her concern. She told him that everyone on base was still in shock over what happened and the fact that no one had located the bad guy. He thanked her again, walked out to his truck, and headed to the gym.

In the middle of the afternoon, the gym was not that busy. He went into the locker room and changed into his workout clothes and hit the stationary bike first for ten miles, watching CNN news channel that was always on. The lead news story was about a holdup in Utah and how the robber was caught in a roadblock on Interstate 80 and the shooting that occurred. It also stated that according to the Utah Highway Patrol commander, they were also on the lookout for any sign of JR. "We had been asked by the FBI to assist in searching for the little boy that was kidnapped this past week. What we did see was a lot of families on vacation, but nothing matched the description of the little boy."

The next breaking news was about a new unknown terrorist group advocating the overthrow of the United States. Patrick only shook his head, wondering why the world was falling apart. He finished the ten miles and went to the leg curls.

This was an exercise he started as a result of his injury in Iraq in 1991. After doing two reps of ten each, he went to the running area where he would jog ten laps then run ten laps.

By the time he was finished with everything, he looked at his watch and knew he had to hit the shower. He had one more stop to make before going to eat and then to spend the evening with Sherrie.

His next stop was his quarters. He knew the FBI phone team was still in the house to monitor any incoming calls that just might lead to the kidnapper.

Instead of just walking in, he rang the doorbell and was greeted by an agent. He identified himself and told the agent he needed to pick up a few extra things for Sherrie, then he would be gone. "By the way, if you have not already done so, the kitchen is open for the teams. No sense in the food going to waste."

"I don't know if you know it or not, but you got some mighty fine cooks in your neighborhood. We have not had to cook a meal yet—all the wives keep coming over with food. Oh, by the way, I am Special Agent Charleston. How is your wife doing?"

"Well, Agent Charleston, my wife is recovering slowly. As for the cooks on this block, you are correct, they are good. During the summer we normally have at least two block parties where they do all the kitchen cooking and the guys do the outdoor cooking. I under- stand the calls have been few and far between and rather drab, is that right?"

"Unfortunately, that is correct. In all the years I have been with the bureau, this is the first time that there have been no phone demands—none, nada, zilch. That is one of the weird things with this case. Special Agent in Charge Abernathy has filled us in on everything so far. Something strange is going on. Well, he has told us one more week in here." He then asked, "Will this put you out?

"No, we will be clearing this quarters for a new one after she is released from the hospital. Too many memories here for her. I will have the move postponed until you guys are finished. A military move is very disruptive even if it is just across the street."

He then went into his bedroom and pulled out Sherrie's robe and slippers from the closet along with some underclothes. He went into the bathroom and put some of her basic makeup in a bag for her. Grabbing his go bag on the way out of the bedroom, he took one last look at his son's bedroom. Fingerprint dust was everywhere, and it was then that he noticed the one photo of the three of them was missing. *Maybe Paul has it*, he thought to himself.

He bid the agents a good night and told them not to eat all the good food that was coming over. It was then that he smelled ribs, but he could not eat ribs in the house. That was one of JR's "good food" along with hot dogs and mac and cheese, of course.

With the items from the bedroom in his truck, he drove off to the Military Airlift Command Terminal, which is like an airline terminal complete with ticket counter and a snack bar. There seemed to be more dependents in the cafeteria and the terminal than normal. Going in, he ran into one of the Law Enforcement Patrols sitting down for dinner, and they asked him over.

Sitting down with his burger, fries, and soda, he asked them about the many dependents. It seems there was a National Guard deployment going out tonight and they were there to see them off—complete with flags, balloons, and red-white-and-blue signs.

They asked him about Sherrie, and he told them just like all the others that ask, "She is recovering as well as can be expected." He then went on to tell them that he had been granted leave time to help take care of Sherrie when she got out of the hospital and moving. Their radio crackled in with a report of a shoplifter at the Base Exchange. They picked up their trays, said goodbye to Patrick, and they left.

"These kids will never learn. They get a call, they go right away no matter how bad it is. They should not have picked up their trays, emptied them, and said goodbye to me." Patrick remembered many calls that interrupted his meals or even a piss break. "Oh well, I am not supposed to be on duty now anyway, and it was not a serious call," he continued to muse to himself.

He went up and got a cup of coffee and watched the aircraft load up with the troops and the families left behind.

He thought back to many of his last deployment in support of Operation Desert Storm and said a prayer for them: "May God watch over you in your deployment. May he let you come home safe to your families and loved ones. Amen." He stayed until he could see the C-141 taxi down the taxiway to the runway. It was time for him to go to his wife and watch TV with her.

22

Sherrie was propped up with the TV on; however, she was not paying any attention to it. In her mind, she kept going over and over what happened when Rod attacked her and then took JR from their home. She remembered back to the birthday party when she last saw him—unexpectedly, no less—at the Brandin' Iron and what Rosie had said about Rod being outside the bathroom door.

Did Rod somehow rape her that night? She remembered how she felt, but she thought it was the booze she had drunk. Then Rosie had been killed in her car after her brakes failed in the parking garage. There was no way she could prove it, but she knew deep down that Rod did it so Rosie could not talk if Sherrie had gotten pregnant.

Then when JR was born, she knew who he looked like, and it was not Patrick. She told Patrick that he did have his eyes and that he looked like her father who had died ten years before, and Patrick accepted that. She knew that JR was Rod's son. He had his looks and his mannerisms, and there was nothing she could do about it.

She thought about the fear that she lived with, always looking over her shoulder to see if Rod was nearby, always wondering if he would show up. She wondered how she would react if she saw him again. Most of all, though, what would Patrick do if he found out the truth?

Well, the time had finally come. Rod had knocked on the door to her home, and though he had a mask on, she knew who it was by his voice. *Stupid me, I let him in. I never thought he would hurt me like he did—but he did. But now, how do I tell Patrick that JR is not really his?* she thought to herself. Just then, there was a knock on the door. She looked at her watch and knew it was not a doc or one of the nurses. "Come in."

Slowly the door opened, and an arm with a bag at the end of it moved through the door. "You can come in, Patrick," she said with a smile on her face.

Patrick came through the door and asked her, "Now how did you know it was me, honey?"

"Silly," she said with a smile. "What gave you away was my overnight bag. Now come here and give me a kiss."

Patrick put the bags down and went to her and kissed her lightly on her full red lips and then finished with their private kiss of rubbing nose tip to nose tip. He pulled the chair closer to the bed and saw that she was still not able to eat as she still had the tube in her nose that emptied her stomach. "Honey, did the doc say how much longer for the tube in your nose?"

"He was in this morning. He told me it would be two more days. Everything has not moved back to its regular location. Then I go on a liquid diet for a couple of days then soft then regular. So we are talking about two more weeks in here." She dropped her eyes then looked back up at Patrick and with tears in her eyes said, "I'm sorry."

Patrick, only guessing why she said that, looked at her and asked her, "Sorry for what, my love?" hoping that now she would tell him what happened.

"I'm sorry for what happened. I should not have let that person in and take JR or do this to me." She then held her arms out, wanting to be hugged by Patrick. She stopped crying, and after dabbing tissues to her eyes, she told him, "The doc wants me to start walking. I need to let them bring me a walker and disconnect me." She hit the Call button to tell them what she wanted to do.

At this bit of good news for a change, Patrick got her house coat ready for her and her slippers as well. "I brought you these as I figured they might help you get better quicker."

It dawned on her that Patrick had gone back into the house for them. "But I thought it was a crime scene."

There was a knock on the door, and in came an orderly with a walker. "Ms. Johnson, I am Airman First Class Roberts. I will be assisting you tonight. Here is your walker for you to use when you are out of bed. However, you can only use this if you have someone with you." She moved to the suction pump to shut it off and then disconnected the tube line just below Sherrie's nose. "Just to make sure you can do things correctly, let's see if you can sit up and swing your feet over the side. We do not want you to fall and tear open the stiches."

Sherrie swung her feet off the bed so that they were dangling over the floor. "Hoo wee, boy, am I lightheaded," she said. "Patrick, I don't know about this right now. My insides feel like they are going to tear apart."

"Ms. Johnson, that is normal to have that feeling. It's noth- ing major. Here, now let's get that robe on you, and afterward, how about if I brush your hair for you to get the tangles out?"

"No, thank you, I want Patrick to do it. He likes to brush my hair when I am not feeling well or when we're watching TV, am I right, Patrick?" With that, all three started to laugh. "I said that you like to brush my hair when I am not feeling good, am I right, or am I mistaken?"

Patrick shook his head as if to clear an image, and he told her that she was right. "Honey, you are correct. However, if the orderly wants to brush your hair, she might give me tips on how to get the bad tangles out."

The orderly, Roberts, told them that she had time and would be honored to walk and do Sherrie's hair. She then told Sherrie that she had to take her time walking.

"She should set a goal each time she gets out of bed even if it is just to the door and back tonight that is a reachable goal."

Roberts paused as she helped her with her robe and slippers. "She should not overdo it. Each patient is different as to how far they can walk." She looked at Sherrie and suggested to both of them, "I think the doorway is fine for today. Physical Therapy will be here tomorrow to help her with her leg strength."

Sherrie took a deep breath, grabbed the walker, and stood up. "Oh damn, that hurts," she said as she moved one foot in front of the other, shuffling like an older person. She reached the door. "That felt like a mile. I need to go back to my bed." Slowly she moved back to bed.

"If that is what it feels like just to the door, how the hell am I going to get out of here?" She looked at Patrick and smiled as best as she could.

Roberts helped her back to bed and told her, "Starting tomorrow, you will need to get up and walk twice a day. The doctor wants you up and moving."

Shortly after that, we can remove the tube and put you on a liquid diet." She wrote out Sherrie's name on a strip of tape and put it on the walker. She asked her if she needed something for the pain. "Hair first, then pain pills when you have time," Sherrie replied.

Roberts brushed her hair and told Patrick how to easily untangle ratted hair. It was all Sherrie could do to nod her head as Patrick moved the big chair closer to the bed and took her hand in his. He looked at her and then at Roberts and said to the orderly, "It looks like another early night for her again."

Roberts looked at him and smiled and told them she would have the nurse come down for the pain shot.

After she left, Patrick told Sherrie that he wanted to stay in the room tonight and watch TV with her except for getting coffee and maybe a smoke. "I know I had quit, but this case has gotten to me, and I can't do anything about it by orders of the old man, and the smokes are calming me down."

"I know you have gone back to smoking again. At least you can get out of this room. I know you will stop again, so I will not harp on it, but you have to promise me no more two packs a day!"

"On my honor, as a loving husband and as an E-8 selectee, I promise to not go back to two packs a day and to cease smoking as soon as I feel possible." He then smiled at his wife and leaned over and kissed her just as the nurse came in.

"Uh, excuse me, but I thought I heard she needed a pain shot and I come in and you two are playing house!" Patrick turned around and saw the nurse smiling at them, for she knew what she saw was the best for Sherrie. "You, out! After I give her a shot, I need to check her bandages and talk to her. Go fill your cup and whatever."

Patrick stood up, looked at her with a straight face, and said, "Yes, ma'am. I'm out of here." He picked up his cup and his blue beret, bent over his wife, kissed her, then rubbed noses together, smiled at the nurse, and walked out, slowly closing the door.

He went to the nurse's station, filled his cup, shot the breeze with Roberts and one other enlisted medical orderly. He then walked outside to the smoke room. As soon as he was outside, he pulled a smoke from the pack and lit it right away, enjoying the clear nighttime sky. He wondered what the nurse wanted to talk to Sherrie about.

He began to run all that he had found out today through his head and came up with the same conclusion. The person was an expert, maybe Special Ops trained, and finally, unfortunately, it was going to be a cold case.

As long as he has been a Security Police investigator, he had used what he called the five W's one H formula, and it worked fairly well in solving cases. The basic W's were who, what, when, where, why, and the one H was how. He knew the what was the kidnapping and assault on Sherrie, when was two days ago, where was his own base quarters, who and why were unknown. How was the detailed planning and execution.

Patrick was thinking more about the what portion. What will it take to solve this and when? He looked around and moved to go inside, but he saw it was crowded with more smoke than he wanted to be around. He knew the place to go.

He went back inside, and after finding out Sherrie was asleep, he told the nurses he would be in the chapel and then the MAC Terminal.

He entered the hospital chapel, and he went to the front pew just as he did that first night. He took a look around, did not see anyone, and started to pray. "God, why did you let this happen to me? Where is JR? I know I only prayed to you when I needed to feel comforted, so I am back again. I know that Sherrie is fine physically and getting stronger, but I need to know that JR is okay and that he was not harmed by whoever took him. Please watch over him and keep him safe, for I know that one day I will see him again. Amen." Patrick then felt a light tap on his shoulder. He jumped as he twisted around, his hands in fists, until he saw the same priest he saw the first night.

"Who are you? Or rather, what are you? The nurses tell me there is no assigned Catholic Chaplain this week." As he waited for a response, he felt a sense of calmness settle over him as the priest touched him again.

"Master Sergeant Patrick Johnson, your son is okay. He is safe. I cannot tell you where he is because that is not my job. However, I am also not a chaplain in the literal sense of the word. What I will say is this: you know who I am, and you read about me as a child in your Sunday school lessons. You were taught to have faith, so have faith in your Lord God. Have faith now, son."

He then moved slowly to the door, and as he left the chapel, Patrick heard songs he had not heard in years as if they were com- ing from heaven. He quickly moved to the doorway but did not see anyone.

Patrick now knew. He had just spoken to Jesus Christ, and his touch comforted him. He knew that everything would be good and that his son was okay.

Even though he felt calm, he was still shaking like a leaf. Patrick left the hospital grounds and went to the Base Chapel. He knew from occasions when he had to take someone for counseling that there was a chaplain on duty until 2200. He arrived at the chapel to find the side door unlocked, and he went in. He went to the chaplain's office and found Father Kelley hard at work. Patrick knocked on his doorframe and asked him "Father, do you have a minute?"

"Of course, my son. Come in." Father Sean Kelley took a closer look at Patrick and asked him, "You are the one whose wife was assaulted and son kidnapped the other day?" Patrick nodded. "Come on in, Patrick, and sit down. Now what can I do for you?"

"Father, this is going to sound like I am off my rocker with all that has happened to me lately, but three times I have been in the Hospital Chapel, and twice I have seen what I thought was the Catholic Priest. The nurses tell me there is no Catholic Chaplain assigned to the hospital this week. First Sgt Brownlie has told me the same thing. Is there a Catholic Chaplain assigned at the chapel this week? I feel so weird about this. This has never happened to me nor anyone that I know."

"My son, tell me exactly what happened at the—everything. I might be able to help you if I know what happened."

Patrick told him exactly what happened the three times he was there including the time nothing happened. "Tonight was different, Father. He touched me, but it was different. This time I heard music like singing from Heavenly Angels."

"My son, what you experienced was something that no one can explain except this way. You did not see a military chaplain. What you experienced was Jesus Christ letting you know that your son is safe and okay. Remember, Jesus is the source of comfort in times of stress and confusion. Does this answer your question, Patrick?"

"Yes, Father, it does. Thank you. I have been in more stressful times than this, and I never saw Him in the flesh before. He had on an Air Force uniform."

Before Patrick could leave, Father Kelley asked him to join him in prayer. Patrick knelt down and bowed his head. He listened to the Priest's words and how they fit the occasion:

"Holy Father, we come to you for a sense of peace in this troubled world, where a distraught husband and father prayed to you and he felt the peace that your Son gave him. He knows now his son is safe and that one day he will see him again. Amen."

Patrick stood up, shook Father Kelley's hand, and thanked him for his time and helping him. "You know, Father, this might be the time to come back to chapel services even if it has been a long time." They both smiled, and Patrick walked out the door into the cool breeze that suddenly appeared. *I need to get something to eat now that that was cleared up*, he thought.

Patrick arrived at the MAC Terminal just as a load of Marines were loading up on two C-141 Starlifters. He got in line at the grill and ordered his meal: a double cheeseburger, french fries, and a soda. *When Sherrie is out of the hospital, I will not get this for a while*, he mused. He sat down just as two LE troops came in, got their food, and sat down with him. They asked him how his wife was doing and if there was any news on his son. He told them there was no news on his son, but he felt that he was okay.

"Sarge, you know that the whole squadron is behind you, right? If there is anything that needs to be done, just ask." Just then they received a call over their radios of a break-in at the BX. "See you, Sarge!" They quickly got up and left, leaving their trash and uneaten food on the table, which caused Patrick to remember those early days of his career.

He picked up their trash with his, put them in the trash bin, and decided to head back to the hospital. Just as he was getting in his truck, he remembered the party tonight with Paul, John, and Don. He wished them well and knew he would hear about it in the morning.

23

That night at the Brandin' Iron, Paul, his wife, Anne; John, his wife, Mary Jane (or MJ); Don and his date, Lydia, enjoyed a chance to unwind. After the major all-out effort to solve the assault and kidnapping case, a standstill now still existed. It was time to relax and unclutter their minds. All three investigators agreed on one thing—no talking about the case.

Once Paul introduced Anne and MJ to Don and Lydia, food and beer were ordered. They sat around eating and drinking until the band started to play.

It was easy to envision John and Paul out there with their wives dancing to a country Western band as they were all dressed in Levi's, Western shirts, and hats. Don, on the other hand, was in his slacks and dress shoes with a sports coat. Lydia was in a skirt and a peasant-type blouse that showed her bare shoulders.

Don and Lydia watched the four dance a couple of dances as they drank their beer and talked about her upcoming move to join him in LA in two weeks.

Don said, "I need to make sure the place is straightened up. It is not so much dirty, but I had to leave real quick to come out here." She laughed and told him she did not think he was a messy bachelor. "You just want to impress me, that's all. Tell me again about your place."

"It is a small three-bedroom ranch with one bedroom converted to an office for me, a small kitchen with eating area, and a fireplace." Just then the other four came back to the table and sat down.

John looked at Don with his arched eyebrow.

MJ knew that look and began to scowl at John while Paul turned his head away as he knew what was coming. "Don, you told us this afternoon at lunch that you and Lydia knew how to CW dance. When are you going to go out there on the floor and show us?"

Don, with a sheepish look on his face, looked at Lydia and explained what that was all about. Just then, the band started to play Texas Two-Step. Don stood up and asked Lydia to join him on the floor.

Arm in arm they went out, and they started to dance the Texas two-step. Much to everyone's surprise, they did quite well. As big as Don was, all the other dancers stopped and at the end gave them a round of applause as they headed back to the table. Don looked at John and asked him, "Glad you did not make a bet with a bookie?"

But John had made a bet and lost to Paul. Everyone at the table could see John give Paul ten dollars. Everyone, including John and Don, had a good laugh—everyone except for MJ, that is. She continued to glower at John, and he knew he was in hot water with his wife.

MJ looked at Don and asked him how he learned to dance the two-step so well.

Don said that he had grown up in Texas, the son of a cattle rancher. "A small town called Tyler and then went to University of Texas." He smiled at John and shrugged his shoulders as if to say, "You never asked."

After that, they all settled down to enjoy themselves. The women moved closer together and talked small talk while the guys ended up talking about the case even though they had all previously had agreed not to do so.

Don wanted to make sure that Paul would keep him updated on anything that came into their office while he promised to keep them updated. "I wonder if Ms. Johnson will ever tell the truth about that day and how her husband will take it?"

Paul thought about it and told him, "Sherrie is, basically, a strong woman. Eventually, she will tell what happened. As for Patrick, he loves her, and he will work with her. I also found out this afternoon that Patrick is going to take the promotion to senior. Since there cannot be two of us with the same rank, he will probably have to leave the office and go back to Law Enforcement duties. If things go right, he will probably be able to stay on station until the base closes."

John picked up and told Don of his and Paul's plan to open up a Cold Case Investigations business after they retire when the base closes. "You can come work with us after you leave the bureau—if you think you can handle working under Paul, that is."

Laughing, he almost choked on a gulp of beer. He looked at MJ and asked her to join him on the floor.

Around 10:00 p.m., they all decided to call it a night since Don had to leave for LA the next morning. As they all left, there was a yell from one of the tables: "Hey, Lydia, who is the big brute with you?" They stopped, wondering how this would play out when Lydia answered, "This big brute, as you called him, is my boyfriend. Come on over and meet Don."

From the table, "Uh, hi, Don. You got a nice gal there."

John and Paul thanked Don for his assistance the past couple of days and promised to keep in touch with him. Anne and MJ said it was a pleasure being with Lydia and that they also would keep in touch especially since she was moving to LA the following week.

Lydia told them then that she was looking forward to the move to LA as it was time for her to move on and to enjoy life and to see if there was truly something called love at first sight as she had never experienced it before.

Anne, having had less to drink than Paul, drove with John and MJ sitting in the back seat. They watched Don and Lydia leave the parking lot, and she told Paul, "I like them. They are a good couple—different, but a good couple."

She dropped John and MJ off at their quarters and proceeded home. She knew Paul was in deep thought and knew what he was thinking. "Okay, Paul, I know you are thinking about Patrick and Sherrie. What is on your mind? You always use me as a sounding board for troubled cases."

"Honey, I love you, and I thank you for offering to let me talk to you about it, but this case is one big ball of wax. Nothing makes sense. The suspect is damn good. He covered his tracks too well, and we do not know who he is or where he is. This case is going to cost me a lot of sleepless nights, and I seriously doubt it will be solved before I retire in two years." He paused and then told her, "Even our excellent brains will not be able to solve this one. Don is not able to solve it, and he is the best they have at his field office." As they pulled into their driveway, he leaned over and kissed her cheek. "Thank you."

24

Two weeks after the attack and kidnapping, Sherrie was finally told she could now go on a soft diet for a couple of days and then a regular diet before she could go home. That afternoon, she told Patrick, "I do not want to see another cup of beef or chicken broth again, nor do I want any sickly green Jell-O again." Then she had many more questions, but she knew she had to wait.

"Honey, we will not be going back to our quarters. We are getting new quarters. In fact, by the time you are out of here, I will have us all moved out and into the new place."

"You mean it will be so I do not have to remember that day as I will not be in the house again?" She grabbed the fork from her mashed potatoes and pointed it toward him and yelled at him, "What the hell do you think I think about every single minute of every day I have been in this damn room?" She laid the fork down and looked at him with a hardness he had never seen from her before. "Get the hell out of here, and don't come back tonight!"

Patrick, taken aback by his wife's fury, at first did not know what to say. He then picked up his blue beret and told her, "As a matter of fact, I do know, or at least I think I know. I hurt for you in here, and I hurt for our missing son, but please do not take it out on me. You have my cell number if you want to contact me."

Just as he turned toward the door, she called him back. "Patrick, I am sorry I said that. I know you hurt, and it must be worse for you as you are a damn good investigator, and you can't do anything to help the investigation. I'm sorry."

Patrick stopped and turned around, went to her, and told her that there would be times like this where they will be like two male cats fighting over one female cat in heat, but it should not set the tone for their relationship. "We have to be strong to get through this no matter how long it takes, no matter what the investigation comes up with." He gave her a kiss on her forehead and asked her "Now do you want me to leave?" He then put on the silly smile he gave her when he was feeling silly. "Or can I stay and watch TV with you tonight with vanilla ice cream and then go to bed in our 'separate beds'?"

"Go get your cup of coffee and come back here. Let's watch TV. Tomorrow you can start to pack up the dishes and stuff like I would if we get transferred." She told Patrick that she wanted to walk to the nurse's station with him, but she needed help.

Patrick pushed the Call button and told them Sherrie wanted to take a walk. They told them it would be a few minutes; they were busy. He pulled his chair next to the bed. They held hands and watched the evening news. Sherrie started to tense up when she heard about a child abuse news item and then relaxed when they said the child was okay. Patrick knew she needed to laugh, so he told her about the FBI agent.

"Hon, you know the FBI special agent that is involved with the case? Well, it seems he took a liking to one of the women in the NCO club—the one who did all the cakes and pies, Lydia, the one that all the guys keep trying to go out with. Well, it seems that she likes him too, and she is quitting her job next week and is moving to LA to be with him. So Paul, Anne, John, and MJ took them out to dinner at some bar in San Berdoo."

"Patrick, the place where they went, is it the Brandin' Iron? Because if it is, you and I have not been there for some years. However, for me, that place is now bad news. I went there for my birthday party with Rose, remember? Then the next day, she dies in an auto accident. I have had bad feelings about that place ever since."

She then drew back into her shell, her arm still in Patrick's as they watched *Wheel of Fortune*, which was one of their favorite game shows.

It was two hours later when the nurse's aide came in to help Sherrie with her walk. "Ma'am, I am sorry it took so long. We had a problem with a postsurgical case."

Sherrie looked at her and said it was okay. "Before we start the walk, I need to go to the bathroom, but I do not want to use the bed pan again." She smiled at both of them as the aide helped her to the bathroom on the walker with the IV stand.

Sherrie came out of the bathroom and commented on how nice it was not to have cold metal under her ass for a change. That got Patrick to chuckle as the three walked down to the nurses' station and Patrick filled his cup with fresh hot coffee. The nurses complimented her on how good she was beginning to look and that she was on her way to getting out of there on schedule.

"Yeah, just as long as it is after Patrick does all the moving himself to our new quarters."

Patrick looked at her, saw how tired she was, and told her, "About face, back to bed for you." Slowly they made their way to her room, this time passing several patients coming in from outdoors with the distinct odor on them. Before she could say anything, Patrick said, "Yes dear, you know I have gone back to smoking. I am sure it is just temporary, and once all this mess is cleaned up, I will quit."

Back in her room, the aide told Patrick he had to leave as she had to change the dressing and get Sherrie ready for sleepy time. Patrick picked up his beret and his coffee cup and went out the door. He headed straight for the smoke room outside.

Once outside, he noticed a fresh breeze blowing from the west, which meant a comfortable day tomorrow. He went into the tent and noticed he was alone. He lit one up and inhaled it, blowing the smoke out his nose, knowing he would have to stop before moving into their new quarters. He heard a step outside the entrance and noticed an old man walk in and not say anything or even light one up. He just looked at Patrick. His face was familiar, but Patrick could not place the old man.

"MSgt Johnson, correct? Do you not know who I am? We have talked a couple of times these past several days."

Patrick looked at him. He was in casual civilian clothes, but he looked older. Calmly, remembering what the chaplain, Father Kelley, had said, "Yes, sir, I do know who you are. You are our Lord and Savior, Jesus Christ, but why do you only appear to me?"

"My son, you have been troubled about the kidnapping of your son, Patrick Johnson Jr., and the attack on your wife. You are troubled because your wife does not tell you everything. You are troubled because you are human. You have to trust me when I tell you that your son is okay—he is safe and well taken care of. He is in no danger, and one day the three of you will be reunited."

Patrick replied, "My Lord, I will follow your guidance and your words."

Before anything else could be said, Jesus got up and walked out just before a young medical orderly came in. "Sarge, you got a light? My Zippo ran out of fluid this afternoon." He looked at Patrick kind of funny and said, "Uh, Sarge, you okay?"

Patrick looked at him and decided not to ask him if he saw anyone. He gave him a light. "You know, Zippo lighters have been around a lot longer than me and have even saved a few lives. I had one in Grenada, and it stopped a bullet from hitting my chest." With that last comment, Patrick put out his smoke and went back inside to finish watching TV with his wife and go to sleep.

Tomorrow will bring new and interesting challenges for me to conquer, he mused as he went to his wife's room. Walking in, he found Sherrie asleep with the TV still on.

He decided to make some noes for what he needed to do to make some notes for what he needed to do to accomplish the move from their current quarters to their new ones. At the top of the list was boxes and newspapers for the dishes and other fragile things. Next would be to rent a truck to move everything once he found out where the new quarters would be.

He watched a crime show then the news. There was nothing there other than the normal daily news about the world in general. He decided to go to bed and said a prayer, thanking Jesus for reassuring him that JR was safe and sound. He then went to sleep and slept the best he had ever since that day.

25

Two weeks after returning home, Rod and Josie were amazed at how quickly the case had been dropped from the media. Rod had hoped that Sherrie was doing okay and knew that the wound he gave her was not life threatening and that she should be able to have another child that would distinctly be Patrick's.

As for JR, it was great having a son with him on his ranch.

JR was full of questions as he toured the land with Rod in a small runabout Jeep he used on the land. He loved seeing the three cows that Rod had decided to purchase and how the machine would milk them and the horse barn, where Rod had told him that he would have his own pony to ride with him *and* Josie next year.

Some of his first questions were, "Are there any Indians here?

Why don't you have a gun?"

"Yes and no, son" said Rod. "We do have Indians, but they are not the ones you see on TV. In fact, several of them work with me on the ranch. As for a gun, I do have some, but they are locked away, and I have no need to use them here. When you get older, I will teach you how to safely use them."

He could see that JR was thinking about that one and then he asked, "How old, Dad?"

Rod laughed. "In a few years, son, when you will understand what guns really do."

As they rounded the last corner of the fifty-acre cornfield, Rod began to make notes about which fence posts needed to be replaced. "Okay, this work is done. Let's go in and get some lunch before Mom throws it out to the pigs".

Before they even got to the house, they could hear the ringing of the bell to tell everyone it was time for lunch.

"I know that you have seen a lot in the past two weeks, and because you have behaved well, we will go out to dinner tonight to one of our favorite restaurants."

"Can I have hot dogs and mac and cheese?" JR asked with a smile on his face, knowing how it made his dad laugh when he did his silly lopsided grin.

Rod was not overly concerned about his son's lopsided grin. After all, he had a normal smile when he was serious. However, just to make sure, Josie was going to take him to see one of the pediatricians at F. E. Warren AFB hospital to have a checkup.

Rod decided to humor him a little with a serious answer to his question. "No, it is not that type of restaurant. It is one with excellent cooked steak and other local menu items. The place is called Little Bear Inn, and in fact, they have the best hamburger in the area. So don't overeat at lunch today. You will still have to lie down and take your nap this afternoon with no temper tantrums, okay, pal?"

"Okay, Dad, but being out here today with you, I am hungry," JR said as he grabbed Rod's arm to keep from bouncing out of the cab of the open side Jeep as it bounced along the rough path toward the house.

Josie knew about the plans to go out to eat, so she had fixed them a small lunch. The field workers who normally ate with Rod and Josie knew of the plans ahead of time, so they brought extra food for themselves. They all loved "Little Rod," as they called him, and marveled at his questions. Even they were amused with his silly lopsided grin when he was having fun with them.

After a light lunch of a hot dog, chips, and milk, surprisingly, without being told to do so, JR went into his bedroom and lay down and watched cartoons on his small TV set. Josie looked at Rod with an arched eyebrow instead of asking him why, so Rod told her what he had told JR about dinner.

"No, not at all, Mr. Osborne, but it will have to be out here. My son is taking his nap." He led Mr. Osborne to the barn to look at his equipment.

"As you can see, sir, my equipment is well taken care of, and to be honest with you, none of my equipment is over five years old. I have a strict policy that after a certain piece of equipment is used, it is cleaned and all the vital parts checked before it goes to work the next day." He took him on a tour of his storage area and let him check the fluid levels and cleanliness firsthand.

"Mr. Duval, I am impressed with how well you maintain your equipment. If more ranchers and farmers maintained their equipment like you do, I will be out of a job real quick," he told Rod on his way back to his truck. He could see Rod was thinking, and he waited for him to speak.

"Mr. Osborne, there is something I might look into in a couple of weeks. I would like to check about getting an old-fashioned hay wagon. I was thinking of taking local kids around the fields on the wagon in the fall after the harvest—not a flatbed trailer but an old fashioned wagon. Think you might be able to help me out?"

"Here is my card. Let me check around for you, and call me in a couple of weeks. I will see what I can line up for you." They shook hands. He got in his truck, and Rod watched him as he left.

As he watched him leave his property, Rod thought long and hard about him. He did seem sincere about his job; however, Rod had a funny feeling about him. Rod decided to call the number on the card to verify who he really was.

He called the number on the card. Human Resources verified that he had been with them for ten years. Rod quickly hung up and, still feeling uneasy, his sixth sense telling him to be wary, looked out his living room window.

Nothing strange out there, but you can never tell. Maybe I will have a couple of the boys keep an extra look out for a while, he mused. He then went to find Josie and remind her the reservations were for six at the restaurant.

He went down the hall to check in on JR and found him under the covers and Josie on top of the covers. *Never have I felt as relieved as I do now, knowing how they get along*, he thought as he opened the door a little and motioned for Josie to come out.

"Everything is okay. I called his company, and he checked out. It seems he is actually employed by Harvester International. However, I still want to be careful of him. I think I will pay some overtime for the next couple of weeks or so by having a couple of the boys stay and watch the ranch at night. How's the little guy doing?"

"He fell asleep as soon as I walked in. He asked me to stay with him. I figured it was the best move to make, considering he has only been here a couple of weeks. Maybe Sherrie did the same thing with him when he took his naps."

"You did the right thing being with him. He is still bound to be nervous with us. We need to make him feel he can trust us when feels confused."

Josie asked him, "What time do you want to get him up for his bath? I was thinking around four, then we can each take our shower while the other one watches him."

"Yeah, four sounds right. Our reservations are set for 6:00 p.m. That will give me another half hour in the barn, and then I will come in. I will tell Hector about tonight and ask him to set up the watch list. I don't think anything will happen, but you never know."

Rod went out to the barn to finish soaping down a saddle that he was going to use the next day and thought more about this "Mr. Osborne" character. Something was not right. He did not know if it was due to suddenly having a small boy here on the ranch or not. Possibly one of his neighbors had talked to someone about it, but he was going to be extra careful. He began to have doubts if Josie could pull it off Monday at the base hospital, but he had to trust her at some point. If she can handle it Monday with no problem, then she will be okay.

At four, he went back to the house and saw Josie getting their son ready for his bath. JR started to run toward Rod completely naked, laughing. Rod blocked the entryway into the living room and scooped him up and nuzzled his neck. "You absolutely cannot go in to the living room with no clothes on." Laughing, Rod put him down and told him to go take his bath, or he would not go out to dinner with Mommy and Daddy.

That got him calmed down, and Rod had to smile when he heard him say, "Come on, Mom, I need my bath."

The sound coming from the bathroom sounded like a pool party with the laughing and the giggling going on. Finally, Josie came out of the bathroom looking like a drenched cat. Rod could not help but laugh at the sight.

"You just wait, mister, until you have to bathe him then see who gets laughed at." But even then, she was laughing so hard it hurt her ribs. "Tell you what, my darling husband, why don't you go get him dressed, and I will shower."

By time Josie was done in the shower, Rod and JR were finally finished. JR had on new blue jeans, cowboy boots, and a Western shirt. Rod looked at JR and said out loud for Josie's benefit, "I won- der who she would rather be out with tonight—you, me, or both of us?"

Josie stuck her head in the room and told them, "Both of you guys. You two gents will be the best-looking guys in there, and every female will be jealous." They all laughed as Rod headed into the shower. Josie had put his clean underwear in there as well. Yes, he was definitely in a good mood tonight, and nothing was going to spoil it. Rod was thinking of what he was going to have for dinner. He decided on Rocky Mountain Oysters as an appetizer before he dug into his brandy rib eye steak that he loved so much. He then remembered what he said about no mac and cheese at the Little Bear Inn. He looked in the mirror and saw his rugged look with his white shirt and string tie with the DDD logo. Yup, he was now ready to step out for the evening with his wife and son. Being a Friday night, he knew some of his neighbors would be there tonight. Many had not seen his son nor even knew he had a son. This will be the biggest test yet of the situation. Before stepping out, he pulled on his corduroy jacket and Western dress hat.

26

At five fifty-five, they pulled into the parking lot. JR was anxious to get inside so he could see the bear that his dad told him about. Up the steps and into the entryway was a bear that stood upright and looks real enough. JR went up to it and touched the fur before Rod could stop him. He looked up at his Dad and asked him if he had to ever fight a bear.

Rod replied that he did not have to fight a bear, "But there were some big guys that were my instructors who taught me to fight bigger guys than me." He then went up to the cashier, and they were promptly seated.

He asked for a Bud Light, a Seven-Up for Josie, and a Coke for JR. Since no one else wanted an appetizer, he ordered Rocky Mountain Oysters for himself.

While waiting for the drinks and Rod's Rocky Mountain Oysters, they looked at the menu while JR looked around at the pictures and other items that adorned the walls of the dining room. He told his father that he was hungry and wanted a hamburger and fries.

When the drinks and appetizer arrived, Josie ordered the rib eye, medium; baked potato with just butter; and the house salad. Rod changed his mind and ordered the prime rib, medium; loaded baked potato; and vegetables. For JR., he ordered the Little Bear Burger with fries.

Before JR could say anything, Rod told him that since this was his first time here, he had to not let his eyes be bigger than his stomach.

"That's funny. What does he mean. Mom?"

With a smile of her own, she told him that some people look at a menu and do not realize what they are eating or how much they are eating. At that point, she looked at Rod and just shook her head as she saw him bite into another Rocky Mountain Oyster.

Just as he finished them, their meals arrived. Rod asked for a cup of coffee for both him and Josie. Rod cut JR's burger in quarters for him and watched him attack his mountain of fries with gusto as if he had not eaten lunch earlier. Josie watched him wipe his mouth of the catsup from his fries and then, leaving some fries, he attacked his burger.

By the time they all finished eating, there was no room for desert, and Rod asked JR if he liked it here. "This is where a lot of ranchers and farmers come to talk business sometimes. Other times it is used to bring their families out for a good dinner, like tonight." He looked at his watch and realized time was moving on, and he called for the check.

While Rod took care of the bill, Josie and JR went to where the bear was. JR looked at it with new awareness of the bear. The three went to the car, and even though the distance was not that far, JR was asleep in his car seat before they got home. Once home, Rod carried JR into his bedroom, and Josie undressed him and put him in his cowboy pajamas that he wanted to wear every night.

"I think it is good that he gets a good sleep tonight as he had had a big day today."

Josie told Rod, "His appointment is at 10:00 a.m. Monday. With no shot records or information on his immunizations, he will have to get them all. I know it is important for him to get them, or he will not be allowed in school."

"I know. Afterward, you can take him to the BX and get him a toy and maybe a stop at Burger King for lunch."

Rod looked at her and smiled at the thoughts of happy family life and the way she was picking up her "mommy role" with JR. "I would love to go with you, but I need to be here Monday, getting ready to harvest the next set of crops. Everything is coming along perfectly." He then went to the kitchen for a cup of coffee and sat down to read the paper.

Josie, on the other hand, went to the laundry room to finish folding and putting clothes away. At 10:00 p.m., they watched the news and then headed for bed.

Thinking of taking JR to the base clinic and then shopping at the Base Exchange and lunch on Monday made her smile. Soon she drifted off to sleep with a smile on her face, remembering when JR had called her "Mom" earlier tonight. Yes, things were going well.

Saturday went by quickly with no problems. Rod went over the plans with his work crew for extra security at night and took JR for a ride on the tractor, making sure he did not touch any of the controls. Sunday morning they all went to church; and then in the after- noon, Rod hosted a barbeque for his hands and their families, with Josie making a cake and homemade ice cream.

Monday morning Josie got up at six, fixed breakfast, made sure there was coffee for Rod, and then gave JR a bath. She put him in his clean clothes, and by 9:00 a.m., both were ready. She called Rod on his cell phone; he told her he was at the extreme northeast corner and would be there in about ten minutes.

When he got to the house, they were waiting for him out by the car.

"Sorry I was not closer. One of the fence posts had come loose and was on the ground. At least the cows are in a different section this morning, so we did not lose any."

He looked down at his son in his nice clean clothes and told him to obey his mom on base today. He bent down and kissed JR on the top of his head and told him he was getting to be a big man now.

Josie put him in the car seat and then kissed Rod goodbye and told him they loved him. Rod waved goodbye to them as she went down the drive to the highway.

In less than twenty minutes, they were at the main gate of F. E. Warren AFB. While waiting to be cleared through the gate, JR asked his mom if he would see any planes today.

"No, there are no planes here. You see those long tubes pointing up to the sky? Those are missiles; that is what this base does. Except for helicopters, they do not fly anything here." She did not have the heart to tell him the rest of the story of the missiles, that they were nuclear tipped. The thought just gave her shivers. "As you get older, you will know about them." She also wondered what was causing the holdup at the gate.

Must have been a recall this morning, she mused to herself. No one was wearing blue; they were all dressed in BDUs.

Then she spotted the armored vehicle behind the gatehouse.

"If not recall, then something happened," she said to herself.

She finally reached the gate and told the guard they had a 10:00 a.m. appointment at the hospital.

The gate guard looked at JR and asked him how old he was.

JR put his finger in his mouth and then held up two fingers and smiled at the gate guard.

The guard told them that his son was also two and for them to have a great day. As they proceeded through, they noticed building signs were in the process of being covered up. Josie made a mental note to tell Rod and hoped that it did not cause the appointment to be cancelled.

Once at the base hospital, Josie was lucky. They found an open spot with no Reserved Parking sign right next to a spot reserved for first sergeants only. She got JR out of the car seat and stepped inside the door, where she had to show her ID card to a door guard. She went up to the sign in window and was told to have a seat.

Five minutes later, a pretty Airman First Class female called out the name of "Roderick Duval Jr." JR picked up his head and looked around and finally he told Josie, "Mom, it's for me. She called my name," which got everyone to either laugh or chuckle and put smiles on their faces.

JR went right up to her and told her who he was and that "You sure are pretty," which again got everyone to smile especially the young A1C. She introduced herself as A1C Dixon and said that the doctor had to go on emergency leave, but he would be seeing Dr. Jackson and that he was waiting to see young JR.

They were in the treatment room no more than two minutes when the doc came in.

"Hi, I'm Dr. Jackson, and who is this young man?" He stuck out his hand to JR, and JR shook it.

"Shake it any harder and my hand will fall off," the doctor said, which got JR to laugh. "Mrs. Duval, I understand this is his first visit here. I see no entries of any other visits nor of immunizations. I need more information."

Josie went on to explain to him how they had just gotten custody of JR and did not have his immunization records. She went on to explain how Rod's sister did not give Rod the records when she gave JR to Rod.

"What is your game plan now, Dr. Jackson? He just turned two the first of the month."

"What I suggest is that he be given all of the vaccines for babies and young children." He looked at JR and saw that he was looking at his diplomas on the wall and looking around the room. "I suggest we start him on the basic baby shots today and then do the rest in stages. In about three months' time, he will be up-to-date."

The doc called A1C Dixon and told her to bring in the needles and medication for basic baby shots. She came in with two syringes and everything else that would be needed. Then she told JR what the doctor was going to do. She asked him if he wanted to hold onto the teddy bear she had with her.

"Uh-huh" was all he said while holding onto Josie's hand.

While the doctor squeezed his upper arm muscle, JR just closed his eyes and gritted his teeth.

Afterward the doctor looked at JR and told him, "Maybe next time I should hold onto the bear," and JR laughed.

"Mrs. Duval, I think we need to see JR in two weeks for his next set of shots. In about two months, it will be all over with except for the annual shots. A1C Dixon will set it up for you." He looked at JR and welcomed him to cowboy country and complemented him on his strong behavior this morning.

Josie thanked him and told him that her husband would be retired from the Army in two and a half months, so they would need to make sure they get JR's medical records for a local pediatrician. Jackson told her it would not be a problem.

Once they had the new appointments, Josie and JR left the hospital and went to the BX for him to look at the toys that were on display. Josie had never been in the BX, so she took her time looking at other things, and then they went to the toy section. Surprisingly, JR did not find anything he really wanted. "Now let's go find Burger King for lunch then go back home."

JR nodded as he looked at all the different people on base in uniform. He said that his Uncle Patrick was in the Air Force also and that he was a police officer. Josie nodded as she located BK and had to hunt for a parking space.

By the time they got home, it was well into the afternoon and past his nap time, so Josie figured to just let him stay up and watch cartoon videos until supper then an early bedtime. When Rod came in at suppertime, he asked her how it went.

Josie said, "He has to go back every two weeks until he is all caught up. He was a good trooper today. We went to the BX, but he did not find what he wanted, so we went to BK for lunch."

Rod asked her if she had found anything she wanted at the exchange. He knew she had not gotten out very much since they got home three weeks ago.

"No, I did not. I had never been in there, so I wanted to see what was there. They have some really nice stuff, but I could not pinpoint what I wanted today." She finished up in the kitchen and told them that dinner would be ready in twenty minutes and to get washed up.

At the table, JR was a little quieter than normal. Maybe it was because of the long day with no nap. After dinner, he went out to the living room and sat in his small rocking chair, staring at the blank TV screen.

"What's up?" Rod asked Josie. "I better go check and see if he has a fever, or he might have a reaction to the shot. Do you have the notice about possible reactions to the shot?"

She came back with the notice and gave it to Rod.

Rod went to the living room and found JR rocking in his chair. Rod put his hand to his forehead, and it felt warm.

"Are you feeling okay? You feel a little warm, and you were not talking much tonight." As a Special Forces "A" Team Medic, he thought he knew what the problem was—a mild reaction—but just to be safe, he called the base hospital ER. He explained what shot he had this morning and his current symptoms.

"The ER doc says it is probably a reaction to the shot. He also said that if his fever is not over ninety-nine, give him two Children's Tylenol every six hours and plenty of fluids tonight. If he is still bad in the morning, bring him in. It is like what we get when we get our annual flu shots—if you know what I mean."

Rod thanked him, went to get the thermometer, and took his temperature. It registered as 98.8, so he got him to take the Tylenol and had him drink a Tippee glass of water. Then he put him to bed, and JR did not fight at all. Rod turned on his night-light.

Rod told Josie that he was sure it was just a temporary reaction to the shot and that he would be better in the morning. They watched a movie then the news. Once again, there was nothing on the news of the kidnapping or anything from Norton AFB.

"I can't believe they have given up this quick," Rod told Josie.

"You must have taken all the pictures and destroyed them like you said you would do." She had a second thought, "Patrick must have had at least a small one in his wallet, and maybe he did not turn it in to the FBI? Let's go to bed. It has been a long day for all of us."

Rod agreed with what Josie said. He put his cup in the dishwasher, turned out the lights, and followed her into the bedroom.

Tomorrow will come soon enough, just as the next few months would, and the longer nothing happened, the easier it would be to accept that they had pulled it off and survived.

27

Over the course of the last two weeks, Patrick had secured new base quarters and had moved everything from their old place to the new one with the help of his squadron mates. The wives of the old neighborhood offered to wash everything for him so that when Sherrie came home from the hospital, everything would be done, and she could make the transition from their old home to the new one. Patrick had made runs to the base commissary, stocking up on items, knowing she would not be up to going to the commissary herself for a while. But there was a big stumbling block—what to do with JR's things.

He had talked to one of the psychiatrists not connected to Sherrie's case. He wanted a fresh new outlook on his questions—questions he did not want Sherrie to know about right away. The one important thing he found out was that he had to not tell her that she was pregnant at the time of the attack and that chances of her becoming pregnant again were very slim.

He also knew he was going back to work next Monday, three days after Sherrie would be coming home from the hospital. Friends from the old neighborhood and new neighbors would be checking on Sherrie to make sure she was okay. He knew that it would be hard not to tell her anything about the case or what was being done. The solution was really quite simple—he went to the commander.

Patrick spoke to him about the problem of JR's items. The commander suggested that he take JR's items to the Airman's Attic, a place for married airmen to obtain items at a low cost. Patrick then spoke about the upcoming commander's call on Friday, knowing it was primarily about his promotion to senior master sergeant the following Monday and that Sherrie might attend if she were up to handling the excitement.

On Thursday, Sherrie came home, and the commander's wife called her and told her that the commander's call on Friday would be for Patrick. She was hoping that if she felt up to it, she would attend as well.

"We will see" was her reply. That night she and Patrick discussed the upcoming commander's call the next day and that part of it would be for him putting on his new stripe on Monday. He would also begin his new job on Monday as well.

She complimented him on how he set up the new place and his shopping although "I can see I have to take you more often when I go to the BX and commissary." Not really knowing if she would be coming home on Thursday or not, he did not take anything out of the freezer earlier. "Do you want to go to the club, or should I bring dinner home?"

"I am tired. I think dinner at home would be better for me. Just let me lie down while you are gone for dinner. Surprise me with what you bring home."

She looked around their new quarters and told him that she knew that many things had changed, and it would take time for her to accept those changes. So with a familiar glitter in her eye, she told him, "Now if you would kindly guide me to our new bedroom, I will lie down until you get home with dinner."

Patrick put his arm around her waist and walked her back to the bedroom. He pulled out an old gown that she wore when she was not feeling well. "Here, put this on, then go to bed."

He told her after she was down, he bent over and kissed her and told her he was glad she was home. He told her he would be back within forty-five minutes.

"I love you with my heart, soul, and mind, my love. Now go. I am getting hungry." She rolled over to her side with a pillow clutched to her stomach, which the doctor had told her she could do to help alleviate the pain.

Patrick looked at her and walked down the hallway, which, unfortunately, passed the room JR would be in if he were here. Patrick had put some thought into it after talking to the hospital shrink about making it into a sewing room for Sherrie or even a small study for him. If they were to get JR back, there was a third bedroom available for him, which was a little bit bigger than this old room. Before he left, he set the table and even put a small flower vase in the center with a long-stem red rose, Sherrie's favorite rose.

Forty-five minutes later, he returned home from the club with Salisbury steak, mashed potatoes, gravy, and green beans. For dessert, he had her favorite ice cream, rocky road. He put the take-home boxes on the table and then set the table. Patrick then lit two candles and turned down the lights. He wanted to have everything exactly right for Sherrie when she came out.

Worried, he went down the hallway and saw her in what would be the new sewing room, her eyes closed, as in prayer. He knew what she was doing, so he waited until she knew he was there. Sherrie turned and looked at him and told him, "Honey, I just did something I have not done in a long time. I prayed, and I now know that JR is okay and we will see him again." Then she smiled and said, "I'm hungry. Let's eat."

She looked at the table setting, the rose in front of her plate, and the lit candles. "Oh, honey, thank you. The rose is perfect, and the dinner looks great. I love the candle as well."

Patrick walked her to her chair and seated her as if they were in an expensive restaurant. He noticed that her eyes twinkled in the candlelight. It was the first time in over three weeks he had seen that. *Maybe it is a good thing we moved to new quarters*, he thought. *But time will tell. Tonight will be an easy night for both of us.*

He began to go into detail about the new neighborhood. "This is a great neighborhood. Actually, though, it is for chiefs only, but they had one unit open, so I took it. Our next-door neighbor is a wonderful couple. They are Chief Master Sergeant Jonathan and

Terri Lombard from Services Squadron. Everyone knows what happened, and since Chief Lombard's wife is a former nurse and not working, she offered to help you if you need any help."

Before he could say anything else, she told him, "Thank you, my love, for doing everything while also having to worry about the investigation. I am sure I will get along with everyone here." She then finished up her dinner, and Patrick picked up the dishes and put them in the sink.

"Patrick, damn you, I have to do something around here, so let me do the dishes." She looked and saw that the dishwasher with a note on it which read, "Sherrie, my love, I know you want to do things, so you can load the first set in here tonight." It was signed "Love, Patrick" and had a smiley face on it. She looked at him and told him to go get his uniform ready for tomorrow and then watch TV.

Patrick went to the bedroom and listened for any untoward sounds, but all he heard was normal kitchen sounds. He would wear his dress blues since he knew the commander would wear his as was his custom. All of his other uniforms now had the new senior master sergeant stripes on, and the extra stripe did look good.

It had taken a lot of hard work over his career for him to put it on. However, he seriously doubted he would put on Chief. *I am not that good*, he mused.

28

By 0900 the next morning, the Investigative Office was open; and since Patrick would be leaving, Paul and John would be starting to screen records of those that wanted to expand their performance in Security Police Law Enforcement and become an Air Force Security Police investigator. It would be a short day, though, as they had to be at the club by 1230 to set up the room for Patrick's frocking ceremony promotion to senior master sergeant and commander's call.

John stuck his head in Paul's office and said, "You need to come out here and take a look at this one guy that just dropped off his paperwork."

Paul picked up his cup of coffee and followed John out to the hallway. There, braced against the wall, at a position of atten- tion, was Technical Sergeant Ronald Overton, who either wanted this job really badly or he was a total smart ass. Paul told him to be at ease. Oh, he looked the part of a Professional Air Force Security Policeman, but this guy took the cake. His uniform was impeccable. His Technical Sergeant stripes were positioned correctly on his uniform blouse sleeves. His name tag was correctly aligned. The only thing that might be wrong were the ribbons on his chest.

His ribbons, displayed in the correct order, were the Silver Star, Bronze Star, and Purple Heart with device to indicate a second award. These were all above his "I was there ribbons"—those that you normally get for serving honorably.

"TSgt Overton, I know that you are assigned to Bravo Flight and your flight is not due to be back on duty until next Tuesday. I want you here at 0900 on Monday morning. I do not mean 0830 or 0915, I mean 0900. Your uniform for the interview will be just as you are now, Class A Dress Blues. You are now dismissed."

"Yes, Sir." He went back to attention and made a sharp left face and exited the office, moving swiftly.

Paul looked at John, and both did everything they could to stop wanting to laugh. "Wait until I tell Patrick about this guy. Guess we will have to wait until Monday. How many applications do we have so far, and when is the cutoff time for applications?"

"Right now, his is the only application turned in. On the way to the club, I will stop by Personnel and request his records and tell them we need it by 0730 Monday."

"Sounds good, John. Let's go outside and talk for a bit in the fresh air." They grabbed their blue berets and ran into Patrick as he was coming in. "Patrick, come with us please," Paul asked him.

They went to their favorite spot for unofficial talking as no one else came out that door except in case of a fire or an emergency. Just as Paul was going to start talking, Patrick pulled out a pack of cigarettes and his lighter.

Paul must have had a funny look on his face as he finished lighting up and then told Paul, "Oh shit, this is the first time since I started again you have seen me do this. I started back up when Sherrie was in the hospital, and I had nothing to do to sooth my nerves. So tell me what you have to tell me."

"Patrick, both John and I have worked with you for some time. You taught us to do quote do everything by the book unquote. I have to tell you there is one part of the investigation we did not turn over to the FBI agent. You gave me a small snapshot of JR and, well, it got mislaid and ended up in the bottom of one of my desk drawers. How should we handle it? Make this your last official instruction before you are relieved this afternoon."

"Paul, you did not turn it over for a reason, and that one reason was that was all I had of JR. Do me a favor—make a copy of it and give me the copy. You know damn well that photo could and probably should be a vital piece of information in years to come if the case is not resolved quickly."

All they could do was nod heads at him. They knew he was right; he taught them that, and the regulations said the same thing.

He put out his cigarette then asked both of them, "I know you did that for a reason. What I do not know, but it is your case, the whole enchilada."

He turned around and told them that he needed to go into the office and finish cleaning out his desk before someone ran off with his important items in his bookcase and on top of his desk before they take "Starlifter wings and fly away."

Both Paul and John, not knowing that Patrick would be in that morning, had already moved his stuff to his office down the hall from the Investigations Office. All they could do was to try and somehow sneak back into the office but to no avail. Patrick was already inside.

They tried to sneak in through the emergency passage, but it was no luck at all. Halfway inside, at the end of the access tunnel, they saw him with his standard "hot under the collar" look that would make any airman basic literally melt under his glare. He crooked his index finger and motioned for them to come to him and not waste any time doing so.

"Just where are my personal items from my desk and the office walls? Who gave you permission to move things?"

Never being on the end of this type of interrogation by him, Paul knew he could break anyone he interrogated in seconds. "Patrick, we, uh, that is, I did not know if you would be in today, so I kinda moved your crap to your new office."

Once Patrick calmed down, they all went to his new office, and he could see that his best friends had set it up pretty much the way he would with a few minor corrections. He smiled at them and thanked them for their thoughtfulness.

Back in the office, they went over the case as best as they could. Knowing that Patrick should not even be involved now, especially since he was classified as a victim, Paul decided to fill him in on his thoughts.

"Patrick, basically, whoever did this act knew exactly what they were doing. Before you say anything, let me tell you what I think, ok?" Paul took a swig of coffee and continued. "One, the knife wound was specific in nature, not meant to kill Sherrie. Rather, he just wanted her to keep quiet while he made his getaway, and two, he knew how long it would take to get off the base. He or she knew when you would be home for lunch, so they must have been following you for several days. Three, he just plainly disappeared into thin air. My conclusion is that he had some sort of Special Forces training. We cross-checked all the branches off to see if he might be discharged and living in the area and nothing."

John picked up and added, "The FBI thinks the same thing. I remember something from a high school buddy. He went into the Army and then Special Forces, and he told me that the only way to survive an operation is to quote hide in plain sight unquote. Does this sound familiar to you?"

"Guys," Patrick began with a mist in his eyes. "There is no other team I would want to do this investigation than the two of you. You both know how the other thinks, eats, and sometimes farts during the day."

"I have been going over my records of everyone I investigated and had them kicked out of the Air Force and those that did not leave. I drew a blank. I know you will not let this rest as an unsolved case, and in my time as an investigator, this is the only one that I could not solve." With that, he got up from the chair and walked out of the office.

John said, "Paul, we have to get this one solved for him, plus it does not look good for us having an unsolved case especially since this bird farm we work at is closing. The entire casefile will be boxed up and shipped for storage. So what will we do now, boss?"

"First of all, lock up everything with the new combination locks I brought in this morning. We are starting to get others in here, and I want nothing removed. Then to the club for lunch and setting up for commander's call at 1400. Who knows, maybe we will run into supercop Overton, and we can have a friendly lunchtime chat with him."

He stopped and uttered, "Oh shit, did you order the flowers for Sherrie?"

John looked at him, his eyes wide open, that told him no.

"No problem, Paul. I will stop by the base flower shop and see what they have. This not being Valentine's Day, they should have some nice long-stem roses. If need be, I will go downtown and get them.

After locking up everything, John headed to base personnel to order Overton's personnel records while Paul headed to the club.

In the ballroom, two airmen were setting up the chairs to cover all but on-duty personnel and had a nice banner up over the stage that said, quite simply, "Congratulations SMSgt Johnson."

"Good job, guys. I am sure he will appreciate it. One thing, though, you have not been here long enough to know this, but MSgt Johnson is a stickler for detail, so make sure the chairs are lined up exactly in line with the chair in front."

One of them looked at Paul and asked what the correct way was to do that. His buddy told him he knew an easy way. He came back with some string and tied it to the front chair and then all the way back. "Now we align each row with this string. Figure eigh- teen-inches separation of each row. and it will be perfect."

"Whatever way that works, guys." He moved into the dining area. Who should Paul run into but Special Agent Abernathy and Lydia? He walked up to Don and asked him if he had any news for them.

"Unfortunately, no. Every rock I turned over was empty or it did not apply to this investigation, but we are staying on top of it." He looked around and added, "I heard there was a ceremony today for MSgt Johnson, so I thought I would stop by just to congratulate him.

No questions on the case—that is a promise." He started to sit down when Patrick came out of the food line and straight to his table.

"Well, I'll be damned. Lydia, have you come back to your senses or are you still with this guy? You left a whole lot of broken hearts." Patrick greeted her with a smile and a hug; he then invited them all to sit down.

He looked at the FBI agent and asked him if he had any good news on the whereabouts of his son and the person who almost killed his wife.

Don gave him the same response he had given Paul. With a crestfallen look, he apologized to Patrick for not solving this case.

"However, that is not the reason we are here today. We were in the area, and I remembered you were being promoted on Monday, so we wanted to come by and congratulate you."

"Yes, I am getting frocked today for my promotion to be effective Monday. My wife is going to be here, and I think it would be best if you were not here when she arrives. Just for the record, Sherrie does not know it, but she also lost her child. Thank you for stopping by." He stepped away from the FBI agent.

Paul and Don looked at Patrick questioningly, so he explained that Sherrie had been pregnant and lost the baby. "She does not know it yet, so I ask that it *not* become public knowledge."

He looked at Don and asked him, "Does this now move it up a notch to include murder?"

"I believe so, but I will have to check. How far along was she?"
"Six weeks or so. Now please go before Sherrie arrives and sees you." He then asked Paul to escort Don and Lydia to the front door

to make sure they were gone before Sherrie arrived.

At the door, Don gave Paul his card and told him he wanted to maintain contact. Paul gave him his card and, on the back, put Patrick's new office and home phone numbers on it. He then wished both Don and Lydia the best in their future together.

Paul went over to Patrick and pulled some of his french fries over to nibble on while they talked. "Okay, Patrick, talk. I know something is bothering you, so talk. We have about ninety minutes before the ceremony begins."

"First things first. No mention to Sherrie about the aborted baby. I have no clue when to tell her. Second, there are some things that just don't add up with this case. One, why the hell did she open the door to a stranger? Two, I was never really concerned about the lack of photos of JR and the fact that he really does not look like me. She always told me that he looked like her father. And three, where is he?"

Paul just shook his head and raised his hands up as if in a sign of "I give up." He felt for Patrick and Sherrie. They were the best friends he has had in his entire Air Force career. *This case tore at my insides, and I wonder if it will ever be solved*, he thought.

Paul had to change tactics on Patrick to get his mind out from the downside, so he asked him about TSgt Overton.

He smiled that crazy smile of his and asked why.

"He is applying for the vacant slot in Investigations. His interview will be Monday morning at 0900. He dropped off his application, and his uniform looked like he had just bought it. His decorations are hard to believe. Is he for real?"

"Paul, I served with him during Operation Fury in 1983. He got the Silver Star for protecting five American students in a building from a Cuban soldier that was trying to burn the hut down. He received his Purple Heart for that action. He received burns on his arms. He also received the Bronze Star in Desert Storm."

Patrick took a drink of soda then continued, "I did not serve with him again until here. You have to believe that his records are correct because they really are. He is the right man for the job. One more thing—he does try to overimpress people. Now let's eat before lunch gets really cold."

At 1300, squadron personnel began arriving for the commander's call. Sherrie was talking with Lt Col Burn's wife and thanking her

After all the hands went back to the field to work, Josie and Rod went to the front porch, made sure the baby monitor was turned on, and talked about the upcoming doctor's appointment on base for JR, with Rod taking the lead.

"Honey, are you sure you have everything well-rehearsed for Monday? Tell me how we came to have JR with only a birth certificate from Ohio?"

He continued by reminding her that this was to get his med- ical records started before he retired from the Army. After that, JR would need to see a doctor in town, and too many questions might be asked.

Trying not to laugh, Josie looked at her husband, whom she loved very much, and said, "Dr. Jones, this is my husband's son who was brought up by his sister in Ohio after his first wife died at child birth. His sister agreed to take him in until he could retire from the Army and settle down as he thought it was best for his son. Now Rod is on terminal leave and will retire in thirty days and now owns a small ranch we have just north of town. We feel he needs a complete checkup."

"Josie, I hope you will be more serious than that. Any doubts and the base might start digging, and we definitely do not want that, do we, my love?" Rod asked with his steely-eye look of a deadly cobra waiting to strike.

"Rod, please don't look at me like that. You know how much I wish I knew the name of the doctor, but I will be fine." She gave Rod a hug, then they heard a truck in the driveway.

"Get inside and make sure his door is closed," he told Josie as he stepped off the porch. This was an unexpected visitor, so he would have to play it real close. He waited until the truck came to a stop and the driver got out.

"Mr. Duval? I am Thomas Osborne, a salesman for Harvester International for all of Laramie County. Mind if I ask you some questions?"

for the support she had given her and Patrick. She looked for Patrick, who was talking with his commander when she noticed both of them come to attention when they were joined by the 63rd Military Airlift Wing Commander, Colonel Wrigley.

She saw Patrick look around the room, see her, and smile. Patrick excused himself and walked over to her and told her that

Colonel Wrigley wanted to talk with her.

Nervously, she walked over to the two commanders. One Lt Col Burns she knew, but not the senior officer on base. With butterflies flying inside her, she hoped she would not pass out.

"Colonel Wrigley, may I present my wife, Sherrie Lee Johnson."

"How do you do, Mrs. Johnson? How are you feeling now that you are out of the hospital? Is everything going okay for you and your husband in your new quarters?"

"Colonel Wrigley, I am doing better now that I am in my new home, thank you. Patrick has done everything he could for me." She paused then continued, "Sir, I have one comment to make about the investigation. The Investigation Unit has done their best. I hope it will reflect in their records for all they have done."

She looked at Patrick and told him that she felt she needed to sit down before she collapsed.

Patrick excused himself from the two commanders and took her over to her front-row seat. Patrick thanked her for her comments to the colonel, then he told her he needed to finish getting ready in the restroom.

He came out at 1350 to find Colonel Wrigley talking to Sherrie. He then mounted the steps alongside Lt Col Burns. Exactly at 1400, First Sgt Penkowsky called the room to attention as the Sixty-Third SPS Color Guard presented the colors. Once they were posted, they were told to sit by the Executive Officer.

Lt Col Burns stepped forward to talk about the squadron and how proud he was of everyone and their accomplishments over the past year. He then spoke of the importance of this ceremony, and even though it is mostly done in the Navy, there have been occasions to do this in the Air Force. It was hard for him not to look at the empty chair next to Sherrie. That was JR's chair. He nodded to the Executive Officer to begin. He stepped back and nodded to the Executive Officer.

"Attention to Orders," he ordered, waiting until everyone rose as if one person. "Effective this day, Master Sergeant Patrick Johnson is temporarily promoted to the rank of Senior Master Sergeant until Monday morning, October 1, 1993. In addition, effective that date, Senior Master Sergeant Johnson will also assume the duties of Senior Enlisted Security Forces Manager."

At the conclusion, Lt Col Burns asked Sherrie to come forward and help pin his new stripes on.

Lt Col Burns and Sherrie pinned on extra-large SMSgt stripes on Patrick's sleeves, covering his current stripes.

"Men and women of the Sixty-Third Security Police Squadron, your new SMSgt Johnson. Congratulations, Patrick."

With that, everyone gave a rousing round of applause until Patrick told them to calm down.

"Members of the finest Security Police Squadron I have served in, as you know, Monday we will no longer be called Security Police. We will be called Security Forces. The mission will remain the same—to serve and protect the mission of the Sixty-Third Military Airlift Wing and the people here at Norton AFB."

He took a deep breath and then moved on. "As you all know, the past three weeks have been hectic, to say the least. Every one of you that was connected with the crime against my family has done the best you could do. Coordination was made with local, State, and Federal authorities in a minimum of time, yet the suspect got away. You could not have done more. Thank you for your professionalism and commitment." With that, he went to sit down with Sherrie as John and Paul got up on the stage.

"Normally," Paul began, "we give out something to the spouse on the retirement of a military member of our squadron. However, if SMSgt Johnson would please escort his wife up here, we have something to present to her, for her devotion to SMSgt Johnson is something else, knowing he will probably be late coming home some nights or will have a call in the middle of the night."

As Patrick escorted Sherrie to the stage and up the steps, Paul paused as John reached behind the curtain. He gave the floral red rose bouquet to Sherrie. "Colonel, with your permission, may we open the bar early this afternoon? The only stipulation is that for those of you going on duty in the next eighteen hours, the bar is closed to you."

"Permission granted" was the response from Colonel Wrigley.

First Sergeant Penkowsky then called the room to attention as the color guard retired the colors. Afterward squadron members congratulated Patrick and Sherrie then headed to the bar.

Sherrie hugged John, Paul, and then her husband to another rousing round of applause. "I am so damn proud of you."

Knowing she could not drink yet, he got her a Coke, and he got a beer from the bar and sat down at a table.

Colonel Wrigley came over to congratulate Patrick on his promotion and his new position. "SMSgt Johnson, I have an offer to discuss with your wife alone, if you do not mind."

Patrick came to attention and told him no problems and left to join the others at the bar.

"Mrs. Johnson, why don't we go sit down in the corner? I have an offer for you that I think you might like."

Once they were seated, Colonel Wrigley first asked her if there was anything that she needed to be done for her recovery.

Sherrie said no, that everything so far had been perfect, and the medical staff was a true group of professionals. However, she did tell him that she still aches for the loss of her son, but she knows that everyone had done their job to the best of their professional abilities.

"Mrs. Johnson, the offer I have for you is to set up a Women's Victims' Rights Office on base. The recent attack and kidnapping only shows that we need to have someone do this. I feel you are the perfect individual for this. I have spoken to the NCO Wives Club president on this, and she mentioned your name right off the bat."

He looked at her and continued, "You do not need to respond now. You need to recover from the surgery. Unfortunately, with the base closing in the near future, it would only be a volunteer job."

"Colonel Wrigley, I accept the offer. I will start in two weeks, but where will the office be located? Will I be able to set my own hours?"

Wrigley smiled and told her that the office would be in the Wing Headquarters building, with a desk and all the accessories, including a computer. He also told her, "Two weeks will be fine. You will also need to get an ID badge to allow you access to the building. The hours are yours to establish." He stood up and helped her up, and they shook hands.

She watched the colonel leave the room, and Patrick went back to her with a questioning look on his face. "What was that about?"

"My super husband, you will not believe it. He offered a position to me that will allow me to be an advocate for women who have been assaulted. I will have my own office in the Wing Headquarters, and it will be furnished to include a computer. I will not be paid but will be a volunteer with my own set of hours."

She also told him that it would help her by keeping active and helping others as well.

Patrick, being the strong inquisitor, asked her how she physically felt and when did she think she would report for duty to her new office. She assured him she was feeling well and she would begin in two weeks.

Around 1700, they joined Paul, John, and their spouses for dinner. When they entered the Enlisted Club Dining Room, there was a round of applause for Patrick, wearing his "frocked" senior master sergeant stripes. Looking sheepish, he tapped a knife against the water glass and stood up. "My wife and I want to thank everyone with the Sixty-Third SPS in addition to all of you noncops."

Many chuckles were heard from the rest of the diners before he went on.

"Many, if not all of you, have heard what happened that day. Well, Colonel Wrigley has asked my wife to set up an advocacy office for women victims of crimes. She accepted and will start in two weeks if she is up to it. If I know her well, she will be there Monday morning by 0800 putting her office together."

As everyone started to clap, he motioned to his wife and kissed her before he sat down beside her.

That day turned out to be longer than he had anticipated for Sherrie's sake, but she was not complaining. They did not leave the club until close to 2100. Sitting outside the door to the club was an SP patrol car and female patrolman who told Patrick that it was her honor to provide escort to his quarters.

"Why, Sgt Jones, is this because I had a beer or two or three or a genuine escort?"

"Sgt Johnson, it is my honor to escort you home. You showed me the ropes when I first got here, and at times, I wanted to give in and just quit. I missed my folks and my hometown. You convinced me this was my new home now, and it truly is my hometown."

She then looked at Sherrie and thanked her for supporting "one of the best supervisors" she has had.

Within ten minutes, they were home for the weekend. It was enough time to finish putting the final touches on their new home before he would start his new job on Monday. It was time to begin to heal.

29

Six months had passed since Rod had arrived home in Cheyenne, Wyoming, with his son and Josie. Even though they had company over, no one had asked any questions about JR that he and Josie had discussed. He explained to them about his sister taking care of JR, but now that he was retired from the Army, he was ready to farm and become part of Cheyenne. In fact, JR was becoming a fast friend with the son of one of their neighbors who was the same age as JR. The neighbor was a volunteer with one of the Cheyenne Frontier Days committees. Rod was seriously thinking of doing the same next year.

Harvest was in full swing now, and they were almost finished with the corn and soybeans. He had told Josie last night that he hoped the corn prices would not go down this year; they needed the money to plant new areas next spring. He told her he would need to go see the Farm Bureau Agent tomorrow.

"I saw on the news earlier tonight that there might be strong storms this weekend. How do you think JR will handle it?" Josie asked Rod.

"I will talk to him about it tomorrow morning before I go out to see the farm agent, Tom Jacobs, and explain to him about going to the basement. He will be okay."

The next morning at breakfast, Rod explained to JR about the possibility of strong storms and to go to the basement if he is told to go there. He told him to mind what *his mom* says and that he would be back later on as he had business to take care of in town.

JR looked at him with a sad pleading look in his eyes that begged to be allowed to go with his dad, but Rod told him no, not this time.

He then gave him a hug, kissed Josie, and put his breakfast dishes in the sink.

He pulled his hat from the hat hook near the back door and walked outside to the yard to get his truck. As he left, he waved at JR, who was peeking out the screen door with his little arm waving goodbye.

During the day, JR stayed in the yard, watching Josie work outside the house. In the distance, he could hear the field hands working on finishing the harvesting; they had heard a storm was coming, and they wanted to get everything put away before it hit. After lunch, Josie put him down for his nap, which allowed her to do some light cleaning and then sit down to take a rest herself. The pressure of what they had been through the past six months was mounting on her, and she hoped that she would not have a breakdown or inadvertently say the wrong thing to a neighbor. She was beginning to fall in love with JR and beginning to have strong maternal instincts to protect him.

Around 3:00 p.m., she heard a car drive up. Not expecting anyone, she went to look out the window and saw it was a newer-model pickup truck.

Thinking Rod had gone out and bought a new truck, she went outside to give him a piece of her mind when she realized the driver was not someone she had met before. Her defenses went up, and she was worried that it might be the FBI. Before he could get out of the truck, Josie was right there.

"Yes, can I help you, sir?" "If this is the Duval place?"

"Yes it is. I am Mrs. Duval. What can I do for you, mister?"

"I am Tom Jacobs of the Farm Bureau. Your husband was out to see me this morning, and I told him I might drop by to see what he has." He started to get out of his truck when Josie pushed against the door, stopping him from exiting his truck.

"Not so fast, sir. I would like to see your ID card please. I do not know many people around here yet, so I am wary of strangers."

At that moment, Rod pulled up behind the agent's truck and got out. He hurried forward and realized that Josie was not being very friendly.

"Honey, this is Tom Jacobs, our farm agent. I agreed to have him come out and look at what we have. I am sorry I did not call and tell you ahead of time. Tom, this is my wife Josie. When I am not around, she kind of runs the place like it is her own little preserve." With that, they all laughed.

Rod took Tom on a tour of the farm, showing him what he had done so far, his equipment, and what his plans were.

Josie went inside the house and made a pot of coffee. Both Rod and Josie had agreed that if possible, they would protect JR from strangers. JR was still sleeping, so she made sure his window curtain and door were closed. She definitely did not need this to come apart now.

Rod and Tom walked through the barn, talking about the age of some of his equipment. As they walked outside, Tom looked at the darkening sky and told Rod he had to get going before the storm hit. "This time of year, it's not uncommon to have a tornado warning or just a hard storm. I suggest you invest in a full home generator and possibly a small one for your barn."

At his truck, he gave Rod a brochure about full home generators and small stand-alone types. "The full home one can be fueled by your propane tank. It's so much easier to maintain, and you do not have to manually start it. It turns on when your power goes off. I strongly suggest you check into it."

After Tom left, Rod went back into the house, looking at the brochures and muttering to himself that he was stupid for not thinking of this. He went to the kitchen, poured himself a cup of coffee, then went to the living room and turned on the TV to the local news channel to see about the weather.

Just then the channel broke in and announced there was a tornado watch for all of Albany, Laramie, and Natrona counties until ten that night. "Strong winds, heavy rain, and hail is possible. If a tornado is spotted, go into your basement or lower floor and away from windows until the threat is over. Stay tuned for further updates."

Rod took a radio, two flashlights, and spare batteries down to the basement then came back and put some water and juice for JR in a cooler with ice and took that down.

Josie put the fresh pot of coffee in a thermos and set that aside as she started to prepare dinner. She also gathered some books and magazines she could read to JR. She found two candles in the kitchen that she put with the stack for Rod to take downstairs when the TV announced a tornado warning.

"A small funnel cloud has been spotted ten miles north of Casper, moving east at five miles an hour. Residents in Casper and surrounding towns are urged to take shelter immediately."

Josie started to run to JR's room when Rod stopped her. "Honey, Casper is one hundred miles north of us. This will not affect us. However, you do need to get JR up so we can eat supper. Try and be as calm as you can. No need to worry him if nothing is going to happen."

He went back to the living room and with one ear on the TV. He started to review the brochures about the generators. He found one he liked; however, the cost for a full home generator was around $5,000.

At the table, Rod told Josie about the idea for a generator. He told her that he would check on it tomorrow and see if they offered a Veterans discount.

"I know the VA will not help, so I will have to do it myself. Hopefully, if they give a discount, it will not hurt so bad when I go to the bank. But if we have one and we lose power because of storms, then it will be worth every penny."

Just then a flash of light lit up the kitchen followed by a loud *crack* of thunder. All three jumped, and JR started to laugh. Rod grabbed his hat to run outside to see if there was any damage from a possible lightning strike. Thankfully, the lighting did not hit the barn or, from what he could see, the property.

Back inside, he heard JR laughing. He asked Josie, "What is so funny?"

Josie told him that "JR thinks the thunder is God's Angels bowling." She went on to tell him that his "Uncle Patrick told him that the first time he heard thunder and was afraid of the noise." She looked at him and said, "So he laughs and hope the angels win their match." They then finished supper.

Just then another lightning bolt flashed, and then the power went out when the thunderclap hit. They then heard the local warning sirens begin their mournful wailing tone.

Rod scooped up JR and said they needed to go to the basement. "Evidently a tornado is nearby. We will be with you."

Once down in the basement, Rod turned on the radio to hear that a tornado had touched down on the east side of Cheyenne, moving east. The radio continued by saying that there were other possible sightings north and west of town. Rod looked at Josie and told her that he definitely was going to look into getting a generator the next day.

As Josie read to JR, they could hear the wind and rain pick up and hammer the house. Within thirty minutes, the radio announced "all clear."

They went back upstairs, Josie carrying JR; and since he was relaxed, she put him to bed while Rod went outside to check on the property again.

Thankfully, all he found were some tree branches that had been torn off some of his trees. He would have to have some of his hands go out and check the land at first light. He went into the barn to check on the animals. The cows and horses had finally settled down. He went back inside to talk to Josie.

The power had come back on, and Josie was watching the special news on the storm. She looked at Rod and told him that there had been one fatality—a truck accident on the interstate that had overturned. Just then, they mentioned the name of the dead motorist. "The name of the dead motorist whose pickup overturned during the storm was Thomas Osborne. He had worked for Harvester International for many years and knew many of the local ranchers and farmers."

They both looked at each other, eyes wide. Josie was the first to speak. "Wasn't he the one that was here that scared the daylights out of us a few months back, Rod?"

"Yeah, he was. I do not know why, but I remember the hair on the back of my neck stood up. That feeling saved my ass a few times in the desert. Wish I knew more about him though."

The weather report showed that the storm had gone east into Nebraska and that no new storms were forecast for that night.

They talked more about the storm and how it affected JR and his remembering his Uncle Patrick. "As long as he remembers him as his uncle, it will be ok. I do not think there will be a problem." He went to the kitchen, drained his cup of cold coffee, and said he was going to bed.

30

As Patrick had promised Father Kelley six months before, he and Sherrie began to attend Mass on a weekly basis. Patrick felt composed and calm in church. Soon Sherrie began to feel the same way.

In fact, she even joined the ladies group that cooked for base dinners sponsored by the base chapel.

Patrick plunged himself into his job, working the base personnel on personnel manning but also with the Air Force Manpower Personnel Center, planning reassignments for when the base closed in eighteen months. Some of the men and women would go to March Air Force Reserve Base in Riverside, California, but most would be sent to other bases.

Sherrie moved into her volunteer job as the Women Victims' Advocate. She would help female family members as well as female Air Force personnel with any assaults or problems they might have. So far she had ten clients, as she called them, and had referred three to the Security Police for sexual assault cases.

She had told Colonel Wrigley that she would submit weekly reports to show him possible problems on base and what she did with each case. So far he had been pleased with what she had accomplished.

So far, all cases had merit, and all ten were resolved peacefully with counseling by supervisors and the Base Chaplain's Office.

Both the spouses clubs had members that volunteered to help Sherrie with the workload. Today she had had a visitor, and she wanted to tell Patrick about it. She called his office, but he was not there. Then her phone rang.

Patrick had gone to the NCO Club to have lunch with his old section friends. He asked Paul how Overton was working out in the

Investigations Unit. He had seen him in the hallway several times since he had moved out of the office, so he was curious how he was working out.

Paul told him that Ronald, "not Ron or Ronnie," was not happy that he had to clean out the files from Patrick's case and check for any abnormalities. "This guy is a stickler for perfection more than you were," Paul said, laughing. "His frames on the wall are exactly one-half inch apart, and none are at an angle." He smiled and said that "He checks them every morning like he does not trust us."

John quickly turned his head away, a smile on his face. Patrick and Paul knew that John was messing with the new guy to see if he could take it or not. So far, he had not lost his temper. He just came in, reset his pictures, got his coffee, then went to work.

Patrick told John, "Better watch out. He is going to get you and get you good, you joker." Laughing, he started to eat his lunch. Then he turned serious. "Has he turned up anything that you guys missed?"

Paul looked at him and just shook his head. "Nothing, de nada, not a thing. He says we covered all angles except for one thing, and you may not like it."

Patrick put his burger down, looked at Paul, and said, "What, Paul? Tell me, dang it."

"Well, Ronald has two questions: One, no pictures of JR and two, who is this guy? That is all he asks—the same questions that all of us have had since day one. And before you ask, he also thinks this perp is special ops trained. He knows some former Force Recon Marines that he is checking with to see if they might know of anyone who might have done this. You never know what he might come up with."

Just then Sherrie came into the club looking for Patrick. She came over to the table and told him that she thought she would find him here since he was not in his office.

"Patrick, could you get me a glass of water please?" She then sat down looking demurely at Paul and John until Patrick came back, which caused John to arch his eyebrow.

After Patrick came back with her water, Sherrie said, "Patrick, you know I have been very crabby and irritable the past month, right?

Well, I had an appointment at the base hospital yesterday afternoon. They called me thirty minutes ago. The rabbit died." With that news, she smiled at all three of them.

Patrick had never told Sherrie that her chances to get pregnant were very slim. Eyes wide opened, he stammered, "When is it due? Are you healthy enough to have a baby?"

"First part of June. I do not know the sex yet nor do I want to know, and yes, the doctor believes I am healthy enough to carry it full term."

Sherrie told him she needed to go to the hospital to pick up some vitamins and that she would see him after work. After kissing his forehead, she left.

Still in shock, Patrick could not get much work done that afternoon. He went through the motion of moving papers around and making official phone calls, but his mind was in three areas: where was JR, his job, and Sherrie.

That night, Patrick and Sherrie ate a simple dinner at home and talked of the new baby. Since they had donated JR's bedroom set to the Airman's Attic, they would get a new bed, dresser, the works.

"Patrick, I miss JR. Every day I wake up expecting to see him with us. I pray for his safety every night and morning."

"Sherrie, I miss him also. I know deep down that he is okay and is safe. I know that if he were here now, he would be thrilled to be a big brother to the baby. Let's clean up and then watch some TV."

"Oh, Patrick, in the excitement about the baby, I forgot to tell you the other good news. The Public Affairs Office wants me to do an interview on the local TV news about my office and how it is helping on base. It will be on tomorrow night's news."

The TV interview lasted only about fifteen minutes, but Sherrie was able to tell her story of the attack and kidnapping. She went on to tell about her volunteer job as women victims' advocate on base and how it was helping people.

The day following the interview, Paul told Patrick, "Maybe it can go national and someone in another state will see it and it will create a new awareness. You never know who might see it."

31

As they had decided shortly after arriving home in Cheyenne six months ago, JR would not watch any national news. This would preclude him seeing Patrick or Sherrie on TV. That night, hours after JR was put in bed, Rod and Josie watched the late-night news. All of a sudden, there on their TV screen was "Sherrie Johnson, Women Victims' Advocate for Norton AFB, California."

Josie went completely white in shock as Rod turned the volume down as the interview unfolded, with Sherrie telling everything about the assault and kidnapping except for her knowledge of who did it.

"Uh, Rod, what if local people put two and two together?" Josie started to ask.

"Quiet, hon, and let me think." Rod then continued, "All pictures I took from there have been burned. The DNA test results we have show JR is my son, and we have a birth certificate that shows I am his father. There is no way anyone can connect us with the assault and kidnapping."

Before they shut off the TV, Josie asked Rod, "Did you hear her say that she is now pregnant? That makes me feel better. Let's go to bed."

Josie checked on JR and saw that he was sleeping peacefully and they went to bed, each with their own different thoughts—Josie wishing she could have her own child, Rod wondering just how long they could get away with what happened. He knew if the truth came out, and since he had still been on active duty, he would be courtmartialed for assault and kidnapping. *Probably get twenty-five to life just for kidnapping alone*, he mused.

They both got up when the alarm went off in the morning, and they both acted as normal as possible around JR. Rod had work to do outside, doing some last-minute work with his hands getting everything ready for the upcoming winter for which forecasters predicted heavy snowfall.

Josie let JR watch cartoons while she cleaned house and did the laundry. When she took the wash outside to dry in the sunshine, JR would try to help her by handing her clothes from the basket. Afterward, she would toss him a soccer ball and watch him try and run after it, smiling at the way he was full of energy.

After lunch, she put JR down for his nap, and she took the monitor with her to the front porch, where she sat breaking down snap peas for dinner. As she worked, she remembered that morning how JR helped her and how she wished she could have a child of her own, preferably a girl. Yet she knew she could not have a child due to a problem she had as a teenager.

Rod came through the house to the front porch to join Josie. "Hi, honey," he said as he bent down to kiss her. He loved Josie very much and wished he had known her much earlier. She would have made a good Army wife, never complaining about anything. "All the snow fences are up alongside the road and driveway. I need to get the plow mounted on the work truck tomorrow so that I can do the driveway when the snow falls." He drank some of his coffee.

"They say it might be a long, hard winter this year, and I am glad we now have a generator to help us if we lose power again."

"Come to think of it, Rod, this will be JR's first snow winter. You do know that you will have to help him make a snowman and show him how to throw snowballs at me," she said with a smile.

"What is wrong with both of us helping him make a snowman, and you will probably throw a snowball or two at me with my back turned," he replied laughing.

He helped pick up the bucket with the snap peas and carried them in for her while she went to wake up JR, who was already up sitting on the side of his bed, waiting for her.

"I heard you and Daddy talking, so I got up on my own this time. He ran out of his room and into Rod's arms. He picked him up and swung him around, both laughing while Josie smiled at them.

While waiting for supper, Rod let JR pick out his favorite cartoon while he told him what the cartoon was about. "It is about a rabbit that lives in a hole and tries to stay away from a funny man with a gun. He always says, 'What's up, doc?' It's funny, Dad."

Rod told him that Bugs Bunny was his favorite when he was JR's age too. He told him that he liked to eat carrots because that is what Bugs ate all the time. He would not admit it, but he still liked Bugs Bunny.

At the dinner table, Rod told them about the coming winter season and the heavy snowfall that was expected. "Have you ever seen snowfall?" he asked JR.

"No."

"Tell you what, both of us will help you build your first snowman when we get enough snow, okay? I promise you it will be lots of fun—the three of us doing it together."

Josie got into the act by offering to make hot cocoa after they build the snowman. "But we have to wait for the snow first."

JR seemed to be excited about the chance for the first snowstorm. "When will that be?"

"They don't know yet. We will just have to wait and see."

After supper, they watched the local news then put on a comedy show to fill in the half hour block that was normally national news. Then they put on *Wheel of Fortune* because JR liked to watch "that pretty girl" walk along the board. Rod figured that it might help JR learn the alphabet and hopefully learn how to spell before he started school in a couple of years.

At bedtime, JR said his prayers and then slid under the covers. Rod started to read him a book on old-time Cheyenne cowboys. However, JR slowly drifted off to sleep.

Rod went out to Josie and told her that JR is probably dreaming about snowmen and snowballs. They watched a movie and then national news to see if Sherrie's story would be on again. It was not. They watched the first part of a late-night show and then went to bed.

The next morning after breakfast, Rod went out to the shed to put the plow on the front of the farm truck with the help of two of his farm hands. The truck was an old one that would not be allowed to be on the street, so he used it to keep his driveway clear along with the pathway to the barn and different sheds.

Josie tried to keep JR calmed down by having him work on his coloring books while she did house work, but he kept running to the window to look outside. She asked him what was wrong.

"I keep looking for snow. My coloring book shows a snowman. I want to make one just like it."

Josie laughed and told him that snow will come soon enough and there may be times when he cannot go outside because of too much snow. "Daddy will explain it better to you."

When Rod came in, JR ran up to him and asked him to tell him why he cannot go out sometimes in the snow.

Rod thought about it and then explained to him that "sometimes snow and wind is so strong that you can get lost in it, or if there is too much snow, you can fall into a big pile and get frozen. You have to do two things: one, pay attention to what we tell you and two, pay attention to the weather. I will explain more as you get older."

"Okay." JR went back to his coloring book until lunchtime.

32

September, October, and early November had come and gone with no snow. JR was beginning to feel as if his dad had not told the truth. His dad had told him to always tell the truth, no matter what. He had been punished one time for not telling the truth. Would his dad be punished? He had gotten everything ready for snow, but none came. He was beginning to feel as if he would never be able to make a snowman as a young boy.

On Halloween, JR's first trick or treat in Cheyenne, Josie made him his favorite cartoon costume, Bugs Bunny, complete with the two big front teeth and a large carrot.

Rod took him out and drove him to all the different ranches and farms for treats. Then he took him to nearby parts of Cheyenne so that JR could see other costumes and get more treats.

When they returned home, they found Josie in a witch's costume including a fake large, crooked nose and pointed black hat. JR told her about all the different costumes that he saw as he dumped his goodies on the table.

They told JR that due to the late hour, he could not eat any candy and had to wait until tomorrow to have some. He was not happy, but he had learned in the short time he was with them that he could not win an argument.

After he went to bed, Rod and Josie went through all of JR's candy. If anything looked like it had a small pinhole in it, it went into the trash. They were not going to take any chances. They ended up throwing out a few candy bars and an apple that he had gotten from a home in town. The rest went into a large bowl.

They also counted fifty cents in assorted change that they would put in his piggy bank in the morning.

Rod told Josie that JR asked if it was cold enough to snow yet. "I told him not yet, but it is getting there. He thinks he will not see snow until he is older. If he only knew what will happen when he gets old enough to handle a shovel."

On Wednesday, November 25th, the early evening news weather report called for a winter storm watch for South Eastern Wyoming for Thursday and Friday.

JR knew that the next day was Thanksgiving, for he had seen the turkey in the refrigerator and had heard Rod and Josie talking about Thanksgiving especially the big parade and football games. "Does that mean snow?"

Rod answered by telling him, "Yes, it means snow, and we will make a snowman—if not tomorrow, then on Friday. It all depends on how heavy it snows."

With a smile, JR went and gave a hug to Rod and to Josie. "I promise to be good tomorrow."

"On Saturday, after I finish my chores, we will go cut our own Christmas tree and set it up. But you have to be good tonight and tomorrow, okay, pal?"

JR smiled and nodded. It all began at the dinner table. JR ate everything on his plate including his vegetables that he normally did not like to eat.

The next morning, he got up and ran to the kitchen door. He stood up on a stool and asked Josie, "What's that?"

Josie came to the door and told him that the white stuff falling was snow. It was coming down so hard it looked like a white curtain had dropped down from the heavens to the landscape. All one could see was snow falling.

JR could hear the truck outside moving the snow and wanted to go outside and be with his dad. Josie told him no and to go watch cartoons while they waited for Rod to come back in. She then returned to the kitchen to work on the homemade dressing that she would stuff the turkey with. It was going to be a traditional Thanksgiving dinner with pumpkin pie, which was one of JR's favorite desserts. Rod and Josie would have mincemeat pie.

Rod came in, stomping his boots on the outdoor stoop to knock off the snow, then removed his boots and jacket. He walked into the kitchen to get a cup of coffee and told Josie, "I'm glad I got a plow and don't have to worry about using a snowblower or paying someone to clear the driveway. I will have to use it for the walkways though. It's still coming down hard."

Thanksgiving went well. JR enjoyed watching the parade on TV, laughing at the balloons, and when Santa Claus came at the end of the parade, JR jumped up from his chair and pointed to the TV and said, "Santy. It's Santy."

Josie and Rod laughed at his enthusiasm seeing Santa Claus in the parade. "Now you have to be real good, or he will not come visit you," Rod told him, which drew a mean look from Josie.

That afternoon, during the first football game at halftime, Rod went out to clear the driveway again. According to the ruler he put in the front yard, they already had ten inches of snow, and it was still coming down. Tomorrow they would build a snowman.

The next morning, after breakfast, the three of them bundled up and went out to the front yard, where Rod showed JR how to make the perfect base of the snowman. JR helped Josie make the middle portion, and Rod made the head. Josie went inside to get an old hat and a carrot for the nose while Rod and JR put small branches for arms and rocks for the face. JR was proud of his first snowman and asked Josie to take a picture of him and Rod standing on each side of the snowman.

That night, they pulled out boxes from the attic of Christmas decorations. Rod checked the lights to make sure he would not have to replace them. Unless one of them asked JR something, he stayed quiet in his chair, watching cartoons. It was hard being good at the age of two, but he was trying.

The next morning, after breakfast and Rod had done his chores, they got in the Jeep and went tree hunting. They found a tree farm where they could cut their own tree. JR pointed to every tree he saw and remarked how pretty they were. Finally, Rod and Josie found a tree they liked, which was an eight-foot fir tree and would fit in the living room away from the fireplace.

They got it home and started to decorate it. Josie popped some popcorn so they could string it and put it on the tree and eat the rest afterward, drinking hot cocoa and singing Christmas songs for JR.

JR was starting to fall asleep, so Rod told him that since he had had a long day, he had to go to bed early. He said his prayers, climbed into bed, and he fell asleep right away.

They watched a couple of Christmas movies then the late news, not really expecting anything new but just to catch up on what was going on and for the latest weather update. The local weatherman stated that Cheyenne had received over a foot of fresh snow since the storm began. No new snow was in the forecast for the next five days.

As far as they were concerned, Thanksgiving weekend had been a success with JR. Hopefully, Christmas would be as well.

33

Since the local TV interview with Sherrie and subsequent national airing, tips had come in for not only the kidnapping but also assaults on women on and off base throughout the local area. Those off base she referred to the local law enforcement agencies. Unfortunately, none of the tips for the kidnapping worked out.

Patrick was busy as well. He was trying to forecast and coordinate with the Wing Security as to what he would need to do when all the aircraft would be gone and the base actually closed. Things were going to get busier for Patrick more than he ever realized he would be.

On October first, First Sergeant Penkowsky had to go home on emergency leave for at least thirty days. Lt Col Burns and MSgt Penkowsky called Patrick in and advised him that he had been chosen to be the interim First Sergeant until either Penkowsky returned or a full-fledged First Sergeant would be assigned.

Patrick, one to never really question an order, asked why he had been chosen to become acting First Sergeant. Burns told him he was selected because he was widely respected not only in the squadron but on base as well by other First Sergeants and those in positions of authority.

He would take over the next day, allowing Penkowsky two days to brief him on his duties and any appointments that he had.

"Patrick, as you know, I have always had an open-door policy. I hope you will maintain that same policy while I am gone. Also, you will have to do both your normal job and First Sergeant duties. So in essence, you will be very busy."

Penkowsky took him to his office and showed him the files and told him that while he would not be wearing the coveted diamond, the emblem of a First Sergeant, he had all the responsibilities.

"One more thing, Patrick, I always attended Guard Mount. In case you forgot when it is, Guard Mount is every day at 0630." He then told him that there was a First Sergeant's meeting that morning at the NCO Club and he would take him. "Then we stay for our monthly 'lunch.'"

Patrick looked at him and said that he would be ready. He just needed to go to his other office and square away a few things including calling Sherrie.

He knew she had a doctor's appointment to see how she was dealing with her pregnancy. They normally had lunch afterward to discuss what the doctor said. So far, the pregnancy was going normally, and the baby would be due in June. The doctor was unable to define a date range yet, but hopefully that would be discussed today. Patrick called her at her office to tell her the good/bad news.

She was thrilled about him becoming a First Sergeant even though it was not an official position nor permanent, but thrilled nonetheless. As for the broken lunch date, it was not the first time, and she took it in stride. She would talk to him that evening.

Patrick then went down to the Investigations Unit to let Paul know what was going on. Paul and Ronald were out on a case, and John had just sat down at his desk. Patrick looked around the room, spotted Ronald's desk, and could see some frames at a slight angle.

"John, you still playing jokes on the new guy?"

John looked at him and with a crooked smile said, "All I did was get a cup of coffee, and I felt a slight wobble. Must have been a small earthquake."

Patrick told him about his new temporary position and to let Paul know if he needed to reach him. He then asked if there were any new leads.

"Yeah, Paul is wanting to talk to you about something. You know how tight Spec Ops are, right? Ronald knows a couple of former Force Recon Marines that live in Utah that know of a suspicious character, one that all of a sudden showed up at home with a two-year-old boy. We already contacted Don, who is working the tip. Don't tell Sherrie yet. It might or might not be your JR."

"Have Paul contact me in either office this afternoon. I have a meeting and then lunch in an hour." He left John and went to the LE Desk to let them know he would be the First Sergeant until further notice. He made sure they had his home phone number as the pager number would be the same as what Penkowsky had.

After the meeting and the lunch, Patrick returned to his office and called Paul. Paul came down with his notebook.

"Now you are a First Sergeant, huh? I never wanted the job. I do not think I could handle the pressure of problems at 0200 on weekends." Paul then put a serious look on his face and told Patrick that it seems that Ronald may have stumbled onto something.

"You do remember that we told you that Ronald knew some retired Force Recon Marines, right? Seems one of his friends from Utah knows this neighbor that showed up about three months ago with a two-year-old boy that might be JR. We contacted Don to let the FBI run with it. Turns out that this neighbor is also an Army Special Forces veteran."

"Yeah, the timing is just about right. The age and sex is right. Hopefully, it is JR, and we can have him home for Christmas." Patrick then added, I am not going to say anything to Sherrie until we know if it is JR. No sense in upsetting her if it is not especially with her being pregnant—a pregnancy that was not supposed to happen."

"Do you know if it is going to be a boy or a girl?"

Patrick looked at his long-time friend and told him that Sherrie had an appointment with the doctor this morning. "She was going to tell me about her visit at lunch today, but I had to go to the monthly shirt lunch instead. I will have to wait until tonight."

That night, Sherrie fixed him one of his favorite meals, meat lasagna, garlic toasted French bread, and a salad for two reasons.

"Honey, I am so proud of you and your new job. I know you will do well, and I know about possible late-night phone calls. The other reason is this: it is going to be a girl, and the anticipated date of delivery is the fifteenth of June."

Patrick was still stunned by the news of Sherrie being pregnant. Sure, they had made love several times. All he could think of was that this was God's will, and he was happy about it. "A girl, huh? I never had any sisters. How am I supposed to raise a baby girl?"

"I stopped off at the base library and picked up a few books on how to raise a baby girl just like I did before with…" She paused as she thought of JR when he was a little baby and the first time she held him in her arms in the hospital. "I miss him, Patrick. I miss little JR. I hope he is okay."

Patrick got up and went to Sherrie, pulled her into his open arms, and gave her a hug. Not wanting to say what Paul had told him, he told her, "Honey, no matter where he is or who has him, Jesus is watching over him, and he is okay. I also know that sometime in the future we will see him again."

After dinner, he cleaned up the kitchen, letting Sherrie rest, and then sat down in his chair in the den to go over some of the papers he had brought home dealing with some administrative actions coming up for two troops that had committed minor mistakes.

The following morning, he went to Guard Mount to brief all the troops on his new status as First Sergeant. He told them that his two main items were that one, he maintains an open-door policy and two, if they went out drinking and felt they had too much to drink, they were to call him, with no problems, regardless of time of night. If they did not call him, his hammer would come down and come down hard. He then asked them if they had any questions.

There were no questions, so he told them to be smart and to be safe. Everyone on base depended on them to do their jobs professionally.

The middle of the month proved to be a downside for Patrick. On the fifteenth, Paul told Patrick that the FBI had concluded their investigation into the possible location of a suspicious child in Utah provided by a friend of Ronald's. "Turns out the child was raised by his grandparents while his dad finished his time in the Army. He got custody through a divorce after his wife left him while he was stationed in Colorado with the Tenth Special Forces group. Seems she could not handle the stress of being married to him."

"It was a long shot, Paul, but it had to be checked out."

"How is Sherrie holding up with the upcoming holidays, Patrick? And most importantly, how are you holding up? I know that you enjoyed taking JR around the neighborhood on Halloween."

"She is doing fine. She is already planning on making outfits for our new baby girl that will be born next June. She misses JR. Hell, I do too. I told her that someday in the future we will see him again and that he is okay and Jesus is watching over him."

On Halloween, with Sherrie dressed as a princess, Patrick was dressed as a hobo, along with other off-duty personnel that were not escorting their kids to on-base housing. Yes, he thought about JR, but he also thought about his new daughter that would be born next year.

On the first of December, Penkowsky notified the commander he needed to extend his emergency leave for another thirty days. If the problem did not resolve by then, he would have to retire early. Patrick would now be the First Sergeant until the first of the year.

On Christmas Eve, Patrick and Sherrie dressed as Santa and Mrs. Claus, visited the Law Enforcement Desk and the main gate to give those on duty some homemade fudge and to wish them a Merry Christmas. The troop's respect for Patrick rose another notch.

34

The new year proved to be busy for Patrick and Sherrie. Patrick stayed on as First Sergeant until January when Penkowsky finally came back. However, the bad news was he was going to have to retire early. He told the commander and Patrick that he was going to retire on April 1, 1994, with thirty days terminal leave.

Lt Col Burns asked Patrick if he would be willing to take over as First Sergeant from that point until the base closed in April 1994. "It will not go on paper until October 1st to work around the working outside your Air Force Specialty Code for six-month rule."

With a deadpan look on his face, Patrick looked at Burns and told him that would not be a problem. Besides, "That is a dumbass rule and does not really apply to cops."

Laughing, both Patrick and Penkowsky went back to the shirt's office so Patrick could get the rest of his stuff and he could take it back to his office. "You know, Shirt, this is one of the best jobs in the Air Force. I enjoyed it. I wish I had taken time to go to the First Sergeant Academy and earn that diamond. Thank you for the opportunity."

On June 15th, Sherrie Leigh Johnson was born. She was a healthy little girl, blond haired and blue eyed. No doubt about it, she was Patrick's little girl. He took the photo of JR from his wallet and put it next to his wife and daughter.

Patrick set up the retirement ceremony for Penkowsky, where he would receive the Meritorious Service Medal. Patrick made sure that all the First Sergeants were invited. They would make a special presentation to Penkowsky of a plaque in the shape of a "1" with a diamond centered over it as a symbol of his time as a First Sergeant.

At the ceremony, when asked to say a few words, Penkowsky looked directly at Patrick and said, "Never give up on your dreams.

Never let someone say it can't be done just because it was never tried." He paused then continued about how great the squadron was and how they all came together as a family when things got worse for a squadron member. He concluded by saying, "Thank God for the United States Air Force."

That Halloween, Patrick and Sherrie took their new daughter out trick or treating in their immediate neighborhood. Everyone thought she was so adorable. In the old neighborhood, those that remembered a year ago did not ask about JR, but you could see it in their faces when they looked out past Patrick and Sherrie.

By Christmas, there were less personnel assigned to Norton due to the base closing the following April. However, the Sixty-Third Security Forces Squadron Law Enforcement was still strong as they patrolled the streets of the base. They still manned the gates and checked the empty houses.

Patrick was everything but an actual full-time First Sergeant. He did all the normal Shirt duties; however, he did not have the coveted diamond. There was nothing that the commander could do to get him the diamond as he had submitted his retirement papers to be effective April 1, 1994.

He would retire the same day as Paul and John would retire. Until then, though, he was the First Sergeant, and everyone in the squadron knew it and respected him. He had very few problems, which made the commander happy.

Sherrie still had her office opened five days a week. However, with less personnel on base, there were less cases to process, and soon she changed her hours to just three days a week. Her weekly reports were submitted to Colonel Wrigley, the wing commander, who had recently been informed that he had been nominated to be promoted to Brigadier General and would move up to 22nd Air Force at Travis AFB upon closure of Norton.

Sherrie turned down a civilian position at 22nd AF doing the same work as she decided to stay home and take care of her new child. She and Patrick had decided to stay in the local area after his retirement.

While Paul and John were making plans to open their Cold Case Investigations business, Patrick did not know what he was going to do except to relax for a few weeks and figure out what he wanted. Until then, Paul and John still had work to do with open cases, most of which were minor. The only major case still open was the kidnapping of little JR, who was now three years old. It was frustrating not being able to close it out. However, they had made copies of everything so that they could have files for when they opened their business after retirement. This was definitely a cold case.

Patrick, still the First Sergeant, still had his late-night phone calls on what he called errant children—the young troops that got into trouble, sometimes without meaning to do so, other times knowingly so. Some involved underage drinking while others were getting lazy in their work habits. He also worked the transfers to other Air Force units based on the needs of the service. Some that wanted to remain in the area were lucky enough to be assigned to March Air Reserve Base in Riverside.

In February, Lt Col Burns asked Patrick, Paul, and John their preferences for their retirement ceremony. All three asked for their ceremony to be held jointly on March 30, 1994, during Retreat at the base flag pole. The commander authorized it and worked out the details with the Wing Commander, who would also attend.

On that day, at 0730, two flags were hoisted to the top of the base flag pole then lowered and immediately folded into the proper triangle. A third flag was hoisted to the top to the tune of "To the Colors".

At 1630, Retreat was sounded throughout the base. The Sixty-Third SFS Color Guard slowly lowered the flag and folded it into the triangle shape and presented it to the Squadron Commander Lieutenant Colonel Burns.

The Executive Officer called out the command, "Attention to Orders," and read off the retirement orders for Senior Master Sergeant Paul Gibbons, twenty-six years active duty; Senior Master Sergeant Patrick Johnson, twenty-two years active duty; and Technical Sergeant John Sommers, twenty years active duty. Each one received a Meritorious Service Medal for their time of service.

Paul and John had agreed that Patrick should receive the last flag flown that day. Then Lieutenant Colonel Burns called the wives up along with Colonel Wrigley.

Anne Gibbons and MJ Sommers walked up to the stage with Sherrie Johnson. Lieutenant Colonel Burns presented each wife a bouquet of yellow roses. Colonel Wrigley made a few comments then asked Sherrie to join him at the podium. He addressed the attendees. "Most of you know what happened here two years ago last month. Since then, Sherrie Johnson has opened an office, at my request, to act as a Victims' Advocate to handle violence in family housing. However, she took it a step further and included all violence against Air Force female personnel. It now appears that this program will move forward to become Air Force wide."

A round of applause was given to Sherrie, who was blushing at all the extra attention she did not anticipate.

He continued, "It is with great honor I give this special wooden plaque, in the shape of our beloved C-141 Starlifter, to Mrs. Sherrie Johnson for her dedication to not only supporting her husband but her support toward the Norton AFB Community as well." He gave the plaque to Sherrie, and then she joined her husband and the other two couples for the playing of the Air Force Song followed by the National Anthem.

Afterward all three couples went to the NCO Club for one last dinner. The club, which would be closed the next day, was packed with diners and those at the bar. Sherrie went out to call their old neighbor, Mrs. Smyth, to check on Sherrie Leigh.

Sherrie came to the table and told everyone that Sherrie Leigh was doing okay with Mrs. Smyth. "I know that her husband is being reassigned too, so maybe we can still use her as a babysitter if we need one." She sighed and asked Anne and MJ if they were all packed up and ready to move out in the next couple of days.

Anne replied first, "Yes, we are ready. We found a nice place just outside of town with a pool."

MJ said that they had found a place not too far from Paul and Anne that had an extra room for John to tinker around in if he wants. "What about you guys, Sherrie?"

"It's a little bit complicated, but Patrick wanted some land so he could raise and board horses. We found a place that used to be a ranch just outside of Bakersfield. He is also thinking of becoming a reserve mounted deputy sheriff for Kern County. When will your business start, Paul?"

"After moving and a couple of weeks of rest, John and I will open for business. We already found a place, not much, but we have to start someplace." Paul did not tell her that their number one priority would be to try and locate JR.

The dinner special that night was steak and lobster since it was the final dinner at the club. Patrick, not a lobster fan, tried to trade his lobster for another steak.

Everyone began eating, each to their thoughts, when an individual stopped at their table.

Paul looked up and almost choked on his piece of steak. It was FBI Special Agent Abernathy and Lydia.

Sherrie clutched Patrick's arm as the agent began to speak before anyone could say anything. "First of all, I have nothing new to report on the case. I know the base is closing, and I wanted to bring Lydia here to say goodbye to those she worked with."

He then continued, "Since you are all here, I might as well tell you I am happy to say that we are engaged and going to get married December 1st."

They all looked at each other in awe—tiny Lydia marrying Don. Sherrie, surprising everyone, hugged Donald then Lydia, looking at her ring. She invited both of them to join them at the table. Everyone started talking as once until Patrick stood up.

He looked at Don, walked around the table, shook his hand, and congratulated him on his engagement. He whispered in his ear, "I hope you do a better job of being married than you did not finding my son." He then smiled at him and sat back down.

Paul and John shook Don's hand, and while the girls all talked, the guys did as well, mostly about the base closing and sports. Don knew about Paul and John's business opportunity but did not know about Patrick's. "What about you, Patrick, are you going to work with Paul and John?"

"No, I am going to raise and board horses and be a reserve deputy sheriff for Kern County. It is in my blood—what can I say? I'm too old for full time."

By 10:00 p.m., the club was empty. They walked to their cars, the women hugging each other and the guys shaking hands and promising to keep in touch. Anne said that the first weekend in June would be a party at their place with swimming and a barbeque. Future addresses were exchanged, and see-you-laters were said.

Patrick and Sherrie got into their car and did not say anything on the ride to Mrs. Smyth's house to pick up Leigh. Each was lost in their thoughts. Patrick thought about not having to get up and put on his blues or BDUs. They were now packed away. His dress blues would be put in a garment bag with mothballs as that was what he would wear when he would be laid to rest.

The next day, the movers came and moved Patrick, Sherrie, and Sherrie Leigh to their new horse ranch in Bakersfield for a new beginning, a new life.

35

JR turned six in 1996, which in Cheyenne was an important year. Cheyenne Frontier Days was one hundred years, and it was a yearlong celebration. For his birthday, Rod got him a pony, and he learned to ride quick. Rod had become involved with the Frontier Days Parade committee and was able to participate that year.

The week before Frontier Days, Rod took JR to see the cattle drive come down the highway into town to Frontier Park. The cattle would be used in all of the rodeo events of the upcoming week.

The first Saturday of the last week of July was the first parade. Josie and JR watched the parade go down the street and saw Rod riding his beautiful white stallion. JR looked at Josie with pride and told her that he wanted to ride in a parade this year. JR mentioned it was just like watching a Western on TV.

After the parade, Rod put his horse in the trailer and took it home to be brushed down and fed. Then they went to Frontier Park, where JR wanted to watch the rodeo first then see the carnival rides.

While watching the bull-riding competition, JR told Rod that he was surprised that they could stay on the bull as it leaped into the air and twisted, trying to dislodge the rider. He also told him that he did not want to do that as he might get hurt.

Rod laughed and told him that it took years of practice to not fall off the bull, and yes, it was a dangerous rodeo sport, but those that make it to the championship round made lots of money.

JR thought it was neat watching the cowboys but also asked if it hurt the animals when they were thrown to the ground as he did not like to see any animal hurt especially for fun. Rod explained that the cowboys do not intentionally hurt the animals, but sometimes they do get hurt but not on purpose.

After the rodeo, JR told Rod he was tired and wanted to go home to eat dinner. Since Josie was not with them, Rod agreed. When they got home, Josie had hamburgers, beans, and chips ready. JR watched some TV and went to bed without being told.

Josie looked questioningly at Rod, and he told her that he had promised to take him to slack time at the rodeo arena right after breakfast. "He is really excited about this week. I know he wants to be in one of the parades. I will have to check it out with the committee chairman."

The following morning, after breakfast, Rod and JR, both dressed in jeans, long-sleeve Western shirts, boots, and cowboy hats, headed out to the park. They watched the cowboys in calf roping and steer wrestling for a couple of hours, and then Rod took JR out to the cattle pens, where the bulls were. Looking at the bulls up close and seeing how big they were, JR stayed close to Rod. "They are real big, Dad. They scare me."

Rod took him around the park, looking at all the merchandise for sale and all the carnival rides. Before he could ask, Rod told him that they did not start the rides and games until noon. There would be plenty of time for him to enjoy the carnival midway in the upcoming week.

That night, both Rod and Josie were dressed up in fancy Western wear to attend the night show with a famous country Western star. JR would have a neighbor's daughter babysit him that night.

Rod told him, "If there are any problems, you will be grounded for the week, which means no parades and no rodeo or carnival." Not that he expected any problems though.

After the show, they went to a local bar to go dancing with some friends. They arrived home around midnight to find JR in bed and his babysitter watching TV. She told them how amazed she was at how quickly JR went to bed when she told him it was time. His only demand was for her to read to him.

Rod laughed, and since she had driven herself over, she left right away and told them she would be glad to babysit for them again if the chance came up.

Josie checked the refrigerator and was surprised to see that only one Coke was missing from the shelf. "I thought we told her to use the fridge if she wanted. The only thing missing is a Coke. When I babysat, I raided the fridge. It's expected," she said.

The following morning was Monday, and the first free pancake breakfast of the Frontier Days week. They got up early so they could be in line early. This was JR's first pancake breakfast, and he was excited. At six thirty, the line started moving.

Walking along the sidewalk outside of the parking lot turned eating area, JR laughed as he saw the cooks flipping the pancakes to Boy Scouts that were catching them. Rod explained to JR that they practice this all the time and they do this breakfast as training in case of an emergency. Once they got inside the lot, they were given sliced ham, pancakes, butter, syrup, and coffee or milk. They then went to sit on bales of hay, and that morning they were lucky to have a local band. "They have this Monday, Wednesday, and Friday of this week, and yes, we will come again." Rod told them before the question was asked.

JR asked when the parade was going to start and if he was going to ride his new pony in the parade.

Rod explained to him that the next parades were on Tuesday, Thursday, and Saturday and that he was going to ride in the parade on Thursday with other children whose parents were on the Parade Committee. Rod knew that the Saturday parade was going to be covered by network TV since it was finals weekend, and he did not want to take a chance on JR being caught on a national network news show.

Tuesday JR rode his pony around the ranch, always with someone watching him, so he could be ready for Thursday. That was all he talked about and dreamed of for the next two days and nights—riding his pony in the parade with his dad.

Early Wednesday morning, after going to the breakfast, Rod told him that there was going to be an air show with the Air Force Thunderbirds doing their stunts. They went to watch the air show, then they went to F. E. Warren AFB to see the different exhibits on base. Rod showed JR how to throw a "buffalo chip" to see if he could land on the number he picked; he did not. They also watched a reenactment of the buffalo soldiers drilling on the field.

The next morning, JR got up early with Rod, got dressed in his best cowboy outfit, and ate breakfast. They went out and put their horses in the trailer, and all three left for the parade assembly area.

Once there, Josie left to get a seat near the end of the parade, and JR looked around at all the other kids riding that day.

Some rode up and talked to him, comparing their horses and names. When asked his pony's name, he simply replied, "Pony."

When the cannon fired at nine, the parade moved swiftly, and JR followed his dad's response to the crowd by waving at everyone. He commented to his dad that there were a lot of people there watching, and he acted as if he was the only one on a horse that day.

As they started up the final street, JR was looking for Josie; but with everyone wearing jeans, Western shirts, and hats, it was hard to find her. Finally, he saw her and yelled out, "Hi, Mom," which drew a chuckle from the others in the group. He kept riding beside his dad until they reached the end of the parade route.

As they dismounted, JR asked his dad if he could go to the carnival that afternoon with Mom, since he knew his dad wanted to go watch the rodeo with some of his friends.

"If she wants to go, it is okay with me," Rod told him and then looked at Josie.

"I'd love to go today. It will give me a chance to look at the different displays they have in the exhibition hall and under the grandstand this year." She then looked at JR. "You will have to go where I go though. We are not going to let you go there alone this year. You are still not old enough."

"Will you go on rides with me?"

"Of course. Now let's get these horses back home so we can go to the park and have lunch before your dad goes to watch the rodeo with his friends."

They got to the park in time for lunch, and Rod made it to the stands in time for the Grand Entry when the national anthem was played. Rod stood along with all the others and put his hat over his heart as the American flag went past the stands.

Josie and JR were in the exhibit hall where she looked at all the different crafts and household items that were on display. She was planning on doing a quilt for next year and wanted some ideas. She had a photo of the two of them taken and even entered some draw- ings for prizes.

Once outside, JR took her to the Ferris wheel and tugged her hand to buy tickets. He had never been on one before. At first, he closed his eyes when they were near the top. Josie told him to open his eyes so he could see everything including the rodeo.

After he got off, he told her that at first he was scared, but when he opened his eyes, he was not afraid, and he could see the rodeo and what seemed to be all of Cheyenne. "This was cool, Mom!"

They walked around the midway until Rod came out of the rodeo. JR took his hand and took him to one of the game booths and asked him to shoot the balloons so he could get a prize. "You told me I am not old enough to shoot yet, Dad, remember?"

Rod watched some of the other dads shooting, picked out the BB rifle he thought was best, and burst five out of five balloons. Rod picked out a stuffed horse and told him, "Next year, you can shoot for your own prize."

By the time they got home, JR was fast asleep in the back seat. "Guess this first CFD is too much for him. Next year he will be ready for more of it," Rod told Josie as he carried him inside and put him to bed and put his horse, which looked like JR's pony, on top of the dresser.

Josie sat in her chair and turned on the TV and told Rod, "I am about worn out the way he took me all over the midway today while you watched the rodeo. Next time, *you* take him to the midway."

Friday was the last breakfast. Walking down the sidewalk near the chuck wagon, JR waved to one of the cooks who was a neighbor. He flipped a pancake toward JR, and Rod caught it and gave it to him. JR told him that he wanted to become a Boy Scout so he could eat all the pancakes he wanted at the breakfasts. Rod laughed and told him he had to be older to become a Boy Scout.

Afterward JR wanted to go see the Indians dance at the Indian Village then go to the midway with his dad. He asked him if he had tickets to the rodeo tomorrow and Sunday. Rod, being a volunteer, could get in for free, but he would see if he could still get tickets.

While at the park, JR and Rod went on all the rides with the exception of the kid rides where JR went by himself. On the Ferris wheel, Rod pointed out the general direction to their home. Rod also checked on tickets for JR for Saturday and Sunday and found out there were none to be had.

While having a corn dog and Coke for lunch, Rod explained to him there were no tickets to be had for the weekend. He also told him that he would not go to the rodeo without his best buddy. Instead, they would go riding their horses together.

That Saturday night, Rod and Josie went to the final night show with the others on the Parade Committee and then went dancing afterward. They arrived home to find the babysitter curled up on the couch watching a movie. She told him that JR was really good and had even read to her out of his favorite book. Rod paid her, and she said she hoped she could continue to babysit JR as he was such a good boy.

The whole week had been a major success for both the town of Cheyenne and for the Duvals, with over 250,000 visitors. There was little crime, and JR got to ride in his first parade. It was a long and tiring week but well worth it.

36

Two years after retiring from the Air Force, Paul and John had established themselves as Cold Case Investigators helping out the local law enforcement agencies with cold cases—except for one, that is. That one case was the kidnapping of Patrick Johnson Jr., son of Patrick and Sherrie Johnson, their best friend while in the service.

All three families had kept in touch and had an annual barbeque pool party at Paul and Anne's place every July. This year, they had invited Don and Lydia, and when they arrived, all were in for a surprise. Lydia was pregnant with twins. Everyone was happy for them, and while their kids played in the pool, the women gathered at one end of the pool deck to talk while the guys gathered around the grill to talk and compare notes.

Paul and John talked about their new building and how it was set up with firearms located in the safe and that two signatures were required to receive a weapon, which included personal handguns for Paul, John, and Janet Beardsley, their administrative secretary.

Patrick asked if Janet still went by the nickname of "Love"—he remembered her from when she worked in their squadron orderly room—and if she had found her true love yet.

With John rolling his eyes, Paul was the one to tell him. "Surely you remember TSgt Ronald Overton from the office? He got transferred to March when Norton closed up. Well, he is now a Master Sergeant, and get this—as an Active Duty Reservist, he is in charge of the Investigations Unit. Janet and Ronald are now dating, and she is hoping that he will pop the question shortly. However, he keeps telling her that he wants to wait until after he completes the Senior NCO Academy."

Patrick looked at Don and asked him how things were going for him and if he was staying at the LA Field Office.

"Yes, I am staying at the LA Field Office. They made me special agent in charge of the region. It keeps me busy, and right now, we are working on several bank robberies that I am sure you have heard about. What about you, Patrick? How have you been doing with your horses?" "I have been busy with the Kern County Reserve Mounted Patrol. Mostly we are in the Kern County fair parade and rodeo. I have been called in a few times to assist in the office but nothing major. As for my ranch, I now have a total of three horses—one for Sherrie, Sherrie Leigh, and my own. I am looking at three mares. I love the ranch and the mounted patrol."

Don looked at Patrick and Paul and told them both, "Look, guys, I know this is eating me alive, but I want you to know that every morning I look at my notepad, and the top item is finding your son. So far, we have tracked down tips on missing kids JR's age, and so far all have proven naught."

He looked at the women then asked Patrick, "Has she provided any information as to who did it? Anything at all? What about to your daughter? You know, girl-to-girl talk?"

Patrick gave Don an icy glare and told him, "Look, I want to believe that you have done all you can with the highly valued and storied FBI always solving crimes, but maybe you have not done everything. As far as Sherrie goes, no, she has not told me anything new, and I still do not push her. She is still under mental health care. As for telling my daughter, she does not even know she has a brother. Someday we will tell her, but not now. She is too young to understand what happened." Paul took Patrick into the kitchen to grab more beer out of the fridge and told him that Don has been in weekly contact with him or John. "Hell, even we are not able to find him, but we have feelers out with every private eye agency in the nation."

They went back out with the beer, and while Paul flipped the burgers for the kids and steaks for the adults, Patrick apologized to

Don. He admitted that he was a crack investigator with the Air Force, and even he can't find him.

On the way home, Sherrie Leigh asked her mom and dad who that "big mean-looking" person was. "Was he in the Air Force too with you and Uncle Paul?"

Patrick gave a forced laugh and told her that no, he was someone they had worked with on a couple of cases a few years ago before she was born.

That seemed to satisfy her curiosity, and when they got home, she took her bath and went to bed, then Patrick and Sherrie joined her in her nightly prayers. Sherrie read her favorite story, *Cinderella*, until she fell asleep. Patrick was out in the living room, reading the paper and had the TV on for background noise. "She asleep?"

"Like the angel that she is," she told him.

Then she asked him the question he had hoped she would not ask. "I saw the agent talking to you. Is there any news at all? What did he ask you?"

"He told me that every morning he looks at his notepad and the number one item is 'find JR Johnson.' He asked me if I had heard anything about JR. He asked me if we had said anything to Sherrie Leigh, and I told him that she does not even know she has a brother—at least not yet. Paul then took me into the kitchen to get more beer for us guys so I could cool off and not hit the SOB."

He then hugged her and asked her what the girls talked about. She told him that MJ had asked if she was still doing victims' advocate work like she did before Patrick retired. "I told her that I was doing some for the county, but I was spending most of my time at home with Leigh. By the way, that is what our daughter wants to be called now. She does not want to be confused with her mom," she told Patrick with a grin of her own.

They hugged as they watched TV, and since the next day was Sunday, they would get up early, go to Mass, then maybe go to the mountains though Leigh was bugging them to take her to Disneyland so she could see all of her favorite characters.

As they got into bed, Patrick told her, "We are going to have to take her one day soon. You do know that, right?"

"Yes, I know. We can't keep denying her something she would enjoy because of memories we have." She turned off her nightstand lamp, rolled over, and kissed him good night.

37

Paul and John were getting settled into their new building, making sure they had the proper fire extinguishers for the vault that stored their weapons and ammunition. Everyone in the office, including Janet, had a personal 9mm handgun that was approved for concealed carry by both the town and county. To be issued one of the rifles, they had to have two signatures—one of which was Janet as the office manager and the other either Paul or John.

It had taken some doing to get these permits. They had to sign agreements that if they needed to take a rifle with them on a case, at least one police or deputy sheriff had to be with them. So far, they had had no need to take one. Both John and Paul had their own personal rifles in their trucks.

Having an inspirational thought, Paul had John brought in the box containing JR's kidnapping case. He went through it and found the copy of the one picture that Patrick had kept. He looked hard at the photo and remembered when he was born how happy both Patrick and Sherrie had appeared. However, Paul was beginning to have stronger doubts that Patrick was JR's biological father.

"John, let me throw out something that was discussed a few years ago. What if, just if, Patrick is not the biological father and the person who took JR and attacked Sherrie is the father? Would Sherrie, knowing this, let him in on her own?"

John replied by saying, "Let's ask Janet and get a woman's point of view on this question, Paul. We never did consider asking a woman's point of view. I'll go get her."

John found Janet crunching numbers of all the costs that were accrued for updating the new office and told her to get a cup of coffee and come to the conference room for a head-scratching meeting.

Janet came in with her cup of coffee and notepad. "What's up, boss? Did I mess up on the balance sheet?"

Paul looked at her, gave a slight chuckle, and told her no. "It is something dealing with the Johnson case. Remember four years ago?"

"Yeah, the one case that the highly valued SPS Investigations Unit and the even higher valued FBI could not close out. Sherrie Johnson was stabbed, and their son was kidnapped, right?"

"Yup, that's the one. Anyway, John and I want your opinion on a scenario that John, FBI Agent Abernathy, and myself talked about but did not follow up on." He paused to take a sip of coffee. "Now this goes without saying this stays here unless I release the information."

She nodded in agreement. "Okay, just suppose—and this is all hypothetical—that Patrick Johnson is not the biological father and the person who attacked Sherrie Johnson and kidnapped JR was or is the biological father. If this were you, would you let him in the house if you were alone?"

"In other words, you are grasping at straws, right? Let me think for a minute." She thought about it and then shook her head. "That could mean one of two things happened to her. One, she cheated on Patrick, but I don't think so. Two, she was raped. I read a report once that said that some wives are hesitant to tell their husbands that they had been raped."

She then added, "Did you ask Patrick if she had gone anywhere nine months before JR was born? Why don't you ask him? It can't hurt."

John looked at Paul and said that she might be on the right track, but they had to come up with a plan to talk to Patrick away from Sherrie. "I know down deep that Patrick feels he is JR's father, but this is something we kicked around before but did nothing about."

"John, you are right. I will invite him to lunch next week. Hell, we just saw him two days ago. Meanwhile, see if you can start tracking down DNA labs and see if someone had requested a DNA test within six months of JR's kidnapping."

Paul looked at Janet and told her it was good work and a raise could be coming in her next paycheck. Going over his old notes again, he asked Janet to talk to Ronald and see if he could come into the office; he wanted to ask him a favor.

Later on that afternoon, he called Patrick at his ranch and invited him to lunch next week on the premise of showing off the new office.

Late that afternoon, Ronald came by, dropped off a box of chocolate on Janet's desk, and asked where Paul was. She called Paul and said Ronald was there.

Ronald was sharply dressed in his best civilian clothes, and he sat down and accepted a cup of coffee. "What's up, Paul? Is it about my dating Janet?"

"No, Ronald, it is not about you dating Janet. Everything is fine as long as she is happy. I have known her for a long time, and she has taken some big hits from assholes. Keep her happy, and I am happy." He took a sip of coffee, looked at Ronald, and continued.

"I am sure you remember the Johnson case back in ninety-two where his wife was assaulted and son kidnapped? John and I have been going over old notes, and it still bugs me that the perp might have had Special Forces or Spec Ops training. You contacted a couple of former Force Recon Marines, and they gave a tip he might be up in Utah. Can you reach out again and go further east?"

"I have a cousin that just retired from Army Special Forces at Fort Carson, Colorado. I will call him tonight to see if he can check on others. He has contacts across the country. You still think the perp is Spec Ops and not someone who had a grudge against Patrick?"

"Yes, I do. It was a well-thought-out plan that showed a lot of training and resourcefulness in what he did. Basically, what I am looking for is some guy who all of a sudden showed up at his home in ninety-two with a two-year-old boy."

"I will call him tonight, but I do not want to limit it to Special Forces. He has contacts with all branches including Air Force Special Ops."

With a smile, Paul said, "I guess I taught you how to be a good investigator. Want a job when you retire? What is your status for the Senior NCO Academy?"

"I received the call just before I left. I report 15 January. Janet does not know yet, so please do not tell her. I will tell her tonight."

He left Paul's office, and he could hear Ronald telling Janet that he needed to talk to her tonight. He would swing by her place around seven. Paul called John in and asked him to narrow his DNA lab test sites to the Rocky Mountain region. It was just a hunch.

That night, Ronald told Janet of his class date for the SNCOA and he would report in on 15 January. He then surprised her, showing her the engagement ring he picked out. "After I graduate, we can get married. Janet, will you marry me?"

"I am not ready to settle down just now, Ronald. I do love you but not to get married. I have to make sure I am making the right decision."

He accepted that, pocketed the ring, and they talked about some of the changes the Air Force was going through, and then he left to call his cousin in Colorado.

38

Ronald called his cousin Eddie that night and said he would check his contacts to see if he could come up with anything. They chatted for a while, and Ronald hung up. He then called a buddy of his that had just retired from the Air Force and was living in Florida.

That Friday, Eddie called Ronald and told him of a retired Special Forces NCO that he knew that was living in Cheyenne, Wyoming, and has a five-year-old son. The name was MSgt Robert Swift III. "I remember him because we used to kid him about him having 'three I's' after his name. He lives near Warren Air Force Base. I do not know what he does for a living though. Sorry."

"This is good, thanks. If this is golden, it just might solve a cold case that has been bugging me since 1992. Anyone else that you might know about? Don't say anything to him though, okay, Eddie?" Ronald called Paul right away and passed on the news to him.

"It may turn out to be like the last one, legit, but who knows. Let me ask you this, Paul—how many guys that you know of would all of a sudden show up with a kid that would be the same age as Johnson's kid that you did not know had a kid?"

Paul took a sip of coffee as he thought of the question and thought of all the guys he knew that had gotten divorced, became widowed, or never married and had kids. "None that I can think of. I will pass this on to the FBI agent and let them run it. Oh, by the way, Janet told me about your so-called marriage proposal. You might be a smart sky cop, but you have no clue on how to talk to women. If you want some advice, call me at home." Before Ronald could reply, he hung up.

He called John into his office. "John, what do you know about Cheyenne, Wyoming? There is a possibility that JR might be there.

A retired Army Special Forces Master Sergeant has shown up in Cheyenne with a five-year-old son that no one knew about. I'm calling Donald now to see how he wants to handle it. I am not saying anything to Patrick when I see him for lunch on Monday."

"Cheyenne, let's see, in July is Cheyenne Frontier Days. Never was stationed there but wanted to. This could be another false lead, you know. Let the feds spend their money. If it is JR, then we get credit for giving them the tip. If not, we do not have egg on our faces looking like fools."

After John left, Paul refilled his cup and called FBI Agent Abernathy.

"Don, this is Paul Gibbons of Cold Case Investigators. Listen, we have a tip on a possible five-year-old boy that showed up in Cheyenne, Wyoming. A retired Army Special Forces MSgt by the name of Robert Swift III. Actual address is unknown. We got the information from a confidential informant. We do not know if it is JR or not. Just hope it won't be like the Salt Lake City tip, a no-go." "We happen to have a field office in Cheyenne. We will put a search out for him and find out what is up. Listen, sorry about what happened at the pool party last weekend. It was not intentional. I am doing my best."

"Yeah, well, I know, Patrick, and sometimes he can be a hothead at times. Don't worry about it. Let us know what you find out, okay?"

"I will, Paul. You take care and be careful with your cases.

There was a PI that got killed back in New York the other day working a cold case for us."

"Yeah, we heard. Both John and I knew him from service time. Let me know what you find out in Cheyenne. Goodbye."

Just then he heard Janet answer the phone, "Gibbons and Sommers, Cold Case Investigators. One moment please."

Janet buzzed him to tell him it was a detective from Riverside PD on the line. "He wants to talk to you about a five-year-old cold case."

"Paul Gibbons, how may I help you, sir?"

"Mr. Gibbons, this is Detective Small of the Riverside PD. We have a case that might be right up your alley. It concerns a person who has been writing worthless checks all over the city and county for the past five years. All the victims say that when he cashes a check, he smiles, so we call him the Happy Paperhanger. So far, he has written over 500,000 dollars of worthless checks. We have no clue who he is or where he is based out of."

"Detective Small, we are quite busy today working on a four-year-old case. I will send my partner, John Sommers, to see you Monday morning at nine if that is okay with you."

After he hung up, he looked at the snapshot of JR and called John into the office. "John, I have two things for you to consider, and I want your honest opinion."

He arched his eyebrow and said one word: "Okay."

"I know you have gotten quite proficient with our new computer system. We have the new facial recognition software, right? I want you to take this photo of JR and add four years to it. I want to take it with me when I have lunch with Patrick on Monday. Let's see what he has to say. Maybe he forgot he gave me this photo of JR. I know the feds can do it, but let's not let Don know we have the snapshot yet. After all, after all, we were supposed to give him everything we had. We will have to come up with a very valid excuse for not giving it to him when we gave him everything else."

"And the second item?"

"Monday morning at 0900 you have an appointment at the Riverside PD Detective Division. They have a five-year-old cold case they want us to handle with them—or rather, *for* them. You are to meet with Detective James Small. No need to come here first. Have a decent breakfast with MJ for a change."

As John was leaving, he turned and told Paul that he had a possible hit on a DNA test that was done in 1992 in Omaha, Nebraska. "It is probably a long shot, but I am still checking. I will work on the photo program now and see if I can come up with something before we go home tonight."

39

The following Monday, while John was with the Riverside PD on a new case, Paul looked at the original snapshot of JR and the facial recognition prints showing four years of aging. "So this is how JR might look now at the age of six. He is quite a handsome devil, but he definitely does not look like Patrick. Now how the hell am I going to approach Patrick with this line of thought?" he muttered to himself.

Just before he left for lunch with Patrick, Agent Abernathy called. "Paul, the tip in Cheyenne is okay. Turns out the guy was never married, but he got his girl pregnant, and she did not want the baby. We checked the birth certificate and court documents that he had filed to have his mom take care of the baby until he retired. His parents live in Arizona, and the kid was raised there. We even checked with the kid's doctor. It is legit. Any other tips?"

"Unfortunately, no. I am having lunch with Patrick today.

Maybe Sherrie has finally opened up a little. I will let you know."

Since it was a two-hour drive for Patrick, they had decided to eat at a small diner in Santa Clara, which was about halfway between San Bernardino and Bakersfield. Paul arrived first and took a small booth at the back of the room so they could both have their backs to the wall and keep an eye on the door and the front of the diner.

Patrick arrived wearing his normal everyday work clothes since he had been clearing some of his land and cleaning the stables.

Paul asked him how he liked being a cowboy now, and Patrick said he enjoyed it.

"Paul, we just saw each other two weeks ago. What's up? Good news, I hope? Are Anne and the boys okay?"

"Yes, everyone is fine, but I hate to say it, nothing yet. I just wanted to talk to you about something that we had talked about before we retired. First of all, has Sherrie said anything about that day yet? Anything at all?"

"No, Paul, nothing at all. Whenever I start to bring it up, she shuts me off like she's holding something back."

They waited until the waitress took their order before Paul continued. "Patrick, I am going to ask you a few things, and I don't want you to get upset and yell at me. We have been friends far too long to have mean words said."

"I agree. If I start to raise my voice, just kick me in the shin. That is why I have my boots on—so you won't hurt me." He laughed. "Patrick, you remember the discussion we had concerning the possibility, I repeat, possibility that you are not JR's biological father?"

Patrick looked at him and asked, "What the hell are you getting at, Paul? And yes I remember the discussion."

"John and I did some brainstorming last Friday. Is there a possibility that Sherrie cheated on you one time nine months before JR was born?" He could see Patrick's face starting to turn red, so he gently tapped Patrick's leg. He could also see that Patrick was thinking.

"Paul, I am trying to think back six years and nine months. It was a crazy time on base with all the heavy airlifts going out to the Middle East. There was no time that Sherrie went out without me. She was home every day for lunch. No, she did not cheat on me. Ahh, here's our lunch, let's eat."

Halfway through lunch, Patrick started to frown and started to shake his head. He put his burger down and looked at Paul.

"There was one time she went without me. It was her birthday, and her best friend, Rose MacDonald, took her to the Brandin' Iron for her birthday party. That night she came home a little tipsy, and I thought maybe it was that she had too much to drink. However, that did not stop her from"—he lowered his voice—"uninhibited sex. I won't go into details, but it was strange."

He bit into his burger, took a gulp of soda, and continued. "Could someone have slipped something in her drink when she did not know it and was raped? Also, Rose died the next day, if I remember correctly, under suspicious circumstances when her brakes failed in a parking garage. If it were someone she knew, that would explain a lot of things including her denial of who did the crime."

Paul looked at his friend and told him he had been thinking it was someone Sherrie knew. "I always did, but you were too close to the crime and you did not want to think of it that way." He finished his burger, and they both ordered a slice of fresh baked apple pie and coffee.

"Patrick, I am going to show you four pictures. You tell me which one looks like it would be your biological son."

He first put down the snapshot of JR, and Patrick looked at it and told him it was the same snapshot he had given him the afternoon of the crime.

"I am surprised you did not turn it over to the FBI like you were supposed to do when they requested all the files."

With a sly smile, he told Patrick, "It was stuck in between bottom flaps of the box that contained duplicate copies of the case files." He then gave the snapshot back to Patrick.

He then laid out three other photos. "These are from a new computer program we now have called facial recognition. We can take a photo, such as the snapshot, and add to it. We added two, three, and four years to it. Take a look at them and see if they look like anyone you might know."

"Paul, you know damn well the boy in these pictures do not look like me other than the hair color. His facial features are not of me. Sherrie told me he looks like her father, who is dead, and she has no photos of him that I know of."

They finished their pie and coffee, and Paul asked him what he thought about Rose's death now that he has had time to think about it.

"Paul, I have no idea. Why don't you check with the PD and see what you can come up with? My guess is if Sherrie was raped in that bar somehow and she saw him, he fixed her brakes. Look at how he covered his tracks after attacking Sherrie and kidnapping JR. Everything fits. Let me know what the PD says. I am sure you have your connections with all the departments."

It was a longstanding tradition between the two that whoever asked the other to lunch or dinner picked up the tab. Paul picked up the bill, and Patrick left the tip.

Outside they shook hands and parted with well-wishes for each other's families. Paul put the photos back inside his shirt pocket and headed back to the office. As he left, he noticed that Patrick was still inside his truck, his head buried in his hands, his shoulders shaking. He pulled off at the corner and waved at Patrick as he drove by.

On the way back, Paul spoke into a tape recorder with what Patrick had suggested about Sherrie being raped and Rose's death. He also recorded his thoughts that the perp, as yet unnamed, who knew Sherrie maybe an old boyfriend?

By time Paul got back in the office, John was waiting for him with an update from Riverside PD. "Paul, this one is strange. Seems this paperhanger is cashing checks all over Riverside, both city and county, for at least the past two years. There is no clear-cut description of him, and the places with closed circuit TV cameras show him wearing a trench coat and a wide-brim hat. He is about six feet, and from what I could gather from the videos I looked at, about 180 to 200. This is the strange part—the checks are for only the total bill plus $10. Never larger."

"Did they squabble over our normal police department rate of $500 per day plus expenses?"

"Detective Small did not even bat an eye. I had to give our contract to the chief of detectives, and he signed off on it. I gave it to Janet so she could put it on the books." He then asked how it went with Patrick.

Paul replayed the tape recording of what Patrick had said and added his thoughts. "I think we need to check into the accident report on this Rose MacDonald person. Do you know anyone at RPD Traffic Division that can take a look at this for us?" He then continued, "Now I need to call Don and explain the snapshot of JR that they still had in their possession."

Just before Paul picked up the phone to call FBI Agent Abernathy, Janet told him that Ronald was on the line for him. "Talk to him while I get a cup of coffee. This is going to be a long afternoon."

"What can I do for you, Ronald?"

"Paul, I have another possible for you. However, this one is a bit strange. It is in Cheyenne again. Eddie told me there are lots of retirees in Cheyenne, and several are former Special Operations types of all branches. He ran into a retired Security Police at the BX yesterday. He was checking out some young kids clothes for a six-year-old son, but he did not know his actual size."

"Ronald, does this SP have a name or a description?"

"Retired TSgt Randall Wyatt, six foot six and around 180. Do you know him?"

Paul sat there, thinking for a minute, trying to run all the different SPs that he knew but nothing. "No, not really, nothing sounds familiar. I will pass this on to Don again and see what shakes from the tree. Anything else?"

"No, nothing. Just trying to help you solve the case. Got to run. My clerk is waving at me." He quickly hung up.

Paul looked over his notes and called John in. "John, we got another tip from Ronald's cousin. Seems he ran into a retired SP by the name of Wyatt. Sound familiar to you? He was in the BX there looking for clothes for a six-year-old boy but not sure of measurements."

John arched his eyebrow and muttered, "Sky cop gone dirty? I don't recognize the name though. You going to call Don?" He then added, "RPD Traffic is going to dig up the accident files and get back to me as soon as they can."

"This one seems stronger than the last one. I will bring in the photos tomorrow to your office. Hopefully, you will have word back by then on this latest tip."

"See you tomorrow then. Goodbye, Paul."

"I was going to call him now about Patrick, so I will make this a long call. What do you have with the DNA testing labs? With the tips we have been getting about Cheyenne, why don't you narrow down to Denver to Fort Collins and east to Omaha. That should cover the territory. Now go, I have a phone call to make."

Paul looked at his notes, picked up the phone, and called the FBI agent. His secretary told him that Agent Abernathy was in a meeting. Paul told her it was extremely important that he talk to him as soon as he returns to his office. Paul hung up and went to get a cup of coffee and a day-old donut.

As soon as he got back to his desk, his private line rang, and he answered it. It was Don. Paul told him about the meeting with Patrick and what they had talked about. He then told Don, "You won't believe this, but in the bottom of the case file box we had packed up before shutting down the shop, I found a snapshot of JR when he was only one-year-old."

He paused, and before Don could say anything, he continued. "John ran a facial recognition program based on that snapshot, adding two, three, and four years. I showed them to Patrick. He admitted that the photos do not look like him."

Don told him, in no uncertain terms, that he wanted that snapshot of JR by noon the next day.

Paul agreed and said he would also give him the new photos as well. He then went on to describe what Patrick's thoughts were about the night Sherrie had her birthday party and the accident involving Rose MacDonald.

"John is working with RPD on the accident investigation. My gut feeling is that if the two events are related, we have one guy that can be connected to a homicide."

"Anything else?"

Paul told him of the latest input from Ronald and his source.

40

The next morning, Paul left early to battle the traffic going into Los Angeles on the I-10 Freeway. Arriving at the FBI building, Paul went through the screening and had to leave his pistol with the guard.

He was given a visitor badge and escorted up to S-A-C Abernathy's office. The receptionist called and told Don his nine o'clock visitor was here and was told to send him in.

Paul was surprised to see how spartan Don's office was. He had presumed that Don, based on his position, would have a large wooden desk and a large bookcase. Instead, he had a normal-size metal government-style desk and one bookcase crammed with files stacked on top of each other. On his desk was his phone, a desk blotter, and a picture of him and Lydia from their wedding.

"Good morning, Paul. Do you have the photos for me? You do realize your holding back the snapshot prevented us from getting a picture out to the media right away. I should charge you with withholding evidence and impeding an investigation, but I won't. Now let me see what your new program came up with. We have the same facial recognition program here, you know."

Paul gave him the photos, the snapshot of JR at the age of one, and the others John did showing how he might look now, four years later. "I showed these to Patrick yesterday. He admits that JR does not look like him except for his blonde hair." He also went on to discuss the possible scenario of Sherrie being raped at the bar where the party was. He discussed the suspicions about the death of Sherrie's friend Rose.

Don looked at Paul and told him that date rapes are not that uncommon, and sometimes the victim does not realize it until it is too late. The possibility that that is what happened to Sherrie, in his mind, was now at about 90 percent. As for Rose, there was nothing they could do unless the RPD called in their technical people. The accident was over six years ago, and the car was probably scrap metal by now.

His phone rang, and his secretary told him it was the Cheyenne Field Office. He motioned to Paul with a finger to his lips. He grabbed his notepad and pencil and started to write down the information he was given over the phone. All Paul heard was "uh-huh" and "Thanks, I'll get back to you." He hung up the phone. "Let's go down to the break room, get a cup of coffee, then I will tell you about the phone call. It is a real doozy, believe me. I will say this though—it closes a relatively short open case in Cheyenne."

Nothing was said on the way down to the break room.

It was busy with customers, so they each got a coffee and a pastry and took them back to Don's office.

"Paul, your informant was spot on with this tip. No, not about JR, but an apparent custody kidnapping yesterday afternoon. Seems this Wyatt character is in the middle of a divorce-and-custody situation. He took the boy on an unsupervised visit but never brought him back to the boy's mother." He took a bite of his pastry and continued. "The local field office tracked his address down and found him as he was packing his car to go out of state with the boy. Evidently, it was a spur-of-the-moment thing. He is now in custody on one charge of kidnapping."

"Is there any reward you can give my informant? He has provided two tips, and one solved the case quickly."

"I am sure there is a reward. Have him contact me on my phone here, and I will take down his information. It will remain strictly between him and me."

"Do you have a spare empty office where I can make a call?"

Don sent him to an office down the hall. He called Ronald and told him the news and gave him Don's number for his cousin to call about the reward. He went back to Don's office and sat down. "He will call you later today. Now what about Patrick's case?"

"Unless something breaks soon, not a damn thing. I have been checking DNA testing databases going back to 1990, but nothing fits the case timeline." They talked about ideas and then promised to not hold anything back. Paul left to drive back to his office.

He stopped by John's office and told him what happened at Don's office with the latest tip. "It wasn't a cold case, but we helped solve it because of Ronald's cousin. He is going to get a reward for it, probably money. It might be something we could do once our cash flow situation improves. Speaking of money, what do you have on the Happy Paper Hanger?"

"Detective Small called this morning. He did it again last night at a liquor store—same description, and the CCTV video does not show his face. He knows it is recording, but not even a side profile. It's going to be a tough one to crack, and, I believe, it will only be solved by luck. There is no way they can station anyone at all stores and banks in the county looking for someone wearing a tan overcoat and a black fedora-type hat. This person hits every place someone can cash a check and even did it at the county library last year. He has guts."

"Anything yet from RPD on the MacDonald accident?"

"Yup, mighty suspicious also, and they are digging into it as we speak. It seems the left front brake hose blew out. They took a photo of both front brake lines and only the left front one had a hole in it. Evidently, she was pulling into a parking space in her townhouse parking garage, and when she applied the brakes, the line ruptured. She hit the retaining wall head on at about five mph. An airbag did not deploy, and her chest impacted the steering wheel. They are going to check the paperwork to see if they had missed that it may have been tampered with."

Paul took a deep breath. "Damn, I wish Sherrie would talk about that night. Maybe she will talk to Patrick. That could…no, scratch that...it would answer a whole lot of questions and possibly find JR. Did Rose have any family that was notified?"

"I asked the same question of Detective Small. She was an only child from San Jose, which coincidentally is Sherrie's hometown. I think they were best friends in school. Her parents died in an auto accident two years prior to Rose's death. I guess it is up to Patrick now, and I sure as hell do not envy him at all.

"Good work, John. You have done a lot. Take the afternoon off and spend time with MJ for a change. She deserves it, and so do you."

"See you Monday. Call me if you need me."

41

That evening, while Josie was fixing dinner, Rod and JR were watching the local news when there was a "Breaking News" notice: "FBI involved in Kidnapping." When Rod saw this, he about choked on a mouthful of coffee.

The FBI Special Agent from the Cheyenne Field Office was speaking. "This morning, at nine, the FBI had a tip on the kidnapping that occurred yesterday here in Cheyenne. We searched the premises and arrested Randall Wyatt, a retired Air Force technical sergeant, on one count of child kidnapping. The investigation is still ongoing, and he will be arraigned in Federal District Court on Monday morn- ing. Information will be released as it becomes available."

JR looked at his dad, whose face was white. "Dad, what's wrong? Your face looks a different color, almost white. Are you okay?"

Josie had not heard the news but did hear JR as she was then at the table. She also saw Rod looking different. "Rod, what's wrong? Your face is real pale, and you are scaring JR and me now. So what is wrong?"

Rod, concentrating on the news program, waved his hand to Josie to keep quiet. The announcer was saying, "Early this morning, the local FBI received an anonymous tip of a possible kidnap victim. The details are still vague to us, but it seems that the victim is a six-year-old boy taken from his mother yesterday in Burns, Wyoming, and was located here in Cheyenne. The child's mother, who wishes to remain unidentified, said the boy was taken by her estranged husband yesterday on unsupervised visitation. We will have more details as they become available."

Josie grabbed JR, hugged him to her legs, and said that she could not fathom how it must have felt to the poor mother when her son was taken. She looked down at JR and told him, "Honey, that will not happen to you. We will protect you from anyone who tries to do that to you, okay?"

"Dad, what's *kidnap* mean?"

His face regaining a natural color and without missing a beat, he told him that "A kidnapping is when someone takes a child from his or her home, sometimes for money."

"Well, do I have to be afraid of being kidnapped?"

Rod reached out to him, pulled him onto his lap, and told him that, no, he did not have to be afraid of being kidnapped, that he and Josie would be there to protect him.

Rod then looked at Josie and asked her if supper was ready. He was hungry after working all day getting ready for the fall season. He knew he had to keep calm and keep things as normal as possible for both Josie and JR's sake.

After supper, they watched a game show where JR was getting to be pretty good at the answers. They then played checkers, where JR beat Rod twice. "Dad, you are not thinking. I beat you two games. Are you okay?" For a six-year-old, he was very astute as to what was going on.

"I'm just tired. Speaking of which, it is time for bath and bed. Now hop to it like Bugs."

JR laughed all the way to his bedroom to get his PJs and then to the bathroom for his bath. He was at the age that he did not want Josie to give him his bath except to dry him off.

Rod told Josie, "I thought that news broadcast was about us. We try to not show JR in town that much, but he is in school now. Tonight caught me off guard. We will have to watch it again later tonight, and hopefully, they will have more detail of what led up to the tip. We might learn from it."

Josie asked him in a low voice, "Rod, what will we do if the FBI comes knocking on the door? I know that we have drilled it into JR not to open the door if we are not nearby."

"Two things we can do—one, *do not* dwell on this one case, it will drive us nuts, and two, we do not let him near the computer by himself. In a couple of years, yes, we will have no choice, but not now."

"What about tomorrow? You promised us we would all go horseback riding while the weather is still decent."

She heard JR calling her, so she left to go finish drying him off and put his Bugs Bunny PJs on. Rod joined them as JR said his nightly prayers and then thanked God for the little boy's safety. After his prayer, and before reading to him, Rod told them, "Tomorrow we will go horseback riding, have a picnic of Mom's fried chicken, play catch with the football, and toss the Frisbee if it is not too windy."

While Rod read to JR, Josie went to the kitchen to make sure the chicken she had pulled from the freezer earlier would be thawed out enough to fry in the morning. She then peeled four large potatoes to boil so she could make JR's favorite potato salad for the picnic.

Rod came out, gave her a hug, and apologized for the short time to prepare for the picnic tomorrow.

"I should have realized it earlier when you suggested it," Josie told him with a hug.

He went back out to the living room to watch TV until the news came on. The lead story was the Burns kidnapping. Nothing more was mentioned than earlier in the evening about the tip or who called it in. They watched the rest of the news and then the weather, which would be perfect for their outing tomorrow. Then they went to bed.

In bed, they decided to downplay the Burns incident. If they overreacted, they could make a mistake. If not, everything was cool. After all, JR was in the big parade this year, and no one recognized him or had second thoughts.

Josie was the first to turn off her light then Rod. Tomorrow would be another day.

42

On the way home from having lunch with Paul, Patrick thought over everything that he could remember from seven years ago. He remembered Rose picking up Sherrie to take her to the Brandin' Iron for her party. There were going to be some other girls there as well, but Rose was her best friend from her hometown.

He remembered how excited Sherrie was when she found out that Rose had found a job nearby in Riverside, California, which was only about fifteen minutes from Norton. They had Rose over several times, and Patrick liked her.

Then they read in the paper that Rose was dead in a single car accident in her parking garage. It seemed that her brakes had failed. But now, Patrick had doubts. Could the person that attacked Sherrie and kidnapped JR have fixed her brake hose to rupture and cause her to hit the retaining wall? If that was the case, then there would be a murder charge added. However, based on experience, that would be downright hard to prove—unless he admitted it, and Patrick doubted this guy would.

The problem was how could he broach the subject with Sherrie away from Sherrie Leigh? Of course, they could get a babysitter and go out, but go out where? All of a sudden, he had the answer. There was to be a full moon tonight with no clouds and temperature around seventy.

He arrived home around 2:00 p.m., put the truck in the barn, and checked on his horses. He went inside and found Sherrie in the living room reading her latest novel.

"Hi, hon, where's Leigh?" he asked as he bent down to kiss her forehead.

"She is in her room, taking her nap. How was lunch with Paul? Anything exciting with his business? How is the family?"

He sat down beside her and told her that Paul's family was fine and they had enjoyed the pool party they had a few weeks ago. He told her about the new case they were working on for Riverside PD, the so-called Happy Paperhanger, who has been writing checks all over the county for at least two years, if not longer, all less than one hundred dollars. "Doesn't make sense."

After a pause, he asked her, "Honey, how about if we go for a moonlight ride tonight on our property. We have not done so in a while, and it is going to be very pleasant out tonight. We can call Betsy to see if she would babysit for us."

"Maybe have a small fire and roast marshmallows? I would love to."

She went to the kitchen phone to call their neighbor to see if she could babysit for a couple of hours that night. "What time, Patrick?" "Make it 7:00 p.m. That will give us time to eat and put the little one to bed."

Sherrie came over to him after she hung up the phone and told him that Betsy would be over at seven, which really meant six forty-five, which was fine with Patrick.

He went out to the barn to gather some dead wood to use for the fire and put three canteens near the saddles. They would do the roast- ing the old-fashioned way with tree twigs. He knew exactly where they would ride—away from the house lights with just the moon and stars to shine for them. Of course, he had his heavy-duty flashlight in his saddlebag that he used with the Mounted Patrol when they were called out to help find lost hikers.

That night, after dinner and the dishes were put in the dishwasher, they told Leigh that they were going out that night but Betsy would be there to take care of her.

"Can I watch TV with her, please, Mommy?"

"As long as you are in bed by seven thirty—no later."

At six forty-five sharp, Betsy drove up and knocked on the door. Patrick told her they were going out for a couple of hours and would be back. She emphasized to her that Leigh was to be in bed no later than seven thirty. Patrick knew she would not have a problem.

Patrick and Sherrie went to the stable and saddled their horses. Patrick, just to be safe, put his .30-30 rifle in his saddle scabbard and picked up the wood and Sherrie put the marshmallows in her saddlebag. They rode off to the east so they would see the moon rise.

After about fifteen minutes, Patrick found a nice clear spot with no overhanging trees or brush that could catch fire and laid out his bedroll. He built a fire ring with rocks and then started a nice small fire. Patrick sat quietly, staring into the fire.

"Patrick, what's wrong? You have not said a word since we left the house, and I know that look. You are thinking of something. Did Paul say something about JR today?"

"Yeah, in a way, he did. No, nothing bad, still nothing as to where he is. However, we talked about a couple of things that did not match up seven years ago, but they just might." He pulled up a twig, scrapped some bark off, slid two marshmallows on it, and put it over the flame tips.

"Seven years ago? Why?"

"Yeah, seven years ago, the day you went out with Rose on your birthday. She took you to the Brandin' Iron. Rose died the next day in a single car accident when her car went into a retaining wall in her parking garage. We read about it in the paper. Did something happen to you that night that you have not told me?"

She looked at him with tears in her eyes. "Patrick, something did happen to me, but at first I did not know what. An old boyfriend was there. I had one dance with him and then I felt woozy and felt I needed to go to the bathroom. He escorted me there. Rose was outside the bathroom. He asked her to check on me. When we came out, he had disappeared."

She wiped tears from her eyes and told him, "Patrick, that is the truth. You have to believe me."

He put his arm around her shoulder, fed her one of the roasted marshmallows, and told her he believed her. He wiped her tears from her beautiful eyes.

"Honey, I have to ask you three questions. One, what is his name? Two, is he the one that came and took JR? And three, is that why JR does not look like me?" He had the pictures but did not want to show them to her by the light of the campfire.

"Patrick, his name is Roderick, or just plain Rod, Duval. Even though he was in a disguise, it was him that took JR, and yes, with the exception of your hair, he looks like Rod. Rose did not like him, much less trust him. She told me that it was suspicious that he was outside the women's bathroom."

She then looked at him and asked him a question she had been thinking of for several years. "Could he have raped me with what they call a date rape drug?"

"It is possible, honey, it is possible. He cannot hurt you now or ever again. We will find him and get JR back. But why didn't you tell us this before?" He knew not to lead her with answers; it had to be her own choice of words to this vital question.

"I was ashamed that I let him in the house. I remember thinking that I should have called you when he was banging on the door, but I did not want to have him wake up JR." She looked up into his eyes then asked him, "If it were a date rape drug, could that explain how uninhibited I was that night with you? I remember how oversexed I was with you, but then I always was—and I still am."

Without a word, they undressed and made passionate love for the first time under the romantic full moon. Afterward, they dressed and looked into the dying flames as she asked him about Rose.

"They are rechecking into her accident. Do you think he could have fixed her car so the brakes would fail and she would die so that she could not talk about what she saw there at the bar?"

"I don't know, Patrick. I really don't know. I remember he worked in a garage when he was in high school. When I saw him seven years ago, he said he was in the Army, Special Forces or something like that, said he was on leave. But how did he know I was going to be there?"

"That I do not know. However, will you be willing to answer questions for FBI Agent Abernathy? I am sure he can talk to you in Paul's office." He kissed her on her soft red lips and told her they needed to head back home. He would call Paul in the morning to set up the interview.

Before they left, Patrick doused the fire with the canteens and spread out the ashes and used the rest of the water on them. They mounted their horses and leisurely rode back to the house one handed while holding hands. They looked at the full moon and how bright it lit up the ranch. It was truly a beautiful night. Sherrie went inside to pay Betsy while Patrick put the horses in the stable and removed the saddles and put everything away. He removed the marshmallows from Sherrie's saddlebag, took them in the house, and said good night to Betsy as she drove off.

"Did Betsy have any problems with Leigh?" Patrick then went to the fridge and get a beer.

"No, babe, but you better sit down. I have something to tell you."

He sat down in his recliner and patted his lap for Sherrie to come sit on his lap. He then reclined back and asked her what is going on.

"I did not tell you earlier, but I had a phone call while you were with Paul." She looked sheepishly at him and then went on. "Babe, you are what now, 42? Well, we had another rabbit die. Yup, you will be a poppa again next April."

"You are joking, right? Hell, I will be an old man when he or she is in high school. Who cares? You make me so damn happy. We fooled everyone. Wait till Paul hears this. I'll tell him tomorrow when

I call him. Will your coming out with the facts now upset you and affect the baby?"

"No. In fact, I am comfortable now that I finally told you the truth. I knew that somehow he was involved in my getting pregnant and that JR looks like him. I know you will still love JR. As far as I am concerned, he is ours, and don't you forget it."

They rubbed noses, and they watched TV up to the late local news and went to bed.

Before they got into bed, they both kneeled on their side of the bed and said their nightly prayer for the safety of JR, their little girl, and their unborn child—their second miracle child.

Patrick's last thought before going to sleep was knowing he was going to get his son back soon and have him as a big brother to two younger siblings. Then he realized he was going to need to expand the house. At least he has plenty of friends in the Mounted Patrol plus Paul and John to help.

43

Even though it was Saturday, Patrick called Paul at home and told him what Sherrie had said the night before. He told Paul that Sherrie might tell more to Don in his office without his being there. Paul agreed and asked Patrick how he felt about the news.

"I feel much better that now we have a stronger chance of getting JR back sooner. Let me know if Don agrees to question Sherrie in your office and when it will take place."

"I will, Patrick, as soon as I hear from him. How did you get her to tell you what happened."

"I won't go into details on how, but my wily old ways of solving a crime worked last night. Oh, and by the way, go easy on her. She is pregnant again—due in April plus, another miracle baby for us."

"Okay, I will call Don now, and I will tell Anne the good news on both counts. I will call you as soon as I hear from Don."

Paul called Don's office and got the agent on duty. He told him he had to talk to Agent Abernathy as soon as possible concerning a kidnapping case he was working on and asked the agent to call him at home.

No sooner had Paul told Anne about Sherrie being pregnant and calling John when Don called.

"Tell me that you have a tip. Sorry, Paul, I don't mean to be so curt this morning. The baby was kicking me all night in the back, and I could not get to sleep—ended up sleeping on the couch. What's up?"

"Patrick called me this morning—early, no less. Sherrie told him everything she knew last night. She is willing to talk to you and me in my office this morning. What time can you be here? Only John and I will be with you. Patrick is going to stay home."

"Make it ten thirty. Have coffee, donuts, and a tape recorder ready."

"See you at ten thirty. I will have everything ready."

He called John and told him to be at the office by ten and to stop and pick up some bottled water for Sherrie in case she wants some. "And tell MJ Sherrie is pregnant again." He then called Patrick and told him to have Sherrie at the office by ten. They would not question her until Don came in.

At nine thirty, Sherrie showed up at the office. John met her at the door and gave her a hug and congratulated her on being pregnant again. Paul came out and gave her a hug and congratulations from Anne.

Paul asked her if she was okay with what was going to happen and if she wanted coffee or water. She told him she was okay, glad to finally come clean with the information, and asked for water. There was a knock on the front door. It was Don with two briefcases and a tripod. John went to help him and escorted him to the conference room.

While John poured him a cup of coffee and got him a couple of donuts, Don set up a video camera and asked Paul if he could do the honors. Paul agreed as John looked it over and arched his eyebrow.

Once they were all settled in, Don advised them that Paul and John could attend the questioning; however, only Don would ask the questions. He also advised Sherrie that the session would be recorded by audio, video, and with written notes and if she wanted a lawyer at any time, she could ask for one. He also asked that the phones in the conference room not ring. John pulled the cord from the one phone in the room.

"Okay, everyone ready?" They all nodded.

Don first had Paul turn on the video camera while he turned on the tape recorder. He then explained to Sherrie that the questioning would be recorded by video, audio, and written notes and if she understood this. She acknowledged that she did, and also if she wanted a lawyer, she could ask for one at any time.

"Please state your full name."

"Sherrie Lee Johnson." "Are you married?"

"Yes, to Patrick Johnson Sr."

"To the best of your recollection, what happened on June 30, 1989?"

Sherrie told them that it was her birthday and Patrick had to work that night. Her best friend, Rose, from high school in San Jose but who lived and worked in Redlands wanted to take her to the Brandin' Iron for her birthday. Management had a table set aside for their small group with appetizers, a bottle of champagne, and some balloons." She paused to sip some water.

"Then this person tapped me on my shoulder and told me that I was still beautiful and wished me a happy birthday. It was a voice out of my long-ago past, but I remembered who it belonged to. He was a former boyfriend from high school. He asked me to dance one dance. We did, and we went back to the table. I emptied the glass of champagne. I guess you might say I did it because of the shock of seeing him. Shortly after that, I felt woozy and had the need to go to the bathroom. I looked for Rose, but she was on the dance floor having fun. He offered to walk me to the bathroom. When I came out, Rose was there and walked me back to the table.

I did not see him again. Rose and I left shortly after that. I remember that on the ride home, Rose asked me if I was okay. I told her I was okay. She then told me that she had seen my old boyfriend outside the restroom door."

"What is the name of your former boyfriend?"

"Roderick, or Rod, Duvall. That is spelled D-U-V-A-L-L. He said he was in the Army Special Forces or something like that."

"Did he say where he was living?" "No, he did not."

"Tell me about Rose's death."

"Two days later, we read in the paper of Rose's death. It was shocking really. She was so young."

"Did your old boyfriend have automotive skills?"

"Yes. He worked in a gas station, and sometimes he did brake jobs for customers."

"Mrs. Johnson, the next set of questions are going to be rough. Do you want to take a break to gather your thoughts?"

"I'm sorry, but I do need to use the restroom. Paul, where is it?" After Sherrie came back, Don resumed the questioning.

"Mrs. Johnson, when your son was born, did it look like your husband?"

"Other than the hair color, no. I told him the baby had his grandfather's facial features."

"Who did the baby look like?"

"Somehow it looked like Rod, but at the time I could not figure out how that could be. I had not had sex with him since we broke up years before."

"Mrs. Johnson, to the best of your ability, please tell us what happened the morning of March 4, 1992."

Sherrie began by describing that JR had a bad night the night before and he was finally sleeping that morning. It was going to be his second birthday, and there was a party planned for later in the afternoon after Patrick got home from work.

She then went on to describe how it was hot that day and she was resting in her recliner with a glass of iced tea when there was a knock at the door. "Several knocks, really. Each one was louder, and I did not want to wake up JR, so I went to see who it was. I looked out the security hole in the door and saw it was him. Even though he had on a rubber mask, I recognized his voice, and he began to talk louder and wanted to come in. I thought about calling Patrick, but I knew he would be home shortly for lunch. He kept banging on the door and speaking louder, so I let him in."

Tears welling up in her eyes, she uttered, "Oh, how I wish I had called him now. But the neighbors could hear him, and I did not want them to call in the disturbance."

Don told her to take her time.

She drained the bottle of water and asked John for another one. She then continued with how Rod first wanted to see JR even though he was sleeping. She told them that Rod had mentioned how happy they could be as a family and squeezed her shoulder. He then asked her for a glass of water. She shut her eyes then began again.

She described how she pulled a glass from the cabinet and poured him a glass of water. Then he grabbed her from behind, and she felt something sharp pressing into her abdomen. The next thing she remembered was waking up in the hospital recovery room and then again in her room with Patrick there.

"Mrs. Johnson, why did you not tell us this when we questioned you in the hospital room the first time?" He looked at his notes. "I asked you specifically if you knew who attacked you and kidnapped your son. You replied, quote I do not know who it was unquote. Please tell us why you did not tell us."

"I was ashamed that I let him in when I knew I should have just called the LE Desk and Patrick. I was ashamed that I let my son be kidnapped."

"You do know that I could arrest you for aiding and abetting the subject and allowing him to escape?"

Her eyes opened wide, and her face went the color of white paper. She thought she was going to throw up.

"Rest easy, Mrs. Johnson, that is not going to happen now or in the future. You have come forward voluntarily, and nothing is going to happen."

Paul stopped the camera and asked Don to step outside. "Don, we did not get a chance to tell you, but she is pregnant again. Let's go easy on her from this point forward, okay?"

"Paul, you should have told me. I would not have said what I did at the end. She has paid a much bigger price for not telling us. We are almost done. I just need to see if she can provide me a description on this guy and see if we can get him."

Going back in, Don could see that Sherrie was composed and ready to continue. Paul got the video camera going, and John turned on the tape-recording machine.

"Mrs. Johnson," Don began. "Can you give me a description of Mr. Duvall?"

"Seven years ago, he had real short hair, deep-brown eyes, about six feet, I guess around 180 pounds. He always loved to wear blue jeans and wore a Western shirt and boots. As for his age, he would be around forty-two or -three now."

"In your quarters, we noticed that there were no photos of JR anywhere. Did you have photos of your son on the walls?"

"Yes, we did. When I came out of the hospital, Patrick had us moved into our new quarters, but I thought he had removed them, thinking it might be too much for me. Rod must have taken them—what a bastard. I hope the son of a bitch roasts in hell for what he did to me and my family."

"One last question—did you know that your husband had a snapshot of JR and did not give it to me? That he gave it to Mr. Gibbons?"

"Funny you should ask. I remember the snapshot. I thought Patrick had given it to you, so I never asked him. I am sure Patrick would like it back."

Don reached into his briefcase and pulled out the snapshot of JR, then he laid out the other photos that showed what JR might look like now.

"Oh my god, is that JR now? That face is almost identical to Rod with the exception of the hair color. Can I have these? Or does Patrick already have them?"

"I'm sorry, Mrs. Johnson, but I need to keep them. We will send them to TV and national news media with the last photo of JR and the description of Mr. Duvall to all field offices as well. You might check and see if this office will give you a copy of the photos. Thank you, Mrs. Johnson. If I have further questions, I will contact you."

Paul and John stopped the recording devices as Don began packing up. "Off the record, I hope we can have JR back with you and Patrick shortly and Mr. Duvall in custody sooner. Thank you for coming forward, and I thank you, Paul, for letting us use your office for this interview. The coffee and donuts were excellent. Goodbye."

As John escorted Don to the front door, Paul talked with Sherrie about the photos. "Patrick has the photos, Sherrie. This is what we talked about at lunch yesterday. I gave them to him. To be honest, I did not know when he was going to talk to you or how he was going to do it. You okay? Do you want to talk to Anne?"

"No, I'm fine. Maybe it was the role of being the victims' advocate at Norton that helped me, but I now know and understand how important it is to come forward right away and not wait years—even if you are embarrassed. Thank you for being Patrick's friend. You mean a lot to him."

She gave Paul and John a hug and told them to say hi to their wives and left for home, thinking how really handsome JR must look.

John waited until he was sure that Sherrie was okay and on the road when he told Paul, "When he mentioned that shit about 'aiding and abetting,' I wanted to reach over the table and strangle him. But I knew he could beat the crap out of me, and MJ would not like to see this loveable puss of mine all beaten up especially since we are going out tonight."

"Yeah, I know what you are saying, and I do not think Janet would like to see blood over the furniture—especially yours. That is why I stopped the camera and took him out to the hallway. Let's get out of here and go get some lunch."

Paul thought about what Sherrie had said about Rod. "John, on Monday, get with Redlands PD and tell him what we found out. I think we now have a murder case. I will check with Don on it on Monday."

"You got it, boss. Let's go eat now, and I will buy lunch since you bought lunch yesterday for Patrick. I won't even put it on the expense account."

44

On the way home, Sherrie thought about Patrick and what he thought when he saw the pictures, and she wondered why he did not say anything to her about them. "Probably thinking he is trying to protect me still," she thought out loud. She stopped to pick up material to make a new dress for Sherrie Leigh. She thought about the child she was carrying, and not knowing yet if it were a boy or girl, she did not bother with anything for the new nursery.

When she arrived home, she found Patrick pushing Sherrie Leigh on the homemade swing set Patrick had just finished. The setup included swings, a teeter-totter, and a small slide. Both were enjoying their father-daughter time.

Patrick stopped the swing so Sherrie Leigh could go to her mother and tell her what a delicious lunch Daddy made for her. "It was PB&J, pickles, and chips. Daddy said after you got home I have to go lie down for my nap. Will you read to me?"

"Of course I will, honey. Go run inside and get ready. I will be in there in a minute."

She looked at Patrick and told him, "We can talk out here when I come back." She then went inside following her daughter.

Ten minutes later, she came out with the baby monitor. Patrick was on his favorite porch chair, his legs outstretched. He looked up at her as she bent over to kiss him. "How was it, babe?"

"It was okay until he mentioned he could arrest me for quote aiding and abetting his escape unquote. Other than that, it was okay. I am glad I have it off my chest now. However, I have a few questions for you, Mr. Johnson, and don't twist the answers."

Uh-oh, he thought. *She has a strange look on her face, and I think I know what it is.* "What question is that, babe?"

"Don't call me babe again until you tell me the truth on these questions. One, did you remove the photos of JR from our old house when I was in the hospital?"

"No, I believe that the perp removed them."

"Two, did you keep the snapshot in your wallet, or did you turn it over to Paul?"

"I gave it to Paul. I did not find out until yesterday that he did not give it to Don."

"Three, did Paul give you facial recognition photos of what JR might look like now yesterday at lunch?"

"Yes, he did. I was going to show them to you last night, but after we talked, we got kind of sidetracked," he said with small grin. "Did you see them?"

"Yes, I did see them. Knowing that his father kidnapped him, does this change the way you feel about him? About JR?"

He looked at her and told her in no uncertain terms, "No, Patrick Johnson Jr. is my son. I loved him as a baby, I still love him and will always love him." He then pulled her onto his lap, and they snuggled and rubbed noses just as they always had.

She told him that by Monday the FBI would release the description she gave Don to all FBI field offices and the latest facial recog- nition picture of what JR might look like now to the media to cover both TV network news and major newspapers.

"Hopefully, someone will recognize one or the other and report it to the FBI," Sherrie added.

Patrick told her, "Let us hope that JR comes home before his next brother or sister is born."

Sherrie agreed and snuggled deeper into his arms. She fell asleep in his lap until their daughter woke up and came out and told them it was time to get up from their naps and she told them that she was hungry.

* * * * *

The following Monday, Don called Patrick and said he would like to do a conference call with him and Paul at ten, before the press release was sent out, to tell them how to handle the media when they contact them. "And, guaranteed, they will contact you."

At the appointed time, Don called and talked to both Patrick and Paul. "Okay, guys, the press release is going out at 1:00 p.m. This will give everyone a chance to broadcast tonight and appear in evening papers as well. Patrick, when the media comes to you, let Sherrie tell as much as she wants to tell, but nothing about Rose's death. That is something we want to keep in our back pocket for now." He then switched to Paul.

"Paul, your business will be mentioned in the release—same instructions as I gave to Patrick. Do not say anything about Rose. If we can prove he damaged her car, then we can get him on murder charges as well. Any questions from either of you?"

Both agreed to what Don had told them. Paul told him that he made sense.

Around 3:00 p.m., a news van from the local TV station followed by three cars arrived at Patrick's place. Patrick, Sherrie, and Sherrie Leigh came out to the front porch. The TV reporter wanted Sherrie to tell her story of what happened four years ago.

Sherrie gave her daughter to Patrick as she came down the steps to talk to the reporters. She was wearing her normal ranch clothes of jeans and blouse. She wanted to look normal and not made up for the cameras. She explained what happened and how she had been attacked.

After she finished, the TV reporter asked her, "Did you know who did this to you—attacked and then kidnapped your son?"

Without hesitation, she replied, "Yes, it was Roderick Duvall—that is D-U-V-A-L-L."

"The press release says that the suspected kidnapper was the boy's father. Is that true?"

Patrick and Sherrie knew this would come up and had thought it best to tell the truth. "My son does look like him, so biologically, yes. Since I have been married to Patrick, who is behind me, there is every indication that Mr. Duvall raped me at my birthday party seven years ago. That is all I will say on this subject."

Other questions were asked, and Sherrie responded calmly and accurately. She then closed out the interview with a plea: "Patrick Johnson Jr., if you see this, know that your father and I love you and miss you. We want you to come home to us. The man you are now with may be your dad, but he almost killed me when he took you." She started to sob and then turned away and went into the house followed by Patrick and Leigh.

An interview was also held with Paul and John at the same time. They had decided that since Paul had been the lead investiga- tor of the crime, Paul would answer questions. He described what the crime scene looked like—all the blood on the kitchen floor, the empty bedroom that JR had been taken from, and how all of his things were gone.

"Were there any witnesses?" asked the TV interviewer.

"Yes, there was one witness who gave a detailed description of the suspect and the vehicle he was driving. Unfortunately, we were not able to locate the suspect. We are still working with the FBI and hope to close this case quickly."

After the interview, John got a phone call from a detective of the Redlands PD. "Our technical guys looked over the pictures and read the report. They feel with 99 percent accuracy that the brake fluid line ruptured from a small pinhole probably caused by a nail. When she hit the brakes that last time, it blew open. The driver was murdered." "Okay, can you send me a written note on this so I can forward it to the FBI?"

"Can do, easy. You will have it by 5:00 p.m. today. Thanks for your tip on this."

John told Paul the news and that they would get a written report that afternoon for Don.

That night, on the evening news, the lead item was Sherrie's interview at her home, her tearful story reaching out to JR for his safe return. They then followed up with the interview with Paul, describ- ing the crime scene and how it affected everyone who was there. Even though Mrs. Smyth's name was not mentioned, it did talk about her statement.

The following morning, the local papers all across Southern California carried the story and the pictures of JR. All hopes for the swift return of JR now depended on the media output.

45

The next night, Josie was in the kitchen, fixing some chicken soup and crackers for JR, who was in bed, not feeling well with a low-grade temperature. She was going to take him to the doctor the next day. All of a sudden, she heard the volume on the TV turn down then nothing. Just as she was going to go out to see what was wrong, Rod came into the kitchen, his face totally white and tears in his eyes. He put his finger to his lips to tell her to keep quiet and took her out to the living room. He unpaused the news broadcast.

There on the TV screen was a computer-generated picture of JR and how he might look today. They put the closed caption on and read that the suspect was a "Roderick Duvall" who was also a suspect in an attempted murder of the mother.

Rod shut off the TV just in case JR came out. He told Josie that they needed to talk but not in the house. They could go out to the front porch. "Go check and make sure he is still sleeping. If he is awake, give him some soup and crackers along with two baby aspirin, then join me on the front porch and bring his room monitor with you. I have to do some thinking."

He went to the kitchen, poured himself a cup of coffee, and went out to the front porch with a notepad. He began putting things down by points as to what he needed to do.

Josie came out with JR's room monitor and said Rod Jr. was still sleeping and she thought his fever had broken. "How the hell did they get a picture of JR to do that new photo recognition? I thought you said you took them all and burned them."

"I don't know. I went through all the rooms to take all the photos I could see—even the ones from their bedroom and off the walls. He must have had a small one in his wallet maybe—I don't know."

"What can we do? He has to go to school. I know that tomorrow he was not going since I was going to take him to the doctor, but is that safe now? Everyone in town watches the local news. Someone will be bound to recognize him or even remember him."

Rod looked at her and said, "We have a problem, he was in the parade this year. All those guys he rode with and all the people watching him especially when he called out to you. Everyone got a kick out of that."

"What are we going to do, Rod? Both of us are going to go to jail for a long time, and you will probably get life for the attempted murder and kidnapping. JR has made me the happiest I have been in my life just as you have made me happy."

"Two things get me. One, I did not know there was a witness, and two, I did not think Sherrie would talk this soon. Somehow, she got some guts. It must have been Patrick who forced her to talk—that son of a bitch!"

"Rod, calm down. You are not young anymore. You are going to have a stroke if you do not watch it. You know you are taking blood pressure medicine now, so please, calm down."

"Okay, here is our initial plan. I will be in the den tonight, going over my military papers, his birth certificate, and the DNA test result to show I am his father."

"What about the doctor appointment tomorrow?"

"If the fever continues to break overnight, then cancel the appointment. No sense in taking him to town if we do not have to. I think he is getting better. Might be just a bug he caught at school."

He then continued, "There was no description of you. As far as the FBI or anyone else is concerned, you were not involved—directly, that is. You will have to go to town more often. If a stranger comes up, just be cool. Don't panic."

Just then they heard JR call out for Josie, so she went inside. Rod continued to try and think things out. He wrote down on his notepad a couple of key questions he had in his mind:

What about our neighbors? Will they put two and two together?

What about the Parade Committee guys? Will they remember JR in the parade?

What about the hired hands?

Anyone in law enforcement in town that I know either on first-name basis or just in passing?

Do we run?

The answers to all but the last were simple. They would just have to play it by ear. The last one was a definite no. Most likely every FBI office and law enforcement agency in the United States has the photo of JR and most likely a description of him from seven years ago.

Josie came out and sat next to Rod. "He just wanted some water and went back to sleep. I felt his forehead, and it felt a little cooler. I hope he is doing okay. I hate the idea of taking him to town tomorrow now." She then put her head on his shoulder.

Rod looked at his phone calendar and saw he had an appointment at the Cheyenne VA Medical Center the next day. He told her of the appointment that was for some routine blood tests.

"Dinner is ready. Let's go in and eat. The news is over, so we can turn the TV back on."

Rod stood up, put his arms around Josie, told her he loved her, and walked inside to eat. It felt strange not having JR with them, but he was still sleeping, so it was best. They needed to keep up a normal routine as best as they could around him. They would start a new rule—no TV during meals. That would cover the morning, noon, and early evening news broadcasts.

The next morning, the sound of the TV set being on startled both Josie and Rod. They went out to the living room to find JR up watching a cartoon tape. "Hi, I woke up feeling better, and I could not sleep, so I came out here to watch my toons. Did I wake you guys up too early?"

With a forced grin, Rod said, "Yes, you certainly did. The sun is not even up yet." He took a long look at JR then asked him how he was feeling. "You must be feeling better today, but I do not think you should go to school. We need to make sure that whatever you have is over before you go back. Okay, son?"

JR had finally learned that if his dad said, "Okay, son?" that meant there would be no argument no matter how he felt about it. Besides, he liked his mom helping him learn his numbers and alphabet.

Josie said that since they were all up, she might as well get dressed and make breakfast. "What time is your appointment, hon?" she asked Rod.

Rod was in the kitchen turning on the coffeepot. "My appointment is at ten, but I have to be there earlier to fill out some papers." They had discussed last night that they would not mention Rod's appointment at the VA to JR.

After eating pancakes and eggs, Rod went out to talk to some of the hands to let them know he would not be home that morning and to see if they said anything about JR. None mentioned the news broadcast to him. He then went back inside, kissed Josie, reminded her to call and cancel the appointment for JR. He then picked up JR, gave him a hug, and told him to mind what Josie told him and he was not to go outside; he needed to stay indoors.

Rod arrived at the Cheyenne VA Medical Center with some trepidation, wondering if anyone would pick up on the name even though it was spelled wrong. Did Sherrie do it on purpose or forgot the correct spelling? No matter, it might be to his benefit.

Rod checked in with the lab, and the clerk asked him if he had seen the news the night before about the kidnapper. "He has the same last name as yours except spelled differently."

"Yeah, there was a guy in boot camp that had the same name, and they always got us mixed up. Drove me nuts. Never saw him afterward and hope I never do again. If he did it, I hope they get him."

He then went and sat down and waited for his turn.

He had some time to kill afterward, so he went to the small Canteen Retail Store and bought an Army Veteran baseball cap to replace his worn-out one. He then went and signed in to see his primary doctor.

He was lucky he had a good provider that listened to him and did not ask personal questions like some do. She called him in and asked how he was feeling and if he had noticed anything different in his health.

"Yes, to be honest, I have noticed that I tire easily and sometimes I feel weak in my arms. I keep thinking it is because of all the work I do on the ranch. Why?"

"Well, Rod, I have to tell you I am concerned about your blood work. Your white cells are a little high, and your red cells are low. As you know, the white cells fight off infections or disease, and red cells are the energy cells. Have you had any headaches or dizziness lately?" She started scrolling through his records on her computer screen as he replied negative to both.

"Were you ever exposed to Agent Orange or other herbicide exposure?"

"There were rumors of it in Honduras, but as far as the other places I served, I have no idea. I know I spent a lot of time in the bush overseas though."

"I am going to do a consult for you to see oncology. Before you get upset, this does not mean you have cancer, but I want to make sure."

"Since I am here today, can I get in to see them today? I have a lot going on at the ranch right now."

She picked up the phone, called, explained the situation, and got him an appointment for eleven. "They will squeeze you in as a walk-in. You will need to have a follow-up, but at least you can get a quick eval this morning. That okay with you, Rod? I want to see you in one month unless I call you."

"Thanks, Doc. I will make the appointment."

Rod went to the appointment desk to check out and make the next appointment. The clerk looked at his name and asked him about the news broadcast. "Must be hell having a name like that SOB, kidnapping a young baby after trying to kill the mother. Must be a sicko."

Rod told him the same story he gave the lab tech—about the guy in boot camp—and agreed the guy must be a sick SOB. He quickly left the room and went for a quick smoke in the smoke room then went back inside to oncology.

He signed in, sat down, and read the local paper. Of course, the lead story was the kidnapping. No one knew where the child was at the present time, but all law enforcement agencies in the US were looking for him. Unfortunately—or fortunately for Rod—there was no picture of the kidnapper, only a seven-year-old description.

Rod was called in by a gray-haired doctor who asked him where he had been stationed and asked him about the herbicide again. "Your blood work is not quite what it should be. Perhaps you might have an infection. You do not have a fever. I want you to come back in two weeks for a more extensive workup."

Rod thanked him and made the appointment for two weeks, wondering if he would still be able to keep it if he was arrested and in custody by then. He got in his Jeep and drove home.

He drove by his place slowly, checking out the driveway and surrounding area to see if there were any vehicles that should not be there. Seeing none, he drove back to his place and pulled into the driveway. Seeing Josie and JR told him everything was okay.

Josie gave him a hug as he got out of the Jeep and whispered in his ear, "No visitors." She asked him how things went at the VA with a questioning look as she could tell that he was trying to formulate his response.

He bent down to pick up JR and told her that he had to go back in two weeks for some tests for the oncologist. He looked at Josie that said, "I will tell you later."

He asked how JR was, and she told him that he was fine, that maybe he should go to school the next day. "The sooner he is back in school, the less chance someone will come looking for him and cause problems in the long run, right, honey?"

Rod was amazed at how calm she looked and how levelheaded she seemed, and she did make sense. However, he also knew that they had to be smart about what they did from this point forward.

He went inside to the den and closed the door, which was a sign to both Josie and JR that he did not want to be disturbed unless it was an emergency. He pulled open a file drawer and pulled out his service record jacket that he had copied before he retired.

He went through the documents to where he had been deployed, Central America. The only place was in Honduras, when he was deployed to help the anti-Communist guerrillas in Central America in the late 1980s and early 1990s. He had also been deployed to the Middle East in support of Operation Desert Shield/Storm.

He then pulled up a list of those who served with him. Many names were crossed off, indicating that they had died. He began to wonder if he were to die suddenly how would it go for Josie and JR? If the FBI showed up, would Josie end up taking the full blame? He decided to write down a full confession so that if anything happened, she would not have to take the full burden even though she did know ahead of time of the kidnapping.

He pulled out his will to make sure it was correct and that the land was to go to Josie first and, in the event of her death, to JR. His life insurance was set up the same way.

He came out of the den and went outside to talk to the foreman, asking him how things were going and to see if there were any problems that needed to be taken care of right away.

"No, sir, everything is okay. Say, do you have anyone in your family with your same name? I saw the news report last night that the feds are looking for a Roderick Duvall. Wait, that cannot be you. You only have one L in your last name."

Rod looked him in the eye and told him, "Yeah, I hope they hurry and catch him. I worry about someone taking JR from me, but with you and the boys around, I feel pretty safe."

That night after dinner and after JR was put to bed, Josie and Rod watched some TV and talked about his VA visit that morning. Rod told her about his blood work being a little off and that he was going back to oncology in two weeks for further testing and workup. "Doc says nothing is for certain, but both my primary care doc and the oncologist want to make certain that there is nothing seriously wrong. It just might be a bad day for my blood work, that's all."

Josie snuggled up against him and told him that she noticed he had been restless for a couple of weeks. She then added, "I know you tire easily like you have a lack of energy at times."

The late news had nothing new about the kidnapping, which made Rod breathe a little easier. "Let's go to bed so we can make sure JR is feeling better and then get him off to school in the morning."

46

Five days after the news release, Paul called the Johnsons' home. Sherrie answered the phone with some trepidation as she saw it was Cold Case Investigators on the caller ID. "Johnson residence, this is Sherrie speaking."

"Sherrie, this is Paul. First off, I have no news for you. I just got off the phone with Don, and he suggested that you get a blood test to prove you are JR's mother when we find him, and we will find him. The test results will be held at the LA FBI Field Office."

"Paul, Patrick and I were talking about this same thing this morning. Where do you want me to do it?"

"I can have a lab tech here. This way we can send it directly to Don's office this afternoon. Can you do it this morning?"

"Of course I can. I will let Patrick know I need to leave now. I'll be there in an hour. Thank you, Paul."

Sherrie went to find Patrick and told him of the call and that she was going there now.

"Babe, I have done everything this morning, and Leigh is a little anxious. How about if we all go, have lunch, and then go to the mall? It's been a while since we went to the mall. Our little girl deserves a treat today."

After Sherrie had her blood drawn at the office and Janet had taken care of Sherrie Leigh, they went to a small diner where they had lunch and then to the mall.

Patrick took Leigh to the toy store so she could pick out a small kitchen she could set up in the house to be with Sherrie when she was cooking. She always wanted to help her out; now she could have her own stove.

Sherrie went to the baby store to check on a new crib and other furniture for the new baby. She saw what she liked, but she would not get it until she showed it to Patrick. The furniture was expensive. She saw what Patrick had bought their daughter and smiled. She took both of them to the baby furniture store and showed Patrick what she liked. Patrick did as well, and they ordered it.

Just as they were leaving the mall, Patrick's cell phone rang. It was Paul.

"Patrick, just to let you know ahead of time so it will not be a shock to you and Sherrie, John and I are on the local news tonight, and Don is trying to arrange us to be on one of the national morning shows hopefully tomorrow or the next day. Hopefully, this will tighten the noose around the guy, and someone will talk and turn him in." He then added, "We are reaching out to all Special Ops guys and gals that might know of anyone nearby that falls into the category of who we are looking for."

"Paul, just a thought—can the FBI access the VA files for any veteran with his last name or any variation of it?"

"Already working on it. The FBI has had to go to court for a warrant. The VA will not release any information without a warrant. He is going for information on *Duvall* and any variation to it just in case the bastard changed his name. With millions of veterans in the system, it might not be as easy as we think it will."

"Thanks, Paul. Keep me informed. By the way, remind John to not to arch his eyebrow and to shave before he goes on TV."

Paul laughed and told him that he had already told John.

As they were driving home, Patrick told Sherrie about the phone call and that Paul and John would be on the local news tonight and possibly one of the morning news shows with Don either tomorrow or the next day. All of a sudden, Leigh shouted, "Ice cream!"

Sure enough, up ahead was a Dairy Queen. They looked at each other and nodded. Leigh got a small cone, Sherrie a hot chocolate sundae, and Patrick got his favorite, a root beer float. They went and sat down. Leigh delighted in licking her fingers from her dripping ice cream while her mom and dad laughed.

After taking her to the bathroom to clean her hands and mouth, Sherrie took her to the truck and put her in the car seat in the back. Once they got home, they put her down for a short nap as she said she was sleepy. Patrick went to the front porch and got into his favorite chair, waiting for Sherrie to come out to join him.

"Babe, we definitely need to get moving to add one more bedroom. JR will need his own room. Where do you want it, on the back of the house?"

"You really think we will get him back, don't you, babe? Put his room on the backside of the house for privacy. This way the baby will not bother him."

47

That night Paul and John, along with Don, were on the local news broadcast, talking about the kidnapping and the status of the case so far. Nothing was said about Rose and her death, but Don did most of the talking since he was the FBI and had control of the investigation. Don led off with a status update as to the progress of the investigation. He mentioned that some tips had started to come in; however, all had been discounted especially those that said JR was in Asia and in Europe. "Those have been checked out, and there is no truth to those tips. We believe he is in the United States." What he did not address was the attempt to get a warrant to research the VA files for any veteran with the name of Duvall.

Paul was up next, going over everything from the beginning to the current status. "We are in constant contact with Mrs. Sherrie Johnson, the mother, to see if her son has made contract with her recently. Sad to say, he has not, but the case is not closed and will not be closed until he is returned home to his mother and father."

When prompted by the interviewer, John basically repeated what Paul had said and emphasized that they would find the person who attacked Sherrie and kidnapped her son, Patrick Johnson Jr.

After the interview, Don told Paul and John that they were to be at his office at 0400 the next morning to do a taping for one of the morning shows that would air in each time zone. "Hopefully, the other networks will pick up on it and replay it. That is what our PR folks are asking for anyway."

John told Don, "Since we have to be at your office so damn early, we have to leave here around 0230. You *are* going to have coffee and donuts, right?" Then with a laugh, "And then Lydia can fix breakfast (at your place)."

"Coffee and donuts, yes. Breakfast is either in our break room, which I do not recommend, or a local restaurant. Lydia is having so much trouble sleeping with the twins kicking her all night long she is not a happy camper when she fixes my breakfast, so I normally eat out." They agreed to meet with him at 0345 to go over what is going to be said.

"One more thing, guys—about Rose, I think we can let it out in general terms tomorrow morning but nothing specific. We will cover it in the morning. I need to get more information first."

The following morning, Paul picked up John and made a quick stop at a twenty-four-hour donut shop for coffee and arrived at the FBI office at 0345. Don was already there, and since they had time before getting ready to go on the set, they went to the break room. Surprisingly, there were several agents there eating pastries and drinking coffee. When introduced to Paul, two of them told him they had been Security Police investigators themselves "back in the day."

Don took them to a back corner and went over what he wanted John to talk about as far as Rose was concerned. "John, I want you to mention that the accident has been reopened as it is possible that her brakes were tampered with. You can say that it appears that it is connected to the kidnapping case and that they are searching for the person of interest. Do not say the name though. We want to cover that after we arrest the guy."

"Paul, you cover the initial assault and kidnapping since it was done on base and you were the lead investigator. I want you to mention the fact that there was an eyewitness who observed him at the door before he went in and when he left. I will take over from there. This morning show interview just might shake a few trees, and we might be surprised at what falls out afterward."

Paul asked him about the source that they used in the past for the last one in Cheyenne. "I am not too keen on talking about that, but he might be a key source for us after the interview."

They decided that it would be beneficial if Don spoke first followed by Paul then John and closed by Don. They each had microphones attached to their coats, and audio tests were performed to make sure they were in the right place. Just before they went live, the network news reporter clarified who was going to talk about what and that they had only five minutes to talk. "If we need to, we can record and add to the live report."

"Good morning, this is Cassandra McCoy reporting from the Los Angeles FBI Field Office. This report is about the assault and kidnapping that occurred in 1992 on Norton AFB here in Southern California. To this date, it has not been solved. With me is FBI Special Agent in Charge Donald Abernathy, Paul Gibbons, and John Sommers, co-owners of Cold Case Investigators. Agent Abernathy, let me begin with you. What is the status of the case right now?"

"Ms. McCoy, right now, as you said, the case is not solved. We are working on several leads, and we are in the process of obtaining a warrant to search the Veterans Administration files for any veteran with the last name of Duvall. I will go into more detail after the other two have finished."

"My name is Paul Gibbons, retired Air Force SMSgt. I was the lead investigator in the assault and kidnapping. When we arrived, we found the victim, Ms. Sherrie Johnson, on the kitchen floor of her on-base quarters. The medics were there, trying to stabilize her for transport to the base hospital. While interviewing her husband, MSgt Patrick Johnson, now retired as well, my partner, TSgt John Sommers, discovered that their son, two-year-old Patrick Johnson Jr., was missing along with his clothes and personal items. A search of the neighborhood was conducted with no results. Due to the crime being committed on Federal property, the FBI and the Air Force Office of Special Investigations were notified. The FBI assumed responsibility for the case with the assistance of my office, the Sixty-Third Security Police Squadron Investigations Unit."

"Good morning, Ms. McCoy, I am John Sommers, TSgt, USAF retired. I worked with Paul during the investigation immediately after we arrived. Unfortunately, I was the one who found the empty bedroom of the young boy that was kidnapped. As Paul said, a search turned up nothing. However, something has recently come to light that might shed more information on this case. A girl friend of Ms. Johnson died two years previously under what are now considered to be unusual circumstances. We are working with the local police department in this regard."

As Don began to speak, the light on the camera went off. Ms. McCoy informed them that they had to go to commercial. They would continue taping for the next half-hour segment, but that would not be live. The network desk had already informed viewers that more would be coming in the next half hour.

She urged Don to expand on the issue of the warrant. "Since it appears that the individual who committed these crimes is a veteran, it stands to reason that the VA has his name. We will be searching strictly for the name that we have at this time."

"What if that is not the correct spelling of the suspect's name?"

"Then we will have to start over again. To search for the one name is one thing. However, to broaden it to search for any similar name is too broad, and the judge may not want to sign the search warrant. We urge anyone with information to contact their local law enforcement or FBI office."

"Mr. Gibbons, do you have anything to add to what Special Agent Abernathy has said?"

"Ms. McCoy, this has been a very frustrating four years for the three of us. We have worked together since the beginning. What makes it hard is that Patrick Johnson was not only the victim's husband and father, but he was also a coworker in our office. Both Mr. Sommers here and I hold the Johnson family in high regard. We are assisting the FBI in this case, and we will find the person who did this."

"Mr. Sommers, can you add anything to what you previously said about new evidence?"

"No, ma'am, I am sorry I cannot add anything else as it is still a pending investigation by both the police and the FBI."

Ms. McCoy looked back at the camera and closed by saying, "I believe it is safe to say that the noose is closing on the person who did this. Back to you in the studio."

The camera light turned off. The mics were removed and packed, and the crew left the building. The three of them talked a bit longer, and then Paul and John left.

After having breakfast, they went back to the office to wait and see what would fall from the tree, if anything. They knew it would be at least three hours before it would be seen on the West Coast.

48

That morning, Josie made sure that JR was feeling well enough to go back to school with no temperature and no cough or sniffles. She packed him his favorite lunch of peanut butter and grape jelly sandwich, homemade chocolate chip cookies, and an apple. Both she and Rod were nervous about JR going back to school after the national news reports, but he had to go so that it would not look too suspicious if he did not go.

After the bus left, Rod went out to the fields to get everything ready for the fall, and Josie poured herself a cup of coffee and turned on her favorite morning show. The lead story was an interview with an FBI agent and two guys about a cold case kidnapping. Not being able to get hold of Rod since his cell phone was being charged, she decided to tape the show so he could watch it at lunchtime.

She knew things were coming to an end. She washed JR's clothes and packed some in his suitcase that was on the shelf in his closet. Every day, since the first news about the kidnapping, things had become harder and harder to deal with; she had come to love JR as her own son, and he would come to her when he was happy or when he was sad.

Rod came in for lunch and noticed the distressed look on her face. "Honey, what's wrong? Did something happen to JR at school today? Is he sick again?"

"No, Rod, nothing from the school, but I taped the morning show for you to see. There was a special interview with an FBI agent and two guys that were investigators on base. Watch it."

Rod fixed himself a sandwich and poured himself a cup of coffee and turned the VCR on. He munched the sandwich and drank his coffee until the commercial break. He paused the tape and looked at Josie. "What's the immediate problem, hon? Like the fed said, they are looking for Duvall with two L's. It will take them time to find out they are looking at the wrong one. Then they have to get another warrant to narrow the search."

"And then what, Mr. Know-It-All?" Josie frostily asked him.

"I have a birth certificate that shows he is my son from my deceased first wife. I have the blood test that proves it. If they come knocking with proof, I am the person they are looking for, and the game is over. We are not going to run. If we suddenly get up and leave Cheyenne, it will only cause more problems for us as it will create greater suspicion. Do I make sense?"

"I guess so, but I am scared, Rod. I don't want to go to prison for the rest of my life as an accomplice to your attempted murder of his mother and kidnapping since I knew about it. Come to think about it, I did not know what you were going to do to her, did I?"

"No, you did not know that part, but you are an accomplice to the kidnapping. Now let's watch the rest so I can get back outside. We still have work to do before winter sets in and it is starting to get cooler."

They finished watching the interview, Josie looking at Rod to see how he was taking it. He had a hard look about him, a sign that he was in deep concentration, trying to figure it out so that they could stay together.

After the interview, Rod got up and put his plate and cup in the sink and told her he was going back out to the barn to work on the old plow truck to get it ready for winter.

As he went out, he told her, "Put on a happy face before JR gets home. We need to be as positive as we can be."

When JR got off the bus at the foot of the driveway, he ran up to Josie and showed her his finger paint project he did at school.

"It's lovely, JR, we will put it on the refrigerator door and start to collect everything you do now. How was your day at school?"

"It was okay. The teacher asked me how I was feeling and if I was okay at home. I said, 'Yes, ma'am.' She is nice. I like her."

Rod came in, all dirty from working on the plow truck, which got JR to laugh. "Bath time, Dad, you're dirty!" which got them all to laugh. While Rod took his shower, Josie fixed supper, and JR was in his room reading his book out loud.

At the dinner table, Rod said things were almost ready for winter and that he needed to put up the snow fence tomorrow. JR talked about his day at school, how he liked to finger paint, and that he was chosen to read a story to the class.

Rod told him how proud he was of his being chosen to read.

"I guess having you read to us helps you out, huh?"

"Yeah, that and Wheel. Can we watch it tonight, Dad?"

"We sure can, but first you have to help clean off the table."

Rod poured himself another cup of coffee, and as they all settled in their chairs to watch Wheel, Rod turned on the TV. There was the end of the interview with Paul talking about getting the bad guy.

"What bad guy, dad?"

Without hesitation, Rod told him the bad guy was wanted for taking something that was not his and it was important enough that the FBI was looking for him.

Thankfully, that was over quickly and Wheel came on and it distracted JR from asking more questions. JR was getting quite good at this show, and Rod wondered if JR would get to be a contestant on the show after he got older.

After JR went to bed, said his prayers, and Josie listened to him read before she turned his light out, Rod and Josie talked on the front porch.

Josie's eyes were red, rimmed with tears as she hugged Rod, telling him how she was going to miss JR as she had grown quite fond of him.

"Calm down, damnit, Josie. If you do not watch it, you will make a mistake in front of JR, and then we will have problems explaining everything to him. The longer it takes, the better off we are. However, knowing the feds, I do not know how much time we have left."

"As usual, you are right. I had promised him to take him on base to the BX this Saturday to look at new clothes. He is growing so fast. What we bought him this past summer no longer fits him. We have to take the chance. Want to come with us and make a day of it for a change?"

"Yeah, it might be fun for a change. Almost all the work is done, and after tomorrow, the snow fences will be up and the truck is ready for plowing. Now let's go inside and watch TV."

* * * * *

The following Saturday, after breakfast and morning chores, Rod, Josie, and JR got into the Jeep and left to go to F. E. Warren AFB to visit the BX. While Rod and JR would get haircuts, Josie would go to the commissary, then they would have lunch in town.

After shopping for clothes, Rod and JR went to the barbershop and had to wait. There was one customer, and Rod could only see the back of the bowed head. He thought he recognized it, but he was not sure. When the head came up, he thought he would have a heart attack. He knew instantly who it was, for he had saved his life one time in the sandbox of Iraq. It was none other than Edward Wolcott, a former A-team member and a person he had not seen in over six years. Last he had heard was that he was living in Colorado Springs, Colorado, near Fort Carson. *What is he doing up here?* Rod mused to himself.

Edward's eyes grew big as he saw Rod in the mirror. "*Yup, that's him all right, that crazy mother—that I saved in Iraq*, Edward thought. After he paid the barber, he went over to Rod, put his hand out, and said, "Rod Duval. It's been six years since I last saw you. How have you been?"

Rod looked at him, shook hands, and said, "Eddie, how have you been? You look great, but I thought you lived down in Colorado Springs near the post."

"Yeah, I do. I came up here to visit some Air Force buddies.

Who is this young boy next to you?"

"This is my son, Roderick Duval Jr. We call him JR so that he knows we are talking to him and not me. He is six years old."

Rod looked at JR and told him that this was the man who saved his life when he was in the war.

JR put his hand out and shook Eddie's hand and said, "Hello, sir."

"Six? I did not know you had a son when you were in the unit. Oh well, must be my old age catching up to me now. I got to get going. By the way, you coming to the reunion next month down at The Fort?"

"To be honest, I had forgotten all about it. I will have to check the calendar and will get back with you. I have your name and address on my roster."

They shook hands, promised to keep in touch, and Eddie left. Rod told JR about the time Eddie had saved his life, and then the barber called JR up for this turn.

"Make me like daddy's hair," JR told the female barber.

She chuckled and gave him an up-and-tight cut with short on top. Afterward, she looked at Rod for his approval, and he nodded.

"Looks like a young trooper to me."

JR got down, and Rod got in the chair. She told him how cute JR was and that he was going to be a heartbreaker when he grew up. "Sure was a surprise for you to see one of your old friends, huh? Did you serve together?"

"Yes, ma'am, we served in Iraq and a few other places together. We were on the same A Team of the Tenth Special Forces Group." He then scolded himself for talking too damn much. Hope she does not watch the news much. After they were finished getting their haircuts, they waited outside the commissary for Josie. Rod got to thinking of the rotten luck to run into that asshole Eddie. He was the team intel specialist and always watched the news. *If he put two and two together, my ass is cooked for sure.* He decided to not mention his concern about Eddie to Josie. No sense in worrying her any further.

Josie came out of the commissary followed by the bagger. They all walked to the car, JR holding onto her hand as they crossed the parking lot.

He told her about Rod's friend he met in the barber shop, "He saved dad's life in the war and is a nice man."

She looked at Rod, who just nodded sheepishly and then got in the Jeep, buckling JR in the back seat. They then went to a local restaurant where they had lunch and then went home.

JR knew he had to go lie down for his afternoon nap, so he took a new comic book with him and went to his bedroom and lay down to read before he went to sleep. It had been an exciting day for him. Rod helped Josie put the groceries away as he told her about seeing Eddie in the barbershop but not about how he watched the news all the time. Then he told her about the reunion next month. "I told him I would get back with him after I checked the calendar. Do you think I should go? I haven't been since I retired."

"Why don't you say yes for now, but you also have your upcoming appointment at the VA for your testing, remember? You can always use that for an excuse to not go. To be honest, I am not comfortable at being here alone now with the news and everything."

"Good idea. I will send him a letter tonight."

49

On his way back home to Colorado Springs, Eddie thought about Rod and his six-year-old son. He did not know that Rod was married or even had a son six years ago when he retired from the Army, but there was something awfully familiar about the face of his son.

When he got home, he turned on the news and saw a report of a kidnapping six years ago from Norton AFB, California, and that it was still unsolved. One of the benefits of being a bachelor was that he could tape all the news shows he wanted to glean off them as he wanted to. This is why he was such a good intel specialist for his A team.

He watched one of the morning news shows from a few days ago, and he saw the conference with the FBI agent and the two Cold Case Investigators. When he heard the name of *Duvall*, his ears perked up. Could this be Rod?

He reached for his phone and called his cousin Ronald Overton, who was still stationed at March Air Reserve Base. This being Saturday, he hoped he could catch him at home. If not, he could leave a message.

Ronald answered the phone on the third ring. "Hey, Eddie, how are you doing?"

"Ronald, have you got a few minutes? I have another tip for you that just might be the one to finally break the kidnapping case from Norton." He heard him tell someone by the name Janet to call Paul.

"Uh, cousin, if you are busy, I can call you back."

"Not if this call is the type I am hoping it is. Go ahead."

He told Ronald about his run-in with Rod at the base barbershop and that he had a kid with him that is six years old. "Hell, I did not even know he was married or had a kid when we were on the same A team when he retired, but his last name is Duval—that is Delta, Uniform, Victor, Alpha, Lima—one L, not two like in the news reports."

Ronald took notes on what Eddie had said. "Eddie, this is the most important question. Where is he living?"

"That I do not know. Unfortunately, my unit listing is not up-to-date, and I have not heard from him since he retired. He was on F. E. Warren AFB, Wyoming, in Cheyenne. He could live any- where within two hundred miles. One other thing, he said his son went by JR, not to confuse with Roderick, or Rod as we called him. This is the best I can give you."

"Eddie, hopefully this is the jackpot. Thank you for calling me. I will pass it on to the Cold Case guys that are working with the FBI on this case. They have been working with them since day one. If you can think of more information, please call me day or night."

"Will do, and give my best to Janet, whoever she might be."

Ronald laughed and hung up. He looked at Janet and asked her if she had got hold of Paul.

"Yup, I told him what I thought it was about, and he said to call him from your home phone. He did not want to tie up my cell."

He leaned over to her, gave her a kiss, and told her it was Eddie and he may have located JR. He quickly called Paul at home and repeated what Eddie had told him. Paul asked him to come to the office and to bring Janet with him. He wanted all this written down before he called Don.

He told him he would be there with Janet in thirty.

Paul then called John and told him to meet him at the office in thirty as well. "Tell MJ you might not be home for supper tonight." Paul got there first. John showed up just before Ronald and Janet. Janet got her Dictaphone device ready to record what Ronald was going to say.

When everyone was ready, Ronald, reading from his notes, told them about the phone call from his cousin. After he was finished, he said, "I think this might be him. The name, the boy's age, and this guy is retired Special Forces. Just like we said six years ago, this guy is good. He covered his tracks well—except for today."

Paul looked at John. "His cousin helped solve a kidnapping right away by a chance encounter. Today was another one. What do you think, John, honestly?"

"Two things, boss. One, let's call Don at home and make his weekend. Two, I wish we had an office in Cheyenne. I want to get this guy, but I know the Feds want to do it, so let them. We still get credit if it is him."

"Janet, print out what you transcribed, please, then you and Ronald can go out to dinner on us tonight. Good work, Ronald. Thanks for calling me."

While they waited for Janet to finish typing the information, the three of them talked and asked Ronald what was after the Senior NCO Academy.

"I'm am hoping to get an assignment to the Pentagon. Janet does not know yet, so please do not tell her about it. She loves this area, and she loves working with you guys. I do not know how she will take it."

He continued with his future goals by telling them, "My ultimate goal is to make command chief master sergeant of the Air Force Reserve."

With this, John arched his eyebrow and asked him if he still kept all of his picture frames exactly so many inches apart.

"I try, but you know how these earthquakes are. They keep moving things on the walls same as at Norton."

With that, they all laughed, and Ronald told John he knew it was him who kept moving his frames around. "The practical joker." Janet came into Paul's office with the typed notes. Paul gave Ronald the business credit card and told him to give it to Janet after dinner.

"You don't really need to do this, Paul, but thank you anyways. Maybe we'll go to Hollywood to eat at one of the expensive places. Just kidding. I will give the card to Janet after dinner."

After the two left, Paul called Don at home and told him he hoped he had his notepad handy, that he had information on the Johnson kidnapping case. He read the notes that Janet had typed.

He then added, "Don, get this—the suspect's name is Duval—Delta, Uniform, Victor, Alpha, Lima—one L not two."

Don told him that he would contact the Cheyenne office duty agent that night and see if they could find the guy.

"No accurate address though? Two hundred miles is large area, but with this spelling, how many can there be?"

"Uh, Don, I just got to thinking—how are you going to handle the boy? He knows this scumbag as his dad for four years. Will you have someone with you to take him? I know he would not recognize Patrick or the two of us, much less his mother, but his mind is going to be messed up real bad when this goes down."

"Normally they have Child Protective Services with them. If not, I can arrange a female agent to go when we bust him."

"How will this go down?"

"Since it is a weekend, if we can find an address on this scum, we can observe his property over the weekend and then go talk to him on Monday morning. That way we will have the manpower. If it looks like the child might be in danger, then we call in local law enforcement to assist us. Stay by your office and home phones this weekend. I will call you as soon as I find out anything. And if this tip is golden, like I think it is, the tipster will receive a reward. Please do not, I repeat, do not contact Patrick yet. I do not want to build his hopes too high on this."

"Okay, and give our best to Lydia."

"I will, and my regards to both Anne and MJ.'"

"I have a feeling this is the end of the road for this case, my friend," Paul told John. "If this tip is golden, then our original thoughts were spot-on Special Ops all the way."

"Looks that way, but the problem that I see is how the kid will take it. After all, like you told Don, he knows the bastard as his dad."

"Let it go, John, let the Feds handle that. We can help out after JR comes home to Patrick and Sherrie. All of them will need help."

Since they could not do anything more now and Don had their home, cell, and business phones, they decided to go home until either Monday morning or if he were to call.

Just as they started to leave, the phone rang. Paul snatched it up right away. It was Don.

"Paul, it's a solid hit. I just got off the phone with the Cheyenne office, and they searched the local phone book. Get this—there is a Roderick Duval in Cheyenne. Yes, that's right, one L and not two."

"What's the plan now, Don?"

"We are going to put him under surveillance until Monday morning. Then we will go in after the kid has gone to school. This even gets better. The agent I spoke to knows him and his son. Seems they are on the same parade committee for the Cheyenne Frontier Days, and they all rode together in one of the parades this year."

"Will he be involved in the raid on Monday?"

"No, based on the fact that he knows him, he will not be at the door; he will be held in reserve. In fact, since he knows his son, he might be the perfect person to take custody of the boy. I think we can get him to bring him home as his escort."

"That is great news, Don. Both John and I are leaving the office now. We will both be in here at 0600 on Monday. That way you can call us as soon as you know how it goes, and we will not tell anyone of this tidbit of news."

"Sounds good. Talk to you on Monday."

50

That night, around nine, Rod came out to the front porch to have one last cup of coffee before going to bed. He noticed a few extra cars on the street but thought nothing of it as he knew there was a party up the street. They had been invited to attend but begged off. Suddenly, a tan-colored Ford slowed down to look at his home then went down the street.

"Now that might be the FBI watching me," he said out loud. "Don't do anything stupid. Don't panic. They have to prove I am the one that did it."

He drained his cup and went back inside to the den. He pulled out some documents. First, he looked at his first marriage certificate and the death certificate of his first wife, Sandra, who died in childbirth on March 2, 1990. He then looked at JR's birth certificate that showed he was born on March 2, 1990, to Roderick and Sandra Duval. He then looked at his marriage certificate to Josie. Everything was in order. Just have to wait now for them to come and question him.

He climbed into bed where Josie was reading a magazine. She looked at him and asked if everything was okay. "You look worried, and I know you were in the den just now."

"Yeah, I'm fine, hon, really I am. I was just checking on a few things like my marriage certificates, JR's birth certificate, and Sandy's death certificate. Tomorrow, I want to go over all of it with you when he is lying down in the afternoon just so you know where things are—you know, just in case." He then opened his book and started to read, but his mind would not stop.

He knew that car was a Ford Crown Victoria, the same kind the FBI uses. It must have been Eddie that called it in. "I know they will observe us for the weekend, and then on Monday morning probably with full force. They will come to see me. "I hope it will be after JR has gone to school," he thought out loud.

Josie put the magazine down and asked him what he said about JR on Monday. "You mumbled. I hope it will be after JR has gone to school."

"Oh, I was just thinking that if the FBI comes, I hope it will be when he is not home. We don't know how it might affect him if he sees several people coming at one time to talk to me, but we can't worry about it now. We need to get some sleep. If you are having problems sleeping, take a sleeping pill."

He continued to read then suggested, "How about if we go horseback riding tomorrow? You know, one more time before next week just in case things go bad for us? You can make a short-notice picnic basket, right?"

"Yeah, sure. Should we invite the Feds if they are watching us?" she asked with a sly grin on her face. "I saw you eyeballing the car as it went by. I looked out the window to see if you were on the porch." She then reached over to give Rod a hug, kissed him, said good night, and turned out her light.

Rod chuckled, shook his head, and continued to read for a few more minutes. Just before he shut off his light, he thought that if they had an extra horse, they just might invite him, but they did not.

* * * * *

The next morning at the breakfast table, Rod and Josie told JR that they were going for one last horseback ride and picnic before the cool fall weather set in. Seeing the expression on his face, Rod knew it was the right decision. He debated within himself to tell JR about the cars acting strangely on the road in front of the house that morning.

While Josie was preparing the picnic basket, Rod told JR that there were some extra cars on the road that morning, but he was to not pay them any attention. "No matter what they do, pay them no attention. They might be looking to buy some property, and they do not want anyone checking up on them. Okay, pal? Just follow what I do."

Rod and JR went out to the barn to saddle the horses as Josie brought out the picnic basket. Rod had made a special carrier to carry the basket on Josie's horse. As they mounted up, Rod took a look down the long driveway and could see a tan Ford Crown Victoria parked across the street with the driver seemingly reading the Sunday paper. That in itself made it look strange, but then they were the FBI.

Before they left, Rod went back inside to set the alarm to the house. It was a force of habit, and habits can save your life. He had learned that in the Army.

They went up their favorite trail to a hill that overlooked their land. They could see for about five miles in any direction. They ground tied their horses so they could eat the grass and ground cover while Josie spread out the blanket and watched Rod and JR play catch with a football. JR was wanting to try out with the local pee-wee football team in two years, and he was learning how to catch a pass pretty well. Josie took both photographs and video of the two of them.

JR ran over to her, gave her a hug, and told her it was her turn to play catch but with the baseball. This was something the two of them had started a year before when Rod was busy working in the fields. When she would drop the ball, JR would laugh, which caused her to make a face at him, but it was all in good fun with no stress on JR.

While they were playing catch, Rod looked down the hill toward the ranch. He could clearly see the house and the car parked across the street. He could not see any other suspicious cars around, and the one agent was still inside his car though he was looking up the hill with binoculars.

After catch, JR asked his dad to pull his reading book out of his saddlebag that he had to read before school the next day. JR had Rod and Josie lay on the ground beside him as he lay on his stomach and began to read out loud an age-old story that both of them remembered.

After reading, JR told them he was hungry.

After lunch, Rod told JR they needed to pack up and head back down so he could take his nap. JR helped Josie fold up the blanket and pick up all the trash while Rod got the horses ready.

On the ride back down the hill, JR noticed the car across the street. "Hey, Dad, is that what you told me about? That car?"

"Yup, just ignore it. I know it is hard, but just ignore it." Once they got back to the house, Rod took care of the horses while Josie took JR inside to get him ready for his nap.

"When you get up, it will be time to watch the Denver Broncos play while I fix supper."

"Yeah, we like the Broncos. Thank you for fun time today, Mom," he said before he rolled over and closed his eyes.

Joie sat at the kitchen table with a cup of coffee, staring at the stuff in the kitchen that JR liked to play with—his board games and his coloring books. Tears started to form in her eyes as she thought of how happy the little guy made her feel.

Rod came into the house and sat down next to her and put his arm around her. There was nothing he could say to cheer her up. The end was near, and they both knew it. Rod told her he was going into the den and did not want to be disturbed until JR got up to watch the game. "I am going to write Sherrie a letter that I will have the FBI give her when he is returned. If everything works out, we will have more time with him." He kissed her on the forehead and left for the den.

He pulled out the pad, and after thinking, he began to write:

Dear Sherrie,

I know that the time has come for me to pay my dues for what I did to you and for kidnap- ping your son. This letter will be delivered to you by an FBI agent upon my arrest and when your son is returned to you.

I know that I am the last person that you want to hear from, but I want to tell why I did what I did.

I knew you would be at the Brandin' Iron for your birthday in 1989; that was the reason why I was there. As you now know for certain, I put something in your drink and raped you while you were in the bathroom. Why did I do this? I wanted my son that I could not have that I always wanted with you when we were going together. You wanted to stay a virgin until you got married, but we broke up before we had a chance at marriage.

My stabbing you was not meant to kill or permanently harm you. It was to keep you quiet while I made my departure with my son. I knew Patrick would not be home until eleven for lunch as he always did. I knew his schedule and felt I could do what I did in time. As it was, I saw him turn onto the street just as I was leaving.

I want to tell you how good our son has been over the past four years. He is now in the first grade and so far is doing quite well. We started him watching *Wheel of Fortune*, and it seems he has picked up on it to the point it has helped him read and spell. We have been working with him on his numbers, and last year he was able to count to Fifteen! I know that you will be proud of him.

> I cannot imagine the hell that you and Patrick have gone through the past four years, but I have seen your picture in the papers and have seen you on television news. I see that you have daughter. She is beautiful—just like you are.
>
> Rod

He came out of the den in time to find JR sitting in his favorite chair, watching the pregame but not really paying any attention to it. "Hi, Dad, almost time for the game to begin. Mom won't be here. She is fixing supper—hamburger and mac and cheese."

After the game was over, Josie took JR to his bedroom and let him pick out the clothes he wanted to wear to school in the morning. "Mom, are you okay? You only let me pick out my clothes on special days."

"Of course I am. It is just that tomorrow is Monday, and you want to look your best at school. That sets the tone for the other kids to look their best also."

While JR took his bath, Rod and Josie went out to the front porch like normal, sat on the porch and talked. When they heard JR was out of the bath and ready for bed, they both went in without a second look at the car out front and put JR to bed.

They both went to bed at their normal time after watching the late news with nothing on that they did not already know. Tomorrow morning would come soon enough, and they both wondered if they would be in jail or free with JR for just a bit longer.

51

When his alarm went off, Rod got up and shaved and showered quickly as he knew that JR would need the bathroom as soon as he got up. He had always thought about putting in a second bathroom but never got around to it. Afterward he went and put his work clothes on while Josie got JR up.

While waiting for JR to finish dressing, Rod grabbed his cup of hot coffee and hat, went out the back door, and headed for the barn as he always did. He took a quick glance over his shoulder, surprised to not see the car parked across the street. "Maybe he got bored," he said to himself.

He went back inside to have breakfast before JR left for school. Josie had turned on the TV for the weather and early morning news. The weather was going to be a typical mid-September day, the high in the seventies, and no rain. It was chilly, so they made sure JR had his jacket with him when the school bus pulled up in front of the house.

As JR got his books, Rod reminded him, "Remember what we have told you before about strangers picking you up from school. If you do not know them, run and tell someone."

JR nodded, gave both a hug, and ran out the door and down the driveway to the bus. The driver waved at them and left, with JR waving at them as he normally did.

They waved and went back inside. Josie went to the kitchen to clean up as she normally did while Rod watched the news and then went outside. Both were waiting to see what would happen.

At nine, there was a knock on the door. Josie, as usual, looked out the front window and saw a tan Ford in the driveway and two men and a woman at the door. She opened the door and said, "Yes?" knowing full well who they were.

"Mrs. Duvall?" I am FBI Special Agent Parker, and these two are Agents Wilkerson and Young. May we come in? I must tell you we have a warrant."

"Sure, but a warrant? Why? Maybe I need to get my husband?" She moved to the kitchen door just as Rod came in.

"Honey, the FBI is here, and they have a warrant."

"I saw the car drive up, but the FBI? Why?"

"Mr. Duvall, I am FBI Special Agent Young. Do you mind if we talk to you someplace while Agent Parker talks to your wife? Afterward we would like your permission to search your home either voluntarily or by us using the search warrant we have. It is your choice, sir."

With a quizzical look, Rod replied, "Yes, of course, but can you tell us what this is all about? We can go outside or go into the den. Which would you prefer, sir?"

Young looked at him and suggested they go outside "So that Agent Parker and Ms. Duval can talk in private."

Rod offered the two agents coffee, which they declined, and he took them out back toward the barn, where the three horses were eating their hay and oats contentedly.

Wilkerson rubbed the flank of JR's pony and said that it was a beautiful horse. Then he asked him, "Mr. Duvall, do you have a child, or is this a horse for a neighbor?"

"Yes, sir, that is my son's horse, 'Pony.' He called it that just out of the clear blue sky. Kids can say the darndest things without thinking, but it has remained 'Pony' ever since then."

Young looked at Rod and asked him, "Sir, are you Mr. Roderick Duvall? How do you spell your last name, and do you go by any other names?"

"Yes, sir, I am Roderick Duval, and the spelling is D-U-V-A-L. I go by Rod or with the workers here simply as Boss."

When he spelled his name, the two agents looked at each other with a look that bordered on confusion. "Sir, did you say you spell your last name as D-U-V-A-L?"

"Yes, sir, that is correct. It has been that way all my life. My Army records even had it spelled correctly."

"Sir, what did you do in the Army? I mean what was your specialty? I myself was an MP during Desert Storm," Young said.

"I was in Special Forces, both the Fifth and Tenth Special Forces Groups before, during, and after Desert Storm. Why do you ask?"

"Sir, you mentioned your son. How old is he now?"

"He is six years old. Why?"

Wilkerson asked, "Sir, do you know a Ms. Sherrie Johnson?"

Rod had what he hoped was a look of concentration on his face as if he were trying to remember a name or a face of females he knew in the past. "No, sir, name does not ring a bell. Why, is someone trying to hit me up with a paternity lawsuit or something?"

Wilkerson replied, "No, sir, nothing like that."

Young then said, "I have two questions, and then maybe we can go inside to look through your house. The first question is have you been to Southern California within the past ten years, and two, how long have you had your ranch here in Cheyenne?"

"No, I can't say that I have been to Southern California in the past ten years. Let's see, I retired from the Army in 1992. I saw the place up for sale around 1990 when I visited Cheyenne during frontier days and I was stationed at Fort Carson in Colorado. I put down a down payment then—so six years now. I have the paperwork inside with the exact date."

"I'm sure you do," Wilkerson mumbled out loud.

Young asked if they could go inside to look at his papers and look through the house if he did not mind.

Rod led the way inside through the kitchen. They heard Josie and Agent Parker talking down the hallway in what appeared to be JR's bedroom, with Josie sounding calm and collected.

They went into the den, and Rod showed them the paperwork on the property sale in 1990. They then asked to see his marriage certificate to Josie and JR's birth certificate. They both watched him closely for any signs of nervousness or undue sweating as he went to the safe and pulled out the certificates they had asked for. "May I ask what this is all about? You never really told me outside."

Young told him that they were investigating a crime from six years ago and that he fit the profile, but so far nothing had been proven. "What happened to your son's mother? Your marriage certificate says you are married to Josie in 1991."

"Yes, sir. JR's mother died at childbirth. Here is a copy of her death certificate. You can see that her death is the same day as JR's birthdate."

Young gave the documents to Wilkerson. "Sir, do you mind if we copy these documents and take them with us? They might prove beneficial to clearing your name. You see, the person we are looking for is a Roderick Duvall, with two Ls. You have only one L. I believe this clears up the confusion. If we have any more questions, we will be in touch."

Rod made the copies, escorted them to the front door, and told them that he hoped they find who they are looking for.

Rod and Josie went into the kitchen as if Rod was getting his cup of coffee before going back outside while waiting to hear the car leave. Once they heard the car start up, Rod looked at Josie and told her to call him back inside in a couple of minutes for a phone call. He grabbed his hat and went out to the barn, looking at the Ford leaving the driveway with all three FBI agents.

A couple of minutes later, Josie called Rod to tell him he had a phone call—only it was a genuine phone call from JR's school. They wanted to know if everything at home was okay as there had been an FBI agent asking questions about JR.

"What type of questions did this agent ask," Rod asked the school secretary.

"He wanted to know if there were any unexplained bumps or bruises on him and if there were any unexplained absences. I told him that he had been sick last week, but he was absent only two days and there are no marks on him."

"Everything is fine, thank you. If anyone else comes asking questions, please contact me immediately, and I will come to the school and answer their questions. Did this agent give his name?"

"Yes, sir, he did. He said his name was Special Agent Parsons. I asked him for his ID before I answered his questions."

"Thank you, ma'am. I can assure you everything is okay here. It is mix-up with my last name. Nothing to worry about."

At the name of Parsons, his face turned white. After hanging up, he looked at Josie and told her to sit down; they needed to talk. "That was a call from the school. It seems my old Parade Committee pal Parsons is an FBI agent out of Cheyenne. He was at the school asking questions about JR to see if there were any unnec- essary absences or bruising on JR. I did not know he was an FBI agent; he was quiet about his job. I never pressed him on it."

He then asked her to tell him about what the FBI female agent talked about.

"She was very pleasant and asked me about JR's health and what type of boy he was. She then wanted to look at his room and the bathroom. I told her that JR was a good boy, never causes us any problems, how he likes to help me around the house and how he tries to make his own bed in the morning. I did not have a chance to straighten it up this morning though." She took a deep breath and continued.

"She then looked in his closet, moving things around a little but nothing major, then went into the bathroom. She could see where we have the small stool for him to stand when he brushes his teeth and wash his hands after going to the toilet. Then she took some pictures of his room, closet, and bathroom. Is this normal, Rod?"

"Yes, since they did not want to use the search warrant. My guess is it was just a cursory check and that that they will be back later this week to execute the full-blown search warrant. We will not change anything. They have already looked around the house. They know what they are looking for."

Rod took a gulp of coffee and then told her what they asked him outside, the interest in Pony, then in the den and what they wanted photocopied. "I think it will take a couple of days for them to check out the death certificate and his birth certificate. We need to be strong and ready for whatever happens."

Just then the phone rang again. They looked at each other with concern. Could it be the school again? Could it be the FBI?

Rod answered the phone. "Yes, this is Mr. Duval. Oh, hi, doc, what can I do for you this fine September day?" He listened with concern etched on his face.

"Yeah sure, I can be there in an hour. Do you want to talk with Josie as well when I come in? Okay, I will see you then."

Rod put the phone down, faced Josie; and with an ashen worried look on his face, he told her that the oncology doctor at the VA wanted to see him. "He said that until he talks to me and explains things, he does not want to see you with me. I think it would be best for you to be here in case the FBI comes back and wants to use the search warrant. If they do, do not stop them or get in their way. Let them search, and only help if they ask for it."

With tears in her eyes, Josie asked him, "Rod, what is wrong? What did the doc say is wrong with you? What if the FBI comes back and they want to search and they want to get inside the safe? I do not have the combination to it. You never gave it to me."

"Honey, all he told me was that he needed to talk to me about my blood work. He deals with cancer of all types, so until I see him, I do not know what is wrong with the blood test." He then gave her the combination to the safe in the den. He knew she would not go into it unless there was an emergency. With this unexpected news from the doc, now was the time to know it.

Just before he left, he jotted down a phone number and told her, "If they do come back and want to execute the warrant, call this number. It is my personal attorney.

52

Parker, Young, and Wilkerson took the photos and documents back to the Cheyenne FBI Field Office to study and discuss with Parsons since he knew Mr. Duval.

"I find Rod to be a smart, intellectual, loving father and husband who loves his ranch and Cheyenne in general. He is supportive of local veterans organizations and, of course, the Cheyenne Frontier Days Parade Committee." Knowing that Young is the aggressive agent, he asked him what he thought of Rod.

"I found him to be very accommodating, very quick with his responses to our questions—maybe too damn quick for me. It was almost as if he had practiced in front of a mirror on how to respond to us."

Wilkerson had the same thoughts. "He also seemed too glib in some of his comments. Something just does not ring true with what he said in his den."

Parker, after listening to what the other two had to say, put in her observation of Josie. "I found Mrs. Duval to be charming, smart, and articulate. She had no problems showing me the boy's bedroom or the bathroom, even the stool he stands on to wash his hands or to brush his teeth. He helps her around the house and even attempts to make his bed before he leaves for school."

She paused to look at her notes then continued, "She told me that she and Mr. Duval work with the boy every night on his reading and his spelling. He even tries to spell out the answers to *Wheel of Fortune*. I found no evidence of child abuse in that home. All I could find and feel was pure simple love."

Wilkerson pulled out the photocopied documents from Rod's safe. They laid them all out: JR's birth certificate, Rod's first wife's death certificate, his current marriage certificate, and the ranch paperwork. "I think we need to check out his first wife's death certificate and the boy's birth certificate from Indiana. Something is not right here—I feel it in my old bones."

Parsons said he would get on it right away.

Wilkerson said he would check into the current marriage certificate and the ranch situation.

Young said he would get in touch with SAC Abernathy in LA and see if he could check out the correct spelling of Duval's last name. He also wanted to check on the status of the warrant issue for the VA files. "I have a strong feeling we will find our person of interest right here in Cheyenne."

While the other agents went to work on their assigned tasks, Young got on the phone and called Don. He explained to him that they had been out to see the person of interest. However, there was a problem. "Seems he spells his name Delta, Uniform, Victor, Alpha, Lima. Yes, that's right—one Lima, not two that we were told to check out. All the paperwork shows it. He also spells his name Romeo, Oscar, Delta, Echo, Romeo, Charlie with no Kilo. Can you dou- ble-check with your sources to check on correct spelling?"

"I will get on it as soon as we hang up. I am working with a cold case private investigator who has been on this case since the very beginning. He knows the victim well, and I will contact him today and get back to you as soon as I can. Anything else?"

"Yes, there is, Don. What is the status of the search warrant? I would like to check out the local VA Medical Center tomorrow if I can get the warrant."

"Bob, no need for you to do it. We got the warrant this morning. It was issued in Washington. They are going through the master files now at the Department of Veterans Affairs. Hopefully, we will have the information by tomorrow. I will let you know the proper spelling as soon as I can get it. Keep me informed."

"Guys, the warrant to search the VA database has been issued and served in Washington. They are now searching their files for this perp. As for the correct spelling of the person of interest, Don is working with a cold case private investigator that has been on this case since the very beginning. He will let us know as soon as he finds out."

Wilkerson gave out a loud snicker and remarked, "What we now have to depend upon is a so-called cold case private investigator? Since when did the FBI farm out its investigations?"

"Wilkie, it is a long story. I have it straight from Don that he has worked with these guys since the crime was committed at Norton AFB back in 1992. He trusts these guys, and I trust him. Now can the sarcasm, and let's all work together to find this perp," Parsons told him.

Wilkerson discovered a flaw in the documents. "Hey, guys, listen to this. According to the Indiana Bureau of Statistics, 'Mrs. Duval did die on 2 March 1990'—that checks. However, they also show that her son, Roderick Duval JR, died two days after birth. If this is true, this must be the original birth certificate of his deceased son."

Parsons asked him, "Okay, what else have you found on this guy's marriage certificate?"

"He did marry her in 1989. He married the current Mrs. Duval in January 1992 just before the kidnapping. This scum is a real piece of work."

"Keep digging, guys. This piece of crap is going down on our watch. I want him picked up *after* we are 100 percent certain this is him. I want all the I's dotted and T's crossed. He will not, I repeat, will not get out on a technicality. Once we have both of them in custody, neither one will see freedom as far as I am concerned." This from Parsons, normally a stoic demeanor.

After telling them to get back to work, he called Don and brought him up-to-date on what they had found out.

53

After receiving the phone call from Parsons, Don called Paul and filled him in on the confusion of the spelling of the last name. "I went over the video and the audio tapes several times, and she spelled it with two L's. Was it an honest mistake, or did she do it on purpose? Paul, you know her and Patrick. What do you think the hell is going on here?"

"Don, it is possible she was rattled and made an honest mistake. I will call Patrick and see if they will both be home and I will go talk to her. On another note, John wants to talk to you."

"Don, this is John. I got off the phone with Riverside PD on Rose's accident. They told me that based on the pictures and the written technical inspection, there is a quote 95 percent probability that the brake hose was intentionally punctured unquote. They have revised their finding on the information we gave them plus their own review. Can a charge of murder be included in the federal charges?"

"That will have to be seen. It may be murder or it may be manslaughter, but he will pay for it."

"Don, this is Paul again. Another point to consider is if, in fact, he was still on active duty even though on terminal leave and he committed these crimes, he can be brought back to active duty and court-martialed at least for attempted murder and assault plus kidnapping."

"Paul, that is a good point. I think that considering the crime was on a military installation, he should be. I can almost guarantee he will not see daylight from Leavenworth. Let me know what you find out from Sherrie on the spelling of this scumbag."

After Don hung up, Paul called Patrick and explained the problem to him. He told him that Sherrie had a doctor's appointment that morning but should be home around 1:00 p.m. "To be honest, Paul, I do not know why she would do it on purpose. She must have been rattled, talking to Don and being on video and audio. Do you want me to ask her?"

"No, I think it be best if I asked her. Do you want me to bring Anne with me? I can bring one of the boys over to babysit, and the four of us can go out to dinner. Or would you rather use your own babysitter?"

"I would prefer our own babysitter if we went out. Sherrie Leigh is very comfortable with her. They get along well—almost as if they were sisters."

"Okay, be there around 1330. Come to think about it, if Sherrie is up to it, how about a gentle ride after I talk to her then go out?"

"We will see when she gets back. It will be good to see you again, Paul, even considering the circumstances."

* * * * *

When Sherrie arrived home, Leigh was taking her nap, so Patrick took her outside to the front porch and told her about Paul coming over to talk to her. "He is coming with Anne as well. If you are up to it, how do you feel about a horse ride with them then out to dinner? I am sure we can get Betsy to babysit."

"The doc says everything is okay with me. All is normal with the twins. Yes, Patrick, twins. He does not know how he missed them. One must have been behind the other. He thinks they will be boys but not sure yet. To be honest, I do hope they are boys." She then asked him, "What does Paul want? And I would enjoy going for a ride. I can talk with Anne, and dinner with them would be nice—but not at that bar."

Since she had come forward with the information, it was decided between the two of them that the name of the bar would not be mentioned nor did she ever want to go back there.

Paul and Anne arrived at the ranch exactly at 1330. It had been decided that after Paul talked to Sherrie and called Don, they would go for a ride and then go out to eat dinner. Patrick had already called Betsy, and she would be there around two thirty.

* * * * *

Patrick and Anne went out to the stables while Paul talked to Sherrie. Anne asked Patrick how Sherrie was holding up especially since she was pregnant.

"She saw her doc today. He says everything is fine. The twins are coming along fine, and he thinks they might be boys. I tend to agree as big as she is. She was the same with JR." As soon as he said that, Anne could see the sadness in his eyes. "But please do not say anything to her I told you. I think she will want to tell you herself." In the house, Paul told Sherrie the problem with the spelling of Rod's last name. "Sherrie, during the questioning by Don about your attacker, you said the person's name was Roderick Duvall, with a K at the end of his first name and two L's at the end of his last name. They found a person of interest."

"Where? Does he have our son?"

"Sherrie, you know that I cannot tell you where or if JR is there or not. However, the names do not match with the spelling you gave Don. I want you to think hard about the spelling of his first and last name. It is very important. Perhaps you were a little rattled talking to Don—I understand that—but think hard, please."

Sherrie thought about it, took a pad and pencil, and wrote down different ways his name could be spelled. Finally, she wrote out the name *Roderick Duval*. "Paul, this is it, this is the actual spelling of the bastard. You are right. I was rattled. What's next?"

"Let me use your phone so I can call Don. He is at his office waiting for my call. By the way, he says that the twins are kicking the shit out of him every night, and he will be glad when they are born so he can get a decent night's sleep. I told him he was really dreaming." As Paul dialed Don, Sherrie started to laugh at the thought of Don being kicked out of bed by his unborn twins and thinking he would get a decent night's sleep after they are born.

"Don, this is Paul. I just talked to Sherrie. She admits that she was rattled, and she wrote out the correct spelling of the guy's name." He spelled it out for Don, who repeated it back to him. He then told Don he had his cell phone and the plans the four of them had for the afternoon and evening.

Afterward they went out to the stables where Paul told Patrick what was going on and the problems Don was having with his unborn twins. "He really thinks he will get a decent night's sleep. He will definitely be surprised."

Patrick looked at Sherrie and asked if she still wanted to ride.

She smiled and said yes, and as Patrick and Paul got the horses ready, Betsy arrived. They told her the plans and that it was time to get Sherrie Leigh up.

"We will be back before we leave to get out what to fix her for dinner tonight. Hope you like mac and cheese. This was kind of the spur of the moment."

Betsy said no problem and went inside to wake up Leigh. Sherrie looked at Anne and told her that Betsy was the daughter of a neighbor and that she got along with Leigh almost like they were sisters. She also told Anne about her doctor's appointment and that the doctor had said that she is pregnant with twins. "If you look at the size of me, it probably will be boys. We both hope so. Next month, I will have the ultrasound done to see for sure."

They rode at a slow pace with Patrick pointing out the features of the ranch and what the future plans were. He told them that he wanted to take about ten of his now fifty acres and make it into a campground for kids from troubled homes and those from sin- gle-parent homes. The area he had picked out included a fairly deep pond that he wanted to enlarge. "However, the problem is with the city. Permits up the gazoo. Hell, all I want to do is help kids and show them a good life."

"Speaking of building, what are you going to do for a new bedroom? Especially when JR comes back."

"Sherrie and I talked about that. We have done up plans for two bedrooms—one for the twins and one for JR. We know that JR is old enough for his own bedroom now. We also need to add a bathroom. Six people and one bathroom is kinda tight."

"John and I can help. We know a former Army combat engineer that helped us remodel our building. I'm sure he will help out. I'll get him to contact you. His name is Bob Youngston. He was the town building inspector. He is good."

"That would be great, Paul. Thanks. By the way, how are the kids doing?"

"Richard leaves for the Air Force Academy next year. I am really proud of him. Robert is still dating John's daughter, Shawna. Both John and I are holding our breath and hoping they will graduate from college before getting married. Robert gave her this thing called a 'friendship ring'—whatever the hell that means. All four of us are happy with that."

The four of them rode back to the stables, with Sherrie and Anne talking about her pregnancy and skirting around the issue of JR. Paul had told her what the status was after hearing from Don. He knew she would not say anything to Sherrie.

When they got back, Paul suggested that the ladies go inside as he needed to talk to Patrick in private.

As they unsaddled the horses, Paul told Patrick that his idea for a camp for troubled kids was a good idea and if he could help him out, he would, and he knew that John would as well.

"Paul, I know you. You have something to say, so say it. I know Sherrie screwed up, but there is something else you want to tell me, so say it."

"Patrick, Don asked me a question this morning, so I did some research. I had to dig out my old *Uniform Code of Military Justice*, which I am thankful has not changed since 1974. The crimes against Sherrie were all done while this guy was still on active duty."

"Which UCMJ Articles, Paul?" Patrick asked with steel in his eyes.

"Let me put them in order. Articles 120—Rape, 118—Murder, 182—Assault with Bodily Harm, 119A—Death of Unborn Child, and 134—Kidnapping. Possibly others as well. Put them all together—this guy is dead meat."

"And Sherrie? Will she have to testify?" However, before Paul answered, he added, "Disregard. That was a stupid question."

"Yeah, she will, but not until after the twins are born unless someone wants to rush it, but I don't see them wanting to endanger the twins or Sherrie for that matter. That might be up to Sherrie though."

"All we got to do now is wait and see what happens with the information she gave to you this afternoon. Any idea where this scumbag is located?"

"Patrick, you know better than to ask me that question, and the answer is no, I do not know exactly where he is."

"Okay, let's go get the girls. I'm hungry, and since it was my idea, I pay tonight. You leave the tip."

Laughing, Paul said, "We are not going to that steak house again, are we? I know it can't be a burger place. They don't accept tips." Slapping each other on the back, they went inside to get the girls.

54

After Paul called Don with the correct spelling, he contacted Ben Parsons at the Cheyenne, Wyoming, FBI Field Office. "Ben, the correct spelling of the suspect's first is Roderic—that is Romeo, Oscar, Delta, Echo, Romeo, India, Charlie. Last name is Duval—that is Delta, Uniform, Victor, Alpha Lima. Actual location is unknown, but I feel the one you guys talked to earlier is him."

"Anything from the VA yet? From the case, I gather this guy is good, but he cannot hide in the VA system. As for his property, that is all legal and valid. However, it turns out that when his first wife died, his son died two days later—and get this, the dead son's name was Roderick Duval Jr."

"One more thing, since this happened while he was still on active duty, I presume that the Army will bring his sorry ass back to active duty and then court-martial him on four or UCMJ articles. Who in your office served in the military?"

"Young was in the Army. I was in the Air Force, working in the Legal Office."

"Ben, you are it then. I want you to research the following articles of the *Uniform Code of Military Justice* for me: Articles 118, 119, 119A, 120, 128, and 134. Article 118 is iffy at best. It all depends on the information we get from the jurisdictional PD on what happened in 1989. If the US Army cannot charge him with murder, then manslaughter will have to do. In any case, do not, I repeat, *do not* mention the UCMJ to him. All we want him for right now is assault and kidnapping. The rest is icing on the cake."

"Don, 119A? That is Death of an Unborn Child. Where is this one coming from?"

"I am sending you all the information with another agent. If my wife were not having problems with her pregnancy, I would be there. Remember, do not discuss the UCMJ with this guy until we have him in custody and arraigned. Make sure everything is by the book." "This guy is not a flight risk. I know him. Young, Parsons, and Wilkerson will pick them up tomorrow morning after the boy goes to school. I will pick up the boy after school when I pick up my son. He knows me."

"Okay, this way you will have a chance to go over the whole file. I will be glad when he is in custody. But knowing how he got away with it, watch him closely—he is good at evasion. My sources tell me he was Army Special Forces. Be careful."

Parsons looked at his crew and told them they would take the Duvals down tomorrow. "I will pick up the boy after school tomorrow. The three of you will go in at 0900. The charges will be assault and kidnapping. Do not say anything extra to them. I will take care of the arrest warrants this afternoon with the US attorney. Any questions?"

Young asked about the status with the VA.

Parsons replied that they were searching through the files now in Washington.

Parsons got on the phone with the US attorney. He explained to him what was going on and that they should have the complete file within three hours or so and he would like to see him that afternoon at 1500 to obtain the arrest warrants.

At eleven, the FBI agent from the LA office arrived with the case file. As he read it, all he could do was shake his head.

"Guys, this one is a real scumbag. He fooled the best that the LA office has to offer for six years. If this sh—gets out, the FBI will be a laughingstock of the country."

At 3:00 p.m., Parsons met with the US attorney and went over the case file with him. He shook his head and verified that all they want was to initially arrest Mr. and Mrs. Duval for assault and kidnapping.

"Yes, sir, the other charges will be tacked on before the court-martial. If the Army does not court-martial the SOB, then I am sure the government can add on everything else since it was a federal crime. In either case, he is going to be locked up for life and in protective custody since he killed an unborn child and kidnapped the two-year-old boy."

"Protective custody—I hate that, but hey, even prisoners have some rights regardless of the crime."

Parsons left with arrest warrants for both Rod and Josie Duval on both counts. Parsons was thinking of the free press that the Cheyenne office would receive from not only local but national and international coverage as well.

He got back to the office and told his crew to be in by 0700 to get ready.

"We have the warrants. We pick them up tomorrow morning at 0900. The US attorney will be waiting to have them arraigned in Cheyenne Federal Court shortly after we have them in custody."

55

That same morning, Rod met with the oncologist at the Cheyenne VA Medical Center. When he checked in, he noticed the clerk giving him a wary look that caused Rod's anxiety level to climb. However, he did not notice any VA security around, so he relaxed a little, waiting to see the doc.

When he was called in, the doc told him that after further reviewing his blood tests and his complaints that he was bruising easily and being more tired than normal, the good news was he did not have cancer of any kind. The bad news was they did not know what was causing his problems. "Considering the fact that you were around herbicides in different parts of the world, you do not have any indications of effects from it. However, I would strongly suggest that you put yourself on the registration list in case something comes up."

"Okay, so what is next, doc? I have a six-year-old son that is active, and I have a working ranch."

"What I am going to do is have your primary care provider give you some medication to counter your bruising. For lack of energy, I am going to suggest that you be put on vitamin B-12 injections. It can be done here at what we call the Open Nurse Clinic. In other words, you come in and wait for an opening, which takes up a lot of time. Once you know how to do it, you can do it at home on your own. You will have three months' worth with four refills."

"I was a medic on my A team. I can give shots, but I cannot do it in my arms. Can I do it in my legs?"

The doc smiled and told him he could give it to himself in his thigh muscles if he preferred. "That should improve your red cells and give you the energy you need on a daily basis. However, the shots are only once a month, normally around the same day of the month."

"I'll take the first one here. Thanks for the good news. I needed it today."

The doc told him he did not need to come back to see him unless his provider thought he should. He also told Rod that his provider would have blood tests done every ninety days to monitor his red cells.

Rod saw the nurse, who gave him the injection of B-12 and then told him to go to the pharmacy and pick up the medicine. "Your script will include three syringes, B-12, and alcohol pads. If you have any questions, just give us a call. We will be glad to help you, sir."

After Rod picked up his new prescription, he left for home. Arriving home, he told Josie the good news that what was wrong was not extremely bad, "Just a royal pain in the thigh," so to speak. All in all, it was not a bad day there. No one had questioned him on his name. He asked her if there were any visitors, noting that there was a strange car parked down the street that he did not recognize.

"No one came to the door or on the property. The same mail-man we have had for months delivered the mail to the box at the end of the driveway. I did notice that strange car earlier today. There was a female in it the last time I looked. Do you think it might be the FBI? If so, what the hell are they waiting for? This waiting is driving me nuts."

"If it is the FBI, they must have called in outside resources. She did not look like the one that was here yesterday. What time will JR be home? Normally, I am out when he comes home. I want to surprise him when the bus stops." He then told her he was going to call his attorney and have him come by in the morning around eight thirty. "Just in case the FBI shows up again."

"The bus should be here in about half an hour. I normally meet him at the end of the driveway. Why don't you do that for a change? I am sure it will make his day."

Rod was on the porch with his ever-present coffee cup when he spotted the bus coming down the road. He got up and went down to the base of the driveway and waited until the bus stopped.

JR saw him through the window and waved at him. He stepped down and ran into Rod's arms with his big grin and said, "Hi, Dad. Is Mom okay? She normally meets me here."

"No, she is okay. I just wanted to surprise you for a change, to do something different." As they walked back to the house, Rod asked him how school was today.

JR looked up at his dad, smiled, and told him he got an A on his first spelling test. "It was easy. I only had to spell five words. Let me show Mom, okay, Dad?"

"Okay, son. She is waiting for you up on the porch."

JR ran up to Josie on the porch and proudly told her he got an A on his first spelling test "even if it was only five words."

Josie looked at him, gave him a hug, and told him it was great news. Maybe she should bake some cupcakes to celebrate and he could take some to school tomorrow. Josie went into the kitchen to start making cupcakes—his favorite yellow with white frosting with multicolor sprinkles on top. Somehow she knew they would not be able to enjoy them the next day, so might as well let JR take some to school. After all, other moms did the same thing.

That night everything was normal, with JR doing some numbers with Rod before dinner. After dinner, Rod and JR played checkers, each enjoying a cupcake. They watched Wheel, then JR went and took his bath and got ready for bed.

In bed, before he read his book to them, he said his prayers and asked God to protect his mom and dad especially now that his dad was sick and had to have a shot every month. He read to them, showing how well he could now handle words, large and small, with only a little help. He then gave them each a hug and said good night.

They both grabbed their jackets since it was now getting cool and went out to the front porch. Rod was the first to talk.

"Honey, I have a feeling tomorrow is going to be the day. This will be the last evening the three of us will be together and definitely the last night for us to be together. I might be wrong, but just in case, know how much I do love you."

Before she could say anything, he continued, "There will probably be things said that I did do that might be correct, things that you do not know about. It is best that you do not know about them so that you cannot be charged as an accessory after the fact. The assault and kidnapping, yes."

"What else, Rod? What else did you do that could connect me to this crime?"

"Like I said, the less you know, the better you will be in the long run. Now let's go watch a movie before we go to bed."

After a movie that had a touch of romance in it, they turned out the lights and went to bed. After they were in bed, Rod told her to not overplay in the morning. "Just be normal and then put the cupcakes in a box and carry them down to the bus stop when you walk JR down, 'kay?"

"Do you think we should have your attorney here tomorrow after he leaves for school?"

They rolled over toward each other, and she told Rod how much she loved him. He told her that he loved her and how happy he was with the way she had accepted JR and loved him as much as he did. They both went to a troubled sleep.

56

On time, the bus came by and picked up JR. Josie gave the box of cupcakes to the driver and asked her to take them into his classroom for him, telling her that they were for his class because she liked to bake them. The driver said it would be no problem.

As Josie walked up the driveway, she heard a car behind her. With alarm, she looked over her shoulder, expecting to see a carload of FBI agents. Instead, it was one silver-haired male, about fifty, who waved at Rod on the front porch. Rod came down and introduced him to Josie as Mr. Perkins, his lawyer.

"Ray, this is my wife, Josie. Come on in. Would you like a cup of coffee and a cupcake left over from last night? I know it is early, but I have a feeling it is going to be a long day for all of us."

Perkins greeted Josie and agreed to the offer of a cup of coffee. After he took his first sip of coffee and bit into the cupcake, he told Josie that Rod had told him what might happen today. "I know what the trouble is. Tell me what you know."

Josie told him of her involvement in waiting for Rod in Sacramento four years ago after he assaulted his son's mother and kidnapping his son. "That's all I know—honest, sir." She then told him of the drive to Cheyenne and the loving household they had set up for JR.

"That is fine. Just don't say anything, no matter what they say. After they give you the Miranda, decline to make a statement until you have a lawyer present. If this goes down, I will get you an attorney. It will be hard for me to defend both of you. Josie, do you understand what I am saying?"

"Yes, sir, I understand, but can we afford two good attorneys?"

"Yes, honey, we will. If we get arrested, the ranch will be sold. Ray here has all the paperwork to sell it."

They sat there, drinking coffee and talking about the ranch. Rod showed Ray and Josie the letter he had written to Sherrie for Ray to give to the FBI to give to Sherrie when JR was sent to his mom in California.

Josie asked about JR's horse, Pony. "Do you think he would want it, or will it remind him of you and me?"

"I don't know, hon. It could work either way for him. He is young enough, and I think he is strong enough that he will recover. Pony might be the right kind of therapy he might need."

Ray mentioned the fact that even though he was not into mental health, Pony might be good for JR. "However, we do not know how it will be with his mother and father."

With that comment, Rod bristled at the thought that Patrick would be considered to be JR's father. "I am JR's father. The blood tests prove it, and he looks like me, not Patrick."

"That may be true. However, you did take him from the parents on his legal birth certificate, and you know it," Josie told him, herself getting upset.

Just then they heard some cars pull up the driveway, multiple footsteps on the porch, and the doorbell rang.

Josie got up to answer the door. She recognized the three FBI agents from the day before. She also noticed there was a van behind the Ford Crown Victoria. "Agent Parker, good morning. What can I do for you today?"

"Mrs. Duval, we are here to execute a search warrant of your entire property. We ask for your cooperation in letting us do our search. Is your husband home?"

"Yes, he is." Josie stepped back and let Parsons, Young, and Wilkerson enter the house.

Rod and Ray both stood up. Ray introduced himself, asking to see the search warrant as he was Rod's lawyer. "What is it you are exactly looking for, Agent Parker?"

"Sir, we are searching for evidence of a crime that we are investigating. Just be seated, and we will not take long. If we need anything, we will ask you to come into the room that we are in."

The three of them sat in the kitchen, with Josie and Rod acting nervous, which would be normal. Ray, on the other hand, was talking about business in town that was going on and the plans for updating his office. Agent Young came out of the den, came into the kitchen, and asked Rod to come with him.

They went to the den, where Young asked Rod to open the safe that was in the closet. "Just unlock the combination and step back, please. Do not open the door."

Rod unlocked the combination and stepped back just as he was told to do. As he did so, he was thinking, *Either they think the safe is booby-trapped or I have a gun in there and they do not want me to pull it out on them. That would be totally stupid of me to do.*

Agent Young asked him, "Do you have any other safes or locked lockers in the house?"

"Only a rifle safe in my bedroom closet, sir. I also keep my son's BB rifle in there along with my ammunition and his spare BBs. This way my son cannot come into contact with them."

Young told him to stay there as he pulled out everything from the safe—life insurance, checkbooks, the certificates they saw the last time, and so forth. He put the certificates into a paper sack and stapled the top and marked it with the date, time, and his initials.

Young motioned to Rod to lead the way to the master bedroom and to unlock the rifle safe and to step back just as before.

Rod looked at him as he pulled out his .30-30 and .30.06 rifles. He then pulled out the BB rifle that belonged to JR. "This your son's rifle?"

"Yes, it is. He likes to have it in his rifle scabbard when he goes horseback riding with us. He thinks he is a real cowboy then."

Young made sure the chambers were empty and tagged all three rifles. He then put the boxes of ammunition and BBs into separate paper sacks and stapled and marked them as well. "Okay, sir, you can go back to your wife now."

Wilkerson came out to tell them that he and Young were now going out to the barn and the shed. He asked Rod to come with them.

Rod looked at Ray, who nodded yes. He would stay with Josie while the female agent finished in the house. They went to the barn, where both agents went through the tack room and used the pitchforks through the hay to see if anything was hidden in the hay piles. Finding nothing, they then went to the shed where the plow truck was parked with the snow plow attached to the front.

They thoroughly went through all the drawers and cabinets, finding only garage-type tools and farm tools, clean and put away in order. "You really take care of your tools, don't you, sir? I mean I have seen some guys that do not clean them after they get finished with them nor do they put them back where they belong. I am impressed." "Thank you, sir. One thing I was taught in the Army was take care of your equipment, and it will take care of you when you need it most. I just applied it after I retired."

They finished looking around and then spotted a shed behind the barn. It was not a large building, about ten feet tall, with a pitched roof and about four foot by six foot. It had a single door in it with a quarter-shape moon on it. Wilkerson asked, "Is that what I think it is?"

"Yes, sir, it is an old-fashioned outhouse, and it is still used even today. I use it instead of tramping in the mud when I am working out here. You can check it out. It was emptied yesterday."

Young opened the door and peered inside, quickly backed out, and told Wilkerson, "Clean as a whistle. Even has a fresh roll of toilet paper, hand wash, and paper towels. Even has a current issue of *Sears Roebuck Catalogue*."

They told him they were finished outside and they could go inside now. As they went inside, Young asked if he could use the bathroom.

Rod showed him where it was. He then went to the kitchen where Josie, Ray, and Parker were sitting round the table, drinking coffee. Wilkerson looked at his partner with a quizzical look, wondering what was going on.

After Young came out of the bathroom, all three agents went outside to discuss the situation. Wilkerson spoke first.

"What the hell is going on? I thought we were going to bust them this morning, not sit and drink coffee with them."

Parker responded by saying, "I was trying to put her at ease so she would talk, but she did not say anything incriminating—even offered me a cupcake to go with my coffee."

Young added he thought they had enough to go on. "At least to the arraignment process. Let's do it and do it now."

Parker waved to the agents in the van to come on in as they would pick up the evidence bags while they arrested both Rod and Josie.

Parker went in first and asked Josie to stand up and put her hands behind her back. Parker said, "Mrs. Josie Duval, you are under arrest for conspiracy to commit an assault and kidnapping." She then pulled out her Miranda card and read Josie her Miranda rights. "You have the right to remain silent. Anything you say can and will be used against you in a court of law. You have the right to an attorney. If you cannot afford an attorney, one will be provided for you. Do you understand the rights I have just read to you? With these rights in mind, do you wish to speak to me?"

Josie replied by simply saying, "I understand my rights, and I decline to make any statement until I see my own lawyer."

Wilkerson then asked Rod to stand up and put his hands behind his back. "Mr. Roderic Duval, you are under arrest for assault with the intent to kill and kidnapping of a minor under the age of five." He then gave him his Miranda rights.

Rod looked at his attorney, advised Wilkerson that he understood his rights and then declined to make any comments or answer any questions at this time.

As they were led out the front door, they noticed a crowd of neighbors, and the local television station was there. The local PD was on hand to handle traffic and crowd control. After Parker put Josie in the van, she went up to the news reporter that was yelling for her.

"Can you tell us what is going on here? According to the neighbors, there have been no problems with this family since they moved here four years ago."

"I have no comment at this time. There will be a press release later on today. Thank you."

Rod was put into the Ford with Young and Wilkerson with Parker in the van with Josie. Josie looked straight ahead, not looking out the side windows at her neighbors or at the TV camera that was pointed at the van. Her face was like a granite wall. Parker got nowhere with her.

Rod, in the back seat of the Ford, also stared straight ahead, not looking at the neighbors, TV camera, or at the local newspaper photographer that had just arrived.

Ray came out as the FBI vehicles departed, locking the front door. The media surrounded him and threw questions at him rapid fire like a machine gun.

"Mr. Roderic Duval and Mrs. Josie Duval have been taken into custody. I have no further comment at this time. I have been assured that the FBI will issue a press release shortly, and I will then make my comments. You all know how good I am at keeping promises to you." The media chuckled as they knew he was right.

That afternoon at 3 o'clock, FBI Agent Ben Parsons went to the school office to let them know that he was picking Roderick Duval Jr. along with his son. The receptionist looked at him and asked if this was in conjunction with his parents being arrested as she had heard something on the radio.

Parsons looked at her and told her the normal FBI line: "I'm sorry, I cannot confirm nor deny what you ask." His son, seeing him through the office window, came in with JR behind him.

JR looked at him with a funny look and said, "Hello, Mr. Parsons.

Are you here to take Timmy home and not have him ride the bus?" "Hi, JR, that's right, and I am going to take you home too, but first I need to stop by my office."

JR looked at him and told him that his dad had told him not to take any rides with anyone unless his dad said it was okay. "Is my dad okay, sir?"

The receptionist was having a hard time with this conversation, so she excused herself. Parsons looked at JR and told him that his dad was okay, and he knew that he was going to pick him up.

Both JR and Timmy got into the back seat, and Ben went to the office. They rode the elevator up to the second floor, went into his office where there was a young lady. Ben introduced JR to FBI Agent Parker.

JR looked at her and asked her if she was a real FBI agent.

"Yes, I am. Everyone calls you JR, am I correct? Would you mind if I talked with you alone, JR?"

"Sure, I guess so. Am I in any trouble?"

"No, you are not, but I still need to talk to you."

"Okay. Is something wrong with my mom and dad?"

Before she could talk to JR, Ben and Timmy stepped out of the office and closed the door so that Timmy could not hear what was being said.

"Before we start, would you like some milk and cookies? I have some milk right here and some chocolate chip cookies." She had found out from Josie his favorite cookies.

"Sure, I love cookies and milk after school."

She got him a small carton of milk and put three cookies on a paper plate. "JR, do you know anyone by the name of Patrick and Sherrie Johnson that live in California?"

"Yes, they are my aunt and uncle. Why?"

"JR, there is no easy way to say this, but they are your mother and father. The people you have been living with for the past four years kidnapped you and brought you out here to be their son."

"No, they *are* my mom and dad! I want to go home to them now." He cried out, shaking his head, tears starting to flow from his eyes.

"I'm sorry, but you can't go back to them. They are bad people, and they are in jail now. It will be on the news tonight. I am sorry to tell you this."

"If they are in jail now, where do I go tonight? I don't want to go to jail to sleep and eat."

"You will go to my home with me. Then tomorrow, while you are in school, I will go to your home here, pack up your things, and then fly to California in two days."

"Okay, but first, can I see those bad people? I want to say goodbye to them."

"I will have to check first, but it might not be a good idea. You will see them later on."

At Parker's home, they turned on the TV just in time to catch the news. She watched him closely as they showed Rod and Josie being taken to the van and car and then the announcer commenting on the arraignment for alleged assault and kidnapping.

JR looked at Parker and asked her what does assault mean. "I know what kidnapping is."

She smiled at him and told him that is when people do things to other people to hurt them.

"I can't believe my dad did this. He is not mean man." Then all of a sudden, he asked, "What about Pony?"

"Who is Pony?"

"That's my horse that I was on in the parade."

"I think we are going to see if we can send him to California to join you. Would you like that?"

All JR could do was nod his head as he watched the TV news about the arrest of Rod and Josie. He shook his head and started to cry as he remembered all the good times that he had with them including the last horse ride.

After dinner of hot dogs and mac and cheese, he asked if they could watch Wheel. He surprised her with his speed of figuring out the puzzles once only a few letters were on the board. She made notes of how well he did this compared to her own slow speed of solving the puzzles.

Afterward, while he took a bath and put on his pajamas that she had brought out of the house without Josie seeing her do it, she made a note to contact the Duvals' lawyer so he could be with her when she went to get his belongings such as clothes and toys while he would be in school the next day.

After his bath, he told her that before he got into bed, he had to say his prayers. She took him into the guest bedroom and listened to him as he prayed that his mom and dad would be okay and asked God to forgive the bad people. He then asked if she had a comic book he could read to her.

"No, unfortunately, all I have is crime novels that are not meant for young boys like you. How about your reading book you brought from school?"

The late news went into more detail of the arraignment that was held that afternoon. Both suspects pleaded not guilty, and considering how much trouble they had caused law enforcement agencies from four states, the FBI plus the Air Force Security Police, they were both denied bail.

As she went to bed, she could hear JR tossing in the guest bedroom, crying out for his mom and dad. She could only imagine the nightmares he was having, the poor kid. "Why do people do this to young kids? I'll never understand," she said to herself as she slid under her covers.

57

"We got them," Don shouted into the phone to Paul that afternoon. "We picked them up this morning without any fuss. They are being arraigned right now, and since they caused so much trouble after the kidnapping, bail will be denied."

"That is great news, Don. I hope they plead guilty so that Sherrie and JR will not have to face them in court. Any idea of how they will plead?"

"My guess is they will plead not guilty. They had a lawyer there with them when the agents went in to search and then arrest them. It appears that Josie will be charged with conspiracy to assault and kidnapping. She will probably get twenty-five to life. Rod, on the other hand, will be handed over to the Army, brought back to active duty, and charged with at least five violations on the UCMJ, thanks to your research."

"What about JR? Was he there during the arrest? How did he take it? I know Patrick and Sherrie will want to know."

"No, JR is fine. He was in school during the arrest. He was picked up after school by another agent that picked up his own kid. A female agent will have him at her place tonight, then, with their lawyer, she will go tomorrow to pick up his things and then fly out the next day to Ontario Airport on Friday."

"Are you going to call Patrick, or do you want me to call them and tell them the good and bad news?"

"Actually, I am going to enjoy calling Patrick—especially the way he was always badmouthing the FBI for not finding his son. One other thing—Patrick still has his ranch, right?"

"Yes, why? You know he does," Paul replied as John and Janet came into his office.

"It seems that JR has a horse he calls 'Pony.' He wants to bring it with him. We will have to move him by horse trailer. One of our agents can do that as he has horses himself."

"One last question before I let you call Patrick. The source that gave us this creep's name—is he entitled to a reward?"

"Yes, he is. Have him call me just as he did the last time. If he keeps giving us tips, he might as well become an agent himself. Speaking of rewards, your office will receive a monetary award for your assistance over the past four years in this case. Thank you, Paul, and thank John for me as well. I will let you know more about where and when the trials will be held."

"Thank you, Don, and if we can be of further assistance in the future, you know who to call. Give our best to Lydia."

Paul hung up, looked at John and Janet, and gave them the good news. "JR will be with Patrick and Sherrie on Friday. The FBI is flying him home into Ontario airport. Both of the suspects are pleading not guilty. He will be brought back to active duty and be court-martialed for violating at least five UCMJ articles. She will be charged with accessory to both assault and kidnapping."

John looked at him and asked what the five articles would be. "This is going to be rough on Sherrie and Patrick."

"Yeah, as far as what Don told me, they charged both of them with the same charges. They did not mention the other three, wanting to let the Army do it for them. This way he gets life with no chance of parole." He looked at his pad and then told them of the five articles.

Fifteen minutes after talking with John and Janet, Paul's private line rang. "Bet I know who it is."

"Paul, Don just called. He said they have the suspects in custody and JR is coming home on Friday. He said they are not going to fight extradition and will be brought back for their trials. He also said, 'The Army wants to yank him back to active duty to court-martial

his ass.' Plus, he said that JR has a horse he wants to bring out here."
"Slow down, old pal, you are going to have a heart attack. How is Sherrie taking the news?"

"Right now she is telling Leigh that she has an older brother that has been away. Leigh is happy she will have someone to play with. JR is only four years older, so it might not be so bad. Sherrie is totally ecstatic about JR coming home."

"And you, Patrick? How do you feel knowing he is not your biological son?"

"Paul, I am overjoyed. JR has my name. I am his father and always will be. The hard part is JR. How will he handle all of this crap? Hell, he is only six years old."

"Patrick, you never know. At that age, he can be very adaptable. Sometimes I thought my boys were like rubber bands, going from one extreme to the other. JR will be okay. It is you and Sherrie that I worry about especially when it comes to the trials. Between the civil Federal trial for Mrs. Duval and the army court-martial for Mr. Duval, she and JR may have to attend along with our only witness."
"What about witnesses that saw them when they were driving to Wyoming? Will the FBI try and track them down as well?"

"That is going to be the FBI's job to backtrack from Norton to Cheyenne. If they are lucky, they will tell them each place they stopped. It's a long shot. As far as this office is concerned, this cold case is closed."

"After JR is back and settled in, I want you, John, and your wives to come over for dinner. If the weather is nice, maybe a barbeque. I will keep you informed. However, I think you and I need to meet to discuss the court-martial. I am curious as to the charges."

"Uh, Patrick, are you clear as far as the phone goes? Is Sherrie near you?"

"I'm clear. I am outside on the cordless phone. Why?"

"One of the UCMJ articles is 119A, Death or Injury of an Unborn Child. Does Sherrie know she was pregnant at the time of the assault?"

"If I remember right, the doc and her shrink both told her that she had lost the baby. Yeah, they did. I remember her almost going into shock when she found out she had been pregnant." He then added, "I am damn glad these things take time. The trials will come after she has the twins, and she found out this morning it is going to be twin boys. We already have the names picked out, but we are not telling anyone until they are born."

"Anything else, Patrick?"

"Yeah, what are the other Articles? I still have my copy of the *Uniform Code Military Justice* in the den."

"Article 120—Rape for raping Sherrie at her birthday party, 118—Murder of Rose MacDonald, 128—Bodily Harm for the assault of Sherrie, 119A—Death or Injury of Unborn Child, which was committed during the assault, and finally 134—Kidnapping of JR. Get this—there might be additional charges but nothing definite."

"In other words, this piece of shit is not going to see daylight for the rest of his life. I sure hope he likes Leavenworth. Too bad they don't make them pound boulders into pebbles anymore."

"Yeah, they said it was not fair for them to be treated like that. Oh well, not for us to worry about."

"Okay, got to go. Need to clean out the empty stall for JR's horse and figure out where he is going to sleep until we can get his bedroom built. I have the plans approved by the city. Do you think you and John can get your buddy to come out here a week from Saturday and start working for a change instead of sitting around in an office all day and getting soft?" Patrick laughed with Paul as they both said goodbye and would see each other later.

Patrick went to work cleaning out the empty stall, putting fresh straw down on the ground. He would not put feed or a fresh salt block in there until the horse arrived. Then he went inside to see how Sherrie was doing.

His daughter ran to him, and as he picked her up, she told him, "Daddy, Mommy just told me I have a brudder. He will be here soon."

He noticed Sherrie looking at them with a smile on her face as he told her that's right, and he was only four years older than her.

He then told Sherrie that Paul, John, and their buddy would be out here a week from Saturday to start adding on JR's bedroom.

"I'm sure he had his own bedroom, so what we might have to do for now is have Leigh sleep with us until we can get his room finished. I will go into town tomorrow to rent a bed, and we can put Leigh's bed in our room."

That night after supper and their daughter was in bed, Patrick and Sherrie went out to the front porch to talk. Patrick settled into his chair, and Sherrie, being heavier than she was with her other children, sat in her chair next to Patrick.

He looked at her and told her what Paul had told him about the court-martial articles. When he mentioned Article 119A, she shuddered and looked at him.

"Patrick, I honestly did not know I was pregnant then. I should have known, but I did not. There is no way he knew I was pregnant. I am okay, and I can talk about it. Will I have to testify at the court-martial or at his wife's trial?"

"Honey, in all probability, yes, at the court-martial since you are the victim same as JR is. As for her trial, probably not. However, JR might have to." He paused and then continued, "As you noticed, I did not watch the news tonight. I did not want to upset Leigh with the bad stuff right now. I will watch it later tonight."

Just then they noticed the local TV station van pull up in their driveway with some other cars they did not recognize. "Damn reporters are here. I am surprised it took them bastards so damn long to get here."

Both Patrick and Sherrie came down the steps, not wanting to have too much noise on the porch to wake up their daughter. Patrick spoke up first. "What can I do for you kind media folks?"

"Ms. Johnson, it is our understanding that your son has been located and the kidnappers have been arrested in Cheyenne, Wyoming. Have you heard from the FBI on this?"

"Yes, we heard from them this afternoon. Our son will be with us in a few days."

"When exactly will he be here? Do you have any idea?"

Patrick answered before Sherrie could respond. "In a few days. When he is here and we have had time to talk with him, we will contact you and hold a press conference, but until then, please leave us alone. We need time to absorb this news."

"Do you have a comment to make at this time, Ms. Johnson?"

Sherrie looked at Patrick then told the reporter, "We are happy to have our son coming back to us safe and sound. For those of you out there that have had their child or children abducted, do not give up hope. It might take years before you are reunited, but it can happen. It has happened with us."

Patrick looked at them and told them that the interview was over and they would contact them when they were ready to give their full interview. "Good night, and thank you."

Patrick and Sherrie went back inside, not saying a word until they heard the vehicles leave. Patrick went to pick up the phone.

"I don't trust them. They will sit out there like damn vultures. I am going to call the Kern County sheriff's office and see if they can post a patrol to keep them away, plus tomorrow all the neighbors will want to stop by and talk to you. We need time to get ready for JR's return, not talk to neighbors and the press."

That night, on the local and late news, the headline item was on finding Patrick Johnson Jr. "kidnapped four years ago and taken to Wyoming." The video showed Rod and Josie being led out of their house and driven away, not looking at the cameras, just looking straight ahead. News of the arraignment came next. They had both pled not guilty to assault and kidnaping. It was also mentioned that Rod was probably going to be called back on active duty to be courtmartialed since he had committed the crimes while on active duty.

Sherrie told Patrick she was tired and needed to go to bed. "It has been an exciting afternoon, and I need to make sure I get plenty of rest before Friday."

Just then Patrick heard a soft knock on the door. He went to the security peephole in the door. He smiled and opened the door.

"Hi, Tom, come on in. Sherrie was just getting ready for bed, but I wanted to stay up a bit longer to keep an eye on the front yard."

"Hi, Sherrie, Patrick. The boss asked me to come by and take the first watch on your place to keep the lookie-loos and the media away. Bob will be here at 0600. We will be here for twelve-hour shifts except for tonight. No one will be allowed on your property unless they are law enforcement or they are cleared by you folks. That okay, Patrick?"

"That's fine, Tom. Do you need any coffee or to use the bathroom before you start?"

"No, thanks, I have everything I need." He looked to make sure Sherrie had left the room then continued. "I have an empty jar if I need to use it." Patrick smiled as he knew what he was talking about. "Good night, Tom. I will see you before you leave. I will have a fresh pot of coffee ready."

Tom left to go back to his car, and Patrick set the timer on the coffeepot for 0530, then went to bed, setting his alarm for 0500.

58

The next morning, Agent Parker got JR up and told him he was going to go to school as she had things to do and he could say goodbye to his friends and his teacher. After she walked him inside, the secretary let her walk him to his classroom. She asked the teacher if she could speak to the class about what has happened. She thought it would be a good idea as the kids were all talking about it.

After the teacher led the class in the Pledge of Allegiance, she introduced FBI Agent Parker.

"Good morning, class, I am FBI Agent Parker of the Cheyenne Field Office. I want to talk to you about what was on the news last night and what is going to happen to JR. Four years ago, JR was kidnapped from his mother and father in California." She had to pause when there were some questions shouted at her. Once the teacher got the students under control, she continued.

"The people that took him lied to him and told him they were his mother and father. They said they took him from his aunt and uncle. Well, as you know, those bad people were arrested yesterday. JR will be flying home tomorrow back to California to be with his mom and dad. Are there any questions?"

One boy raised his hand and asked, "Why did they do this?"
"They knew his mom and knew she had him. They wanted a little boy to raise as their own. I am not able to tell you how we found him, but we did."

The teacher told the class that JR would be in school all day, but it would be his last day and to treat him with respect.

Parker left the room to go to the office and told them she would pick up his school records when she picked him up after school. "And no one, I repeat, no one is to pick him up after school. If you have any questions, please call me." She handed over her business card with the FBI number on it.

She went to her office to call the Duvals' attorney, Mr. Perkins, to ask him to meet her at the house so she could pick up JR's clothing and toys. She also mentioned that JR was concerned about Pony not being fed this morning.

He suggested meeting her at 10:00 a.m. She agreed as she had some paperwork to catch up on. Right on time, Perkins showed up at the house. Unfortunately, there was a crowd there of neighbors and residents of Cheyenne wanting to take a look at the crime scene. There were two Cheyenne police cars with one Laramie County sheriff car to keep people off the property and to keep traffic flowing safely.

Parker slit the Do Not Enter tape that was put up yesterday. She would replace it after they come back out. Once inside, they both went through the house, checking the windows to make sure none were open or broken.

They then went into JR's bedroom, got his suitcase from his closet, which already had clothes inside, and in a paper sack, Parker collected some of his toys including his baseball glove and the pony from the top of his dresser. They both wrote down what she packed, and then both signed both lists for their files. This way there was an accountability for items taken from the room.

As they neared the door, with Perkins carrying both suitcases and Parker carrying the two paper sacks, Perkins told her that Rod had asked where JR had spent the night last night.

"I told him that JR was being taken care of and for him not to worry about it. Strange, though, he did not ask about the welfare of his wife."

"Not so strange. He evidently is more concerned about JR and how he is going to adapt as time goes on. If he asks again, tell him he is flying home to his mother and father tomorrow. Whether JR sees him again will be up to his parents."

Outside the front door, Parker replaced the crime scene tape. The press hollered out to them asking what they had taken from the house. Both Parker and Perkins ignored them as they put everything into Parker's car and the police cleared a path for them as they pulled out of the driveway.

"Damn it all," Parker said to herself as she reversed herself and drove back to the rear of the house to the stables. She fed the horses fresh hay and made sure they had plenty of water. All three horses looked healthy. "Wonder what will happen to you guys," she said to the two older horses. She heard a noise behind her, and she spun around to see the ranch foreman.

"You must be the FBI agent. I am Bob Smith, the ranch foreman. Mr. Duval asked me to make sure the horses are taken care of in his absence. I will make sure they have plenty of feed and water until a decision is made. Mr. Duval is a good man—really, he is."

She went back to the office, gave Parsons the inventory sheet of what she had taken from JR's bedroom, and asked Parsons about the horses. "Are you going to be able to drive his pony out to him? What about the older horses?"

Parsons looked at her and told her that he had been approved to take official travel to California to deliver Pony to JR.

"He rode that guy well during one of the FD parades this year. They were made for each other. As for the other two, we can only put them into a boarding stable until the trial. I am sure we will find a good home for them."

"JR was real good last night. He ate supper, then he asked if we could watch Wheel. At first, I did not know what show he meant until I asked him if he meant *Wheel of Fortune*. He said yes, but he could not say the big word. That kid can spell." She took a gulp of coffee and told him how he could figure out the words with only a few letters up on the board.

Parsons laughed and told her that his son, Timmy, told him that JR is the smartest speller in his class. "He is going to miss him. So what is the plan for tomorrow? I know that Don is sending one of the Gulfstreams today."

"Yup, we leave tomorrow morning at 0900 and arrive at Ontario Airport around 1100 or so. Once I turn JR over to his parents and have them sign for him, I will speak to Don about the transfer of the prisoners."

"The Army Special Forces feel that Mr. Duval has given them a very black eye, so they want him back on active duty for court-martial. He will be sent to March Air Reserve Base for confinement until his trial. Mrs. Duval will be sent to San Bernardino County Jail for Women until her trial."

Parker just remembered, "I forgot to fix JR a lunch. I am not used to this. I hope the school will give him lunch and I will pay them when I pick him up this afternoon."

"Don't worry about it. I will call the school for you and set it up. This happens a lot of times."

Parker went to her desk and went through the toys that she collected from the house. She had the baseball glove that would soon be too small for him, his pony from his dresser, his Frisbee, and a few odds and ends of farm vehicles. "I just hope that these toys do not bring unpleasant memories for him," she said to herself as she processed paperwork for her trip to California in the morning.

At two thirty, she left for the school to pay for the lunch and to pick up his school records. When she arrived, there were two police cars in front of the school with their roof lights flashing. She put the FBI placard on the dash and ran up to the door.

One of the officers stopped her. She showed him her badge and ID card and went inside to the office, expecting the worst.

JR was sitting in the office, looking sad until he saw Agent Parker walk in. The secretary told her that JR had been told by an older child at afternoon recess that he was going to a reform school because his mom and dad were in jail. "The boy's parents were called, and they were informed that their son was suspended for five days. No other child said anything to JR."

"Why the police? Did they get into a fight? How did JR take it?"

"JR stood his ground and told him that he was glad he was leaving because he was a bully, which the boy is. However, the parents threatened to call the paper and have them come out here to bother JR and the rest of the school, so the principal erred on the side of caution and called the police. JR went back into class and finished the day like a real trooper."

Parker asked if the records were ready, and the secretary gave her a sealed envelope. "These are all of his grades from last year and this year up to today."

She looked at JR and told him, "JR, it has been wonderful meeting you. I wish you the best of luck in your new home and school."

In the car, Parker told him that she wanted to take him to her office so they could take a picture to send to his mom and dad so they could see how grown up he has become before he arrives at home tomorrow. "Then we will go out to eat, okay?"

At the office, he asked her if he looked okay for a picture. She combed his hair and said he was fine. They took the photo and then showed him how it would be sent to his mom and dad through Don at the LA Field Office with the fax machine.

After eating, they went back to Parker's place where they watched news which showed a picture of Sherrie and Patrick on the front porch with Sherrie holding her daughter. She told him that was his mom and dad. He asked if he had a sister and why is his mommy fat.

Parker laughed and told him that, yes, he now has a sister, and his mommy is fat because she is pregnant with a baby brother or sister.

All JR could say was *wow*. Then he asked her, "Can we watch Wheel now?"

After watching Wheel, he took his bath and got ready for bed. As usual, before getting into bed, he knelt down beside his bed and said his prayers including his sister and his fat mommy. He also prayed for safety in his first plane ride tomorrow.

After he said his prayers, Parker listened to him read his book. She left his door open a crack so that she could hear him if he had any bad dreams. She went into her bedroom and went to bed.

She lay there, wondering what it would be like to have a child of her own, but then, would she leave the FBI? She did not know the answer to that question. She did know, though, that tomorrow would be a long day, so she fell asleep thinking of a child of her own someday.

59

That same day, after Don received the photographs of JR, he called Patrick and asked if he would be home in two hours. He had something to bring out to them. Patrick told him that they would be home and that it had better be good news or he would not be responsible for his actions.

Don arrived at the house at 5:00 p.m., and after showing his badge and ID to the deputy sheriff at the driveway entrance, he went up to the front door. Sherrie opened the door before he could ring the doorbell and invited him in.

"Don, we are getting ready for tomorrow morning. Patrick is moving furniture from Sherrie Leigh's bedroom to our room, then he will move furniture into her room for JR. What happy news do you have for us?"

Patrick came out and joined them, offered him a cup of coffee, and sat at the dining room table. "Okay, Don, what do you have for us?"

"Thanks for the cup. First of all, as you know, Agent Parker from the Cheyenne Field Office will be flying JR in tomorrow, arriving around 1100 at Ontario Airport on one of our Gulfstream jets."

"Yes, we know that, Don. I also know that is not why you came out here."

"Okay, hold your shorts. This afternoon, Agent Parker sent us two photos of JR." He gave them the photos, then he told him how JR stood his ground at school to the bully.

There were tears in Sherrie's eyes. Patrick had a strong determined look in his eyes and thanked Don for the pictures. "He looks so grown up now even though he is six years old," Sherrie said.

"Mommy, why are you crying?" Leigh asked her as she tried to climb on her lap.

Sherrie, getting bigger by the day with the twins, could not have her sit on her lap, so Patrick picked her up and showed her JR's picture. "This is your big brother. He is the one we will pick up at the airport tomorrow. Remember, we told you about him last week?"

"Is that why I will be with you and Mommy?"

"Yes, that is why. He will be in your room until we build his bedroom. It is just for a short time, honey."

"Okay. Will he leave my dolls alone?"

Patrick and Sherrie laughed and told her that JR would leave her dolls and animals alone, that he would have his own toys to play with, and he would be busy working with daddy, taking care of the horses. "Just like you work with Mommy in the kitchen."

Sherrie asked how Lydia was doing with her pregnancy and if she was having any back problems like she was.

"Not really, but my back is going out sleeping on the couch as the twins are taking turns kicking me in the back at night. I hope I can sleep after they are born. But from what some of the guys are saying, I might not. All I can do is hope they will be okay."

Patrick smiled and told him that each night would be different at first. "Read up on twins, my friend. I have, and I have learned quite a bit about how they work as a team, trying to see whether it is Mommy or Daddy that gets up all the time."

"I know it is suppertime for you guys, so I will be on my way, and see you tomorrow morning at the airport. By the way, the jet will be flying into the General Aviation side. Agent Parker will brief me then will go back with Agent Parsons after he delivers JR's Pony."

Patrick walked him to his car, thanked him, then came back in and hugged Sherrie. "You do know it is going to be a big change here. Next week we will have to get him enrolled in school. By the way, I found his old chair that he used to sit in. I wonder if he will use it?" Sherrie, even though excited, knew she had to eat, so she was fixing supper. "I guess it will be a wait and see. I wonder how well he can read now. I mean, I do not know how they worked with him on schoolwork," she said as she put supper on the table.

After supper, they watched the news, and of course, it was about JR coming home tomorrow. "Will they leave us alone, Patrick? I mean will we ever be without the media at our doorstep all the time?" "Honey, until the trials are over with, there will be no real peace for us. That is why I have asked the county to help us out. All we can do is try and protect our JR from the press. The kids go nowhere without you, Paul, John, or me except for school—at least until the clamor is over with."

After the news, they watched *Wheel of Fortune* as they always did. Then they put Leigh to bed, with Patrick kneeling beside her as she said her prayer. Just before she said amen, she added, "Be with my big brudder tomorrow. Amen."

Patrick tucked her in and kissed her on her forehead. Sherrie did the same then turned out the light, leaving on a small night-light, and closed the door. She followed Patrick out to the living room, where they agreed that it seemed things would work out.

They went over the plans for the two new bedrooms and the new bathroom that would be added on. "First, though, is JR's room—next Saturday—then the bathroom followed by the twins' room."

"Patrick, my love, after the twins are born, I think I will have my tubes tied. I do not think I could go through this again. We can't afford more kids especially with your plans for the local kids."

"I was thinking of the same thing. In a few years, maybe we should build a new house, not just adding a room at a time but a new house. If I went to work with Paul and John and kept my part-time job with the County Mounted Patrol, we could do it. That way, each child could have their own room."

Sherrie told him that it was time to think about JR first. "Your ideas can wait, my dear. You are no longer a young spring chicken, you know. JR will need you as he grows up."

He laughed and they watched some of their favorite TV shows, excited and not able to go to bed just yet even though they had to get up early. The late news made only a brief mention that "the boy that was kidnapped four years ago is coming home tomorrow." There was no mention of how or when or where he would arrive.

In bed, Patrick rolled over to snuggle with his wife and told her that the circus would start tomorrow once the press found out he was definitely home. "One important item we have not talked about is his mental wellbeing. Will he need mental health care? How bad is he screwed up?"

"Honey, let's worry about that when it happens, okay? We can't dwell on something that we have no control over tonight. My fear is will he remember me as his mother and you as his father?" Sherrie replied. She then turned off her light while Patrick opened his latest crime novel and read about five pages, but his mind kept wandering back four years ago.

*****

The following morning, the Johnsons got up early and had a light breakfast since they were all nervous—even Leigh, who ate only half a bowl of cereal. She asked questions about JR that her parents could not really answer.

By 0745, they were all settled into the car and left. They told the deputy they were on their way to get JR, and since he had a key, he could use the indoor plumbing if need be. He laughed and waved to them.

They arrived at the General Aviation Terminal at 1030, meeting up with Don and Paul. Don told them that the jet was about thirty minutes out, so it would be on time. Patrick asked Paul why he was there as it was supposed to be just the FBI and family.

"Patrick, I am hurt. I am family. I am JR's godfather after all. Does that not make me family?"

Patrick smiled at his longtime friend and told him it most certainly did make him part of the family. Sherrie took Sherrie Leigh into the terminal to use the bathroom while Paul and Patrick talked about the bedroom job next week.

Patrick told him he had the lumber and concrete at the ranch.

He asked when he and his crew would be out tomorrow.

Paul asked him if he was certain that he wanted everyone there tomorrow when he needed to be with JR.

"Second thought, why don't we hold off until next Saturday. This will give us a week to bring him back into the fold and have less disruption. It will be bad enough with four people and one bathroom, but we can handle it. I meant to mention the change in plans. Sherrie and I had discussed this same option."

Just as Paul agreed with him, Sherrie and their daughter came out of the terminal. "I wish he would get here. I am so nervous." She shaded her eyes and looked toward the east, hoping to catch a glimpse of the jet. However, it was not to be. The sun was too bright.

A few minutes later, Don, using binoculars, spotted a jet over the San Gabriel Mountains. He did not say a word until he was sure. "I think it is them. They are about five minutes out."

Sure enough, within five minutes, the Gulfstream was visible to the naked eye, and it touched down exactly at 1100. The engines screamed in reverse so loud that Sherrie Leigh put her hands over her ears to try and blot out the noise.

It rolled down to the end of the runway, turned around, and taxied back to the waiting group. Leigh was laughing and jumping up and down with the excitement that was felt by all who were waiting for JR.

As the jet rolled to a stop in front of them, they could see a young boy peering through the window, his eyes wide with either excitement or fear. He looked at Agent Parker and asked, "That's my mom, dad, and sister, but who is the big man?"

Parker laughed. "That is the agent who has been trying to find you all these years. He is a friend. Make sure you shake his hand and thank him. As for the others, yes, that is your mom and dad and your sister. I do not know who the other person is though."

He was so excited that he forgot to unbuckle his seat belt once the engines spooled down and the hatchway was opened. Parker pulled him back down in the seat and told him to slow down while she unbuckled his seat belt. He ran to the doorway and then waited for Parker to walk with him down the steps.

At the base of the steps, he looked at his mom, a faint flicker of recognition in the eyes of both of them. He ran up to her, looked at her, and said one word: "Mom?"

She looked at him and, with tears in her eyes, said, "Yes, son, I am your mom."

He wrapped his arms around her legs as she bent down a little and put her arms around him. "I have dreamed of this day for four years. I never gave up hope."

JR stepped back and looked at Patrick. "Are you my real dad?" "Yes, yes, I am. You are Patrick Johnson Jr., or JR, as we called you when you were a baby. But you are grown up now. You may not want to be called JR, but we can talk about that later."

"Who is she?" JR pointed to Sherrie Leigh.

Patrick smiled and told him, "It is your little sister, Sherrie Leigh. She is sometimes called Leigh. Your mom is pregnant with two brothers who are not born yet."

"You mean I have to share everything with them? I have never been around girls before except for school."

That got everyone to smile a little as Don came over, kneeled down before him, and told him that he was the agent who had been looking for him all these years.

"I will need to talk to you in a couple of weeks about your time with the bad people." He then stuck out his hand and shook JR's hand and told him that he had been a very brave boy and that his mommy and daddy love him very much.

Patrick called Paul over and introduced him to JR as his godfather. "He has been searching for you as well all these years, son. He worked with me in the Air Force."

"Thank you, sir." He then gave Paul a hug.

Paul, as if he had something in his eyes, turned away. He did not want anyone to see the tears that were there. This homecoming was turning out to be better than they had all thought.

As Don unloaded JR's bags, JR gave the toys to him and told him "That bad man gave me these. I don't want them. I miss Pony though."

Patrick looked at Don and shook his head no, not to say anything yet. He took the bag from Don and told him he would call him tomorrow.

Don agreed, gathered Parker, who was talking with Sherrie, and escorted her to his car. Before they left, JR ran up to her to hug her and thank her for taking care of him "and keep watching Wheel."

Patrick, Sherrie, and the kids got into the car, with Patrick making sure JR was in the seat tightly and Sherrie putting Leigh in her car seat. "We need to get a car seat for JR tomorrow, but first, we need to measure him when we get home. He may just fit the requirement for not needing a car seat."

On the ride home, both JR and Leigh tried to talk to each other, asking questions. JR laughed at his sister's stumbling over words, and Patrick had to tell him to stop, that it is not nice to do that.

They finally arrived home to find a gaggle of cars and vans, many with TV transmitter antennas. The Bakersfield PD, called in by the deputy, cleared the traffic so they could go up to the house. JR stared out the window at the crowd of media trying to thrust their cameras close to the windows to take his picture. Both of the kids started to cry and said they were scared.

Patrick drove up to the front of the house and had Sherrie take the kids inside. He went to the edge of the driveway and talked with the deputy. He reached inside the patrol car and handed signs to Patrick. He asked him if he had a hammer in the trunk. The deputy handed him the hammer, and Patrick nailed a sign to the edge of the fence. He then addressed the crowd.

"Folks, this is private property. Anyone caught trespassing will be shot and then arrested. These notices, like the one I just put up here, are posted all around my property. I ask that you give us time to get reacquainted with our son before we hold a news conference. The FBI will contact you when it will be held. For now, though, go home or back to work and enjoy the weekend as we want to do. Thank you."

He turned away, ignoring the yelled questions as he walked up to his front porch, where he turned and waved at the media and went inside.

Sherrie was talking to JR and showing him his temporary bedroom and helping him put his clothes away. She explained to him, "This is just temporary. You are going to have your own bedroom built in a couple of weeks."

Afterward they came out and the kids had PB&J sandwiches and Sherrie had vanilla almond ice cream. Patrick had a cup of coffee. They made idle talk until it was time to put Leigh down for her nap. JR told them that he was too excited to nap.

The three of them went out the back door to the porch where they could talk in private, away from the cameras that were still out front. JR saw the stables and asked if they had horses.

"I had a pony with the bad people. I miss my Pony."

Patrick told him they knew he had one.

"Do you want Pony here? We have room for him, or do you want a new pony?"

"I think so, but I am sad. That bad man makes me sad."

"I need to know something. What did he call you? We called you JR as your name is Patrick Johnson Jr., after me."

"He called me JR also or Rod Junior. I don't like that name now."

"Well, if we call you Patrick, everyone will wonder if it is you or if it is me they are talking to. How about just plain Pat? Would that make you feel better?"

"Yeah, I'd like that. You are my real daddy, I think. I like Pat."

Sherrie had gone back inside to bring out the bag of toys for Pat to look at. Sooner or later, they would have to go through them. She knew it had to be done, and she thought the sooner the better. She gave the sack to Pat and asked him to go through it and tell them what he did not want to keep from his Wyoming time.

The first thing he pulled out was the pony that he had on his dresser. He looked at it and threw it on the ground along with the coloring books and Frisbee. He looked at the baseball glove and threw that on the ground as well. "I don't want any of it. They bring back dreams of playing with the two of them. I want new toys from you." He then turned toward Sherrie, hugged her, and started to cry.

"The only thing I want is Pony. I miss Pony."

Patrick looked at him and told him that Pony should be there within the next two days. "We already have his house all set up for him. There is one more thing we need to tell you, son."

"What's that?"

"You are going to need to see two doctors. One is so that you can go to school, and the other is to make sure you are adjusting from the bad experience you have just gone through."

Patrick looked at Sherrie and told her he needed to call Don. "We need to find out his doctor's name was so we can get his health records. It will postpone JR…I mean Pat…from going to school."

Don told him he had thought of the same thing after talking to Parker. "The Cheyenne agents are talking to Josie Duval now, and she is willing to give up the information. How is JR doing?"

"He no longer wants to be called JR. He gets confused with that bastard, so we now call him Pat. Every time we call him Pat, he brightens up." Patrick paused then continued. "The media circus was here when we got home. Can you schedule a press conference for Monday here at the ranch? I would like you, Paul, and John here as well."

"I can do that. Maybe have Parker and Parsons there also with his horse. He does want Pony, correct?"

"Yes, he wants Pony. That is the only thing he wants from there. He says Pony makes him happy. To be honest, I am afraid to leave the ranch right now. I don't trust the media horde even though I have posted No Trespassing Private Property around the ranch and we have a deputy at the driveway. Once we have the press conference, they should go and find some other morsel to chew on—or at least I hope they will."

60

The next morning, after breakfast, Patrick asked Pat if he wanted to go for a ride to see the ranch. After he enthusiastically smiled and said yeah, Patrick told Sherrie that he and Pat were going out for a ride.

He took Pat out to the stable, showed him where Pony would go, then told him he would have to ride his sister's horse as the other ones were too big for him.

"But that's a girl's horse!"

"True, but I think you will like it anyway. And besides, it is just for one or two days until yours gets here. Okay, pal?"

Patrick saddled both horses while Pat looked around the stables, seeing how neat everything was just like the last place he was at. Pat looked at Patrick, trying to remember him but had only vague memories. He seemed like a nice man though.

They left the stables and headed north, away from the house and the crowd outside the driveway. They rode in silence until Patrick stopped at a small pond and told Pat, "Let's sit here and talk a little, and we can let the horses drink."

Patrick told him that this was his favorite spot to come and think because it was so quiet and peaceful. He asked Pat what it was like where he was.

"It was okay. He had lots of land, and we each had our own horse like you do. He grew corn and some other things. He let me ride with him in a parade this year. That week was fun. I forget the name of the rodeo, but it was a full week." He paused. Patrick knew not to rush him to talk.

Pat continued, "Sometimes he let me do things with him, other times he did not, and I had to stay in the house. Do you have snow here? We had lots of it. I learned how to make a snowman, and one year we had one for each of us."

"Did he ever hit or beat you or punish you if you did anything wrong?"

"Nope, he never did. If I did anything bad, he just kind of laughed about it. One thing we did do, the three of us, was watch a show every night. It was called Wheel. I got to learn how to spell with it. Do you watch it?"

"We watched it when you were a baby, and you had your own chair to sit between the two of us. And yes, we still watch it every night. Your sister tries to watch it but gets bored. Maybe you can help her spell since you do so well. That is what big brothers are supposed to do. I never had a big brother, but I wish I did."

"I will try. I like to spell, and I really liked the school I was in. I had a good teacher. She was pretty and smart too."

Pat looked around at all the open land and then asked him some questions. "Is all this yours? What do you grow here?"

"Yes, this is all mine. Well, actually, it belongs to the bank, but I am buying it from them. No, I am not growing anything. It is all open land. I plan to create a camp for troubled children. They will be able to camp and fish just to get away from their problems."

"Do you work?"

"Sort of. I retired from the Air Force two years ago, and besides the ranch work, I am also with the Kern County Sheriff's Mounted Posse as a Reserve Deputy Sheriff."

"Those bad people told me you were my uncle and mom was my aunt. When we went on the Air Force Base, I remember saying that my Uncle Patrick wears the same blue clothes." He looked at him with a sad look.

He looked at Patrick and asked him the one question he could not truly answer. "Why did they take me away from you and Mom?" "I do not really know why, son. Someday, we will find out. We all need to be ready for the answer though. Some people do this type of stuff for money or for revenge. However, it does not appear to be either of those two reasons."

"Can we ride some more? I want to see more of your land. It looks so big and wide open."

"Sure we can. Mount up. After we get finished, it will be close to supper. Do you still like mac and cheese?"

Pat got on his horse, and he told Patrick he loved mac and cheese along with hamburgers and hot dogs. They rode for about two more hours as Patrick showed him the rest of the ranch, then they headed back to the stables.

After Patrick took the bridles and saddles off the horses, Pat went ahead and started to brush the horse he had ridden. Then he made sure it had enough hay to eat. Patrick was impressed with the way he was around horses.

They went inside, and Sherrie was just fixing lunch of PB&J for the kids. Pat made a face and asked for hot dogs and mac and cheese instead.

His mom told him they would have that for supper. "It is too heavy for your stomach just before you lie down in the afternoon for your nap."

Pat looked at her with a downcast look and said, "Yes, ma'am." Seeing his downcast look, Patrick told him, "Your mom knows what is best for you, son. You will learn you cannot argue with a woman—especially your mom."

Leigh started to laugh as she bit into her sandwich. She had jelly smeared all over face which made Pat laugh. "You look like a funny clown."

After the kids were lying down, Patrick and Sherrie went out to the back porch to talk. He told her how the ride with Pat went that morning and that he was happy that they did.

"It appears that they did him no harm and were very conscientious about making sure he was learning things before he started school. They watched *Wheel of Fortune* together, which he says helps him spell." He paused to collect his thoughts before continuing.

"We talked about him helping Leigh spell as I told him that was what big brothers do. He accepted it. He loves Wheel. He handles himself well on the horse, and when we got back to the stable, after I took the bridle and saddle off, he brushed her down as best as he could and made sure she had plenty of hay. I have a feeling that he will be okay."

"What about school?"

"With the press conference on Monday morning, it will be all over the place. After the conference, I will go to the school and talk to the principal and see how they want to work it out. Hell, I might go with him the first day and talk to the class. He will be okay."

"What about toys? He did not keep any of what he came with except for the baseball glove. We sure can't go shopping with him now. The press would follow us. What about church tomorrow?"

Patrick thought about what she had just asked. Her questions made sense. "Tomorrow morning we get up, eat breakfast, and go to Mass like normal. I am sure Father O'Malley will enjoy more people at his service tomorrow." He then added, "We have to get back to living normally with a full-size family. Who knows, maybe we will become the family of the year for the state of California or some other silly contest."

Sherrie laughed and told him, "That is one of the reasons why I married you—such a sense of humor in times of stress."

Leigh came out and tried to climb on her mother's lap, rubbing her eyes, "I could not sleep any more. I want my bed."

"Honey, it is only for a short while until we get your brother's bedroom built. Then you get your room back, okay? They are going to start building it next week."

Pat came out a short time later and asked his dad if they could take a walk and talk some more.

As they started walking, Patrick asked his son, "What is it you want to talk about? About what we talked about this morning? I have one question for you. Did you go to church or Sunday school back there?"

"I'm bored. I do not have any toys here to play with, and all that is in the room are dolls and girl stuff. We went to a big church once in a while at Easter and Christmas. Why?"

"Tell you what, you and I can go into the barn and go through some boxes of my old stuff. Maybe I can find my old baseball glove and we can play catch. Monday afternoon we can go to the toy store and buy you some new toys that you can pick out, okay? As for church, we go to a Catholic church, and we are going tomorrow. We go every Sunday morning."

"Okay, if you find your old stuff, we can play. I don't want to play with the other stuff."

"Anything else you want to talk about?"

"I lay in the bed and tried to remember you and Mom, but it wasn't clear. You told me about a chair I used to sit in. I kinda remember something like that. They had one for me there that I sat in between the two of them. Was it a bad dream?"

"No, son, it was not a bad dream. It really happened to all of us. Let's go back and see what we can find in the barn."

Once in the barn, Patrick pulled down some boxes, and before Patrick could stop him, Pat started to go through them. At first, he found nothing of interest, but in the second box was a stack of comic books—*Superman*, *Batman*, and then he found some *Easy Company* comic books. "Hey, Dad, what are these about? I know *Superman* and *Batman* but not these other ones."

"Those are Army comic books. They are about a unit in World War II. If your grandpa were alive, he could tell you about that war, but you are too young to know about it now. Hopefully, when you grow up, there will not be another war."

He then found his glove, and behind that box was his bat. "This is what I played with before I met your mom. I was younger then."

As Pat ran inside to get his glove, Patrick went through one more box. It had all of his Air Force photos in it beginning with his basic training photo up to his retirement photo. There were photos of when he was in South Korea, Germany, and Iraq. He gathered up the box and decided to show them later to the kids.

Pat came out with this glove and ball. They played catch, and every time Pat caught the ball, both his mom and sister applauded him, with Patrick giving his verbal encouragement. However, he wondered why he always threw the ball underhanded.

"That's because that is the way she told me to throw the ball, not like they do on TV. She told me this was an easy way to play catch."

Patrick knew that it was going to take time to change the way he did some things, but the way he took care of the horse after the ride was perfect, plus the fact that he sort of made his bed this morning was good news in itself.

Sherrie went inside the house to start supper of hamburger with mac and cheese while Leigh watched cartoons.

"Mommy, where has he been?"

Sherrie explained that he had been taken away from her four years ago by some bad people that wanted him to be their son. "We will know the reason soon enough. All we can do is love each other and help him recover, and that includes you, my little darling."

Patrick and Pat came in, talking and laughing at what they had found in the barn. Patrick sat the box of his photos on the floor and told everyone that after supper they would go through the box, and he would show them what he looked like over the years.

Pat grabbed some of the comic books and took them to the living room, sat down, and began to go through them. He was so absorbed in a *Superman* comic that he did not hear his mother call him for supper. Not even the odor of hamburgers got his attention, but telling him that mac and cheese was getting cold did get his attention. He quickly put the comic down, went and washed his hands, and went to the table.

After supper and the kitchen was cleaned up, Patrick started to go over the photos with the kids. Pat seemed to be more interested in his photos showing him in his BDUs in Korea and in Iraq than in his blues.

"Is that your rifle? Did you ever have to shoot somebody with it?"

Patrick thought about the answer before he responded. It was a hard question as he still sometimes remembered that night. "Yes, I did shoot it, and yes I did have to shoot some bad people. I was protecting some of our men when the enemy tried to kill us." His mind remem- bered that night, and his body still remembered that piece of shrapnel as it penetrated his leg. He then continued, knowing his next question. "If you want to know the truth, I do not know if I killed anyone. Your mom knows that I was injured. I will tell you more after you are older when you can understand better."

"That bad man had two rifles. Do you have any guns? I had a BB rifle."

"Yes, I do have a rifle and a gun. I wear the gun when I am with the sheriff's posse, and the rifle is for when I go hunting."

"Can I get another BB rifle? I was real good with it before."

"We will see. We will see."

Sherrie's eyes showed that she was not happy with the answer.

Patrick kept digging in the box and came out with some loose wedding photos. "I thought you put all of these in the book, hon."

There were two photos of them rubbing their noses together, which caused the kids to look at each other and laugh.

Leigh said that it looked like two animals kissing. Pat agreed with a laugh.

Pat asked about photos of him as a baby. Patrick and Sherrie knew this would be asked as they had pictures up on the wall of his sister.

"No, son. When you were taken, the bad man took the pictures we had of you with him. He did not want your picture to be put in the papers or on TV so that no one would recognize you and call the police. He probably destroyed them." Patrick pulled out his wallet, and he showed Pat the only photo of when he was a baby.

"I was sure small."

"Yup, that you were. And speaking of small, it's time for both of you to take your baths. Leigh, you go first and then Pat."

"Yeah, Leigh, girls go first," Pat said to her. Then he went back to the living room and read more of his comic book until it was his turn. He took the comic books to his bedroom so he could read them in bed.

After the kids were in bed, Sherrie told Patrick that she was happy Pat was with them, and calling him Pat was so natural. They decided that after church the next day, they would go to their favorite steak house and enjoy a nice Sunday dinner so that Sherrie would not have to cook.

The next day passed uneventfully, with the exception of the media parked outside their home. At church, some of the media followed them in, and Father O'Malley welcomed the extra attendees that morning, which brought about a slight titter from the normal parishioners. He then welcomed home Patrick Johnson Jr. He gave a special prayer in honor of Pat's homecoming.

After church, Father O'Malley spoke to Patrick and told him that he would like to talk to Pat someday soon after all the hubbub was over with.

They then went to eat, and Pat told them about Little Bear Inn with the tall brown bear in the lobby. He teased his sister about the bear, telling her how tall and mean it looked. Leigh gave a sour look at him and then at her mom.

"Pat, that is not nice. Now apologize to your sister."

Pat looked crestfallen as he did not think he had done anything wrong. He still had to get used to having a sister all of a sudden. "Leigh, I am sorry."

They finished eating with no further problems and left for home. When they arrived, they saw a strange vehicle just inside the driveway off to the side. The driver was talking to the deputy that was still there to control the media. As they got closer, they saw it was a horse trailer behind a pickup truck.

Pat yelled out, "It's Pony!" as he tried to unbuckle his seat belt.

Patrick told him to wait until the car was parked before he got out. He pulled up to the deputy and asked him what was going on and who was the driver of the truck.

"This is FBI Agent Parsons from Cheyenne, Wyoming, with a horse. He says it is your son's horse."

Pat was jumping up and down with excitement to see Pony, and he urged his dad to open the trailer ramp and let Pony out. Parsons opened the back ramp and guided Pony out of the trailer.

Pat went up to Pony and patted his flank and neck. He asked Parsons if Pony was okay after the long ride in the trailer.

"Yes, and I think he missed you too. I think he needs to rest a bit, though, on firm ground before you ride him. He took the ride here well. He is a good horse."

Sherrie and Leigh looked at Pony, and Sherrie marveled at how well Pat loved the horse. The media, just outside the driveway, was eating this all up for the night's news.

Pat took the bridle and walked Pony back to the empty stall. He made sure he had fresh hay to eat then went back out front to his dad and Agent Parsons.

Pat shook Parson's hand and thanked him for bringing Pony to him. Then he told Patrick that he had been in the parade with him and that he has a big horse.

Parsons and Patrick exchanged tales of the parades they had been in, and each invited the other to attend their town's celebration in the future. Then Parsons told him about the press conference.

"Since I am the lead agent at the Cheyenne office, I will answer questions about the arrest. Agents Abernathy and Parker will be here as well. We have heard the Army will call him back to active duty and court-martial him for the five charges I believe you have been briefed on. He is also being charged with conspiracy to obstruct jus- tice. They will be announced tomorrow."

"What about Mrs. Duval?"

"She will be charged with Accessory to Conspire to Commit Assault after the fact, since she knew afterward what happened, Conspiracy to Kidnapping and Conspiracy to Obstruct Justice. The last charge has been recently added as she did nothing to provide information to the other two charges. If she is found guilty, she will get twenty-five to life. Unfortunately, your son may have to testify at her trial but not the court-martial."

"Why at her trial?"

"Her lawyer wants to show that Mrs. Duval did not harm the boy and that she had worked with him on his schoolwork and showed genuine love for him."

"Which trial will be held first? His or hers?"

"That we do not know yet—probably hers since we have to go with when the Federal court has an opening. The court-mar- tial will be held when the Army has everything locked up. If he is found guilty of all charges, he will get life with no chance of parole at Leavenworth under protective custody. He'd probably be happier at Super Max in Florence, Colorado."

After Parsons left, Patrick went inside to find Pat had changed into jeans and wanted to go riding. Patrick told him that Pony wanted to rest after his long ride, but he could ride him the next day. Then he called a family meeting.

Patrick told them some of what Parsons had told him such as who was going to be there for the press conference including Paul and John. Everyone would be at the house by 0830 for the conference, which would begin at 9:00 a.m. He told Pat that some of the media will shout questions to him and for him to answer their questions if he could. "If you do not understand the questions, ask me or your mom." The next morning at eight, Paul and John arrived, and Pat took them out first thing to see Pony. The FBI agents showed up at 0830. Pat went up to Parker and gave her a hug and shook hands with the other agents. Don told them that the International Press was now included in the gaggle of reporters. He looked at Pat and told him, "You are a young hero, young man."

At 0855, the deputy let the media in up to the front porch. Everyone inside came out. Don spoke first, introducing everyone on the porch including Sherrie Leigh, who was trying to hide behind her mother's dress. Then the questions began.

"Mrs. Johnson, can you tell us how you feel now that your son is back?"

"I am extremely pleased and thankful to both the FBI and the Cold Case Investigators who assisted the FBI in solving my son's kidnapping."

"Mr. Gibbons, you were involved from the beginning, correct?"

"Yes, you are correct. I was the lead investigator."

"What was your role in assisting the FBI?"

"We gathered information from various sources that led to the arrests."

"This question is for the young boy. Were you mistreated by the ones that took you away?"

"No, they did not hit me or spank me."

"How do you feel about being back with your mom, dad, and your little sister?"

"I like it. I did not even know I had a sister. She is okay."

"Agent Parker, you had the boy after the kidnappers were arrested. How did he sound to you?"

"He appeared perfectly normal for a six-year-old. As you can tell, he seems to be like a rubber band, very flexible."

"Agent Parsons, what was in the horse trailer you pulled in with yesterday afternoon?"

"That was Patrick Jr.'s horse, Pony. He had said he missed it, so we decided to bring it out for him. If you were here yesterday afternoon, you would have seen how happy he was to see Pony—and yes, the horse's name is Pony."

Don raised his hand and said that there would be only one more question.

"Agent Abernathy, as the Special Agent in Charge of this case since the beginning, can you tell us the actual charges that are being brought forward for each individual?"

"I will answer this in two parts. The first is Mrs. Josie Duval. She has been initially charged with Conspiracy to Commit Assault after the fact and Conspiracy to Commit Kidnapping. She has had one additional change, and that is Conspiracy to Obstruct Justice. She will be tried in the United States District Court in Los Angeles with the date to be determined."

He looked at them and then added, "Mr. Roderick Duval is being recalled back to active duty to face a General Court-Martial. The charges so far are Conspiracy to Commit Assault, Conspiracy to Commit Kidnapping, and one more has been added—Conspiracy to Commit Obstruction of Justice. The Department of the Army will conduct the General Court-Martial at March Air Reserve Base. They will put out a release as to when and the exact charges as they are considering other charges as well."

He looked at the media crowd and thanked them for coming, then the Johnsons and the others went inside to wait for the crowd to leave. Pat wanted to take Parsons out to show him how happy Pony was. "You can see how happy he is now that he is back with me again." He tugged his hand and said, "Please?" All the men went out the back door to see Pony, who was happy to see Pat and Parsons, for that matter.

Parsons looked at Patrick, who nodded, and he went back to the trailer that was parked near the stables. He came back with Pat's BB rifle and scabbard. "I forgot to give you this yesterday, but your dad says you can have it as long as you are careful with it."

Pat thanked him and went to his dad and thanked him for letting him have it. "Now when we go riding, I can be a cowboy again," which got everyone to laugh.

Parsons noticed that the media crowd had thinned out, so he hooked up the trailer to his truck and asked Parker if she was ready to go back.

She looked at Pat with tears in her eyes, went to him, gave him a hug, whispered in his ear, and gave him a kiss on his cheek. She thanked Don for putting her up since Friday, thanked Paul and John for their assistance, and climbed into the truck. Parsons pulled out with both of them waving goodbye.

The other three left with Patrick and Pat still at the stables. Patrick looked at Pat and told him that even though the BB rifle was his, it would be locked up in the safe with his rifle and guns.

"You can use it only when I am with you. Okay, son?"

"Same rules, huh, Dad? Safety first?"

"That's right. Now let's go inside and have lunch." Patrick let Pat carry his BB rifle while he put his hand on his son's shoulder.

Yes, everything is going to work out just fine, Patrick thought to himself.

61

Two days after Parsons and Parker returned to Cheyenne, Duval's attorney, Mr. Perkins, provided the letter Rod had written and asked that it be given to Mrs. Johnson before either of the trials started. He told Agent Parsons, "This does not justify what he did. However, he wanted to let her know why."

Parsons told him that he would pass it on to the LA Field Office and ask the Special Agent in Charge to give it to the Johnsons. Before sending it to Don, he read it and shared it with the other three agents involved in the case. All they could do was shake their heads. All remained quiet except for Wilkerson.

"This jerk wad thinks he can write this crap and hope he can justify what he did to that poor woman and her family? My god, he killed an unborn child. I hope he rots in hades."

Parsons chided him, "Calm down, Wilkie, this guy has only had an arraignment on three charges. He does not know about the other ones that the Army is going to slam his ass with, so chill out!"

Parsons faxed the letter to Agent Abernathy along with the request from Duval's attorney to pass it on to Mrs. Johnson. He also asked, on behalf of the crew at the office, how Patrick Jr. was getting along. He closed by asking that they be kept updated as to how things go in California.

Two days later, the FBI office in Cheyenne was tasked with providing manpower to escort both Mr. and Mrs. Duval to California for pretrial confinement. Considering the publicity that they had received over the kidnapping and the other charges, it was deemed necessary to transport them in separate FBI aircraft.

Special Agent Young would escort Rod Duval to March Air Reserve Base in Riverside, and Special Agent Parker would escort Josie Duval to the Metropolitan Detention Center in Los Angeles. They would both be met by FBI agents from the Los Angeles area. Even though they would fly out of the Cheyenne airport, they would not see each other nor had they seen each other since their arrests.

Josie arrived first, wearing blue jeans, a Western shirt, sneakers, and handcuffs. She was met by the local newspaper and TV station. Parker had warned Josie that the media might be there and for her not to say a word to them, not even to answer their questions.

Once onboard the jet, Parker strapped Josie into her seat and lowered the window shades so that Josie could not see Rod arrive at the airport.

Young, having advanced knowledge of the media at the airport, went straight up to the perimeter gate in an attempt to bypass the press. The media saw it was Rod in the car, and they swarmed around it, trying to take pictures of Rod inside the car.

Once inside the gate, they drove right up to the jet. As Rod stepped out of the car, the photographers were able to take pictures of him in his full dress Army uniform since he had been called back to active duty for his court-martial.

Once on board the jet, Young did the same thing as Parker had done, securing Rod in his seat and lowering all the shades except for the window by Young's seat. Rod knew it would be a long flight especially if he could not look out the windows. It was just like flying in a military transport, he thought.

Josie's jet arrived at Los Angeles International Airport and taxied to the private hanger used by the FBI. She was taken to the detention center and placed in protective custody due to the kidnapping charge. Her trial would start in forty-five days.

Rod's jet arrived at March Air Reserve Base for security reasons, and he was placed in confinement immediately. He changed from his dress uniform to a set of fatigues and was placed in a cell by himself.

He would not be out of his cell except under armed guard—more to protect him from other prisoners than to prevent him from attempting to escape.

The next day, Sergeant First Class Roderick Duval, US Army (Retired) had two visitors. One was his Army Defense Counsel, Captain Adams, and the other was his civilian attorney, Mr. Perkins. It was Perkins that introduced Adams to Rod and told him that Captain Adams had bad news for him.

"SFC Duval, you have been previously arraigned in Federal Court for assault and kidnapping. However, the Army is going forward with the following Articles from the *Uniform Code of Military Justice*. You will be formally arraigned tomorrow from the military judge. We are going to advise you of all the charges."

At the words *all the charges*, Rod's face turned white. "What do you mean 'all the charges'? I was arraigned on two charges in Cheyenne. What's going on here?"

Captain Adams continued, "Articles 120—Rape, 118—Murder, 128,—Assault Resulting in Bodily Harm, 119a—Death of an Unborn Child, 134—Kidnapping, and 131b—Obstruction of Justice. For the two murder charges, if found guilty, you could get the death penalty. I believe we can get you life without parole."

"Murder? What murders? I did not kill anyone," Rod protested loudly. "Sherrie survived. I saw here on TV. So who did I kill?"

Perkins looked at Captain Adams and nodded his head for him to tell him since it was the Army bringing the charges of murder.

Captain Adams looked at his sheet and told him that he was being changed with the murder of Ms. Rose MacDonald. "On or about 30 June 1989, you did puncture the brake hose on Ms. MacDonald's car, causing her brakes to fail and causing her to crash into a wall in her parking garage at her home, which resulted in her death, in violation of Article 118." He paused and then continued with the second murder charge. "On or about 4 March 1992, while committing the assault on the victim, you caused her to lose her unborn child, in violation of Article 119A."

At this, he slumped in his seat, his face suddenly drained of color. He looked around the room for something in case he lost his cookies. Instead, he swallowed the sour bile rising in his throat and said, "I did not know she was pregnant." He then asked what was next.

"Tomorrow morning, you will go face the Military Judge, Colonel Mark Conyers, who will read all the specifications to you.

You will be asked to state your plea to each charge and specification." He paused before he continued.

"Both Mr. Perkins and I strongly urge you to plead guilty to all charges, and you will receive life without parole. Otherwise, you face the maximum penalty for the two murders that you are being charged with. Granted, the second one was unknowingly. However, you still allegedly caused the death of an unborn child. That may count in your favor."

"If I plead guilty, will that prevent the Johnsons from attending? Will I have a choice of it being publicized?"

"I am afraid that due to the enormity of the crimes that you are being charged with, keeping the victim's family away is not going to happen—plus the fact of the damage you have brought forth against the Army, the media will want to be in attendance as well."

Rod looked at Perkins and asked him how his wife was doing and how she was going to plead.

"Your wife has an excellent lawyer, well versed in both Federal and local laws. Mrs. Duval is as well as can be expected, like you, in a cell by herself. From what her attorney, a Mrs. Matthews, has told me, she is going to suggest she plead guilty to the three charges and will get twenty-five to fifty years with no parole."

"Can I write or talk to her?"

"Not until both trials are over with. This is standard procedure," Adams said. "Think about what we have suggested, and we will see you tomorrow morning at 0900 when you see the judge."

* * * * *

At the same time Rod was meeting with his defense team, Josie was meeting with her lawyer, Ms. Matthews, at the detention center. Since her trial would be after Rod's court-martial, she had more time to prepare her defense of being an accessory to the assault after the fact since she did not know exactly what had transpired prior to Rod taking JR.

Matthews explained to Josie that she would go in front of the judge the next day to be arraigned on the additional charge of Conspiracy to Commit Obstruction of Justice and would enter a plea. "At that time, I will ask the judge to let you plead not guilty to Conspiracy to Assault After the Fact and guilty to Conspiracy to Kidnapping and Conspiracy to Obstruction of Justice. Those two guilt pleas will get you at least twenty-five."

"How is Rod, and when does his trial start? Will I be called to testify against him?"

"As far as I know, Mr. Duval is doing as well as can be expected. He is like you, in a cell by himself. You cannot testify against your spouse in California, and I would not recommend it anyway. That is a double-edged sword. His attorney, Mr. Perkins, has advised me that he will be seeing his military judge tomorrow for all the charges against him. His charges are far more serious than yours."

"Will I be able to see little JR? Will he have to testify?"

"This is something I wanted to talk to you about," Matthews replied. "How was he with you when it was just you and the boy? Did you ever have to punish him for the smallest problem?"

"No, he was a good boy right from the beginning. He caused no problems that he needed to be punished for. Together we worked on his coloring books, and I started working with him on how to read and spell. Both Rod and I encouraged him to read aloud to us from his favorite books. I loved him as if he was my natural son."

"If you want him to testify in court, I will have to clear it with his parents. It might help your case some, but I will not guarantee it. We do not know how he will react seeing you again, knowing what you did."

"When do I go see the judge here? Tomorrow?"

"Yes, tomorrow morning at ten. I will bring you clothes to wear tomorrow. Think about what I said about pleading tomorrow. I will see you just before you go into the courtroom. Be prepared for the press, and do not say anything to them. Nothing is to be uttered out of your mouth to the press, am I clear?"

"Yes, you are clear—absolutely clear."

62

Later that afternoon, Paul received a phone call from Patrick concerning Rod's arraignment hearing on all the UCMJ Articles. "Paul, we just received a phone call from that scum's attorney about the hearing. Evidently, it is open to the public. Do you and John want to join us? After all, you guys were the investigators at the beginning. You guys helped close the case."

"Yeah, I'll go. John is working the Happy Paperhanger cold case I told you about. This perp has the cops going nuts in Riverside County. So far, he has not left the county that we know of."

"Hope you can catch him before he moves to another county like Kern. If he does, maybe I can brush off my investigative skills and catch him myself. Oh, by the way, Pat is looking forward to helping us build his new bedroom. He says he is tired of looking at 'dolls and other girl stuff.' He is a remarkable kid, adjusting easily."

"I was going to ask you how he was doing. Is he going to need mental health monitoring? Maybe the court will have Duval pay for it out of his forfeiture of his retirement pay if he is found guilty."

"Sounds like a damn good idea to me. I will have to ask. We are due to meet the Army prosecutor, some major by the name of Davidson. Can you do a check on him for me? I don't want to abuse my position with the Kern Country Posse."

"Consider it done, my old friend. I will give you the info tomorrow morning. I'll meet you and Sherrie at 0830? What about the kids? Need a babysitter? I am sure Anne would love to come out to the ranch to help." "Thanks, Paul, but as soon as we got the phone call, Sherrie called Betsy, and she will skip her classes at the junior college and be here—some sort of 'parenting classes.' This way she gets hands-on training, so to speak, and the kids love her."

"John just came in with that damned arched eyebrow of his. See you tomorrow at 0830."

Before Paul hung up, John came into his office and told him he had some news on the paperhanger.

"Paul, first, what is at 0830 with Patrick and Sherrie? Something happen to them?"

"No, that scum's UCMJ arraignment hearing is tomorrow. I understand it is open to the public, so I am going to be there, and so should you since we were the first investigators. So what's up with the arched eyebrow?"

"This guy hit four towns this past week—Palm Springs, Indo, Hemet, and Blythe. He also wore the same disguise, struck at different times of the day, and always had his face covered up. One clerk told the Hemet PD that his left hand was wrapped up in gauze that covered his fingertips. This guy is crafty. Do you have any ideas?"

"No, John, not really. It seems he is branching out. Maybe we need to call in some outside help on this one. How about Patrick once his case is finally finished?"

"What about his part-time job with Kern County? Won't this cause a conflict even though it is in a different county? How about if I search for other private investigators in the areas that he is hitting now? Can't hurt none, boss."

Paul thought about it, not wanting to hurt his own business, but it did make sense. "Go ahead, search for a *reputable* PI, one that is in our directory, and see if they can help us out. Just remind them we are the lead PI in this case as we have a contract with the PD."

After John left, Paul pulled out his old copy of the UCMJ to look at the maximum penalty that Mr. Duval could receive if found guilty on all counts. He saw that for the charges of rape and murder, the maximum penalty was death. He doubted he would get that, but

Duval would probably wish he could get it. It would be much better than isolated confinement for the rest of his life.

It will be very interesting tomorrow, he thought to himself.

He then opened his computer to check on Major Davidson, the US Army prosecutor.

63

The next morning, Paul and John met Patrick and Sherrie at the at March Air Reserve Base Legal Office. Patrick and Sherrie had just come out of their meeting with the Army Prosecutor, Major Davidson.

Patrick told them that Davidson still had not heard how Duval would plead. "If he is smart, he will plead guilty to all charges. That way he will get life without parole."

John, raising his eyebrow, which made Sherrie giggle, mumbled under his breath, "Life is too good for that sum na bitch."

They all went into the courtroom, which was packed with reporters, other Army personnel, and some Special Forces troops. At the front behind the prosecution table were four empty chairs.

At 0859, SFC Roderick Duval was escorted in by two Air Force Security Police with his two attorneys. Rod was in his dress uniform including his Green Beret with the Fifth Special Forces flash. He glanced at Sherrie out of the corner of his eye but did not smile at her or show any emotion.

At exactly 0900, the room was called to attention as Colonel Mark Conyers marched in and took his seat. He ordered everyone to be seated. He told the spectators that there would be order at all times and there would be no opening statements or witnesses. This was an arraignment for the charges under the *Uniform Code of Military Justice*. He then asked the defendant to rise.

"Sergeant First Class Roderick Duval, you have been called back to active duty by the Army Chief of Staff to face a General Court-Martial for the following offenses under the UCMJ that you committed while serving on active duty. You will plead your status guilty or not guilty after each individual charge. If at any time you do not understand the charge, you may consult your attorney. Do you understand these instructions?"

"Loud and clear, Sir!"

"SFC Duval, you are charged with Rape, in violation of UCMJ Article 120. How do you plead?"

"Guilty, Sir."

"SFC Duval, you are charged with Murder, in violation of UCMJ Article 118. How do you plead?"

"Guilty, Sir."

SFC Duval, you are charged with Bodily Harm, in violation of UCMJ Article 128. How do you plead?"

"Guilty, Sir."

"SFC Duval, you are charged with Death or Injury of an Unborn Child, in violation of UCMJ Article 119A. How do you plead?"

His shoulders sagged as he replied, "Not guilty, Sir."

At this, Sherrie uttered a gasp, and Patrick held her tightly, comforting her.

Colonel Conyers paused for a moment then continued. "SFC Duval, you are charged with Kidnapping, in violation of UCMJ Article 125. How do you plead?"

"Guilty, Sir."

"SFC Duval, you are charged with Obstruction of Justice, in violation of UCMJ Article 134. How do you plead?"

"Guilty, Sir."

"SFC Duval, you may be seated."

Patrick whispered to Sherrie to ask if she was okay or if she needed to leave the room. He was obviously concerned over her reaction to Duval's not guilty plea to the Death of an Unborn charge.

While her eyes bored into the back of Duval's skull, she nodded her head that she was okay and wanted to stay in the courtroom and see the entire proceedings.

Conyers called the prosecutor and both defense attorneys to the bench. He covered the microphone and covered his mouth so no one could read his lips as he talked to them. He then had them step back. The defense attorneys, Adams and Perkins, then explained to Duvall what would transpire next.

"The defendant will rise," Convers ordered.

"SFC Duval, you have this one opportunity to change your plea to UCMJ Article 119A, Death of an Unborn. Do you wish to change your plea of not guilty?"

"No, Sir, I still plead not guilty to this charge."

"Your defense team has explained to you the maximum punishment you face if found guilty of this charge?"

"Yes, Sir, they have. I understand the maximum punishment if I am found guilty."

"Based on your 'not guilty' plea, you are hereby remanded to the confinement facility here at March Air Reserve Base until your General Court-Martial is convened." He looked at his calendar and then continued. "Your court-martial will convene thirty days from today." He brought down the gavel, stood, and left.

Rod conversed with his attorneys and then was escorted out between two USAF Security Policemen, not looking to either side, just straight ahead, as if no one else was in the room.

"Well, if anyone deserves to die, it is him. Too bad they won't put him in a cell with some big burly guy that is looking for a cell wife," John observed.

"John, shut up for a change," Patrick told him as he looked at Sherrie and began to escort her out of the courtroom through the media that was crowded outside the doorway.

As soon as they started to hurl the questions, Sherrie looked at them with a stern look and told them in no uncertain terms, "I have no comment at this time." The four of them, under escort of two burly SPs, walked through the media gaggle.

By the time they finally left the Base Legal Office, they decided it was lunchtime, so they went to a small diner outside the gate and found a small booth in the rear. Both John and Paul had their backs to the wall so they could see the entry door while Sherrie and Patrick sat along the sidewall.

Everyone was silent until Patrick asked, "Anyone have thoughts?" Sherrie was the first to speak up. "Guys, I know this sounds crazy, but if I did not know I was pregnant, then how could he have known? How can they charge him with this crime if he did not know?"

Paul was the first to answer. "That is why he is pleading not guilty. He is hedging his bets on the death penalty that since he did not know, he will not get death. With everything else he has pending, and his admitting to Rose's murder, I will venture to say he will be found not guilty of this one but will get life with everything else."

"Do you think I will have to take the stand and testify and relive that horrible day again, this time to everyone including the press that I know will be there?"

Patrick looked at her and told her that she might have to testify. "I just hope it does not cause you to go into premature labor. A courtroom packed with a bunch of service people and the media is definitely not the place to have twins."

John piped up and told them, "With all of them SF folks, they all have medical training. She would not have to wait for medical help to arrive."

They ate their meals with Sherrie picking at her salad, not really wanting to eat.

To change the subject, Patrick reminded them that the project to build Pat's room would get into full swing Saturday morning. "He is willing to help. Though I seriously doubt he can swing a hammer hard enough yet, he can still be our 'gofer' person. You have it set up with your Army buddy to come along as well? I know I will need him for the electrical job."

Sherrie asked if Anne and MJ were coming as well. "The three of us plus Sherrie Leigh will make sure there are sandwiches for lunch, and Patrick said he would grill steaks and burgers. Right, Patrick?"

"Well, since you reminded me, I guess I am cooking that night. Guess I better not drink too many beers then," he said, which got everyone to laugh.

Patrick then asked Paul what was new with his latest cold case, the Happy Paperhanger.

"Patrick, this guy is branching out to places like Hemet and Indio. He is altering his disguise to include rubber gloves and wrapping gauze on his hand that covers his fingertips but still wearing a trench coat and a brown fedora despite the weather. No one knows where he will strike next. We need some extra help."

"What businesses does he hit? Liquor stores? Supermarkets? Anything else?"

"Gas stations, small stores only. No banks, post offices, nor supermarkets."

"Maybe you need to swallow your pride, Paul, and ask for outside help. The PD swallowed theirs and asked you to help them—or perhaps another investigator?"

John quickly jumped in and told Patrick, "This is exactly what I suggested yesterday. He says he is thinking about it but needs to know what happens with your job in Kern County? Will that cause a conflict of interest for you if you come work with us?"

"I do not see a problem, but I will have to check on it with the county attorney and the county sheriff. I will get back to you. Speaking of which, we have to get back. I have a posse meeting tonight."

Since it was not really a business lunch, they divided the bill three ways, and Sherrie threw in the tip. Outside they agreed to meet at Patrick's at 0900 Saturday with wives and tools.

On the way home, Sherrie looked at Patrick and asked him, "You miss working with them, don't you? You miss the camaraderie that the three of you built up. Be honest with me."

"Yes, I do miss it. Sure there are other veterans on the posse, but I never worked with them before. I will check with the posse boss tonight and see what he says. I love you, honey."

"I love you too, and I am really okay with what happened today."

64

The following Saturday at 0830, Paul, John, and their wives arrived with Bob Youngston. Youngston had told Paul to tell Patrick not to purchase any electrical items, that he would do it and bring exactly what he would need based on the drawing Paul had shown him. He would charge him only cost and no labor since he was doing a BBQ for everyone that evening.

Patrick had already laid out the foundation and had poured the concrete so that it would be set by Saturday. Both Patrick and Pat wrote their names in the concrete.

Anne and MJ went inside, carrying bags of food items for the day and to help Sherrie around the house. Both Anne and MJ loved Sherrie Leigh, and she showed them her doll collection that she had moved into her parents' bedroom so that her brother would not destroy them. No matter what Sherrie told her, she was not convinced.

Patrick had set the guidelines for Pat to help out—no tools— and if someone needed him to move out of the way, he had to do it quickly. He would be the gofer, and Patrick even got him a hard hat to wear.

Pat went to John and told him he was going to be a gofer. "But what is a gofer?"

John looked at Pat and raised his eyebrow, which always made Pat laugh, and told him, "A gofer is a young boy who has to go fer whatever is needed."

The first thing that had to be done was to build the frame of the room. Pat was kept busy getting extra nails when asked and ensuring that everyone had something to drink. By twelve o'clock, the wall frames were done, and everyone broke for lunch. Pat exclaimed that he did not know what the hard part was—"Watching you do the work or getting what you needed."

The girls came out with sandwiches, chips, and coffee or water. It was then that Paul asked Patrick if he had thought about coming to work for him and John as a Cold Case Investigator and if he had spoken to his posse chief.

"Yeah, I spoke to the posse chief, and he says as long as it does not interfere or cause a conflict of interest with Kern County, I can do it. Sherrie and I have talked about it, and she thinks it would be great for me to join up with you and John again."

Paul told him that he missed the camaraderie that the three of them had set up back in the Cop Shop, as they called the squadron. "It will be great to have you with us. Come by the office Monday, and Janet can do the paperwork. By the way, did you have a background investigation done when you applied for the posse?"

"Yes, and it has been updated this year. You should be able to use it."

Patrick looked at his watch and told everyone that break time was over, and it was time to get back to work.

"Same old slave driver," John mumbled with a smile.

"Never thought I would miss it."

By 3:00 p.m., the wall frame was up and secured. Paul and Patrick went to work on the roof while Bob began to install the wiring. John put up the Sheetrock against the outside wall studs. Just as the sun was going down, the roof was up, and the room was enclosed from the outside.

The timing was good as it was time for Patrick to start the fire in the grill. It was an old-fashioned brick barbeque grill big enough for ten medium-size steaks. That night it would be seven steaks and two burgers. He used some mesquite from his land and wood chips that he had been drying out for just this purpose.

The guys washed up while the girls brought out the potato salad and told Patrick that the corn on the cob would be cooking as soon as he put the meat on.

While Patrick was cooking the meat, Pat asked his dad if he could sleep in his own room tonight since it had walls and a roof.

Patrick laughed and said, "No, the room is not finished yet. One night, this coming week, you will. We have to finish the inside walls, make sure the electricity works, and we need to put a door in." "Okay, but can we hurry up? I'm tired of looking at dolls all over the room and the sissy stuff on the walls."

By the time everyone was finished eating, both Pat and Leigh were falling asleep where they sat. Patrick carried Pat in and came out for Leigh. Anne and MJ took the dishes inside while Paul, John, and Bob put the tools inside the new bedroom.

They told Patrick they would be back the next day at noon, knowing that Patrick and Sherrie would go to early Mass.

* * * * *

When Patrick and Sherrie arrived home after Mass, they found the three guys working. "How did you get inside to get the tools? My house was locked."

John looked at him sheepishly and told him, "There was no glass, so I climbed in the new window." Paul and Bob both laughed at John's expression.

Patrick and Pat both changed and went outside to see how things were going. Patrick joined Paul and John putting up the out-side wall that matched the rest of the house while Pat was in his new room, trying to help Bob hang the bedroom door. Bob showed Pat how the wall plates over his light switch and electrical sockets were attached to the walls. Bob hung a light from the ceiling that looked like a lamp from an old Western bunkhouse, which made Pat very happy.

Sherrie came into the new room with wallpaper that showed a Western design of cowboys and horses. "Yes, I think this will go perfect in here. It will match his new bedroom set and the view outside his window."

Bob offered to hang the wallpaper for her. By 8:00 p.m., the room was finished, and the bedroom furniture would be put in the next day. The guys sat around outside, talking, having a few beers, wondering how they got it all done in two days.

Bob said it in two words *team work*. He took a slug of beer and said,

"By the way, your town building inspector will be out here tomorrow to check it out before Pat can use it. That is a rule here in California—electrical work needs to be certified and signed off before use."

"That makes sense, Bob. By the way, how are you with bathrooms? I need to add another one especially with twins on the way." Paul told Patrick that Bob was good with bathrooms that he helped replace the one in the office. "Army combat engineer, almost as good as our red horse and prime beef that we have in the Air Force, right?"

"If we knew anyone in the area that was red horse or prime beef plus Army combat engineer, we could build a new home in a matter of time, but I do not think that Sherrie or the kids are ready for hardback tents, and I certainly do not want to be in one again if I can help it," Patrick replied.

Everyone laughed and agreed with his comment as they all had spent time sleeping in those quarters in the field. Bob was the first to leave as he figured that the other three wanted to talk.

Paul asked Patrick to come to the office by 9:00 a.m. and asked him if there were any restrictions on his working five days a week with them.

"The only restriction is if I am called in for posse duty for a search-and-rescue mission or for any other reason. Also, when the twins are born, I will not be at work. Don't worry, I will not ask for family medical leave as I know that I will not be there long enough to accrue the time I want."

"It's a deal then, pal. Welcome aboard. Both John and I need to get going. See you at 0900."

Patrick picked up all the empty beer cans and took them inside. He went to look at the new bedroom from the inside for the first time. He liked how it looked and admired the job Bob did with the wallpaper. He explained to Sherrie that the town building inspector would be by the next day to sign off on the electrical work, and then they could move Pat's new furniture into the room tomorrow night.

Sherrie told him that Pat was excited about the room and could not wait to sleep in it. They looked and figured out where the bed, dresser, and desk would go. Bob had put in an outlet near where the desk would go for the desk lamp.

"What about the twins, honey?"

"They will sleep in our room at first just like JR. I mean Pat did when he was born and just like Leigh did when she was born. We can add their bedroom later or just build a new home."

"Why not keep the ranch and buy a bigger home? We do not have to rush into it now," Patrick told her.

The next morning at 0900, Patrick showed up at Cold Case Investigators to have Janet fill out his paperwork. She gave him the paperwork to take to the SB PD for his concealed permit until he showed her that he was carrying his permit card from the state of California. Since he was a reserve deputy sheriff, he was cleared.

She showed him the layout of the building and where he would be working.

"Where is John? I understand I am going to be working with him on the paperhanger case."

She took him back to John's office, where he was on the phone with a half-eaten donut on his desk with a frown on his face.

He looked up and waved Patrick in and hung up the phone.

"You are not going to believe this, Patrick. This guy walked into the Indian Wells PD and pays a $100 fine last Thursday. The check was deposited Friday morning. It bounced, and this time he wore a blue Dodgers baseball cap and windbreaker. Had his right arm in a sling and bandages up to his fingertips."

"I suggest we go talk to the Indian Wells PD and see if they have a closed circuit TV system."

John told Paul where they were going and did not know when they would return. They were hoping that they might be able to look at a CCTV video.

65

The days that followed Patrick starting to work for Paul Gibbons went fast. There were still multiple items that needed to be done as far as Pat was concerned.

The FBI was able to obtain Pat's medical records from both the hospital at F. E. Warren AFB and the private doctor that took care of him. With these showing that Pat was current with his shots, Sherrie enrolled him at the local elementary school.

Sherrie followed the arraignment of Josie Duval, hoping that she would not plead not guilty, for that would mean that Pat might be called to testify. As it would happen, she pled guilty to Conspiracy to Commit Kidnapping, Conspiracy to Commit Assault (after the fact), and Conspiracy to Obstruction of Justice. Her sentencing would he adjudged after Rod's Court-Martial.

Sherrie also made an appointment for Pat to see a juvenile psychologist to see how the past four years had affected him. So far, at home there were no indications of problems, but she and Patrick wanted to make sure.

The psychologist interviewed Pat at length to ask him about his four years with the Duvals and if they had harmed him in any way—either physically, verbally, or emotionally. He spent forty-five minutes with Pat and then spoke to Sherrie about his findings.

"Your son is remarkable for his age. I do not see any emotional damage that is sometimes evident after a major trauma like this with kids. However, I do recommend we have a few more follow-up sessions just to make sure that he is okay and is able to participate with other kids his age. He was alone for the past four years with the exception of a few times he told me he was with neighbor kids and his school friends."

"I do not care how long it takes or how many sessions you need. I just want to make sure my son is mentally okay for the future. He now has his own room, and he is happy. He is in school, and so far, we have not had any problems."

The psychologist told her that it was probably not a good idea to have him at the court-martial of his abductor. "We do not know what type of reaction Pat might have if he were to see him again. You have told me that Mrs. Duval has pled guilty to her charges, so he will not have to testify at her trial as to how they raised him. In a strange way, this might be her way of convincing herself that she loves him and wants to spare him the agony of seeing her again."

"How often do you want to see him for the near future?"

"I think every two weeks to start off with, and we can go from there. If he starts to have problems with his sister or at school, then maybe once a week, but let's take things one step at a time." He paused then continued, "How is your daughter accepting Pat? Any problems with her? Anything I should know about?"

"At first, she was upset because Pat was staying in her room, but now that they have their own rooms, she is fine. In fact, Pat is trying to teach Sherrie Leigh how to read comic books though not the type little girls would read."

He chuckled and said he would see Pat in two weeks and for her to make the appointment.

* * * * *

Ten days before the court-martial, the Army Prosecutor, Major Davidson, called Sherrie and said that he would like to meet with her, Patrick, and Paul the next day at the Base Legal Office at March Air Reserve Base. "I just want to iron out some details. I realize you are pregnant., Will you be up to testifying?"

"Yes, I will testify."

When Patrick got him, Sherrie told him of the phone call and that Davidson had asked her if she would testify. "Of course, I said that I would testify."

Patrick called Paul to tell him of the appointment the next day. He had no clue what it was about, just that Davidson wanted to "iron out details."

"Good. See you tomorrow at 0900. Goodbye."

* * * * *

The next morning, the three of them met with Davidson, who asked questions about the assault, what Patrick had discovered when he arrived home, and what Paul first saw. Then he added one important piece of information.

"We will also call Colonel (USAF Ret) Dr. Thompson who will describe the damage that caused the death of your unborn child. I know it will be rough for you, and if you wish to be outside the room during his testimony, you can be."

"No, I want to be in that room when the doc describes the result of what he did to me. I want to see that bastard's reaction."

"That may be the case now, but I will have the judge allow you to leave the courtroom if you do not desire to hear the testimony of Dr. Thompson."

He looked at the three of them and told them to be there in his office at 0800 on the day of the trial for any questions that might come up by either him or the defense counsel. Patrick asked him if the judge could order him, through Duval's forfeiture of pay, to have it used to pay for any and all mental health expenses incurred by either Pat or the family.

Davidson said that was already presented to the judge and the defense attorneys. "No one has objections to this proposal."

Sherrie thanked him for talking to them and for the kind offer he made to allow her to leave the room during the trial when Dr. Thompson would testify as to the damage done due to the assault. Leaving the base, they decided to stop at a local donut shop.

Patrick and Paul had coffee and a frosted donut while Sherrie had water. Patrick looked at her and asked if she really wanted to be there during the testimony by Thompson, thinking of how far along she was with the twins.

"Yes, Patrick, I will be fine. I want to see his reaction when Thompson gives his testimony. I don't care if he did not know I was pregnant. That does not alter the fact of what he did to me." She took a sip of water and had them tell her about this paperhanger case.

Paul let Patrick tell her since he was working with John on the case.

"Honey, you would not believe it. This guy has got some real balls. His latest targets have been two different police departments in Riverside County. He has altered his disguise and has no fingerprints on one hand, and his other hand is completely covered up with gauze. He changes from an overcoat to a windbreaker and baseball cap." He stopped as Paul had nudged his leg with his foot and nodded over toward the wall near the door.

There sitting by himself was a male, about six feet and about 180 pounds. He was wearing a blue LA Dodgers ball cap and a blue Dodgers windbreaker. He also noticed one arm was wrapped in gauze that was in a sling. "Paul, that fits the description from the PDs that got hit. Their CCTV video does not show much though."

He noticed they were looking at him, and he got up suddenly and left, not running but in a hurry as if he were late for an appointment. He went out the door and turned left, where he mingled with a crowd of young people all wearing Dodgers caps and blue windbreakers and all heading in the same direction.

By the time they got to the door, he was gone, lost in the crowd. Then they saw a blue Vespa scooter with the operator having both hands on the handle bars with one hand completely wrapped in gauze and the sling flapping against his back.

"Did you get the plate number?" "No, did you?"

"Nope, he is long gone now. Obviously, his arm problem is a fake. I think we need to contact Riverside PD and tell them what just happened," Paul told Patrick.

"Roger that. You're the boss. You tell them the best PIs lost their suspect," Patrick said with that crooked smile of his.

They got back to the table, and while Paul went to call the PD, Sherrie told Patrick, "See, I told you that you missed working with them."

"Yes, dear, you were right. Thank you for letting me go back to work with them.

66

Finally, the day of the General Court-Martial of Sergeant First Class Roderick Duval had arrived. Sherrie, Patrick, Paul, John, and Doctor (USAF Colonel, Retired) Thompson arrived at the Prosecutor's office exactly at 0800. Major Davidson outlined the way it would go. "Due to the anticipated crowd of media and military personnel that have begun to show up, the court-martial will be held in the old base auditorium. To prevent any undue influence in witness testimony, until you are called in to testify, you will have to wait in the lobby, where you will not be allowed to talk to other witnesses. There will be Military Police to ensure you do not talk among each other. Once you have given your testimony, you can either have a seat behind my table or leave the auditorium." He paused and then looked at Sherrie.

"Mrs. Johnson, since you will be the first one called, you will be in the lobby only a short time during opening statements. Following you will be your husband then SMSgt (Ret) Gibbons then Doctor Thompson. Any questions so far?"

"Seeing as there are none, after the four of you are finished, I will rest, and then the defense will take over. It is unclear if SFC Duval will testify or not. It is possible that he will not. If he does not, then the judge will give instructions to the jury, which will consist of five officers and two enlisted. He will then recess the trial until they come back with a verdict. The judge may or may not impose sentence right away. Any questions?"

Thompson motioned that he had a question. "How detailed do you want my testimony to be? I can give explicit details as to the injuries that Mrs. Johnson received, or I can give the bare minimum, but it will still have the same effect."

Davidson told him, "Answer the questions in nontechnical responses if possible. Remember, the jury are not medical personnel. I will ask about how the unborn fetus died. You will need to be exact in your answer on that one."

He watched to see Sherrie's reaction to his comment. He reminded her of the option she has, and she declined to remove herself from the trial.

Sherrie asked if the judge did not impose sentence right away, would she have to come back?

Davidson stated that the answer is no. "There would be no need to have you come back for sentencing. "Now if there are no further questions, I suggest we all head over to the auditorium. Witnesses will wait in the lobby, and remember, no talking. Mr. Sommers, you can go right on in and have a seat in the front row behind me."

On the way to the auditorium, they could see all the media vehicles parked outside, the TV news vans from the major networks, plus cable news proved it would be a circus, and Patrick was glad he was not in charge of the security.

Once inside, their ID was checked against the witness list, and they were told where to sit. John, not being a witness, was told to go inside and sit behind the prosecution table on the right-hand side.

"Room attention" was called as Colonel Mark Conyers marched in and sat behind a raised podium that had the appearance of a judicial bench. He called in the jury of five commissioned officers and two enlisted soldiers. Once they were seated, he called in the defendant.

SFC Duval marched into the room, looking straight ahead to where his attorneys were seated. He then did a smart right-face movement to face Conyers. He said nothing, just stared at a point above Conyers's head as he had been trained to do during his career. Conyers told the court, "Sergeant First Class Roderic Duval, you are being tried today for your not guilty plea of the charge of Death of an Unborn Child, in violation of Article 119A, *Uniform Code of*

Military Justice. Do you wish to change your plea at this time? This is your last chance."

"No, Sir, I do not desire to change my plea."

"Captain Adams, have you briefed your client on the maximum penalty if he is found guilty of this one charge?"

Captain Adams came to attention and replied that he had advised him of the maximum penalty.

"Very well, SFC Duval, be seated." Conyers waited until Duval sat down and then asked Davidson if he was ready to proceed.

"I am, your honor. Prosecution calls Mrs. Sherrie Johnson to the stand."

The MP went to the lobby and called Sherrie. He escorted her to the front of the room, where she was sworn in. She was asked to state her name and occupation.

Not looking at Duval, she replied, "I am Mrs. Sherrie Johnson, and I am a housewife and mother."

Davidson asked her to describe to the court exactly what happened on March 4, 1992.

Looking straight at Davidson, she explained how she was resting after being up the night before with her son, Patrick Johnson Jr. She described how Duval had begun banging on the door and beginning to raise his voice. "I looked through the security hole in the door, and even though he was in an outfit that changed his appearance, I knew who it was. I had thought about calling my husband, but I did not." She stopped to compose herself as Davidson asked her to continue.

"I did not want him to wake up JR or cause a scene with the neighbors. I let him in. I was hoping that Patrick would come home for lunch early."

"Mrs. Johnson, can you point to the individual whom you let into your home that morning and how you knew it was him?"

Sherrie pointed to Duval and told the court that he had been her boyfriend years ago in high school and that he had raped her in 1989 at her birthday party.

Captain Adams jumped up to object, "Your honor, he is not charged with rape here today. I request this response be stricken."

"Overruled. I will accept it unless it affects the outcome of this trial."

"Your Honor," Perkins jumped up.

"I said overruled. Sit down, Mr. Perkins." He nodded for Sherrie to continue.

She explained how Duval wanted to see JR, how he had put his hand on her shoulder and told her how they could have had a family. "He then told me he was thirsty and wanted a glass of water. He followed me into the kitchen, and after he drained the glass, he grabbed me around my chest and I felt something sharp going into my stomach area. That is all I remember until I woke up in the hospital room after my emergency surgery."

"Mrs. Johnson, did you know you were pregnant at that time?"

"No, I did not know it. I had missed my period the month before, and I had mood swings. I was planning on going to see the doctor the next week."

"I have nothing else your honor."

"Capt Adams, your turn" Conyers stated.

Adams stood up and declared he had nothing to ask this witness.

Conyers told her to step down and for Davidson to call his next witness.

Sherrie stepped down and sat next to John behind the prosecution table. He patted her hands and winked at her.

"Prosecution calls Senior Master Sergeant Patrick Johnson, USAF (Ret), to the stand."

The MP escorted Patrick to the stand where he was sworn in and was asked to identify himself and his occupation.

"SMSgt Patrick Johnson Sr., US Air Force, Retired, former Security Police investigator, Sixty-Third Security Police Squadron. I am now currently employed as a Reserve Deputy Sheriff with the Kern County Mounted Posse. I am also employed as a part-time employee as a private investigator."

"SMSgt Johnson, would you please tell us what you saw when you arrived home for lunch on March 4, 1992."

Patrick described seeing a red pickup truck leaving his street as he turned onto it and what he found when he went inside his home. With tears in his eyes, he described seeing Sherrie on the kitchen floor, lying in a pool of dark-red blood that was flowing out of her abdomen. He described how he tried to staunch the flow of blood by using a kitchen towel and holding it with one hand while calling the Law Enforcement Desk.

"Almost immediately, I heard sirens, and I told my wife to hang on, help was coming. The medics arrived and kept the towels on but also put a pressure bandage over them. They told me that I had probably saved her life."

"Did you know that your wife was pregnant at the time?"

"I had thoughts she was, but I was not certain. I know that she had mood swings just like when she was pregnant with our son, Patrick Johnson Jr., but I was not certain. So my answer is no, I did not."

"I have nothing further, Your Honor." "Capt Adams?"

"Defense has no questions to ask at this time, sir."

Conyers told Patrick he could step down and asked Davidson if he had any more witnesses to call.

"If it pleases the court, I have just two more witnesses to call." "Go ahead."

"Thank you, Sir. Prosecution calls SMSgt Paul Gibbons, USAF (Ret)."

Paul was escorted up front, was sworn in, and was asked to identify himself.

"SMSgt Paul Gibbons, USAF, Retired. I was assigned as the lead investigator for the Sixty-Third Security Police Squadron at Norton AFB and was the lead investigator at the Johnson crime scene. I am also part owner of Cold Case Investigators."

"SMSgt Gibbons, you were one of the first to arrive at the scene, is that correct? Please tell us what you saw when you arrived."

"As the first investigator to arrive at the scene, I was designated as the lead investigator for the crime. When my partner, Technical Sergeant John Sommers, and I arrived, we found the medics still there taking care of Mrs. Johnson, who was still lying on the floor in a pool blood. The medics put her on the gurney and took her to the ambulance and left for the hospital."

"Did you see a weapon anywhere?"

"No, sir, I did not. I looked after SMSgt Johnson left the kitchen. When I went to the living room to interview him, I asked him if he had seen a weapon. He told me he did not see one, but he did not look for one."

"You are also a close friend of the Johnson family, are you not?"

"Yes, I am. I have known SMSgt Johnson and worked with him for several years. In fact, I am their son's godfather."

"I have nothing to add, Your Honor."

"Defense, do you have anything you wish to ask?"

Perkins stood up, buttoned his blue suit coat, and strode over to Paul.

"Sir, you just said you are a close friend of the victim's family, am I correct?"

"Yes, I did, and yes, you are correct."

"Did you know if Mrs. Johnson was pregnant at the time of the assault?"

"No, sir, I did not know that she was pregnant at the time." Perkins went back to his seat and told Conyers he had no further questions.

Conyers nodded toward Davidson.

"Prosecution calls Doctor Thompson to the stand." After he was seated and sworn in, he identified himself.

"I am Doctor Bertrand Thompson, Colonel, USAF, Medical Corps, Retired. I was the Hospital Commander at Norton AFB and the Chief Trauma Surgeon."

Davidson asked him to relate the events of March 4, 1992.

"I was in my office finishing up on some paperwork when I heard the call come in over the radio of an assault victim with what appeared to be multiple knife wounds. The ambulance was dispatched immediately, and I was in the ER waiting for it to arrive. When they came in, I directed them into the first cubicle that was used for trauma victims. The victim had what appeared to be kitchen towels under a pressure bandage that were completely soaked with blood. She was rushed upstairs to the OR where the staff was waiting." He had to pause before he continued.

"We had to remove her spleen as it had been damaged by a sharp instrument, definitely a knife. It was then that during a check of her other organs that we discovered she was pregnant."

"How far along was she?"

"She was two months along. The instrument that was used in the attack nicked the sack, which caused the fetus to go into shock. There was no way to save it."

"I have nothing further, Your Honor."

Adams stood up and stated that he had nothing to ask. Conyers told Thompson he could step down and have a seat. "Prosecution rests, Your Honor."

Colonel Conyers asked Captain Adams if the defense would have any witnesses.

"No, Sir, defense rests."

Conyers looked at his watch and stated that it was 1100 and stated that if there were no objections, they would break for lunch and reconvene at 1200 for closing arguments. "Court is recessed."

Everyone stood as Conyers and the jury left the room. The MPs escorted the five witnesses and John out through the media horde until they were outside.

By 1145, they had returned and were allowed back inside, sitting in the same chairs, waiting to hear the closing arguments. John whispered to Patrick that he thought the jury would be back before the end of the day and sentence would be imposed today. "I bet he gets life even if found not guilty for this one charge."

Exactly at 1200, Colonel Conyers and the jury came in followed by Duval, his SP escorts, and his attorneys.

"Major Davidson, are you ready for your closing argument?"

"Yes, sir, I am."

"Gentlemen of the jury, I thank you for your time and your patience in this heartbreaking case. You have heard from the victim and the witnesses what happened that day. True, neither she nor her husband knew she was pregnant. However, that does not negate the fact of what SFC Duval did to the victim. If he had not assaulted her the way he did, there is a strong possibility that a four-year-old child would be among us today, a brother or a sister of Patrick Johnson Jr. However, due to the assault on Mrs. Jonson, that child was taken from her before it was allowed to be born. Even though no one knew she was pregnant, you have to return a verdict of *guilty* for the death of an unborn child. The death of that unborn child was the result of SFC Duval's action four years ago. The only finding you can find is *guilty* of the Death of an Unborn Child." He returned to his seat and looked at Sherrie behind him.

Captain Adams stood up, tugged at the hem of his blouse jacket, and proceeded to the front of the jury. He looked at all seven members, making eye contact with them. He knew that the decision of life or death hung in the balance. He needed to convince the jury of five officers and two enlisted soldiers.

"Gentlemen, I too thank you for your time and patience in this trial. Yes, the unborn child died as a result of the assault committed by my client. However, no one, not even the victim, knew she was pregnant until after the fact. It was not known until the emergency surgery that she was pregnant. Since it was not premeditated, you have to find SFC Duval *not guilty*. True, if he had not assaulted Mrs. Johnson, the child would be among us today instead of us deciding my client's fate. You have no choice but to bring a verdict of *not guilty*! If he had known that she was pregnant, would he have assaulted her the way he did? We do not know that answer. You *must find him not guilty*! Thank you." He returned to his seat and patted Rod on his shoulders and smiled.

Colonel Conyers addressed the jury and gave them their instructions. "Gentlemen of the jury, you have heard the testimony today of both the victim and witnesses. The decision is yours to make. Is the defendant, SFC Roderic Duval, guilty or not guilty of Death or Injury of an Unborn Child, in violation of Article 119A of the UCMJ? You are now dismissed to the deliberation room to discuss your reasoning for the verdict."

The jury was led out of the room and into a side room by a Military Police escort that would stand in front of the door until a verdict was reached.

Colonel Conyers announced, "The court is in recess until the verdict is reached. All attorneys are to be near their phones until further notice. This court is in recess." Everyone stood until Conyers departed the room.

67

Once the jurors were in the deliberation room, they all sat back in their chairs, took a deep breath, and exhaled. They had heard information that affected them all. Three of them were fathers, and one was waiting to find out the sex of his unborn child. However, they knew they could not let their personal feelings decide the fate of the defendant.

As they all drank some water, each in his own mind, still absorbing what they heard that morning, the jury foreman first told them that they had all been selected by the convening authority, Colonel Conyers. "I know that he reviewed over one hundred personnel files. You were chosen based on your education, both military and civilian, your training, your performance reports, and your professionalism, plus none of you served with Sergeant First Class Duval." He then told them that before they go any further, he would summarize Rule 921 of the *Manual for Courts-Martial*.

"I want to summarize Rule 921, Deliberations and voting on findings of the *Manual for Courts-Martial*. Again, this is just a summary. If at the end you have any questions, feel free to ask." He paused to take a sip of water.

"Subsection a—we are to be alone in here. It also states that rank superiority is not to be influenced in our discussions here." At this point, he removed his service dress blouse and rank from his uniform to preclude intimidation. All other members of the jury did the same.

"Subsection b—our discussion is full and free-flowing based on the merits of the findings. In other words, there will be no influencing because of rank, no matter what the discussion or voting shall be. Questions?" There were none.

"Subsection c—voting will be done by secret ballot. Since this is a charge punishable by death, a guilty finding must be found by all of us. There is more, but it is dry legal stuff that would only bore you to death. If the situation comes up, we will review the applicable section. Questions?"

One of the enlisted members raised his hand. "Sir, I do not mean to ask a stupid question, but how will we do this? I mean do we write down our verdict as I have seen in some movies, or do we make a verbal comment?"

"First of all, son, in this setting, no question is stupid. The old adage of 'the only stupid question is the question not asked' applies." He paused to let this sink in especially with the officers.

"Okay, this is how we will do this. Each of you has a stack of 3X5 size paper in front of you. You will write down your finding, fold it, and put it in the box in the center of the table. The last person will pass the box to me. I will add my finding, close the lid, and shake the box to mix them up. I will draw out one piece of paper at a time and read the finding."

The jury foreman watched as each person thought about his finding and put his folded slip in the box and slide it down toward him. He put his slip in the box, closed the lid, and shook the box to make sure the slips were all mixed up. Before he opened the lid, one of the enlisted members raised his hand.

"Sir, what happens if we do not reach a unanimous verdict of guilty? Do we discuss and vote again, or do we go with our first vote?" "Let us see how the voting goes before we discuss that situation."

He shook the box one more time, opened it, and read the findings as he pulled each slip out of the box: "Guilty, not guilty, not guilty, guilty, guilty, guilty, guilty." He paused and took a deep breath.

"It seems that we do not have a unanimous finding. If anyone wants to discuss the case and revote, we will. Otherwise, we will let the judge know we have reached a finding of not guilty."

One of the other officers indicated that he wanted to speak.

"How can we convict him of murdering an unborn child if he did not know she was pregnant?"

"If he had not assaulted the victim in the first place, the fetus would not have died" one of the other members stated. Several others agreed with him.

The other enlisted soldier stated that "No matter how we cut it, a death resulted in the assault. I ask that we vote again."

With no objections from the other members, the jury foreman passed the empty box down to the end of the table and waited until each member placed his folded slip inside the box. He added his slip, closed the lid, and shook it up, making sure they were all mixed up. Without looking inside, he reached in and pulled out the first slip of paper.

Once again, he read off each slip and put them face down on the table. "Guilty, guilty, guilty, guilty, guilty, guilty, guilty." He took a sip of water, looked at each member of the jury panel, and asked them if anyone had any questions now that this vote was unanimous that Duval was guilty of killing an unborn child.

Seeing as there were no questions, he contacted the bailiff and told him that they had reached a verdict and asked him to notify Judge Conyers of their decision.

"Gentlemen, we now wait until the judge has reconvened the court. I suggest we sit back, relax. I presume that he will poll us as to our individual finding, so be ready to state your finding individually."

The talk around the table became something that all members of the military do when they become relaxed after a hectic and pressurized situation. They shot the bull.

Someone started with the old saying "There I was…" that was soon followed by "Believe it or not, but I…," which got everyone to laugh. It settled down to stories of their past assignments—the good and bad places and supervisors.

68

Since it was still before 2:00 p.m., Patrick, Sherrie, and the others adjourned to Major Davidson's office, hoping for a speedy verdict. "A quick verdict may not always be what you want to hear. However, with his guilty pleas for the other charges, I seriously doubt he will see freedom again. Even then the judge can override, and for a guilty ver- dict, it has to be unanimous to convict in a General Court-Martial." He looked at all three Air Force vets and told them that while it was comfortable here, he could not wait to get back to his post at Fort Hood Texas.

John could not help himself. "Texas, gawd, I hated Fort Bliss during SP training. It was too damn hot and dry for my liking. I will take California any day including the smog."

They all laughed at his comment when the phone rang. Davidson picked up his phone and listened for only a few seconds. "Yes, sir, we are all in my office. We will be right there."

He looked at them and told them that the jury has reached a decision and the judge would reconvene in fifteen minutes. "The media never left, so we will go in by the back door. No matter what is decided, you will have to face them afterward."

A combination of AF Security Police and Army Military Police surrounded the auditorium as they entered from the rear. Upon arriving, they noticed that Duval was already present at the defense table with his two lawyers. They quickly went to their seats just before the room was called to attention, and Conyers entered and took his seat at the quasi bench.

"It is my understanding that the jury has reached their decision. Before I let them in to announce their finding, I want to make it perfectly clear this is a court of law, not some damn circus ruled by the media or emotional outbursts. Anyone, and I repeat, *anyone*, acting in negative manner will be held in contempt of court. Am I clear?"

After seeing several heads nodding up and down, especially from the press, he called the jury in.

Sherrie noticed that as the jury marched in, Rod tried to make eye contact with them, his head moving from one person to the next, only to find as they entered the box they looked straight ahead, making no eye contact with him or with the prosecutor.

Colonel Conyers looked at the jury and asked them if they had reached a verdict.

The jury foreperson rose up and replied that they had. He handed the finding to the bailiff, who gave it to the judge. He looked at it and gave it back.

With a stoic look, he made the monotone comment, "Will the defendant please rise?"

Rod slowly stood. That he was unsteady on his feet was clearly evident as those in the front rows could see his bloused trouser legs moving as if there were a breeze in the auditorium.

Conyers looked at the jury and uttered the words that would seal Duval's fate. "What say you?"

"We, the jury, find the defendant, US Army Sergeant First Class Roderick Duval, guilty of violating Article 119A of the UCMJ, Death or Injury of an Unborn Child."

There were some gasps heard in the room including from Sherrie. However, since they were quickly subdued, Conyers did not invoke his threat.

Conyers stated that since a guilty verdict required a unanimous decision, he would have to poll the jury to ensure that requirement was met.

He began with the senior ranking member, a Colonel—"Guilty," a Lieutenant Colonel and a Major—"Guilty" while another one replied, "Guilty." A First Lieutenant replied, "guilty." Both enlisted members—a Master Sergeant and a Sergeant First Class—both replied, "Guilty."

With this, Duval collapsed on the floor. An Air Force medic rushed up to him and gave him a dose of smelling salts and checked his blood pressure.

It was so quiet in the auditorium one could have heard a coin drop on the carpeted floor. Everyone looked at the judge. Adams and Davidson both knew that the judge could overturn the guilty verdict based on the evidence. Perkins, not strongly familiar with military law, did not know what would happen next. He was already planning on appealing the death sentence.

Patrick and Sherrie, on the other hand, showed no emotion. It would hit them later that night.

Adams and Perkins stood on either side of Duval, his face a pasty white, his stomach threatening to lose all that he had inside of him. He wished now he had changed his plea from not guilty to guilty. He looked at the jury, three of whom were fellow Special Forces, even though he did not know them. He knew about the Colonel; he was a fair and nonjudgmental person from what he had heard.

Conyers looked at the Jury then at Rod. He then surprised everyone by looking at Sherrie.

"Mrs. Johnson, I see that you are still here with us. Do you have anything you wish to say before I pass judgment?"

Sherrie looked at Patrick and at Rod, who had turned to look at her with pleading eyes. She then stood and looked directly at Colonel Conyers and told him in a strong, steady voice, "No, Your Honor, I do not wish to say anything." She then sat back down.

Adams quickly turned Rod around to face Colonel Conyers, who was staring at him. "SFC Duval, before I pass sentence, do *you* have anything to say to the court? That means to me, not the audience."

Duval straightened up and at rigid attention replied. "Sir, I meant no disrespect to the court. As for my wanting to say something, yes, sir, I do. I had no idea she was pregnant. I did not mean to kill her baby."

Conyers looked at him and shook his head. "While that may be the case, the end result was the same. You caused the death of an unborn child." He paused and then formally continued. "Sergeant First Class Roderick Duval, you have been found guilty of violating Article 119A of the *Uniform Code of Military Justice*, to wit, Death or Injury of an Unborn Child, by a jury of your peers. The maximum penalty for this charge is death. However, you did not know the victim was pregnant, nor did anyone else, for that matter. Since that appears to be the case, I am going to overturn your guilty conviction and, based on your guilty pleas to your other charges, sentence you to the United States Penitentiary, Leavenworth, for the rest of your natural life without chance of parole. Your actions have brought discredit upon the United States Army and, specifically, our nation's elite Special Forces." He took a sip of water before continuing.

"Before leaving this courtroom, you will surrender your Green Beret, a symbol that was entrusted to you to preserve and protect in the highest honor. Furthermore, you are hereby reduced in rank to E-1 and will forfeit all pay and allowances exceeding $50 per month that will go for paying mental health expenses of Patrick Johnson Jr. and to help set up a trust fund to pay for his college education." He took another sip of water.

"Your sentence begins immediately." Conyers ordered Rod to be taken into custody and held in confinement at this location until he could be transported to Leavenworth. "You will now surrender your beret to your defense counsel, who will present it to me."

Rod looked at the coveted symbol of his entire career in the US Army Special Forces and gave it to Captain Adams, who presented it to Colonel Conyers.

Conyers told Adams to stay in front of the bench. He then pulled out a pocketknife and cut into the Green Beret to cut the Special Forces Flash insignia from it, causing a hole to appear in front of the beret. He gave it back to Adams.

"You will now wear this defaced piece of cloth as your head cover as long as you live at Leavenworth to remind you of the disgrace you have caused."

He then had Rod escorted out of the courtroom, tears streaming down his face as he looked at his now defaced beret, a symbol he had worked for and worn with pride for over twenty years.

Conyers then addressed the jury, thanking them for their service and releasing them. Once the jury was gone, Conyers then declared the trial over, stating, "Court is adjourned." He immediately left the room followed by his MP escort.

Immediately the media surged forward, hollering questions, having no sense of common decency. Finally, they calmed down.

The first question for Sherrie was how she felt about the final outcome.

"He did not know I was pregnant. I did not know I was pregnant. The question remains, though, if he had known I was pregnant, would he have still assaulted me in some other way? We will never know. I feel the judge was correct in overturning the jury's guilty verdict. I feel the punishment he was given fits all the crimes he committed against me and my family."

Both Patrick and Paul were asked how they felt about the crime scene.

They looked at each other and declined to answer the question with "No comment."

After fifteen minutes of questions, Davidson stopped the interviews and escorted all out of the building to their cars. Patrick told Paul that he and Sherrie would meet him at the office after they escaped the media circus.

Sitting in the breakroom at the office, everyone except for Sherrie, who drank water, enjoyed a glass of champagne to celebrate the end of the four-year nightmare for all of them. The first topic to come up was Rod's punishment.

John wondered what would last the longest—Rod or his now-defaced beret? He asked the question that was paramount in everyone's mind: "How long do you think he will last living by himself twenty-four hours a day, never talking to anyone but his guards?"

Patrick said that Rod would have plenty of time to think about what he had done and if it was worth it.

Sherrie admitted that she was glad he did not get the death penalty. "The appeals would have dragged on for years."

Paul mentioned there was still one missing piece of the completed puzzle that needed to be put in and the case finally closed. "And that is Josie Duval. Her sentencing is tomorrow. Don is to call me as soon as she is sentenced. She did the right thing by pleading guilty, saving Pat from testifying."

John asked a question that had been messing with his mind the past several months. "Paul, has Don said how much they will pay us for helping to solve the cold case? I mean we put in a lot of time for him, and it was because of us and our connections we helped solve the case."

"Thanks for reminding me. I need to call him and tell him the news. I will talk to him about it then. Now let us relax a little. Patrick, take the rest of today and tomorrow off. Go home and take it easy. I will call you tomorrow after I hear what happens to Mrs. Duval."

69

Josie Duval had requested a TV set be placed in her cell as she was not allowed to watch TV shows in the prison dayroom with other inmates due to her status. She was having a hard time coping with being alone all the time. The only ones to talk with were her guards. The local morning show talked about the court-martial and what might happen if her husband were to be found guilty of Death or Injury of an Unborn Child. Most legal analysts suggested that he could receive the death penalty, but appeals, unless he waived them, would take years. Some said if he was found guilty, the judge might overturn the verdict and sentence him to life in prison for all of the other charges.

That noon, she heard of the testimony of the witnesses. She heard that Sherrie did not know she was pregnant. If Rod had known she was pregnant, would he have assaulted her anyway to get his son? Why would he have gone to that extreme?

Later, while watching a soap opera, the local channel broke in with breaking news. It simply stated that Rod had been found guilty of killing an unborn child; however, the judge overturned the verdict. More would be on during the evening news.

She saw the evening news, where the reporter stated that even though the jury had found Rod guilty, the judge overturned the verdict and gave him life in prison at Leavenworth without chance of parole. They also described what the judge had done to his Green Beret and the order for him to wear it at all times due to the disgrace he had brought to the US Army and the Special Forces. She felt no sorrow for him; instead, she felt relieved that he did not get the death penalty. Her main concern now was how would his sentence affect her hearing the following morning? Her attorney, Mrs. Matthews, had all but assured her that she would probably get fifteen years for the Conspiracy to Commit Kidnapping of a Juvenile and five years for the Conspiracy to Obstruction of Justice.

The next morning, Matthews arrived at eight to talk to Josie. "I brought you a nice dress to wear today. It gives the judge a better impression than if you wear your prison outfit. Your sentencing begins at 10:00 a.m. Do you have any questions before we meet again in court?"

"Yes, I have a couple of questions. First, how will Rod's sentence yesterday affect my sentencing today?"

"That I do not know. However, his trial was much different than yours is. His sentence was based on all of his guilty pleas. Remember, you are charged with conspiracy to commit Assault after the fact, conspiracy to commit kidnapping, and conspiracy to obstruction of justice. Those are the only ones you need to worry about."

"Second, where will I be serving my sentence?"

"That I do not know yet. I have not heard. However, I believe it is safe to say that you will not be remaining here—probably one of the other two Federal prisons here in California."

"Third, after I am sentenced, can I still write to Rod? What are the rules for this especially since we are still married?"

"That will be up to the judge to decide. There are extenuating circumstances in your case since you are still married. It will be up to him and the warden at Leavenworth. If you have no other questions, get dressed. You have thirty minutes."

Matthews stepped out of the cell and waited until Josie got dressed and had Matthews brush her hair. "I have some makeup you can put on after you get to the courthouse."

Josie was taken downstairs to the garage to board the Federal Bureau of Prison bus for transportation to the Federal courthouse for her sentencing. All the while, she kept going over in her mind the prayer that she remembered JR saying at night to protect all those that he loved.

When she arrived, she saw the media, thicker than ants at a July picnic, crowding around the front entrance. The bus went into the underground garage that was protected by Federal officers. She was whisked up to the third floor where the courtroom was located.

The only two people inside were the Federal prosecutor and her attorney, Mrs. Matthews. They were both in an animated discussion until Josie was brought in by her prison escort, who took her to her table and removed her handcuffs and stepped behind her.

Josie looked at Matthews and asked her if the Johnsons would be there to see her get punished.

"I do not really know, Josie. It is my guess the media is hoping they will be here. However, yesterday must have taken a heavy toll on Mrs. Johnson. As to any others that were involved, who knows? However, the media outside is hoping that someone will show up."

A few minutes before ten, FBI Special Agent Donald Abernathy and the agents from the Cheyenne Field Office that were involved in the arrests arrived. Agents Parker, Wilkerson, Young, and Parsons sat with Don behind the Federal prosecutor.

At 10:00 a.m., the Federal marshal called the now-packed courtroom to "all rise" as Federal Judge David Blunt came into the room and sat down. He looked around the room, which was over three quarters filled with media. He took a sip of water and gave out a stern warning.

"Ladies and gentlemen, this is a courtroom, and we deal with the rule of law. All respect will be made to this bench. Any outbursts or loud comments will not be tolerated, and I do not care if you are the press or a law enforcement officer. If you violate this warning, you will be held in contempt. Afterward, if you so desire, you can go to the first-floor administrative offices where there will be a press release. There will be no, and I repeat no, press conference in this building. Is that understood?" He waited a few minutes before he continued.

"Now that I have issued fair warning, Mr. Edwards, are you prepared to present the government argument?"

"I am, Your Honor. While Mrs. Duval has pleaded guilty to the charges of Conspiracy to Commit Assault after the fact, Conspiracy to Commit Kidnapping, and Conspiracy to Commit Obstruction of Justice, we ask that she be sentenced to twenty-five years to be served in the Federal Prison in Dublin. Remaining here in Los Angeles puts her close to the victim of her crime." He then sat down.

Judge Blunt then looked at the defense table. "Ms. Matthews, are you ready?"

"Yes, Your Honor, I am ready. Ms. Duval fully accepts the second and third charge. However, she did not know the method of how he was going to take his son until after the fact. True, she did not report it, but she should not have to pay the price of committing that crime. Defense asks for a sentence of fifteen to twenty years. Thank you, sir."

Judge Blunt looked at both the prosecution and defense tables, took a sip of water, and then had had Josie stand with Matthews.

"Mrs. Josie Duval, you are guilty of conspiracy to commit kidnapping and conspiracy to obstruct justice. I am almost tempted to overturn your guilty plea to conspiracy to commit assault after the fact since you did not know how your husband was going to carry out the kidnapping of Patrick Johnson Jr. However, since you did not report it, you are guilty of the crime." Before he passed sentence, he looked at his notes and took a sip of water.

"Mrs. Duval, I am sentencing you to twenty years at the Federal Prison in Dublin, California. You will be eligible for parole after ten years if you remain on good behavior. I am also going to issue you a warning. You are not to contact Mrs. Johnson's family at any time. If you attempt to contact them during your sentence, you will not be granted parole, and you will receive additional time. Is that clear?"

"Yes, Your Honor, very clear."

"Do you have any questions before you are escorted out?"

"Yes, Your Honor. Will I be able to write to my husband while we are both in prison? Will I ever get to see him again?"

"You can write to him and possibly even talk to him on the phone, but that is not a guarantee. As for seeing him again, it all depends on the warden where your husband is going to be incarcerated."

"Thank you, Your Honor."

Blunt had Josie escorted out, wearing handcuffs by the same female Federal Marshal that brought her in. She looked at the agents from Cheyenne, nodded toward Parker, and mouthed the words *thank you*.

After Blunt left, Don thanked the visiting agents and told them that Patrick Johnson Jr., now called Pat, was adjusting well and in school. "In fact, I have to call the Cold Case Investigators that helped us solve this one. How about if I see if we can all come out to see him? I am sure he would love to see you again, Parker."

As they left the courthouse, Don answered some of the questions from the press, stating that he was happy with the two sentences. "Justice has been served." They then went to Don's office so he could call Paul.

70

When Paul told Patrick the news, he also mentioned that the agents would like to see Pat one last time. By the time they got to the ranch, Pat would be home from school. He told Paul to let Don know it was okay. "It might do everyone good to see them one last time and thank them."

Pat came home from school with a smile on his face. He ran up the driveway and burst inside the house to show his mother his spelling test—fifteen words, fifteen right answers. She put it on the refrigerator door and gave him a big hug.

"Your dad is at the stables. He has something to tell you. Go tell him your good news first," she told him.

"Dad, I got an A in school today. It was spelling—fifteen words and no wrong words," he told Patrick with a beaming smile. "Mom said you had news for me?"

Patrick pointed to a bale of hay and told Pat to have a seat. "We are having company in a little bit. It is people from Cheyenne that you met before you came out here. They want to see you one last time and say hello before they leave to go back."

"Is it the bad people? I thought they were in jail. I saw it on the news last night."

"No, to us they are not bad people, but some people do not like them. They are the FBI agents that arrested the bad people. One of them that is coming is the woman that brought you home."

"Really? I like her. She is pretty, and she took care of me at her place before we got on the jet for my first plane ride. I really like her."

Patrick smiled. "Yes, she is one of them, and Agent Parsons, the one that brought Pony out here, he is also coming. They all are."

Fifteen minutes later, a dark-colored Ford Explorer entered the driveway, and all five agents got out. Patrick, Sherrie, Sherrie Leigh, and Pat came out of the house and waited for them on the porch. Patrick invited all inside for coffee and water.

Pat went up to Parker and gave her a hug while Patrick and Sherrie thanked all the agents for everything they did in Cheyenne once they found out where Pat was.

Just then, a car pulled into the driveway and parked behind the Ford. Paul and John bounded up the steps into the house, not wanting to miss the celebratory party.

As soon as Don saw Paul and John enter, he walked over to Paul and gave him a check for five thousand dollars for helping to solve the cold case. "You can help us out anytime we have a cold case, and we have several. I owe you and John a debt of gratitude for your help from the beginning."

John arched his eyebrow, which caused Parker to laugh and the others to grin, when he heard Don. Parker quit laughing and asked him if he always did that along with the quizzical look on his face.

"Only when I am confused or I think something is wrong—or sometimes when I want a pretty woman to laugh."

Pat went up to each agent and shook their hands and thanked them for what they had done to bring him home "to my real Mom and Dad and to put the bad people away for a long time. I was happy then, but I am happier now."

Don asked Paul if he had told Patrick and Sherrie all the detail of today. Paul said he had not.

"Ms. Duval will be at the Federal prison up at Dublin for twenty years with eligibility for parole after ten years. She is not to contact any of your family, and if she does, she goes back to prison for additional time."

Sherrie, holding onto Pat and Sherrie Leigh, with Patrick beside her, said it bluntly to everyone in the room. "Justice has been finally served. Our son is back, and we have more on the way!"

ABOUT THE AUTHOR

Merrill Vaughan was raised in Monrovia and Duarte, California, graduating from Duarte High School in 1967. He served in the Air Force from 1971 to 1993 when he retired as a Master Sergeant. His duties included aircraft maintenance, personnel, administration and as a First Sergeant. He served numerous overseas assignments and several state side assignments. He attended Franklin Pierce University graduating in 2012 with his B.S. Degree in General Studies which he used as a substitute teacher at his local middle high school. This is his first novel.